VAN B   W9-CCI-053   Y
DEC   MICHIGAN 9045

DISTRICT LIBRARY

SAINTS AND SINNERS

of OKAY COUNTY

SAINTS ᴬᴺᴰ SINNERS
of OKAY COUNTY

A Novel

Dayna Dunbar

BALLANTINE BOOKS
New York

Dun

This is a work of fiction. Names, characters, places, and incidents
are the products of the author's imagination or are used fictitiously.
Any resemblance to actual events, locales, or persons, living or
dead, is entirely coincidental.

A Ballantine Book
Published by The Random House Publishing Group

Copyright © 2003 by Dayna Dunbar

All rights reserved under International and Pan-American Copyright
Conventions. Published in the United States by The Random
House Publishing Group, a division of Random House, Inc.,
New York, and simultaneously in Canada by Random House
of Canada Limited, Toronto.

Ballantine and colophon are registered trademarks
of Random House, Inc.

Grateful acknowledgment is made to Sony/ATV Music Publishing
LLC for permission to reprint an excerpt from "Blue Eyes Crying in
the Rain" by Fred Rose. Copyright 1945 Sony/ATV Tunes LLC. All
rights on behalf of Gold Hill Music administered by Sony/ATV
Music Publishing, 8 Music Square West, Nashville, TN 37203. All
rights reserved. Reprinted by permission.

ISBN 0-345-46039-1

Text design by Barbara Sturman

Manufactured in the United States of America

104
gift

For my mother, Linda Rose Dunbar,
with all my love.

Acknowledgments

I am deeply grateful to the following: Brenda Adelman, for her constant love and support. Pamela Lane, whose brilliant assistance on this novel has made all the difference. The University of Santa Monica class of 2001, and specifically my project team members and friends—Wendy Brenner, Kim Pflieger, and Noah Jordan, whose support and encouragement helped make this book a reality. Ron and Mary Hulnick, dedicated, wise, and compassionate teachers who helped give birth to this project and loaned me a computer to work on when I was desperate. My father, Fred Dunbar, and my siblings, Debi, Darron, and Dustin, who were there with me the whole way. The Roses, Logans, and Mannings—my Oklahoma family. Laurie Goldstein, who gave me the inspiration for the opening chapter. My agent, Bob Tabian, for finding me a wonderful publisher. My editor, Maureen O'Neal—thanks for getting it. Finally, many thanks to Reverend Michael Beckwith and Agape for the retreat that turned me around.

The
SAINTS AND SINNERS
of OKAY COUNTY

Chapter One

By the time Aletta realized the bitter smell drifting out her front door was burning kolaches, it'd been too late to save them. Inside the house, two sheets of blackened fruit-topped pastries emerged from the veil of thick smoke like a magic trick. She plunked herself down on a bar stool, a dish towel still dangling from her fingers, and watched wisps of smoke rise off the kolaches. She couldn't help but draw unkind comparisons to her own life— singed beyond recognition, stinking to heaven's pearly gates, and most likely irretrievable. The kolaches had been a shot at making a little cash, but this was the third batch she'd ruined, the first dying from a baking powder overdose. She still wasn't sure what had gone wrong with the second.

Outside, the Okay Czech Festival paraded right in front of her house on Main Street. The yearly summer festival caused the population of Okay, Oklahoma, to swell from five thousand folks just getting by to forty thousand out for fun. When the bill for the mortgage had come in the mail the day before, she knew it meant a near end to her checking account, so she'd decided to make some grocery money off her location. She hadn't realized making Czechoslovakian desserts required some kind of baking miracle.

Honking horns and whoops and hollers made her glance out the kitchen window. Men with round bellies tucked against their thighs and tasseled hats covering balding heads raced around in toy-size sports cars. Aletta let out a chirp of a laugh. The parade had started.

"Mama, what's that smell?" Ruby yelled from the front door. In another moment, she stood in front of Aletta, her face painted with a daisy on one cheek and an American flag on the other. In the summer of 1976, it seemed all of Oklahoma was into America's bicentennial.

"I burned the kolaches," Aletta said. Her eight-year-old looked so scared, it made Aletta think the girl must've heard wrong.

"Does that mean we have to move?" Ruby asked.

"Where'd you get that crazy idea?" Aletta's pale green eyes had to fight back the surprise of unexpected tears.

Ruby looked down at her flip-flops. "I heard you talkin' on the phone."

"Now, that's grown-up talk, Ruby. We're not gonna lose this house if I have anything at all to do with it, so there's nothin' to worry about. I'm just gonna make some lemonade to sell." She reached out with both arms, inviting a hug. "You go on and have fun. I'll be right out."

Ruby held her mama's pregnant belly, her fine blond hair spilling across Aletta's breasts. Aletta hadn't realized just how much their daddy's leaving and her fears about money were affecting her kids until she'd seen that scared look on Ruby's face. She smiled as Ruby pulled away, but inside she was cussing Jimmy again, unable to pretend he'd left for something more complicated than going middle-age crazy at thirty-four.

On the card table in her front yard, Aletta set out a pitcher of powder-mix lemonade, a small ice chest with ice cubes from her fridge, and some Happy Birthday cups left over from Randy's sixth birthday party. She turned over the notebook paper that said *Homemade Kolaches - fifty cents for one or three dollars a dozen* and wrote *Lemonade - ten cents*.

Her house was on the far west end of town, at the beginning of the official parade route. People lined both sides of the street farther down, but here Aletta could watch the marching bands in their snazzy tasseled outfits and the floats carrying firemen or the bowling league right from her front yard. Just as she finished her sign, she looked up and saw Jimmy. Her husband stood on a float that looked like an enormous football. He and several other men of varying ages and waist sizes wore red-and-white Okay letter jackets and waved to the crowd. The 1940s red tractor that pulled the float carried a banner reading OKAY ATHLETIC ALUMNI ASSOCIATION.

Aletta couldn't decide if the pain in her belly was the baby or her stomach pitching a fit. Inside, she felt a humble brew made up of equal parts shame that he might not want her anymore, revulsion that she cared, and fear that he'd really stay gone forever. A voice in her head told her clear—as clear as the ringing of the Jesus Is Lord church bells at noon every day—that she couldn't make it all alone.

As always, Jimmy stood out from the other men. His six-foot-two frame was topped off with black hair and sideburns that made his handsome face look rugged, but it was his smile that made people watch him that extra second. He kept his back to her until the float passed their house, then turned for just a moment, flashed her that smile, and waved. She raised her hand, but instead of waving, she pushed her shoulder-length strawberry blond hair behind one ear and then sat frozen in her chair until he finally turned away. How could he smile like that? As if there wasn't a train wreck lying between them, twisted and smoldering.

From his perch down the street, the PA announcer called out, "And now we have our athletes. Y'all are sure to recognize Okay's only all-state basketball player, Jimmy Honor." Across the street, Aletta saw Ruby and her little brother, Randy, watching their daddy with mouths hanging open. They seemed unsure what to do until the people watching the parade cheered for Jimmy, and then they started running alongside the float. Aletta wanted to yell at them to stop. Instead, she put her hand to her mouth as their daddy tossed them little plastic basketballs. They finally stopped running and waved good-bye as he tossed more of the orange balls out to scrambling children in the crowd.

"I'll take a lemonade if you're still sellin'."

The powerful scent of her daddy almost pitched her from her chair as Aletta turned toward the stranger. The weather-beaten cowboy held the reins of a beautiful quarter horse. He smelled like milk and hay and farm animals.

The impression of her father remained after the cowboy took his lemonade and went to join the rodeo contingent. Aletta closed her eyes. "Oh, Daddy, what should I do?" she whispered.

"You're one smart girl makin' some money with this location," Joy called from her driveway, "and I for one am in desperate need of a kolache." Joy lived next door with her husband Earl behind her beauty salon, Joy's Femme Coiffures. This month she happened to have red hair, flaming and high, and her Merle Norman pancake makeup hid any hint of a pore. She hated the natural look that was "in" these days and made it very clear to her customers that she intended to keep the "femme" in all their coiffures.

"Come on over," Aletta called back.

Joy sashayed across the lawn wearing tight-fitting Capri pants, a sequined American flag blouse, and gold-strapped high-heeled sandals.

"I couldn't make a kolache to save my life," Aletta said, opening a metal folding chair for Joy.

"I'm sorry, hon. When Randy told me you were tryin', I have to admit I said a little prayer," Joy said.

Just as she situated herself on the metal chair and put a cigarette to her lips, a tiny red Corvette raced by, passing the parade on the other side of the street. Joy's husband, Earl, held onto his tasseled hat with one hand as he sped along, an impossibly serious look on his face.

In an instant, Joy was running after him. "He musta missed the start," she shouted.

Aletta laughed as she watched Joy zigzag around a line of people waiting to buy brisket and beer, then hop off the curb and race between the Okay Marching Band and last year's homecoming queen waving from a yellow Thunderbird convertible. She chased after Earl, her gold two-strap shoes somehow staying on as she ran, until Aletta could no longer see her.

A flash of light caught Aletta's eye, and she turned to watch her eldest daughter's twirling team march into view. Sissy and the other girls wore white Keds, sequined one-piece outfits, Supp-Hose, and big smiles. They tossed their batons high in the air, light glinting from the silver metal. Aletta stood up and cheered for her pretty fourteen-year-old. Pride swelled inside her chest, and she thought that maybe she was doing something right.

Ruby and Randy ran toward Aletta. Randy's face paint was smeared across his pudgy cheeks, and bits of cotton candy clung to his home-cut bowl-shaped hair.

"Do you see Sissy?!" he yelled.

"I see her. She's doin' great," Aletta said.

"Sissy!" Randy screamed, waving frantically.

"Not so loud, honey. How much sugar have you had?"

"A ton," Ruby said.

Not two minutes after Sissy marched by, the Burning Bush Battle Church banner approached. Aletta wanted to run inside to avoid her mama, one of the brightest of the Bushes. But when she saw Reverend Taylor, she sat stuck in her chair. At first she thought he must be attached to the float by a rod up his backside because of the look on his face. It was a mix of holier-than-thou and y'all are my people, a tricky combination. Plump in his gray leisure suit, he waved and beckoned.

Behind him, a man dressed as a lion with a huge head full of sharp teeth battled with a sheet-wrapped teenage boy. They wrestled so fiercely that Aletta feared one of them was going to fly off the flatbed trailer. Strapped onto a cross behind them, Jesus overlooked the fight. He was sweating so badly that his fake blood had turned pink and ran in rivulets onto his drooping beard and down his chest.

Spreading out from the float, several dozen people dressed in their church clothes handed out pamphlets. Odiemae Sharp caught a toe on the curb as she beelined toward Aletta, causing her to do a little skippity-hop on her way across the grass. She was darned fit for a lady of her age.

"Here y'are, Aletta. We look for you ever' Sunday, you know," she said, holding out a pamphlet.

Aletta noticed Odiemae's silver hair coming in beneath her brown dye job, but her hazel eyes were clear as a child's. It was just her mama's friend, but still she felt the old pang of guilt for not being the daughter she was supposed to be.

Aletta took the pamphlet but made sure their hands didn't touch.

"Thanks," Aletta said, looking past Odiemae. "Where is she?"

"Oh, she stayed home, complainin' of old age."

"But she's strong as a mule." Aletta hadn't seen her mama in almost five months. It seemed they just couldn't be around each other anymore without a bitterness rising up like a wind before the rain.

"Well, I gotta run," Odiemae said. "How long before the little one comes?"

"Just a couple more months."

"I'm sure your mama's proud. She's a saint of a woman, you know."

Aletta looked down at the full-color pamphlet in her hand. *The Burning Bush Battle Church,* it said across the top, *Battling to Save Your Soul.* Below a painting of a bush aflame, there was a Bible quote: *Whoever brings back a sinner from the error of his way will save his soul from death and will cover a multitude of sins. James 5:20.* Aletta tossed it onto the table without opening it.

Near the end of the day, Eugene Kirshka walked up and slid a quarter across the table. "I'll take one, please," he said, his rounded cheeks making him look boyish despite six feet of lanky, milk-fed build. His light brown hair looked unruly without the cap that normally sat on his head.

"You're an awful big spender," Aletta said.

He took a sip of watery lemonade. "How you holdin' up without him?"

"Not so good," she said, her smile fading. He was the only one to ask her about Jimmy all day. People around here handled hard times, especially emotional ones, by not talking about them, unless of course they had anything to do with bad weather or surgery. "You're his friend. You tell me what he's doin'."

"If we were still friends, I'd have to kick his tail from here 'til

Tuesday for what he's done to you, Aletta. Only way I know to help is to fix your car. Wish I could do more." He hooked his thumb into a belt loop of his Wranglers and looked down.

"That's more than enough, Eugene. I don't know why that car's been such trouble," she said. He'd been working on her pink '57 Chevy for free since Jimmy had taken off a few months back.

"What I don't know is why it makes me feel guilty him leavin' like that," he said.

Aletta laughed. "At least one man feels bad about Jimmy's behavior, and it sure ain't him."

At the end of the day, Aletta figured she'd lost over ten dollars on her kolache bake. To make it worse, she gave Sissy money to buy good kolaches from the ladies down at Czech Hall because, as all three of her kids argued, it's not Czech Day without them. As Aletta folded her card table to close up shop, a woman who looked to be in her fifties walked toward her, smiling. She reminded Aletta a little bit of an older Doris Day. Before Aletta could pull away, the woman grabbed her hand.

"I just had to come tell you how lovely you look. You've got the glow. I've been noticing you off and on all day," she said.

The images flashed in Aletta's mind as the woman held her hand—cars strewn over the highway, a horse trailer on its side, a big rig in a ditch. Finally Aletta pulled her hand away. She felt afraid and unsteady. The images had been so strong. Avoiding touching people outside her family was just second nature to her now, but when it did happen, the images were usually weak and easy to dismiss, but not this time.

Feeling off balance, she sat down on her chair.

"Are you all right, hon?" the woman asked, concern in her voice.

Aletta smiled weakly up at the woman, shading her eyes from the sun with her hand. "Where you from?" she asked, unable to get the images of the accident out of her mind.

"Over in Chickasha. Me and my husband just came down for the day. He's on a horse somewhere around here. I prob'ly ought to go find him." She glanced over her shoulder, scanning the crowd.

"Don't take the highway home," Aletta blurted. The words

had jumped out before she could stop them. *Now what am I gonna do,* she thought.

"Excuse me?" the woman asked.

"Just promise me you won't get on the highway tonight. Take the back roads."

Aletta's heart thumped as the woman cocked her head to one side and studied her for what seemed like a very long time.

"I'll tell you one thing, hon," she said finally. "I ain't gonna ignore the advice of a woman with child."

Aletta sighed with relief. "Thank you."

After the woman left, Aletta sat back in her chair and watched an old couple walk past wearing matching FORD FOR PRESIDENT T-shirts.

It surprised her that she felt numb, even calm. She'd just revealed herself to a stranger, after all this time of hiding, and it hadn't been that bad.

The next day was Sunday, but Aletta felt too tired to go to church. She spent the morning folding the laundry and folding the possibilities over in her mind. There simply wasn't enough money to pay the bills, let alone buy food or gas. She knew it would take months to get any from Jimmy. It was impossible for her to go back to cashiering at the 7-Eleven as pregnant as she was, not only because of the hours of standing on her feet, but also because she couldn't lift cases of beer anymore.

She sat in the living room with piles of clothes around her, watching Bugs Bunny cartoons with Ruby and Randy until the twelve o'clock news came on. While making peanut butter and jelly sandwiches in the kitchen, she heard the newsman talking about an accident that had happened on the highway the night before. She hurried back into the living room just in time to see a semi truck buried in a ditch like a pig in mud.

"The driver of the truck allegedly fell asleep at the wheel," the man on TV said. "The truck hit one other car before going into a ditch just outside of Chickasha."

Aletta drew a sharp breath and put her hand to her mouth. The horse trailer wasn't there. The woman at the parade had listened to her. She didn't let that breath out until she was back in the kitchen sitting on a bar stool. She stared at a smear of ketchup on the refrigerator door while fear and excitement wrestled inside her like the boy and the lion in yesterday's parade. When the phone rang, she started.

"Hi, darlin', it's me." Jimmy's voice was calm. When he'd started calling her in high school, that voice would give her stomach the flutters every time. Jimmy was fun then, a basketball star, a dreamer. Now the same voice made her feel nauseous.

"I need some money, Jimmy," Aletta said. She tried to sound neutral, like she didn't feel anything for him one way or another. The truth was she wanted to scream at him to grow up and come take care of her and the kids. But she knew it was the responsibility that had driven him away. When he'd told her about a month before he left that he was starting to feel like his daddy—a joyless, bitter man who'd worked himself into the grave—she'd gone into the bathroom and cried.

"I'll come over. We'll talk about it," he said.

She could tell he felt guilty, but that wasn't enough for her to trust him. "No, don't come over. These kids can't handle much more. Just send some money."

"They're my kids, Lettie. Did you see 'em run after me at the parade? They need me. The new baby needs me, and so do you."

"Then why'd you leave in the first place?" she asked.

"I'll come over," he said.

Not knowing what to do, Aletta just hung up the phone. In spite of her anger, a little sprout of hope started up inside her. He loved his kids. That meant something. She glanced down at the bills stacked on the kitchen bar and felt the sprout retreat back into darkness.

She made her decision the next morning. At a little after ten, Ruby dragged in the door with the skin scraped off her right knee, wheezing and crying.

"I . . . fell . . . off my bike," she said. Her words labored to get out between raspy gulps of air.

Aletta sat her down and gave her a pill for her asthma. "Calm down now. The doctor said if you relax, it'll help, remember?"

As Aletta cleaned and bandaged Ruby's skinned knee, she listened to each breath her daughter took to make sure the asthma was getting better, not worse. It suddenly occurred to her, what if Jimmy's drinking got so bad he lost his sales job at Southwestern Bell? They wouldn't have insurance anymore.

The doorbell rang. Aletta could tell Ruby was improving, so she answered it herself. The Doris Day lady from Chickasha stood on the porch wearing a flowery summer dress. For a moment, Aletta was sure she was in trouble.

"I figured you must live here since you had the lemonade stand out front," the woman said, extending her hand. "I'm Beverly."

Aletta looked at Beverly's hand for a moment but didn't take it. "I'm Aletta. Come on in. I'm sorry, my house is a mess."

One eyebrow rose slightly, then Beverly let her hand fall to her side. "No, no, I don't want to bother you, so I won't come in. I just had to drive down and thank you myself. Did you hear about the wreck out on the Interstate?"

Aletta held the screen door open as they talked. She was nervous. "On the news. Big truck, wasn't it?"

"That's the one you warned me about. I knew as soon as Ottillie came over from next door and told me about it. You saved my life, and my husband's."

Aletta's face flushed. She had no idea what to say. Nothing like this had ever happened before. "I'm real glad y'all got home safe and sound," she said finally.

"How long you been able to see things?" Beverly asked, her eyes warm and gentle.

"I don't know. It's not something I even think about." Aletta glanced across the road to avoid those eyes. The wall of shame she'd hidden behind for twenty-two years made her want to shut the door, but the feeling of helping someone made her feel like giving this woman a hug.

Beverly smiled. "Well, I have to tell you I feel like the Lord just smiled on me. It's so funny 'cause I noticed you so much at the parade."

"Well, thanks for comin' by. Chickasha's a pretty far drive," Aletta said, closing the screen door a little. She needed to be alone.

After Beverly left, Aletta sat in the rocking chair, pushing back and up, back and up, for an hour. She thought about her kids and how she had to take care of them no matter what the consequences were for herself. Jimmy treated responsibility like a tax audit or a bad cold, something you avoided if at all possible. Aletta treated it like it was a cross she had to carry on her back 'til she could put it in the ground and hang on it for all to see.

She got up and called Eugene.

"You have any wood layin' around? I need to make a sign," she said.

"Sure, I got some stuff out back that'll most likely work," he said. Aletta was grateful that he didn't ask any questions. She liked Eugene. He was simple, and she appreciated that.

An hour later, she hollered to Sissy with a determination in her voice that brought her daughter faster than Aletta had seen since Sissy transformed, like a character in a science fiction movie, into a teenager two years ago.

"You gotta drive me down to the auto shop. My belly won't fit behind the wheel of Eugene's loaner truck no more," she said.

Sissy's mouth fell open as she stared at her mother.

"Don't look at me like that," Aletta said.

"Like what?" Sissy asked.

"Like you're thinkin' about how to use this to your advantage."

Sissy rolled her eyes. "I have to go change first." She wore cut-off shorts and a long-sleeved shirt tied in a knot at the waist.

"Do you wanna drive?" Aletta asked.

"Yes."

"Then wear what you got on."

"Go real fast, Sissy!" Randy yelled as he and Ruby scrambled into the back of the pickup. It was so hot out, the metal on the truck burned them when they touched it, so they sat carefully on the edge of the tire humps.

Aletta shot down the idea of going fast with a glance as they backed slowly away from their olive-green three-bedroom house with a wide front porch and a slamming screen door. They lived across from what was now an empty used-car lot that had moved to a bigger location east of town. Theirs was one of only three houses on Main Street. The fact that it happened to be located where it was could have you arguing for dumb luck or providence, depending on your philosophical bent.

As Sissy headed east on Main, Aletta leaned toward the window, letting the hot, moist air blow on her face until a bug glanced off her cheek. She wished she were lying down with her feet up and a fan blowing.

Her eyes scanned Bass's Dress Shop and the Ben Franklin Five and Dime with their faded awnings and glass storefronts. Okay had started out a farm town, a place for the hard folks who came for free land to sell crops and buy supplies. The town sat in the middle of miles of flat farmland on every side, sun-cooked in the summer and frozen mean in the winter, the wind blowing without cease or concern for the season.

Aletta closed her eyes, her imagination returning to the sign and how it would look and what it might bring. "Oh, boy," she sighed with the weight of her thoughts.

"What'd you say, Mama?" Sissy asked.

Aletta turned to look at her oldest daughter and saw Randy's face pressed against the glass, his tongue and nostrils splayed out flat. She laughed in spite of herself, then scolded Sissy to keep her eyes on the road.

Aletta turned to look at Ruby sitting on the tire hump in the back. She admired the way her tough little girl handled her asthma, never letting it slow her down for long. "Hi, Pappy," Ruby called.

The kids waved at the bronze statue of Jeremiah T. Pappe, the founder of Okay, which stood near the hulking flour mills at the end of town. He had been one of the soonest of the Sooners back in the land run of '89, laying claim to almost half the county before the other settlers even heard the starting gun.

The burnt-orange truck creaked and moaned the three minutes across town to Eugene's shop next to the Hilltop Diner. The diner was a squat building the color of dried mud. Its name was an inside joke among the people of Okay, given that there wasn't anything that could be classified as more than a rise for at least ten miles around.

Sissy pulled the old truck in front of the worn stucco of Eugene's Auto Repair Shop, careful not to hit the wooden posts that marked the place where the old gas pumps had stood when this was a Mobil station and Route 66, Okay's Main Street, was part of the main artery through the heart of America.

The kids hopped out of the back of the truck before it came to a lurching stop, and ran to Eugene's dog, Rascal.

"Hi, I hope we're not interruptin'," Aletta said, approaching Eugene, who was bent over the engine of an old Ford Fairlane. As usual, he wore coveralls over his T-shirt and jeans, and Aletta noticed again that while his hands were dirty with grease, the rest of him stayed pretty clean. It was the same with his shop. There were broken-down cars and engine parts everywhere, but somehow the place seemed organized, like there was a reason why he'd put them there.

"Not at all," he said, smiling.

He led her out back, past her pastel Chevy that stood with its hood open next to the '66 Mustang he was always souping up.

"I tried to fix that radiator without havin' to replace it, so I was gonna give her a spin today to see how she goes," Eugene said as they passed Aletta's car.

He picked up the large piece of plywood and the post that were leaning against the back of his shop. After Aletta had called earlier, he'd hopped in the car and gone to Logan Lumber and bought the wood she'd asked for.

"Let me get these for you," he said, and carried the lumber to the truck.

"Thanks, Eugene, this is exactly what I need," Aletta said.

"Whatcha got planned?" he asked.

"If you're out in my car later, come on by and see for yourself."

When they got home, Ruby watched her mama open the small cans of purple and white paint they'd picked up at the Otasco. Aletta turned the air-conditioning up even though she was trying to save money. She decided she had to not sweat for a few minutes.

She carefully moved the cheap deer and rabbit statues that made up the centerpiece of the dining room table, then laid down some crusty newspapers she'd found in the garage and put the plywood on top.

The quiet in the house was strange, and it added to Ruby's feeling that something important was happening. Sissy talked on the phone in her bedroom and Randy watched TV, but Ruby hovered near her mama, keeping an eye on her as she painstakingly outlined letters and filled them in with paint. Ruby stayed quiet so she wouldn't be told to go play. As the letters slowly formed, purple on white, she read them upside down, trying to see if she could find something in them to let her know if her mama might leave her like her daddy had done.

Just as the sun was turning the late-afternoon blue into an early-evening lavender, Eugene pulled up in Aletta's Chevy. She saw him out the kitchen window and walked out to meet him.

"There's still somethin' goin' on with her," he said, closing the car door behind him. "Might be a water pump. I'll get it fixed, though, if you don't mind waitin' a little longer."

" 'Course not. How can I argue with free?" She smiled. "Hey, would you mind diggin' a hole in my yard?"

"All right. What you up to?"

"You'll see. I just need it deep enough for that post you gave me."

The kids saw Eugene shoveling the ground and came out to help. Sissy opened the garage door where the sign leaned against an old mattress. She and Ruby and Randy carried it to where Eugene was digging the hole in the front yard. They buried the post in deep. Aletta insisted on getting down on her knees and packing the dirt around it herself. With her enormous belly and her hands in the earth, she looked like she might be performing some Indian ritual. After Sissy and Eugene pulled her up by the elbows, she stood back, put her hands on her hips, and examined her work.

ALETTA HONOR
PSYCHIC READER
DROP-INS WELCOME

"Oh, boy," she said.

The next morning, the kids ate breakfast at the kitchen bar. The white Formica counter with little gold starbursts was the center of the Honor beehive. It served as a desk for bill paying and homework, a place to visit over coffee or to doodle while talking on the phone. It separated the kitchen from the dining room. They ate every meal there except when guests came over, and then they'd venture three feet over to the dining room table. The bar could fit only four stools without blocking the passageway, so when their daddy was there, they'd pull one in from the garage. But they hadn't had to worry about that for a while.

Randy performed his usual ritual of smashing a toasted Velveeta cheese sandwich with his hands until it was as flat as a plate. He ate the crust first, nibbling around the outside, then chewing through the middle and ending up with two halves that went down one at a time.

Ruby pushed him. "Mama, Randy's being weird again."

"Leave him alone." Aletta stood at the sink doing last night's dishes, wishing for one of those automatic dishwashers so she wouldn't have to be reminded so much that she didn't have two dishes that matched in the whole house except the china she'd gotten from her mother as a wedding present. That set was in the hall closet, where it was going to stay.

"You're weird too, Ruby," Sissy said, pouring two-percent milk over her cereal. "We all are. It runs in the family."

Aletta turned from the sink, the water still running, and leaned toward Sissy. "Sissy, I know what you're gettin' at, and you can just stop. Eugene can fix cars. Joy can do hair, and I can tell things about people. I doubt if anyone's even gonna come, so don't worry about your reputation just yet." Her voice had that mix of bone-tired, worried, and it'll-all-work-out. The cross felt really heavy today.

Sissy was picking at her Cap'n Crunch when the doorbell rang. They all froze. Two distinct ticks tocked from the electric mini–grandfather clock on the counter before anyone moved.

Ruby ran to the door. "I'll get it!"

Randy was right on her heels.

Outside stood a young Hispanic woman looking nervous and small with a baby in her arms. Pointing to the sign out front, she asked, "Is the lady in?"

"Who is it, Ruby?" Aletta yelled.

Ruby ran back into the kitchen. "It's a lady asking about the sign. She wants to see you."

Sissy groaned and stomped off to her room. Reaching for a towel to dry her hands, Aletta knocked a jelly-jar-turned-water-glass off the counter, shattering it all over the orange-and-yellow linoleum floor. The pain between her shoulder blades crawled like stinging insects up into her neck.

"Dammit all." Aletta stepped over the glass as she headed to the door. "You and Randy put your shoes on 'til I can clean this up."

Ruby stopped her and whispered, "Mama, are you sure you can do what that sign says?"

"I sure hope so, honey."

Aletta didn't know. She didn't know if the images would keep coming or if she'd be able to make sense of them or if they'd be true. She went to the door unsure of everything except the belief that she had no other choice but to try.

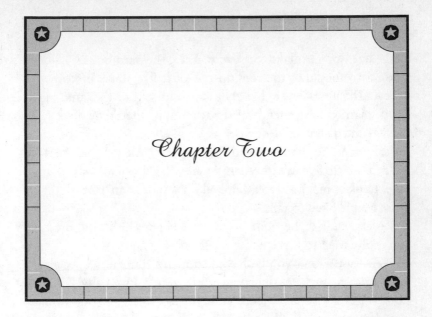

Chapter Two

It had started when Aletta was Ruby's age. An old woman who reminded her of the burned-out tree down by the creek, with its dark skin and bony angles, had walked into Aletta's bedroom and sat down as if she were an old friend.

"Who are you?" little Aletta asked sleepily. The woman smiled wide enough to show she had no top teeth.

"I'm Tessie Jones Maple. And you are?"

Aletta laughed a little. Maple—just like the tree. And Miss Maple had a voice the sound of which Aletta had never heard. It was deep and rich and raspy.

"Aletta Marie Jacobs. I'm eight."

"Special girl. Aletta Marie. Hmmm, a special girl, yes indeedy."

Tessie looked around the room at the little school desk and the homemade hickorywood dresser, but her gaze seemed distant.

"You live around here, Miss Maple?" Aletta was easy around adults. People said it was because she was an only child.

"Tessie, Lord, just Tessie. Used to live not far from here, but not in a lovely big house like this."

Aletta never thought of the two-story farmhouse as lovely, although it certainly was big. It sat in the middle of Okay County with acres of farmland on every side. The farmhouses seemed natural to the land, to grow up out of it like stalks of corn and wheat. The people were like that too, born out of the land, raised on it, married to it, then buried back into it when they died.

"Worked that land down yonder like you wouldn't believe." Tessie waved her hand toward the window. "All my life, fourteen kids I bore. Too many. Too damn many. Died when I was seventy-one. Look at me, just look. Look like a hundred an' one, don't I?" Miss Maple liked to talk.

Aletta pulled the quilt up around her neck. "A hundred an' one." She tried to make her voice sound like that.

"At least. Don't you be havin' so many younguns, special girl. Don't do it. Suck the life right outta you. I loved my kids, but couldn't ever give any of 'em enough. Too many for one woman. Preacher told me what I needed to do was stop sleepin' with Maple. I looked at that man an' just laughed an' laughed. That the important advice you have for me? That there is special. Then I can raise all these chil'ren by myself 'cause my husband done run off?" Tessie's laugh was far away now.

Aletta didn't understand much of what Tessie was talking about, but it had the effect of a lullaby on her. And in the place between awake and asleep, Aletta kept thinking that Tessie was that old tree and that her runaway silver hair was a gray squirrel sitting in the top of it. Aletta smiled as her eyes closed. She liked Tessie the Maple Tree.

★

Aletta opened the door still wiping her hands on the dishrag, Ruby and Randy hovering around her legs. She recognized the young woman on the porch as a waitress from down at Poquito de Mexico (known as Pakita's to the locals). The only minorities in Okay were the Mexicans who owned and worked at Poquito's and the few Chinese who worked at the four-table China Palace restaurant out near I-40.

Aletta hadn't seen the woman around in a while. Seeing the

tiny baby, she knew why. "Hello, I'm Aletta Honor. Come in." Her voice sounded high and strange, so she cleared her throat as she opened the screen door for her first customer. The young woman stared at Aletta's massive belly as she came into the house.

Aletta rubbed the round tightness of her stomach. "Seven and a half months. What's your name?" Aletta wished the girl didn't look so scared. It didn't help her confidence at all.

"Silvia. This is Miguel."

First name only, Aletta noticed. "I don't really have a room set up yet, but we can talk in here."

"How much is it?" Silvia blurted out, shifting Miguel from one arm to the other.

"Is five dollars okay?" Aletta said weakly. She hated the way it came out. It felt like begging somehow.

"I don't have any money, really. My husband, he's gone. I don't know what to do." Big tears popped from Silvia's eyes like liquid diamonds.

"You kids go get Sissy and tell her to come take this baby." Aletta herded Silvia into the living room, picking things up off the floor as she went—a box of Saltine crackers, a baton with pink tassels, Ruby's flip-flops. "Here, sit right here."

Silvia fell onto the tan-and-rust corduroy couch as Aletta took Miguel and handed him to Sissy. He let out one of those cries that sound like a buzz saw starting up, and Silvia instinctively reached into her purse and handed over a pacifier. Sissy took the baby, plugged in the pacifier, and went off cooing at him.

Randy came in with a wad of toilet paper for Silvia's tears.

She smiled at the chubby, tanned child. "Thank you. How old are you?"

Randy held up six fingers. "Goin' on seven." He turned to leave, then stopped in the doorway. "Our daddy left us too."

Silvia looked up at Aletta, a little embarrassed.

"Thank you for that update. Go on and play now." Aletta felt the hot-cold of regret in her chest again and tried to stop the endless loop of thoughts about how she was screwing up with her kids and what she could've done differently with Jimmy. She was glad Silvia was there so she didn't have to think about her own problems.

After Randy's announcement, something changed between the two women. They sat on the couch facing each other, knees almost touching.

"I'd like to say a little prayer first if it's all right with you." Aletta had written it down just before she went to sleep last night. She took a deep breath, trying to relax just a little.

Silvia nodded and touched the Virgin Mary pendant around her neck as they bowed their heads.

"Heavenly Father, we ask You to bless us in this sharing, and that anything revealed here be helpful to Silvia in her time of need. We give thanks for all that we have today, knowing that we live by Your mercy and love. Amen."

They opened their eyes and sat for a moment in silence. Aletta gathered her courage like she used to when she was a kid before she jumped off Mackey's Bridge into the river. Finally, she reached for Silvia's hands. "So what would you like to know?"

Silvia sniffled. "Where is he? Why hasn't he come home? Is he alive?"

The impressions came to Aletta as they always had, flowing in like random thoughts. She had become a master at pushing them away if she touched someone accidentally, so that they became as unreal as a forgotten dream as soon as they passed. Even when the images and visions were strong, she'd never acted on them or told anyone. Until the parade, of course, and again right now.

When she closed her eyes and actually focused on the impressions for the first time as an adult, it was almost overpowering. Silvia gasped as Aletta swayed backwards, grabbing the top of the corduroy couch to stay upright.

"It's all right. Just give me a sec to adjust." Aletta tried to make her voice calm, but she felt like a boat she'd seen in a storm in Galveston on her honeymoon, rising and falling with the waves.

At first, the combination of her own fear and Silvia's was so strong she almost couldn't see past it, but then images of a man came through, choppy and quick. "Drives a truck, a big one." Aletta thought it was strange that the two times she'd seen something, there was a big rig involved. But this was a different truck altogether.

Silvia's eyes became huge. "Yes, yes. He's a truck driver. He was supposed to be back three days ago."

"I see a motel." A dark man with a big mustache who looked several years older than Silvia was with a woman, a prostitute by the looks of her. He stumbled, drunk. The woman tried to seduce him and get to his wallet, but he kept pushing her away, crazy with booze and fear. "He's drunk, he's scared." Then two men are there, wanting something. They say he stole something from them. They beat him up and leave him sprawled out on the floor. "He's hurt, in trouble, Casa de San Antonio." The images jumped around while she tried hard to focus. This was something she needed to work on.

Silvia pulled her hand away. "San Antonio! He was supposed to be going to New Orleans. What kind of trouble? How bad is he hurt?"

The waves stopped and Aletta came back to the room. Later, she realized the impressions ended when she couldn't handle any more physically. She had worn out fast.

"That's all there is. You should call that place." Aletta breathed deeply. She hoped, if she had to keep the sign out, it would get a lot easier than this.

"Yes, yes, I must find him." Silvia's tears were flowing again as she jumped up and ran out the front door.

"What about Miguel?" Aletta called after her, struggling to her feet.

After a moment, Silvia burst back through the door and pushed five wadded-up dollar bills into Aletta's hand. She hugged her from the side to avoid her belly. Sissy brought Miguel to her, and she flew out the door, saying "Thank you" over and over.

Aletta could see Silvia talking to herself as she started her huge baby-blue Impala and drove away.

Chapter Three

"Lettie, come on down, your mother's got breakfast on." Aletta's daddy, Clovis Jacobs, always woke her after he came in from milking the cows. He had a low, rumbly voice. The rumble woke Aletta every morning, not the words. It was the first of May, a big day on the farm, so she quickly put on a long-sleeved blue cotton dress and tried in vain to smooth her rumpled hair. Downstairs, she followed the smell of sizzling bacon, eager to see the farmhands who had just arrived to bring in the alfalfa. In a couple of weeks, they'd plant the cotton. It felt almost like Christmas as she walked into the big warm kitchen.

"I don't know, Mrs. Jacobs, I'd probably come here and work just to eat your food. Clove wouldn't even have to pay me." Johnny Redding had worked for her daddy during the harvest since Aletta could remember. He charmed everyone with his mischievous blue eyes, his big laugh, and his compliments.

"I'll take ya up on that, son," Clovis chuckled. Her daddy was taller than most of the other men, and thinner too—his overalls never quite filled out completely, especially his backside, which was flatter than one of her mama's pancakes. The black hair on his head was getting little patches of silver at the temples.

"Yes, ma'am, your cookin' beats all, but you won't mind if I go ahead on and take my wages, I hope," Chubby Lute said as he stuffed a whole dollar pancake in his mouth.

"Didn't you tell 'em Clovis?" Nadine Jacobs turned from the stove with a skillet full of hash browns. "This year, they're all workin' for breakfast and dinner." She saw Aletta standing quietly watching them. "Hi, big girl," she said. Nadine had her light brown hair pulled up in a bun as usual. Unlike Clovis's overalls, her apron was filled out pretty well, most of all around her middle.

The farmhands saw Aletta with her big sleepy eyes and blond hair swooping up on one side and laughed warmly. They were big guys, men with hands like baseball mitts and arms strong enough to toss huge bales of hay around for a living. To Aletta, they were larger than life, men with wild stories, stubbled faces, and big hearts.

"Lookee here, it's the princess of Okay County," Johnny said. His teeth were tobacco-stained but still a stark contrast to his sun-browned, leathery skin.

"Hi, honey, I'm Pete. It's good to make your acquaintance." Pete was the only one of the three men Aletta hadn't met before. He was younger than the others, so his face was smooth.

Although she was thrilled to get the attention, she stayed quiet. Her mother had taught her how to be a nice girl, and a big part of that was being quiet.

"Nadine, you better go fix her hair 'fore she goes to school," Clovis said.

"Not before I get a hug," Johnny said. Aletta walked over to Johnny, her face pink from shyness. He gave her a big hug, then took the point of her hair that stood straight up and tried to put a little curl in it. He smelled like coffee and dirt and chewing tobacco. One of his hands was as wide as her back.

In the bathroom, Nadine asked Aletta if it was all right with her that Johnny had hugged her.

She nodded her head. "He reminds me of Uncle Joey. I like him. Ouch, Mama, that hurts!"

Nadine was trying to drag a comb through Aletta's rat's-nest hair. "Just a little bit more, honey."

"Mama, do you think I'll ever have a baby brother or sister?"

"Remember what I told you about that?"

"Not really." Aletta did remember. She just wanted to hear it again.

"You were like a miracle to me and your daddy. The doctors told us we'd never have a child, and for years and years we didn't, but then when I thought I was way too old to have a baby, I had you by the grace of God. But I can't have any more, honey. One day you can have your own babies, though, I promise."

"Miss Maple had fourteen, but she said that was too many."

"Fourteen children? Oh, my, that's a lot," Nadine said. She'd never heard of a Miss Maple storybook, but of course a lot had changed since she was a child.

"Maybe I'll just have ten, then, or maybe eight," Aletta decided.

A few days later, as Aletta walked the mile to the bus stop, she passed the creek and saw Johnny far down the line of trees off the tractor, bending over something in the ground. She thought about how he treated her like "the princess of Okay County." She loved that. She'd been thinking about asking if he would be her brother, or pretend he was anyway. She yelled to him, but he couldn't hear her. She couldn't wait to get home after school to see what he'd found. Maybe it was an animal, like the tiny baby possum she'd found the year before under a fallen tree trunk.

After Silvia left, Aletta shooed the kids outside and sat down at the bar to look at the bills again. Her reading with Silvia had been rough, both physically and because Silvia had been so scared, but it showed her that the images would come when she wanted and made her think she might be able to do this, even if she didn't want to.

"Yoo-hoo!" Joy called through the screen door.

"Come on in." Aletta gratefully pushed aside the stack of bills. Joy swept in smelling, as always, of hairspray and cigarettes.

"I just put Kathy Kokin under the dryer and had a few minutes, so I thought I'd come say hi." She took out a long cigarette and lit it with a slim gold lighter.

"I didn't see you again after you chased down Earl at the parade," Aletta said. "That was some show."

"His car wouldn't start, the poor baby. I thought I'd seen him at the start. Ain't that awful, I couldn't tell him from any of the other pot-bellied old farts? After I caught him, we had to go get consoled at the Silver Spur."

Joy glanced out the window at the sign with just her eyes. Aletta could tell she was forcing herself to be casual.

"Did Jimmy show up?" Joy asked.

"Nope, but he called. He says the kids need their daddy."

"Better off without him, if you ask me." Joy exhaled puffs of smoke with each word.

"Maybe we shouldn't have had kids so young. Maybe he needed more time to be young." Aletta wanted to believe that if things *could* have been better between them somehow, then there was still a chance they might be.

"So he could cat around and drink like an Indian? You must still love him if you're talkin' like that."

"I don't know," Aletta said. And she didn't. Between the anger and frustration and resentment, she thought she sometimes still felt love for him. She'd adored him when they were younger, and that feeling she knew was long gone, but there was something left. She wasn't sure if it was love or maybe just need.

Joy rolled her eyes in answer. "Okay, girl, I've been polite long enough." She put out her cigarette in the beanbag ashtray that sat on the dining room table. "What's up with the damn sign in the yard? The girls shoved me out the door to come over here and get the lowdown. I've had three drop-ins already this morning asking questions." She tapped a red-nailed finger on her temple. "The talk is that this whole thing with Jimmy has got you touched in the head."

Aletta looked hurt, even though she'd expected as much. "I just needed some money is all."

"But Lettie, sweetie, do you think it's such a good idea?" Joy asked with a dramatic swoop of her hand. "I mean, if people are payin', they're gonna expect some real information. You can't just tell 'em things you learned out of a book and expect . . . well, I'm sure you could fool a bunch of these folks, but not all. Aren't you afraid of the consequences?"

Aletta reached out and took hold of Joy's forearm. "Ask me something you want to know about."

Joy looked down at Aletta's hand on her arm, and her carefully etched eyebrows turned into a V. "I just told you. I want to know why you're pullin' this stunt."

"You're concerned because you're afraid people might turn on me and then you'd have to decide whether or not to be my friend, and you don't want to have to do that because you like me and my kids."

"Well, hell's bells, darlin', that was easy." She grabbed Aletta's hand and looked at her, begging her to understand. "That's what I mean. It wasn't mind-readin'. That was just plain old female intuition. Any woman with her head unfamiliar with her ass coulda told you that."

Aletta closed her eyes and felt the wave swell up in her. She wasn't so nervous this time because Joy was a friend, but she still didn't like the feeling. It was almost like nausea, and she'd had more than enough of that from morning sickness. When the wave died down, she got images. She was surprised at how clear they were, laid out like a picnic on a blanket for her. Maybe if she was able to stay calm like this, it'd be easier.

After the images stopped, she opened her eyes and spoke. "When you were twelve, you fell out of a tree and tore your leg open on the way down. There was a deep cut on your thigh with white fat bulging out of it. You decided just before you passed out to get thin and never be fat again. And look at you now." Aletta opened her hands toward Joy's slim figure.

Joy popped out of her seat as if it were in flames. "Oh, my God, I've never told that to a single soul, not even my mother.

Wait a minute. Was I twelve? Oh, good Lord-a-mercy, that's exactly right because I was in love with Harley McQuarrie then, and
he moved over to Mustang a month before my birthday." She
rubbed her hands on her arms and hopped around. "Ooh, ooh, I
just got the chills all up and down me. How'd you do that?"

"I don't know. It's just something I've always been able to
do." Aletta pushed her hair behind her ears. "I didn't want to put
the sign out, or even be this way for that matter, but I need the
money, Joy. I don't know how I'm supposed to feed and clothe
four kids and keep this roof over their heads." Her voice became
quiet and small. "This ain't what I signed up for."

"Well, of course you should make money offa this." Joy put
an arm around Aletta's shoulders. "It's the American way, by
God. Don't worry, honey. It'll all be just fine. People are going to
love it."

Aletta let herself lean against Joy. She felt helpless. "I just need
to take care of my kids."

"You gonna be okay, hon?" Joy asked.

"Yeah, go on, I'll pull my fat self together. I feel like a big old
sad sow." Aletta laughed at herself.

"I gotta get back to Kathy before her rollers melt, but I'll come
back over this afternoon to check on you, all righty?"

"Thanks, Joy." Aletta got up to fix some canned creamed corn,
a craving she'd been having for three days. She thought about the
sign up in the room at church where the old men went for their
alcoholic meetings. "One day at a time," it said. "How 'bout one
minute?" she said aloud as she cranked open the can of corn, the
Jolly Green Giant beaming at her from the label. "What're you so
happy about?" she asked him.

Joy walked out the front door and past the window, then
broke into a sprint all the way back to the salon. She was breathing hard as she stepped inside. Eight pairs of mascaraed eyes
turned to her with anticipation.

"Girls," she said, placing one fist on each hip, "We've got us a
real live psychic right next door."

* * *

Aletta made frozen fish sticks, frozen French fries, and another can of creamed corn for dinner. Silvia had been her only customer all day.

"What did that lady with the baby say today, Mama? Did you read her mind?" Ruby asked for the third time. They sat at the bar in their usual places, Aletta closest to the stove and Sissy closest to the phone.

"Ruby, I told you it's private business what happened with her, and you should respect people's private business."

Ruby swiped her fish stick through a puddle of ketchup on her plate, but just before shoving it in her mouth, said, "Why didn't you start reading minds 'til now, Mama?"

"I just didn't want to." Aletta placed a fallen French fry back onto Randy's plate.

"Did you read that lady's mind?" Ruby pressed on.

"Janice says her mom reads her mind all the time. She says she can't lie to her, because her mom knows it, but Mama never reads our minds," Sissy said.

"Many people have an ability," Aletta said, "especially with their own family and loved ones, but mine is the opposite. I can see things about strangers but never have been able to see anything about my own or myself. But I'll have you know I can always tell when you're lying. That just comes with being a mother."

"Mama, I need a new bike. I really do. I can't even sit on the seat anymore, mine is so small. That's why I wrecked," Ruby said.

"Well, I need a new bathing suit first. Mine from last year doesn't fit anymore and it's ugly," Sissy said, more to Ruby than Aletta.

Randy just sat quietly.

"Listen here, y'all know that your daddy's gone, and we can't afford things for a while. We're just gonna have to make do with what we have. I don't have any idea how I'm gonna pay for the bills I'm behind on now, let alone a new bike, so you're gonna have to grow up a little bit and help me out by not askin' for stuff so much. I need more help with this house too, especially with this baby that's comin'. I can't do it all by myself and y'all are big enough to do more things around here."

Aletta's worries were spilling out again, and while she knew she shouldn't make the kids worry too, she didn't know how else to handle it. If she was honest with herself, which mostly she wasn't, she had to admit that sometimes she felt like a child too, not sure how to handle things or manage life.

The kids were quiet for a few minutes under the weight of their new burden, but Aletta realized Randy had been quiet the entire dinner. He wasn't one to play ball or go fishing like his dad always wanted, and now his dad was gone. Just as the familiar worries about her son started gaining speed, she smelled something. Sissy sniffed the air.

"Gross-out. What's that smell?" Ruby crinkled up her nose.

Randy started laughing and covered his mouth with his hands as Aletta got up to track down the origin of the sickly sweet, rubbery smoke.

"Randy, what the hell're you up to?" Smoke was seeping from the oven that was set to 450 degrees. Aletta yanked it open and saw a cookie sheet with five wads of chewed-up bubble gum melted and burning. Randy was by her side, admiring his creation.

"I'm making kolaches," he said proudly.

Aletta took a deep breath. "And burning them just like your mama," she said, and laughed. She fished the cookie sheet out of the oven with a dirty dish towel and put it out in the garage to cool off.

Later, lying in bed feeling her baby kick, Aletta prayed, "Thank you, God, for all my kids and this one that's on the way. I pray I can stay strong for them. Amen."

It relaxed her enough to let herself fall asleep and to dream.

In her dream, Aletta ran around asking everyone she saw, "Have you seen my baby? Where's my little girl?" The people spoke, but she couldn't hear anything they said. The distant sound of a doorbell ringing made her wonder if it was someone bringing her baby to her.

In order to sleep, Aletta required a fan blowing on medium, earplugs, about six inches of blankets, and aluminum foil covering the windows behind the curtains in her bedroom. That was her favorite thing about being alone—she didn't have to accommodate Jimmy's sleeping needs, which were a far cry from her own.

From inside her dream-heavy cocoon, she realized it was her own doorbell ringing.

"Shit." She threw back the covers and tried to jump up, but her heft said no, so she grunted and lay back down. Trying again, she rolled out of the bed sideways, stood up slowly, put on her robe, and went to the door. Glancing at the clock in the kitchen, she saw it was seven-thirty in the morning.

A man and woman in their sixties stood at the door smiling. The woman held a tiny Chihuahua, and when the three of them saw Aletta, they burst out all at once. The couple laughed, and the dog barked.

"Ooh, Vera, look there. I think we came to the right place," the man cooed.

"Josie, be quiet this instant," the woman scolded the bug-eyed dog, then turned to Aletta. "Hello, are you the psychic of the house?" She smiled like she'd won something as she admired Aletta's belly. In fact, neither one could take their eyes off her roundness for long.

Aletta nodded, noticing the RV sitting outside. "Yes, but it's really early."

Ruby peeked around her mother. "Who is it, Mama?" She pushed the screen door open and reached for Josie. "Can I hold him?"

"Why, of course you can, young lady. What's your name?" Mrs. RV asked.

Jesus, these people are chipper, Aletta thought.

"Ruby Rose Honor." Ruby took the squirming dog. She laughed as it barked and licked her face.

"Come on in," Aletta finally said. "You'll have to excuse my robe."

She led them into the tiled entryway and turned them to the right into the living room, away from her messy kitchen. It was a tight fit for three adults in the small living room, already crowded with the tan-and-rust corduroy couch and matching love seat, her wooden rocking chair, and the ancient Panasonic TV with aluminum-foil-wrapped rabbit ears.

When they got situated, her customers on the couch and Aletta facing them in her rocking chair, she asked what they wanted to know. She felt less nervous because these people were out-of-towners, and she figured she wouldn't see them again.

"Well, first we want you to prove that you're a real psychic, right, honey?" Mr. RV looked at his wife, getting the final go-ahead with a nod. "Then we want you to tell us if we're ever gonna have any grandchildren."

The Mrs. added, "Our two kids don't seem in any hurry, and we're about to bust. By the way, I'm Vera and this is Harold."

"Nice to meet you. What proof would you like?" Aletta asked.

"Um, what year did we get married?" Harold asked, and Vera nodded.

Aletta chose to take Vera's hand, to avoid touching another woman's husband. The images came. They were visions of moments, fleeting and swift. She had no idea why she got the particular things she did, but if she began to think about it, the images would fade, so she just allowed them to come as they might and hoped for the best. The story the images told were confusing, so Aletta kept her eyes closed and thought for a few minutes.

Aletta opened her eyes and pulled her hand away. "I don't get dates, really."

"Oh." Vera's smile dropped from her face.

Harold shifted on the couch. "Well . . . hmmm."

"You were divorced for a little while, weren't you?" Aletta asked.

They looked up at her at the same moment, their expressions changing so quickly Aletta almost laughed. She had to admit she enjoyed it.

"Well, yes, we were," Vera said.

"But you got back together and had another wedding," Aletta said. "Y'all are ornery asking me a trick question like that!"

Vera laughed. "Yes, but we couldn't fool you!" she exclaimed, and clapped her hands. "That was just wonderful."

Harold leaned forward, excited as a little boy. "Now, what about grandkids?"

Half an hour later, they walked out the front door damn near whistling a jig. Aletta put the ten dollars they'd insisted on giving her into her wallet as she watched the RV drive away. For the first time in weeks, she felt a small sense of peace. She made a cup of Sanka—caffeine made her feel sick when she was pregnant—and tried to figure out where she could fit HOURS 9AM TO 6PM on her sign.

Eugene stopped by at noon, standing at the door with his cap in his hand. "Just wanted to come let you know about your Chevy. I've ordered a water pump."

"I feel bad you doin' all that work for free, Eugene. It must be all kinds of trouble," Aletta said, pushing open the screen door. "Come on in."

Eugene sat down at the dining room table. "I have fun with it, Lettie. She's a pleasure to work on. I just wish I had more time to do it is all."

Ruby, dressed in blue leather chaps and a vest with two six-shooters in her holster, chased Randy into the room. He was wearing her cowgirl hat. "Mama, he stole my hat!" she bellowed.

"I'm supposed to be the bartender of the saloon. I have to wear it, Ruby!" Randy yelled back.

"You kids stop running right now!" Aletta shouted.

Ruby tried to snatch the hat, but Randy took it off and threw it across the room. It landed at Eugene's feet. He picked it up, took off his cap, and put the tiny blue hat with white rope trim on his head. Ruby and Randy laughed in their high-pitched, little-kid way. Aletta had to laugh too. Finally, Ruby marched over to him and put her hand out asking for her hat back.

He tipped the hat to her. "Howdy do, ma'am. Do you know how to use those pistols you've got there?"

"You look funny!" Randy blurted out as Ruby twirled the pistols on her fingers and shoved them back into place.

"I'm Jesse James," she finished with a flourish.

"I bet you get thirsty after a few bank robberies." He caught the hat as it slipped forward and replaced it on top of his head. Aletta laughed again.

"I drink whisky," Ruby said.

"Got it right here!" Randy pulled a pitcher of grape Kool-Aid out of the fridge.

"Whisky sounds good to me. Can I buy you a drink, Jesse?" Eugene asked. "Wait a minute, I think we have a problem. I don't see a bartender anywhere."

"I'm the bartender! It's me!" Randy called out from his perch on the cabinet shelf he was using as a ladder to reach the glasses above.

"Let me help you, honey." Aletta pushed herself up from the table. She felt like she hadn't slept all night.

"You don't look like a bartender to me. How do I know you're the real thing?" Eugene asked.

"I know! I know! That's what I was *saying*! I need a hat or something," Randy agreed.

"Okay, but only while he's the bartender. That's it," Ruby said.

"Sounds fair to me." Eugene extended the hat to Randy.

Aletta sighed gratefully. Eugene had rescued her from having to play policeman.

After Eugene left, Aletta spent the rest of the afternoon in bed except for the many trips she made to the bathroom to pee. *This baby better grow up to be the president,* she thought as she shuffled down the hall. In the evening, she was barely able get up long enough to make TV dinners for the kids because of her swollen feet and ankles and sore back. She went back to bed while Sissy, Randy, and Ruby ate their Salisbury steaks and mashed potatoes and watched the movie *Jesus Christ Superstar* on television.

Sissy kept adjusting the rabbit ears and balling up the aluminum foil in different configurations to get a clear picture, but other than "No, the other way was better" or "Yeah, right there," they sat in rapt silence. In their world, Jesus had long hair and a beard, but he didn't sing rock and roll, and he definitely didn't dance. They liked this Jesus a lot better.

The next morning, Joy was ratting Iola Little's slightly purplish hair when she saw, in the reflection of the mirror, Kathy Kokin, in sunglasses and straw hat, sneaking up Aletta's front walk.

"Give me two shakes of a lamb's tail," she said to Iola, and tiptoed over to peek out front. She looked up and down Main Street for Kathy's white Cadillac Eldorado, but as she suspected, it was nowhere to be seen. She smiled and said under her breath, "Hypocrite."

When Joy had made her announcement about Aletta's ability the day before, Kathy Kokin had been the loudest naysayer in the group, arguing that Aletta was just trying to get attention. Joy returned to Iola and got out the huge pink can of Aqua Net. She couldn't wait to ask Aletta about this one.

Sissy and her best friend, Angie, answered the door. Kathy took off her hat and sunglasses, revealing her most prized possession, her face. Lavender-blue eyes smoldered above her defined cheekbones and full mouth.

"Is your mother here?" Kathy smiled sweetly and pushed her way into the house. "I just wanted to come and see about her condition."

"She's in bed, not feeling very good," Sissy said between sneezes caused by Kathy's sweet rose-petals-and-jasmine perfume.

"Good thing I came by to see her, then. I'll just go look in, all righty?" Kathy walked to the closed bedroom door at the beginning of the hallway. "In here?"

Sissy nodded, and she and Angie rolled their eyes at each other.

"Knock, knock," Kathy said in a high voice, opening Aletta's door. Aletta looked up, taking the earplugs out of her ears. "My God, Kathy, what are you doin' here?"

"I just wanted to check on you, and it looks like a good thing I did, too. Your girl said you were feelin' pretty punk."

"I'm having some cramping, and I'm dog-tired, but I need to get up." Aletta did her roll-over-and-stand move. She still had creases on her face from the pillow. "Give me a minute, and I'll be right out."

Kathy waited in the dining room, trying to decide exactly how many colors were in the hideous shag carpet. She came up with at least five—blue, gold, orange, brown, and turquoise.

Aletta came out, looking pale. Just about the last thing in the world she wanted to do right now was visit with Kathy Kokin.

"I'm gonna be all right, Kathy, but thanks for stoppin' by."

Kathy had been after Jimmy since even before her husband Lonnie Kokin, the car dealer in Oklahoma City, died from a heart attack last year. "Lonnie K Cars—we love folks" was heard over the TV set regularly. He'd been thirty-three years older than Kathy, so it was no surprise to anyone she ended up a widow at thirty-eight.

Aletta realized she was straightening her ridiculous pink bathrobe over her round belly as she looked at Kathy in her perfect makeup and expensive taupe pantsuit. "Would you like a cup of Sanka?" she asked, and dropped her hands to her sides.

"No, thank you, dear. . . . So I hear you're some kind of psychic or somethin'. Is that the truth?" Kathy asked.

"I try," Aletta said.

"So if I wanted to find something out, something particular that I'm wonderin' about, I could ask you and you'd know the answer?" Kathy tilted her head, looking at Aletta sideways.

"Well, not always, but most the time, yes."

"How much do you charge for this service?"

Aletta sat down. She had to get off her feet. "Oh, five dollars usually, but I'm feelin' dog-tired right now."

Kathy opened her purse, pulled a ten-dollar bill out of her wallet, and laid it on the table.

"What do we need to do, light candles or call on the dead or something?" she laughed. "Oh, Lonnie, honey, where are you? Oh, no, you better not listen after all."

"I don't think I have the energy today, but . . ."

Kathy pushed the ten closer to Aletta and lowered her voice. "I know you need this money. I just have one little question."

Aletta looked at the bill, swallowed the "no" on the tip of her tongue, and sat down next to Kathy. The rose-petals-and-jasmine perfume tickled the inside of her nose. "First I have to pray," she said, rubbing her nose with the palm of her hand.

"Whatever you need," Kathy said.

"Heavenly Father. . . ." Aletta said her prayer, then looked at Kathy. She couldn't get over the feeling she shouldn't be doing this. "What, um, what would you like to know?"

"Who's gonna be my next husband?" Kathy smiled, having fun.

Aletta took Kathy's manicured hand and closed her eyes. After a long silence, she opened them, looking even paler than before.

"I'm not seeing anyone clearly," Aletta said finally. She pulled her hand away a little too quickly. What she'd seen she didn't want to talk to Kathy about. *It's not my business,* she told herself. *I might be wrong anyway.*

Panic played on Kathy's face. "What do you mean?" she asked.

"It might not mean a thing, Kathy," Aletta fumbled. "I'm just not seeing anyone." *That's true,* Aletta thought. *I don't see her next husband, and that's all she asked me about.*

"Well, try again, I know you're tired. I mean, I'm dating two or three very eligible men right now." Kathy laughed nervously and pushed her soft hand back into Aletta's trembling one.

Aletta held it for a moment and then withdrew. "No, nothing. I'm just not seeing anything today is all."

Kathy's face turned red as she stood up and looked around the cluttered house in disgust. "I don't know what came over me to believe such nonsense, but I know you're desperate, so why don't you keep that, dear." She glanced at the ten-dollar bill, then turned and walked out, the screen door slamming behind her.

After Kathy left, Aletta sat looking around her house, thinking again how small it was for four kids. She looked at the worn-out kitchen linoleum, the dent in the front door where one of the kids, she couldn't remember who, had crashed into it. Everything seemed flawed right down to the faded, cheap upholstery on the arm of her chair. Closing her eyes, she could still smell the pungent decay underneath the sterile, antiseptic aroma of Lysol and medicine as the vision of Kathy's future faded away. The smell that came with the sight of Kathy lying alone in a hospital bed had been the most difficult thing for Aletta to take. That smell and the scent of Kathy's perfume lingered with Aletta as she wondered why Kathy was in the hospital. When it came down to it, though, Aletta decided she didn't want to know. It was none of her business or any of her responsibility.

It could have been a few minutes or half an hour later when Ruby walked in the front door bouncing her basketball.

Ruby sang to herself a song about blood money Aletta hadn't heard before. Ruby spun around.

As she walked by, Aletta grabbed her by the arm and spanked her once on the butt. "I told you not to bounce that damn ball in this house, and stop singing that song. Where'd you learn that?"

Ruby's tears were silent at first. "I heard it in the Jesus movie last night!" she wailed. The basketball thumped across the shag carpet.

"Just don't bounce that ball in here anymore," Aletta said. "Mama's havin' a rough time right now, so you need to be a good girl."

Randy walked in from the living room. "What'd ya do, Rube?"

"I didn't do anything, stupid!" she screamed.

Randy started to cry.

"No, no, it's okay, Randy," Aletta said reaching out to hug him. As she did, she heard Ruby stalk back to the room she and Randy shared and slam the door.

Once Randy calmed down, Aletta slipped into the bathroom and locked the door. She dug through the piles of makeup and hair curlers in the bottom drawer and found her pack of Salem menthols. Jimmy hated her smoking. He still jogged every day and was adamant about her not smoking around the children. But she needed something and he wasn't here, so she put one of the flattened cigarettes in her mouth, struck three matches until one lit, and inhaled.

Realizing she hadn't opened the window, she held in the drag until she could unlock the window and push it open. Finally she exhaled, and immediately leaned over the toilet and threw up. She waited, bent over, to make sure she wasn't going to throw up again. She watched pieces of creamed corn floating in the green-brown chunks of vomit and noticed that the porcelain toilet bowl had a black ring around the inside.

Aletta started to cry.

Finally, after deciding she wasn't going to throw up again, she flicked the long ash of her cigarette on top of the vomit and flushed the toilet. She closed the lid, sat down, and really let go, endless tears streaming down her face as she sobbed aloud.

God, she thought, *I'm not a good mother. I love 'em, but it ain't enough. I've tried to be a good wife, but I've even screwed that up. And I'm not a good daughter, God. That's it, isn't it? I've never been a good daughter.*

In the next room, Ruby pressed her face against the wall, listening to her mother cry. "I'm sorry, Mama," she whispered.

Chapter Four

That day at school, eight-year-old Aletta decided to tell her class of eleven children and her teacher, Mrs. Vandehay, about her visits from Miss Maple. They sat in a one-room schoolhouse that was painted a dark burgundy red on the outside with stained wood floors on the inside.

Aletta sat in her little desk near the front, close to Mrs. Vandehay. "She's real old and has dark skin and fuzzy gray hair. She doesn't have many teeth, and she said I shouldn't have lots of babies."

Mrs. Vandehay was not amused. "Aletta, I don't know if you had some crazy dream last night, but I do know that your parents would never let such a creature in their home, and that she certainly wouldn't talk to you about having babies. So I suggest you sit down and reconsider your story and remember that nice girls don't lie."

The other kids laughed at her, and at recess they called her Crazy Lettie. Gerald Clemmons, who was a year older than Aletta, called her Crazy Lettie all the way through high school. To him it became a term of endearment, and he even told her once he'd forgotten why he'd started. But she never forgot.

Sitting around the dinner table that night, Aletta waited until nobody else was talking, then said to Johnny, "I saw you out there diggin' in the ground. What did you find?"

The spoonful of mashed potatoes he held stopped before it reached his mouth. He laughed nervously and glanced at Clovis. "I didn't find nothin', darlin'. You musta been seeing things. Or maybe it was the call of nature."

Lute and Pete laughed.

"What's the call of nature?" she asked.

"Never you mind, honey. Just eat your dinner," Clovis said.

She went to bed that night confused about a lot of things.

★

"What'd Kathy wanna know?" Joy asked as she drove the half mile to the grocery store. The air conditioner in her Buick blasted out blessedly cool air.

Aletta leaned her head back on the headrest, completely exhausted from crying so hard. She felt exposed and vulnerable, so she avoided Joy's gaze. "Now, I don't tell that, Joy. You wouldn't want me tellin' her about your business, would you?"

"Ah, hell's bells, Lettie honey, I wouldn't tell a soul," Joy pleaded.

"I can't, Joy. I made a promise to the Lord." Aletta closed her eyes.

Joy clacked her wedding ring on the steering wheel a few times as she considered. "Well, I saw her runnin' outta there like hell shot a goose, so it must not 'a been very good, I know that much."

An image of Kathy when she was told there might not be any more husbands came up behind Aletta's closed eyes. Hell shot a goose. She started to laugh and then to giggle uncontrollably.

"What, what is it?" Joy said as she pulled into the IGA parking lot. There were only a few cars, all of them massive four-door sedans driven precariously by the elder population of Okay.

"Nothing, I'm sorry, I'm just delirious," Aletta said. She tried to stop laughing, but couldn't.

Joy parked her two-tone tan-and-brown Riviera but kept the

engine running. "See, I knew it was somethin' juicy. It's juicy, ain't it?"

"No, no, it's me," Aletta said through her laughter.

Joy lit up a cigarette and shook her head while Aletta laughed.

"Everything's turnin' brown from the heat already," Joy commented, and blew smoke out the sliver of open window.

Aletta roared with laughter. She'd let go of reason and responsibility for a moment, and it felt great.

Joy smiled. "Girl, you *are* a little touched," she said.

When she finally stopped laughing, Aletta felt lighter. Inside the store, even the looks of pity from old ladies who knew that handsome Jimmy Honor had left her when she was as big as a barn didn't bother her so much. She spent every penny of the twenty-five dollars she'd made from her psychic readings on Hamburger Helper, Lucky Charms, and all of her kids' other favorites. On the way out to the car, the gangly blond grocery boy who carried out her bags asked her if she was the psychic lady.

Joy answered first. "Rusty, meet Aletta Honor, real live psychic reader." Then to Aletta, she added, "He's Betty and Frank Conway's son."

As Rusty loaded the bags in the car, Aletta touched his shoulder. He turned. "You ought to keep playing your guitar, Rusty. Practice as much as you can," she said.

He almost dropped the bag he was holding. "Really? You think I could be a rock star or something? I want to be in a band like Led Zeppelin or Journey." His blue-gray eyes danced in the June sun.

Aletta smiled. "Just keep playin', hon."

They drove away and Aletta could see him walking toward the store. After a few steps, he broke into a run and jumped up to touch the top of the door as he went inside.

From two hundred yards away, Joy and Aletta could see the van parked in Aletta's driveway.

"What on God's green earth is that?" Joy asked.

Aletta didn't know what it was, but she knew who. Her heart

was lodged squarely in her throat, making speech about as likely as squeezing her bulk out the car window and flying away. She *wanted* to fly away, or at least tell Joy to turn the car around, but she couldn't take her eyes off that van. It was red, white, and blue with huge stars and stripes, an enormous hot-rod American flag. As Joy turned into the driveway, the back doors of the van flew open. Randy and Ruby sat inside on the red velour seat surrounded by red, white, and blue shag carpet.

"Mama, look, isn't it groovy?" Ruby yelled before Aletta even opened her door.

Jimmy walked out the front door of the house, smiling that beautiful smile. Sissy was right behind.

Joy grabbed Aletta's hand. "You all right?"

Aletta nodded. Joy got out of the car and put on a show of helping Aletta heave herself onto her feet.

"Well, look what the cat dragged in," she said as Jimmy walked up.

Aletta noticed her sign was gone.

"Hello, Joy," Jimmy said. He turned to Aletta and turned on the charm. "Hey, sweetheart. God, it's so good to see you. You look great." He hugged her and laughed with delight at how big her belly was. He reached out to touch it, but Aletta turned and went to the trunk. She picked up two bags of groceries, using them like a shield in front of her as she tramped inside.

Joy picked up a bag and started to follow, but Jimmy took it from her. "Thanks, Joy, but I'll get this. I need to talk to Aletta."

"I bet you do." Joy let him take the bag but walked to the house anyway. She found Aletta in the kitchen putting away groceries.

"I'll stay if you want me to, babe."

"It's all right, Joy. Thank you," Aletta said. She didn't want to burden Joy with her problems. Anyway, it was embarrassing enough to have other people know about her broken marriage and broken life. She certainly didn't want them to see it firsthand.

"Come by tomorrow for a free manicure, okay?" Joy said.

Aletta nodded.

"Promise me." Joy put her hands on Aletta's shoulders.

"I promise."

Joy walked past Jimmy, who'd been standing holding the groceries, waiting. She shot him the meanest look she had, the one that caused Earl to do whatever she demanded, the one she pulled out only on special occasions.

"Here, honey, why don't you sit down? I'll put these away," Jimmy said. But Aletta kept mechanically opening cabinets and drawers and stuffing things inside. She didn't know if she should listen or leave, if what she was feeling was hope or fear.

"I'm sorry I had to leave for a while, baby."

Sissy came in the front door. "Hey Dad, can I have a slumber party and sleep in the van?" she asked.

"I need to talk to your mom for just a minute, Sis. We'll talk about it later."

Sissy walked back outside where the neighbor kids were gathering around the van as if it was sending out a homing beacon.

Jimmy put the groceries down on the kitchen bar. "I love you, Lettie. I want to be with you and the kids. I've been thinking about it a lot. That's why I had to leave for a while, to think about my life and get my head together. When I saw you at the parade the other day, I knew I had to come back." His voice shook slightly as he spoke. "I got the family a present. Do you like the van? It's brand-new, custom-made for the Bicentennial. I traded in the Ford for it. That car was fallin' apart. I thought we could all go on a trip."

"Where were you?" Aletta asked with her back still to him.

He walked over, put his hands on her shoulders, and kissed her neck. "What'd you say? I couldn't hear you."

Angry that her skin still tingled when he kissed her, she pulled away and faced him. "Where the hell were you, Jimmy?"

"I told you, I was stayin' with Vic at his apartment in the city. I was thinkin'."

"You were partying. Don't you think people tell me when they see you out at the bars two-steppin' with other women?" Aletta folded the grocery bags as if she had something against them.

"I had to see if that was the kinda life I wanted, Aletta." He led her to a chair and gently coaxed her into sitting. He knelt on the floor in front of her and looked into her eyes.

"What kinda life *do* you want, Jimmy?" she asked. "Whatever you say, you better tell the truth. I can live with most anything, but not with lies."

"I want a life here with you and Sissy and Ruby and Randy and this little guy," he said, touching her belly lightly. "It's what I really want. Will you take me back?"

In spite of herself, she could feel the cluster of tightness in her chest softening, the little sprout of hope pushing its way to the surface. She knew she needed him to help her with the kids, the bills, the house. She looked at him and prayed to God to please let him be telling the truth.

"I married you, didn't I?" she said taking his face in her hands. "But don't you ever leave again. We're broke." She let go of him, her voice strained and angry. "I had to put that sign out in the yard to make enough money for us to have food in the house. The electric bill and the mortgage are past due, and I was worried to death. I think I have enough to do around here without havin' to worry about food."

His light brown eyes seemed distant and sad as he stood up. "I'll take care of it. You don't have to worry about makin' money with that psychic crap anymore. The place looked like a whore-house or somethin'."

He walked outside. She sat there staring at the empty spot that had just been filled with her husband. Her head felt like a teakettle with the whistle going off. She didn't move until the wave of anger subsided. It wouldn't help to say anything. Anyway, when she really considered it, she was glad to have that sign put away.

Aletta finally walked outside and looked closely at the van along with everyone else. The inside had a sink, a tiny refrigerator, and a small table with fake wood trim. Jimmy was folding the table down to make a queen-size bed out of the back. The front bucket seats were blue velour, while the back seats were reversible—

blue vinyl on one side and red velour on the other. Even the ceiling had red shag carpet. On the hood there was a huge bald eagle with its wings spread and a ribbon in its mouth. Underneath it read BICENTENNIAL: 1776 TO 1976.

Joy walked out on the front porch of her shop cleaning out a hairbrush. Aletta walked over and joined her.

"Looks like George Washington took a crap in your driveway," Joy said.

"That's just about what I was thinkin'," Aletta said, laughing. "The kids love it, though."

"I bet 'the kids' do," Joy said.

Aletta knew she meant Jimmy.

"I think he really means it, Joy. He's back for good. He went and tried out bein' a playboy, and it wasn't for him," Aletta said. She was trying to convince herself as much as she was Joy.

"I hope so, honey. For you, I really hope so."

"Come on, darlin'! Let's go for a ride," Jimmy called.

Aletta smiled weakly at Joy, then went to join her family.

Joy went back inside the salon. "A man that good-lookin' is pure trouble," she announced to her two hired beauticians and three customers.

Even the ladies who didn't know who she was talking about nodded their heads in agreement. Joy's husband, Earl, who'd been setting mousetraps under the building, poked his head through the back door of the salon. Like most of the men in Okay, he was unwilling to enter the sea of mauve and mirrors and gossip. Joy had chosen the pink hues because she said it made her customers (and herself) look rosy and slightly flushed, a very beneficial beauty trait.

"Can I get somethin' to drink 'fore I go?" Earl asked.

"Sure you can, honey," she said, and took him a Coke. "Now this is a man that never has to worry 'bout gettin' in trouble, ain't that right, ladies?"

The ladies giggled behind their magazines. Earl took the Coke, shook his head, and left.

* * *

The Honor family cruised down Main Street in the new van. Ruby and Randy waved at people out the back windows.

"Everybody's lookin' at us!" Randy yelled.

Sissy opened the curtains on the side windows a little wider, and even Aletta checked her hair in the visor mirror.

Jimmy put Glen Campbell's new eight-track in the player and turned it up as they drove out to Braum's Ice Cream forty minutes away in Oklahoma City. When "Rhinestone Cowboy" came on, Jimmy couldn't help thinking Glen was singing about him.

They passed the VFW on Portland Avenue. Aletta pointed out the window. "Remember comin' over here to the sock hop?"

"How could I forget? I thought I was too cool to be at a sophomore party," Jimmy said, smiling.

"I was so mad. Big Mister Senior, you wouldn't take your shoes off and dance with me."

He laughed. "I needed a beer to loosen me up."

"God forbid," Aletta said and looked out the window. They didn't talk again until they got to the restaurant.

For the next few weeks, Jimmy settled back into being at home. He only drank a little, and never inside the house. Most of his free time was spent on the living room couch watching baseball or reading the paper. Aletta tried not to ask him to do too much, but she wished he would help her more. *Give it a few months,* she thought, and tried to be pleasant when they were together.

Sissy came in one night flushed from running home from Angie's so she wouldn't be in after nine, her parents' weeknight curfew. "Daddy, can I have a slumber party in the van?"

Jimmy didn't look up from the sports page. "No, you sure can't, honey."

"But some of the junior cheerleaders have asked. It might help me at tryouts. Please?"

"You want some cheese with that whine? I said no. It's the only thing that ain't messed up around here."

She stalked off, unaccustomed to her father saying no to her.

One evening after work, Jimmy brought home a kid's baseball glove and bat. He opened the garage door before entering the house so he could stop and take a drink from the bottle he kept hidden in an old chest of drawers out there. He grabbed his own glove and a ball and went to find his son.

"Come on," he said to Randy, who was lying on the living room floor watching *The Gong Show*.

Ruby was in the room too, but he didn't notice. She followed them out to the front yard. It was a small yard, but since Jimmy had come back home, the grass was green, mowed and trimmed neatly again. He had taken plugs of grass from the backyard and filled in the hole where the sign had been. It was almost completely grown over now.

"I got you somethin' today, Randy," Jimmy said. He was walking backwards and leading him out to the grass, holding his gifts behind his back.

Randy ran toward him, excited. "What is it?"

"It's time you learned how to play ball like your daddy." Jimmy showed Randy the glove and bat, and the little boy's smile vanished like it had been stolen right off his face. He stood there, arms at his sides, until Jimmy took his hand and put the glove on it.

Jimmy backed up about five feet and tossed the ball underhand to his son. "Catch it, slugger," he said, but it thudded across the grass.

Jimmy rolled his eyes. "Get the ball and throw it here."

Aletta watched from the kitchen window and saw Randy pick up the ball and toss it about two feet with a flick of his wrist.

"Put some arm into it, for God's sake," Jimmy said. He picked up the ball and tossed it back to Randy, who waved his glove as it dropped at his feet. Jimmy shook his head.

"Okay, son, really throw it hard this time." Jimmy pounded his glove and crouched into a catcher's position to receive the blast, but once again Randy flicked his wrist and the ball fell limply to the ground.

Jimmy's face turned red. "Goddammit, you throw like a damn girl!"

"I don't like playing ball!" Randy threw the glove down and ran inside crying.

Jimmy watched him go, dropped back onto his butt, and sat on the grass.

Ruby walked over and picked up the discarded glove. She grabbed the ball and backed up from Jimmy about ten feet.

"Here you go, Rube. Throw it here," Jimmy said halfheartedly.

Ruby reached back and threw the ball at him as hard as she could.

He had to reach above his head and snatch it out of the air before it went through the van window. He smiled and got back into a crouch.

"That was a hell of a throw. Try it again."

She easily caught the ball he tossed to her, then threw it wildly back at him.

"You can throw hard! We just need to work on your control a little," he said.

Aletta checked on them through the window as Randy helped her make dinner. She didn't mind that Randy didn't want to play ball and wanted to be near her. He was definitely a mama's boy. She could see that Ruby was throwing the ball hard, and, with Jimmy's coaching, closer and closer to his poised glove. When Aletta called them in, Ruby took the glove off, picked up the bat, and handed them to her dad.

"I'm a girl, you know," she said. She looked up at her father towering over her for a moment, and walked inside.

After that, Jimmy and Ruby played ball together often. He bought her her own glove and bat, saving Randy's in case he wanted to play some day. Jimmy also taught her how to make a jump shot. She seemed to love basketball the most, just as he did.

One night, he went out after work with his college buddy Vic, and while working on his third vodka-and-seven, opened up about Randy.

"I'm not sure about that kid, and I don't think he knows what to think about me either," he said.

Vic was Jimmy's only real friend, because he approved of everything Jimmy did. Aletta couldn't stand him. Now, as usual, Vic listened.

Jimmy took another sip of his drink. "I mean, I don't know what to do with a boy who doesn't act like a damn boy. I never saw anything like it. I sure as hell don't want to encourage his sissy behavior either, so I try not to be too nice. Maybe he'll turn around."

"Sure he will," Vic said.

On the way home that night, Jimmy felt like crying. *"What in the hell's the matter with you?"* he asked himself aloud as he cranked down the window, letting the night air blow on his face. He couldn't stand Randy acting like a weakling, so he sure wasn't going to let himself get away with it.

Chapter Five

On July second, Jimmy took off work early and they all loaded up in the van to go to Grandoak Lake where Aletta's high school friend Shirl Barber and her husband, Tom, had a little cabin. They went to Grandoak at least once every summer. Aletta had been packing for two days, and the van was stuffed so full Jimmy couldn't get the back doors closed.

"The raft and this box have to come out," he said.

"Nooo, that's our flippers and masks," Ruby whined.

"Yeah, and our bucket and shovel," Randy chimed in.

"Here, give it to me," Sissy said. "I'll hold it on my lap."

"That's nice," Aletta said. "Thank you, Sissy."

Ruby and Randy looked at her appreciatively. The two siblings had agreed a few weeks before when they were deciding what to put on their All Time Favorites list that Sissy won Best Big Sister easily.

Finally they pulled away, heading west on Main, then turning south onto Cemetery Road toward Interstate 40. Cemetery Road marked the western edge of Okay, with small- to middle-size houses on one side that became newer the farther from downtown you went. Okay High School interrupted this progression just a few blocks down. On the other side of the road, the small cemetery planted with elm and poplar trees was the only thing to break up the expanse of wheat fields and open pastures.

As Jimmy turned the van onto the highway, Sissy called from the back, "Put it on K J103." The Bay City Rollers rocked them down the road.

In the tiny town of Minko, they stopped for lunch at Bob's BBQ, a rundown double-wide trailer on a concrete slab where people drove from all over the state for barbecued ribs, beef, and chicken with sides of pinto beans, coleslaw, and potato salad, enormous bricks of curly fries, and huge pieces of peach and blackberry cobbler.

They sat at a big folding table draped with a plastic red-and-white-checked tablecloth. The waitress, just as much a fixture of the place as the bird-dog oil paintings and the mounted bass and catfish, pulled off being both sweet and pushy at the same time as she took their order. Randy couldn't sit still and kept ducking under the table between bites. He tickled Sissy's ankle, making her yell and almost jump clear out of her seat thinking she had a spider on her.

"Will you please discipline your son?" Aletta said to Jimmy.

"Come on, Randy," Jimmy said, putting two more ribs onto his plate.

Aletta grabbed Randy by the collar and pulled him into his chair. "You could try a little harder than that," she said to Jimmy. "A father's supposed to discipline the kids."

Jimmy glanced across the table toward Randy, who was now gorging on cobbler. "Look, he's fine."

Aletta just wanted to relax on this vacation. She didn't want to have to police the kids or nag Jimmy. So far, it wasn't working out. After another minute, Randy was up again before Aletta could catch him. He came back with a piece of paper in his hand.

"That lady was tellin' me they're havin' a turtle race an' stuff," Randy said. Aletta looked at the flyer:

✪ MINKO 4th of JULY CELEBRATION 9am to 5pm. ✪

Celebrate the USA's two hundred year anniversary.
Lots of Activities all day for the whole family,
which include some of the following:

Craft Booths ✪ Live Country Music
Cowboy Poetry—On Stage
Jefferson County Antique Tractor Show
Tractor Rodeo—Fairgrounds
Chicken Bingo—Main Street 4:30pm
Chuck Wagon—6pm—Legion Hut
Horseshoe Tourn.—Legion Hut yard
Water Balloon Toss/Egg Toss—2pm
Dunking Tank—All day—west end of Main
Baseball Throw—10am to 5pm
Fireworks Display
45th Infantry—Taps—before fireworks
Domino Tourn.—Domino Parlor
Turtle Race—Behind Bob's BBQ—10am
Frog Jump—Behind Bob's BBQ—10am
Pie Eating Contest ✪ Cow Calling Contest
Adult Baby Contest
Basketball Tourn.—East of City Hall
Downtown Parade—11am
Decorated Bike Contest (in Parade)
Poems by Preachers ✪ Cake Walk

"There must be some farmers comin' to town for all this to go on," Aletta said.

"The whole damn county'll be here for it," Jimmy said.

"Can we come to it, Daddy? Pleeeaase," Ruby said after she read it.

"I dunno, we'll have to see what Tom and Shirl and their kids wanna do too. Remember, they got a boat," he said.

Outside, there were six or seven people standing around the van, gawking at it.

A shirtless, skinny boy in tattered blue jeans stared at Sissy and asked, "Damn, didju paint dis like 'is jis' fer the Fourth?"

"It was painted like this for the Bicentennial," Sissy said, speaking as clearly as possible to make it known she was not like him.

Bob of Bob's BBQ walked up to Jimmy and shook his hand. "This is some set a' wheels you got here. Hey, don't I know you? I'm Bob Tilson."

"Jimmy Honor. Don't believe we ever met," Jimmy said.

"Honor," Bob said. "Aren't you the ballplayer from over at Okay?"

Here we go, Aletta thought. She half smiled when Bob looked at her with the beaming look that said how lucky she was to be with such a great man. This happened often with the old-timers.

"Looks like you got a little guy over there to take after you, and some pretty girls too, and another one on the way, I see," Bob bellowed.

"Yep, that's right," Jimmy said.

Randy hid his face in his mother's legs and Ruby kicked a rock across the road.

"You used to come in here and beat the pants offa our team. I tell you what, we hated you but we couldn't help but respect the way you played. You played baseball too, had a helluva arm I recall," Bob said.

Aletta loaded the kids in the van while the men talked. She pulled Sissy to the side before she climbed in. "I think that boy likes you," she whispered.

Sissy rolled her eyes. "He asked if he could kiss me."

"You just barely met him, and you're way too young." Aletta pointed a finger at Sissy but pulled it back when she remembered how she'd hated it when her mama did that to her.

Sissy climbed into the van. "Don't worry, Mom, I wouldn't let him near me. He's a skank."

Aletta laughed. "What in the world is a skank?"

"The exact opposite of a fox."

Jimmy shook hands with Bob and swung into the front seat with a huge smile on his face. He turned around and looked at the kids. "Guess who's gonna be in the Fourth of July parade?" he asked.

"Who? Who?" they shouted.

"We are! He wants us to lead off the whole thing." He looked at Aletta. She just smiled, amazed once again at the power of being able to play with a ball.

Aletta was nodding off, sleepy from the heavy food, when Jimmy drove through the entrance to the lake, but the sight of the water revived her like some wonderful drug. The kids jumped from seat to seat in the back of the van as Jimmy inched along the dirt road leading across the dam so the van would stay clean.

The tiny lake was pretty, with lots of trees and sloping green lawns rimming its shore. Most of the cabins that dotted the hillsides were rustic little shacks, but not the ones right on the lake.

"That's where the rich people live," Jimmy told them, about the big cabins near the water. "They're not like you and me."

Boats buzzed across the water and old men fished from shore. At the swimming area across the lake, kids jumped off the diving board and scrambled onto the dock that floated in the middle of the water. Aletta breathed in the smells of moss, summer, and rich red earth. She felt her body begin to relax a little.

They pulled up to the Barbers' one-room yellow cabin that was ringed with tall elm trees. Aletta sighed at the sight of the outhouse set among some trees not far from the cabin and ran her hand over the baby that was sitting on her bladder. Jimmy laid on the horn that played the first few bars of "Yankee Doodle." The Barbers came out to greet them, all of them tanned and wearing shorts.

Aletta's kids went to see the catfish the Barber kids had caught that morning. Tina was seven and Terry fourteen. Tina, Ruby, and

Randy took turns touching the whiskered fish that swam lazily around in a metal tub.

"Wanna go see my rope swing?" Terry asked Sissy as they stood mesmerized by the fish. "Goes way out over the water."

Terry was skinny, but his long sandy-brown hair was nice, and he made Sissy laugh, so she liked being around him. "Sure," she said, grateful to leave the ugly fish behind.

"I should tell my dad where I'm goin', 'cause we were about to put the boat in."

Aletta hugged Shirl and just kept talking as the images came through and then slipped away like wisps of smoke. She didn't want to know anything about Shirl or read her, but she did notice the colors were brighter and clearer since she'd had the sign out for those few days.

They stood at the side of the cabin, taking advantage of the shade. "We're so glad y'all are here," Shirl said. She was a big gal—big-boned and big-boobed, with enormous brown eyes. She was the kind of person who'd do anything for someone she loved, but she was a straight talker too, not too polite to get in the way of getting things done. She and Aletta had hit it off the minute Shirl moved to Okay their junior year.

Her husband, Tom, who had a half-inch layer of fine, curly hair over his entire shirtless torso, opened an enormous ice chest. Dozens of gold Coors cans glistened inside.

"Would you like a beverage?" Tom asked Jimmy.

"Are those just for you and me?" Jimmy laughed.

"Hell, no. These are mine. I was just gonna give you one 'cause you're my guest, but from here on you gotta get your own," Tom said. He smiled like a little boy and cracked open his third of the day, dropping the tab down inside the can.

"Well, I'll take that one beer soon as I get back from my run," Jimmy said. "But I guess you'll be drinkin' your own tonight when I'm takin' all your money." They had plans to play poker with some other men.

"What you got?" Tom asked.

Jimmy led Tom to the van, opened a hidden compartment inside the cabinet under the sink, and pulled out three bottles. Jim
Beam, Smirnoff regular vodka, and a Smirnoff cherry vodka that
was already opened.

Terry stopped Sissy behind him as he turned the corner of the
cabin. "Wait," he whispered, pointing to their dads trading the
shining bottles back and forth.

"What is it?" Sissy asked, craning her neck around him to see.

He leaned close to her ear. "It's liquor."

Jimmy went for his run while Shirl showed Aletta her garden
behind the cabin. They walked through rows of tomatoes, squash,
carrots, cucumbers, lettuce, potatoes, and bell peppers. Aletta
couldn't bend to inspect the plants, but she inhaled the scent of
the sun and the growing things. She closed her eyes. The smells
brought back her mama's garden so clear, she felt like she was
there.

Aletta helped her mama around the house most every day before and after school. Her favorite chores were tending the garden out behind the farmhouse and feeding the chickens. The
garden was enclosed with high wire fencing to keep the critters out,
so from the outside it didn't look like much. But step through
the gate, and there was a treasure of color and touch. Depending
on the time of year, it held smooth, pale green watermelons and
drops of ruby red tomatoes, hairy yellow squash and callous-
skinned cantaloupes. To Aletta, the garden was like a red dirt cake
with green icing and multicolored candies on top. Today, they
were yanking weeds under the midday sun when they heard the
old truck pull up in front of the house.

"I wonder if the wheat's ready yet," Nadine said, glancing up
from under her bonnet. Her father had been a wheat farmer and
had lost more than his fair share of crops to storms and droughts,
so she was always nervous about the wheat.

"Nope, needs two more weeks," Aletta said, pulling a spiky-
leafed weed out of the ground.

"You think so?" Nadine smiled at her daughter.

Clovis walked around the house to the garden. He wore striped OshKosh overalls and a long-sleeved shirt. Aletta ran to him and gave him a hug, getting the red dirt that was on her hands all over him. She breathed in the smells of her daddy—milk, farm animals, and hay.

Nadine stood up and wiped her hands on her apron. "What do ya think?"

"When you think the wheat's ready, go fishin' for two weeks," he said. "I'm gonna wait."

Nadine looked at Aletta. "Two weeks?" her mama asked.

"Yep," he said. "It'll be good and ripe by then."

Nadine just shook her head, "All righty, well, your daughter certainly agrees with you."

Aletta smiled a squinty smile. She soaked up the warm feeling of knowing things about the world just like she soaked up the sunshine.

✪

Jimmy got back from his half-hour run shirtless and sweating. He chased Randy, Tina, and Ruby around the yard, trying to hug them as they screamed, "It's the sweat monster! Gross, run from the sweat monster!"

Aletta bit her tongue as he opened a beer and drank half of it in one pull. She and Shirl and the younger kids loaded up in the van and drove the three minutes to the swimming area while Jimmy, Tom, Sissy, and Terry walked down to get the boat. The pale green Bayliner ski boat was tied up at the Barbers' dock down the hill from the cabin.

Tom motored out to the middle of the lake and threw the ski rope to Terry. Sissy checked Terry out. He looked cute in his cut-offs and those bands of leather around his wrist and neck. She lay back on her seat to get her tan started, but sat up and smiled as Terry whooped and rose up out of the water on his ski. He sliced his way through the water, jumping back and forth over the wakes behind the boat. He used one hand on the turns and sprayed the boat docks with water from his skis as he went by.

After Terry finished, Sissy jumped into the water. She adjusted her life jacket nervously as she waited for Tom to throw the two skis out to her. She gritted her teeth as the boat sped up, crouching over the skis through the warm water. She smiled triumphantly as she stood up on the first try. With one hand, she carefully reached down to pull at her bikini bottoms, making sure each cheek was covered.

The men took turns skiing. Sissy knew they had to go now before they had too many more beers. The boat had a big Evinrude motor, but it still had a tough time pulling out a muscular two-hundred-pound man who was fighting it the entire way. Sissy laughed as her daddy stayed crouched over his skis, his face contorted, as he dragged through the water for about thirty yards before the boat had enough speed to finally pull him up.

Aletta and Shirl sat on banana lounges on the beach watching the kids swim and the boat go around. As Tom dragged through the water, holding with all his might to the ski rope, Shirl said, "That looks like a Go-Kart trying to pull a longhorn." She and Aletta laughed, not the first or the last laugh they had at their husbands' expense.

"So, Jo Lynn Parks called me outta the blue a few weeks back," Shirl said casually as she dog-eared the page in her paperback mystery. Aletta was halfway through *Jonathan Livingston Seagull*.

"What in the hell was Jo Lynn callin' you for? Y'all can't stand each other," Aletta said.

"It was a surprise to me, believe me. Nosy little snit, she wanted to see if I knew anything about some sign you had out in your yard about psychic somethin' or other."

Aletta closed her book and groaned. "Good Lord, she coulda just come on in and found out for herself. It wasn't like I was hiding anything."

"That's when Jimmy was gone, wasn't it?"

"I gotta get outta this sun." Aletta stood up and moved her lounge chair under a silver maple tree a few feet away. She stretched her lower back and looked down at the enormous blue swimsuit she had on, the same one she'd worn through all of her pregnancies.

"I look like a giant blueberry, don't I?" she asked.

Shirl smiled. "Oh, I was thinkin' more like a marble, or maybe a gumball."

"Hey, be careful now." Aletta sat down and they were silent for a few moments, just watching the sun glinting off the water. Aletta listened to the sounds of the children playing and the boats buzzing around the lake mimicking the bees that buzzed around their heads every so often. It was a moment in which there was a decision being made, not a thought one, but a felt one. Shirl's silence provided the answer. It spoke to Aletta of loyalty and acceptance that gave her the space to move into.

"I'm psychic, or clairvoyant, or whatever you want to call it," Aletta finally said. "Always have been, or at least since I was a kid."

"I thought you might be somethin' like that," Shirl said.

"You did?"

"You've always known things, little things, but hard to deny. Like Gary Felton," Shirl said, smiling up at her friend. " 'Course, that wasn't too little."

★

Gary Felton was a rich boy, the quarterback at rival Putnam City High School, who was after Shirl when she and Aletta were seniors in high school. Aletta warned Shirl to be careful of him, but Shirl was giddy with excitement that someone like Gary Felton would want to date someone like her. Just before their first date, Aletta brought over a .38 caliber pistol she'd taken out of Clovis's old gun case. She didn't know if it worked, and anyway she couldn't find bullets for it, but she insisted that Shirl carry it with her in her purse that night. Shirl thought Aletta was going crazy, but she took it because Aletta had a fierceness about her she had never seen before.

They went out to the movies, and Gary tried to feel Shirl's breast as his hand dangled over her shoulder. She pushed it away and he stopped. After the movie, they drove out to Lake Overholser in his '56 Dodge convertible to look at the moon.

Gary leaned toward her for a kiss, but she turned her head away shyly. She wanted a good-night kiss before he took her home, but she knew it was important to hold out. He put his hand on the back of her head and pulled her to him.

"Hey you, stop that," she said, lightly putting her hand on his shoulder.

"Come on now." He smiled at her but pulled harder. When she resisted him again, he shoved his mouth onto hers, his tongue writhing all over her face. He crawled on top of her, pinning her against the seat.

"Stop it!" she screamed, and pushed on his face with her hand as hard as she could.

He ripped her dress at the shoulder, then unzipped his pants.

His hands were hurting her badly, so finally Shirl stopped fighting. Instead, she whispered in his ear, "Stop for just a second so I can take off my panties."

"That a girl," he said, and rolled off her.

Shirl reached into her purse on the floorboard and pulled out Clovis's gun. She pointed it straight at Gary's head. "I'll kill you. I'll shoot you right in your head," she said, wishing like hell the gun had bullets in that moment, and grateful to God it didn't in years to come.

"Get out," Gary said, sweat glistening on his forehead.

Shirl opened the door behind her with one hand while she held the gun on him with the other. She grabbed her purse and scrambled out of the car. Tears streamed down her face as Gary screeched down the road in his fancy car, leaving her standing there still shakily pointing the empty gun.

Shirl's parents went to Mr. Johnson, the principal of Putnam City High School, and he gave his word he'd take care of Gary Felton. But when it came down to it, he decided he would just wait until after the football season, then really punish him. Gary got a scholarship to Oklahoma University to play for Coach Wilkinson, who said the kid had enough talent to make it to the pros. There never seemed a good time to bring up that old business, so when Gary graduated, Mr. Johnson shook his hand extra hard, looked him in the eye, and said, "You stay out of trouble now, you hear?" and that was that.

★

"You saved me on that one," Shirl said, turning on her side on the banana lounge to look at Aletta. "You knew, didn't you?"

"He shook my hand when we met," Aletta said.

"You could see that because he touched you?" Shirl asked, curious.

Aletta took a bottle of Coppertone out of a bag on the ground and spread the lotion on her arms. "Yeah, sometimes I know things anyway, but mainly it's touching." Putting on the suntan lotion gave her something to do besides looking at Shirl.

"What's it like when you know things?" Shirl sat up on the edge of the lounge.

"Pictures," Aletta said. "I get pictures that come into my head mainly, just like watching TV but more jumpy than that, kind of one at a time. Sometimes they go real fast." She'd never spoken to anyone like this. She felt unsure of herself and vulnerable.

"That's just amazing, Aletta. Why you been hidin' it so long?"

"Oh, it's just a pain in the ass, Shirl. People don't understand. It's brought me nothin' but trouble." Aletta finally looked up at her friend. "I needed the money, though, with Jimmy gone, and it's the only thing I could think of doin' sittin' on my butt at home. I wish I never done it."

"Do you really?" Shirl asked. "Seems like somethin' that oughta be used."

That afternoon, Aletta made Jimmy stay on shore while she went out in the boat with Tom and Shirl to watch her kids ski. She said there wasn't enough room, but the truth was she didn't want him to be in the boat drunk. He and Tom had been drinking beer all day. Somehow, with Tom, you could never tell if he was drunk.

The only real sign was that he got quieter and more focused when he drove the boat, which didn't bother Aletta at all.

He stood at the steering wheel with a cigarette dangling from his lips and his eyes squinting against the smoke and the sun. As Aletta helped Randy put on his life jacket, she saw Shirl checking out Tom's hairy chest and tanned legs. She smiled to herself. Shirl caught his eye as he killed the engine and turned to watch Randy jump into the water. She whispered, "Nice butt," and the three of them laughed like they were sixteen again.

That evening, two other couples who lived at the lake came over, and after a dinner of burgers, potato salad, garden veggies, and watermelon, the men gathered around the beat-up old picnic table at the side of the cabin to play poker. They drank vodka and whisky and gin, and the language they used was as hard as the liquor.

The kids fished down at the dock and caught perch with balls of Rainbo bread until the orange-and-pink sunset turned to night. Tina, who was very small and seemed almost frail, caught the most, screaming with fear and delight each time she pulled the string out of the water and let the colorful perch do flips on the end of the line. After dark, they took turns catching fireflies with a net.

The women did the dishes, carrying the neighbor's well water in buckets to the porch and teaming up to wash, rinse, and dry. Afterwards, they sat down inside the cabin in front of the tiny window air conditioner that blew blessedly cold air.

"Once again, Lyle stuffs his face and then walks away," Jackie Harding, a woman with striking blue eyes, said as she fell into one of the mismatched vinyl chairs and lit a long, skinny cigarette that seemed to match her thin, sinewy frame.

"It's how they were raised, you know," Aletta said, trying to get comfortable on the brown sleeper sofa with saggy cushions and soda-pop stains.

Shirl poured herself a bourbon and 7-Up. "Tom's a neat freak. He can't stand anything out of place. It's hard on the kids, but I guess it could be worse."

"That's a problem I'd love to have. I'm lucky if Lyle picks up his underwear off the floor," Jackie said. She blew two streams of smoke out her nose, then added, "So, what do y'all think about these women goin' without their bras?"

"Are you kidding? Without a harness, I could be headed in three different directions at the same time." Shirl cupped her large bosom in her hands. They all laughed, except for Minnie Trehorn, a pretty and petite woman with dark hair and serious eyes.

"What do you think, Minnie? Would you go braless?" Aletta asked.

"I think the Scripture makes very clear that women are meant to serve their husbands, so I try to live by that," Minnie said.

The only response was Shirl taking a long slurp of her cocktail as the women glanced at one another. Aletta wanted to ask Minnie if she'd missed the last ten years completely. Women were supposed to be getting free. At least that's what she kept hearing.

In the silence, they heard Minnie's husband, Burl, bellowing drunkenly, "Goddammit Tom, that was my hand! I'm barin' my ass here, ain't I?"

Jackie put out her cigarette, turning her head away. She tried to hold it in, but a snort of a laugh escaped. Shirl and Aletta laughed at Jackie's snort.

"Well, I think there's somethin' to be said for women's lib myself," Shirl said. "I mean, I appreciate your devotion, Minnie, but don't you want to be treated like an equal?"

Minnie uncrossed and crossed her legs. "Equal to what?" she asked quietly. "I don't want to be equal to *that*."

"Now there's a point!" Jackie exclaimed.

No, she wants to be less than him, Aletta thought. *She's brainwashed to think she's less than a man.* She remembered Jonathan Seagull and what she'd read that day. He was trying to fly faster and farther than other seagulls ever had, but he failed and crashed miserably. He decided he should forget trying and accept that he was limited.

"What about you, Aletta?" Jackie asked.

"I wouldn't mind spreadin' my wings a little bit," Aletta said.

"I think it's high time women got more respect for all we do." She thought again of Jonathan, who, after his defeat, was back at it again, vowing that he did not have to be ordinary. *Maybe I don't have to accept the ordinary,* Aletta thought. *Maybe I don't need to be like everyone else.*

"That a girl!" Jackie whooped. "Let's go start a fire out back."

Outside, Terry sneaked into the bicentennial van and took the cherry vodka from its hiding place. Sissy waited for him at the side of the cabin. After he came back, they entered the woods behind the cabin. The almost-full moon spread a soft glow of light through the trees, so they could see fairly well.

Sissy's stomach growled loudly as it always did when she was frightened or excited. Tonight she was both. The child inside her was scared to be out there in the dark woods knowing she would be in big trouble if they got caught. But she was also a young woman who was thrilled to be taking a journey toward some unknown, daring experience with an attractive young man.

"You hungry?" Terry whispered as he pushed a spiderweb out of his way.

"What? No, no, I'm just fine." Her voice quivered a little. The air was thick with humidity, adding to Sissy's sense that the woods were alive.

Terry turned and smiled. "Hope you're thirsty."

"Maybe a little."

They ducked under tree limbs, their feet crunching the underbrush with each step.

Terry stopped at a fallen log and sat down. "I found this while I was lookin' for deer the other day," he said as Sissy sat next to him. He looked around, making sure they hadn't been followed, then unscrewed the lid and took a big drink out of the bottle. He puckered up his face and exhaled like fire might blow out of his mouth.

Sissy laughed at him, took the bottle, and sipped. She held the burning liquid in her mouth for a second before she could convince herself to swallow. It was the cherry flavor that helped it go down.

"Prob'ly some snakes out here, don't you think?" he asked.

Sissy looked at him sideways. "I don't know, but I'm not gonna think about it, that's for sure."

Terry scooted closer to her. "You wanna kiss?" he asked after a few more drinks.

Sissy hesitated for a moment. She wanted to know what it was like to kiss a boy, but she was really nervous.

"All right," she said finally, "but no French kissing."

He got close enough to her so their thighs touched, then kissed her stiffly on the lips. She tried to imitate the people she saw on TV, moving her head from side to side. They stopped, and each of them quickly took another drink. She was starting to feel giddy and loose.

"Have you ever French kissed before?" Terry asked.

"Yeah, once or twice, what about you?"

"Sure, some, a few times," he said. "Why don't we just try it? What's it gonna hurt?"

Sissy turned to face him and took his shoulders in her hands. "You won't tell a single soul? Cross your heart and hope to die, stick a thousand needles in your eye?"

"I swear on the Bible," he said, smiling, excited.

Sissy looked away, her gaze resting on a bird's nest tucked into the V of two tree branches. *Could be now or never,* she thought. "Okay, just once."

Sissy hoped he wasn't lying like she was about French kissing before, because she had no idea how to do it, except that you were supposed to touch tongues. He leaned toward her with his tongue out, so she stuck hers out too. They rubbed their tongues together for a few moments with their eyes closed. Both of them peeked to see if the other was watching.

"What did you think?" Terry asked when it was over.

"It was nice," she said. She didn't want to hurt his feelings, but the truth was she thought it was the grossest thing she'd ever done outside of putting her hand down the hole at the haunted house and touching brains. "But I don't think we should do it again. What about you?" she asked.

"Cool," he shrugged.

She could tell it was a letdown for him too, and she knew without a doubt she had been his first just like he was for her.

"Time for bed! Woohoo! All you kids come on in now!" Shirl's voice floated to them through the woods.

They jumped up and rushed toward the cabin, Terry holding the bottle under his T-shirt. He looked exactly like a teenage boy trying to hide a bottle of liquor, so when they got to the edge of the woods, giggling and whispering loudly, Sissy went and did surveillance around the van before motioning him to run over. He hid the bottle, only about two-thirds full now, back in the secret compartment.

Sissy avoided her mother and quickly got her toothbrush. She stood outside and juggled a coffee cup full of water, a tube of Crest, and her pink toothbrush, spitting the foamy evidence onto the ground.

Aletta escorted the kids to the outhouse with a flashlight one last time and then put them to bed on old army cots on the screened-in porch. Outside, the crickets chirped so fast and loud, it seemed like they were racing, the first to a thousand wins.

Tom decided he wanted to go gig some frogs and talked Jimmy into going with him. The kids begged to go along.

"Oh, come on, Shirl, we're on vacation," Tom said. So Tina, Ruby, and Randy put their sneakers back on and followed the men down the path to the boat dock and along the water's edge.

Tom held a big orange flashlight in one hand, and he and Jimmy both carried poles with metal points on the ends.

"Y'all keep quiet now," Tom said, scanning the edge of the lake and the path in front of them with a beam of light.

The ground was moist and covered with leaves and underbrush beneath Randy's sneakers. The smell of moss and trees was strong, stronger at night than when the sun was out. To him, it seemed like a secret and important thing they were doing, like in the Hardy Boys or Nancy Drew. Then Tom caught a huge bullfrog in the light. The bumpy green blob of flesh sat frozen by the brightness until Jimmy stepped in and speared it through the back.

"We're gonna have frog legs for supper tomorrow," Tom said.

Jimmy held the frog up on the spike while it jerked and flailed. "That's a big ol' boy."

Randy was horrified at the sight of the dying frog, the moonlight shining off its rubbery skin. He could tell that Tina and Ruby felt sorry for it too, but they kept quiet.

"Daddy, can I go back to the cabin?" he asked.

"You begged to come along, so now you have to stay with us," Jimmy said, his words all slurred together.

Randy stayed behind as they moved toward the deep rumbling hiccup of another frog. He didn't want to see any more animals get killed. He waited until he realized he was alone in the heavy darkness, then ran as fast as he could through the roots and mud to catch up with the lights. Frog-killers were bad, but not as bad as the dark.

Aletta was already asleep when Jimmy crawled into the van next to her.

She yawned. "You smell like a swamp."

He snuggled up against her back, smelling her hair. "You smell delicious."

He moved her hair aside and kissed her neck softly at first, then nibbled a little. He ran his hand along her tight, round belly and up to her breasts, touching them lightly. Aletta's body was tense when he started. She didn't like it when he had been drinking. But tonight his hands and mouth felt like they might be the answer to all her concerns. Besides, they were on vacation, and she had been touched so little lately with him gone before and her late in her pregnancy now. She missed making love. She missed feeling sexy, feeling like a woman. As his hand moved between her thighs and his warm, moist mouth found hers, she relaxed and surrendered, letting go of the past and not caring about the future.

Chapter Six

A rooster crowing from across the lake woke Aletta and she went inside to prepare breakfast with Shirl, feeling better than she had in months. She decided that sex and a vacation were just what she'd needed. She wanted to do Cheerios and sweet rolls for breakfast, but Shirl insisted on eggs, bacon, and buttermilk pancakes. Once they started cooking, the smell of bacon worked better than a cowbell to call the sleepy-eyed, sunburned children to its source.

"Everything tastes better at the lake," Ruby said.

And they all agreed that everything was better at the lake.

Aletta looked at Jimmy. "That's for sure," she said.

"No doubt about it," he answered, and winked at her.

"Except for the mosquito bites," Tina said, scratching her leg.

The women cleaned the breakfast pans while the men loaded the boat and the kids changed into their suits. It was already hot by the time they got to the water. Jimmy had a hangover, so he went for a run to the swimming area to sweat it out before opening his first beer.

At the end of a path that started at the swimming area and went through some cattails and tall grasses, there was an enormous oak tree with a big hole in it from which the lake got its name. Aletta's group stationed themselves near the trailhead as usual. After lunch, the kids had to wait thirty minutes before they could go back in the water, so Randy wandered down the path to look at the big oak tree. He crawled inside the small cavelike opening and made himself as little as possible. Even though it was hot and the sun was shining brightly, it was always cool and dark inside the tree. He loved being alone, because when he was, he thought of magic powers and imagined beautiful things. This time, as he sat inside the tree, inhaling the smell of moss and warm wood, he imagined himself a prowling cat like the magnificent leopard he'd seen at the zoo with his grandma last summer.

Because everyone who came to Grandoak Lake *had* to go see the grand oak, it wasn't long before some people started down the path. It was a middle-aged couple who looked as if neither one of them had been outside in years. They were softly fat and pinkly white, so by the time they reached the oak tree, they were huffing and sweating from the heat and the thirty-yard walk.

Randy heard them as they approached, and he cocked his head like a cat.

"Oh, my, it's big," the Mrs. said.

"Yes, it is. It's big all right," Mr. answered.

As soon as they got close enough to peer into the hole, Randy inhaled deeply and let out a hiss that was so angry-sounding, he almost frightened himself.

"What the hell . . . ?" the man asked, backpedaling, but his wife was already running down the path. Almost stumbling, he turned around and ran after her.

Randy peeked out of the hole in the tree and watched them go. For a moment he was still, his dark green eyes big and round. Then he covered his mouth with his hand and laughed, his eyes flashing with delight.

The couple ran back down that path so fast and were so white that when Aletta saw them, she almost laughed too.

"I wonder what the hell happened to them?" Tom asked. He chuckled, watching them enter the pavilion in a flurry, their bodies gelatinously moving in all different directions at once.

As Jimmy and Shirl continued their conversation about the

parade that was to take place the following morning, two girls and a boy, about nine or ten years old, headed down the path toward the tree. The Barbers wanted to go to the parade too, so they were trying to figure out how to fit everyone in the van.

Suddenly screams pierced the air, and the three kids shot back up the path, eyes as big as moons, sandals flying off their feet.

"There's something down there!" they yelled as they ran to their parents.

Out of the corner of her eye, Aletta saw the lake's sixty-eight-year-old sheriff walk with purpose out the screen door of the pavilion where the pink couple had entered a few minutes before. He flicked his cigarette and touched the butt of his pistol, making sure it was still in its holster on his skinny hip.

Aletta looked around frantically. "Where's Randy? I thought he went to the bathroom. He said he was going to the bathroom."

Sheriff Lloyd was almost to the group now, clearly headed for the path.

"I think I saw him go down the path a while ago," Ruby said.

"You did? Are you sure?" Jimmy asked. He and Tom ran down the path. Shirl, Aletta, and the sheriff followed them, Aletta holding her belly as she ran.

"Randy?! Randy?!" Jimmy called.

He and Tom got to the tree and approached it slowly. They heard an uninspired hiss.

"What the hell was that?" the sheriff called from behind Aletta.

Tom smiled and pointed into the hole, mouthing the words "He's in there." He put his fingers to his lips to shush the rest of the crew as they ran up.

"Sounded like a big cat to me, what do you think?" Tom said.

Randy hissed again, this time a little more effectively.

"Whoa," Jimmy said. "I think you're right. We're gonna have to stick a knife in that thing and skin it and eat it."

He reached into the hole and grabbed Randy's bare shoulder.

"It's me! It's just me!" Randy yelled. After the frog hunting, there was no doubt in his mind that his daddy and Tom would kill anything that moved.

Randy was grounded for the rest of the day, but since everyone, especially Jimmy and Tom, laughed so much about it, he was back in the water by late afternoon. The scared kids glared at him and their parents glared at Aletta. They never saw the pink couple again.

That evening, as the sun was setting, they took the boat out for one last ski. Shirl insisted that Aletta go out with Sissy, Jimmy, Tom, and Terry while she prepared hamburger patties and a big salad from her garden. Tom asked Jimmy to pull Terry so that he could watch his son ski.

Aletta squirmed, knowing that Jimmy had been drinking all day, but after going back and forth in her mind, she said to him, "I guess it's the least we could do for Tom after he's worked so hard for us. You'll do a good job, right?"

Jimmy glanced at her standing on shore while he pulled a T-shirt over his head. "Just get in, dear."

She sat shotgun next to Jimmy while Sissy and Tom watched from the rear seats. Terry signaled from the creamy-looking evening water and Jimmy pushed the throttle down. It wasn't enough, and Terry dragged along for a bit, then let go of the rope, exasperated.

"Throw it all the way down, Jimmy, just like with me," Tom said as they circled back around.

"Okay. I thought since he was so much lighter . . ." Jimmy said defensively.

"Give it some gas, old man!" Terry yelled from the water.

Jimmy circled Terry, his face reddening with anger. This time when Terry yelled, Jimmy pushed the throttle down hard, and Terry got up easily. Jimmy made sharp turns at full speed, but Terry ate it up. He jumped the wakes, then glided out beside the boat. When he got to the end of the rope, he lay out almost flat on the water, then whipped his ski around and headed to the other side.

Aletta and Sissy clapped at each turn. "He's so good!" Aletta said, thrilled at how fast he went.

"He likes to put on a show, that's for sure," Jimmy said under his breath.

"That a boy!" Tom called.

After three times around the small lake, Terry finally threw the rope up in the air and slid across the water, slowly sinking in, two thumbs up in the air.

"He's down," Sissy said.

Jimmy pulled up on the throttle a little, then swung the boat around to go after him. He headed straight for Terry, who bobbed in the water in his life jacket, holding his ski with one hand, smiling and breathing hard. Terry leaned his head back in the water, closed his eyes, and smoothed his long hair back with his free hand.

Jimmy gave the throttle a nudge.

When Terry looked up again, he saw that the boat was really close now and still bearing down. Aletta, frozen in her seat, was near enough to see the disbelief in his eyes.

"Jesus, Jimmy, turn the boat!" Tom shouted.

Jimmy finally yanked on the wheel, but it was too late. The boat went right over Terry's head.

"Oh God! Oh God!" Aletta screamed. Panic consumed her like a fire.

"Terry!" Sissy wailed and scrambled to the front of the boat where he had disappeared.

Tom grabbed the top of the outboard motor while it was still running and pulled as hard as he could. But his hands slipped off the wet surface, and the propeller buzzed away about three feet under water. "Kill the goddamn engine!" he yelled.

Jimmy turned the key to stop the engine but otherwise stood motionless and pale. Aletta almost fell as she tried to lean over the side, her eyes frantically searching for her best friend's son.

"Terry!" Tom bellowed and plunged into the water. He came to the surface just as Terry burst up, gasping for air.

"That fucker tried to kill me!" Terry screamed.

Later, they found out that Terry had pushed himself off the hull of the boat with his hands and dived down as deep as he

could go with the life jacket on. He said he just knew he was going to get chewed up by the propeller, which passed over within
inches of his body.

Jimmy tried to laugh it off, but it was easy to tell he was scared
as hell.

"Hey, buddy," he joked with Terry when he and Tom got in the
boat, "I didn't think I was that close. I sure as hell wasn't tryin' to kill
you, okay?" he turned to Tom. "I wasn't, Tom. I just screwed up."

"Whatever, man." Terry sat exhausted and dripping with water. He wouldn't look at Jimmy.

Neither would Aletta. She sat watching the shoreline as Tom
took them slowly home. She felt numb inside, as though the part
that feels had been pulled out and just emptiness had been left
behind.

Dinner was quiet even with Tom's frog legs going around. Afterwards, they all went to the dance down at the pavilion where the
jukebox played everything from Johnny Cash to Donna Summer.
It was a long, low building with concrete floors and windows lining both sides. Two window air conditioners pumped in cold air
and dripped condensation into buckets underneath.

The party really took place outside because there was no
drinking allowed inside the pavilion. Sheriff Grady saw to that.
"No permit," he reminded people as they pulled their bottles out
of bags and purses. They'd go outside near the big wooden lifeguard stand and picnic tables to drink their booze and watch the
teenage boys shine flashlights at the shoreline of the lake. From
the land, it dropped off about three feet to the water. During the
day, it served as a docking area where people would pull their
boats in to have a foot-long chili cheese dog or an ice cream cone.
At night, though, the boats were all parked at their own docks,
and it became a favorite hangout of the long gray-blue water moc-
casins that inhabited Grandoak by the hundreds. The lights from
the pavilion drew them in, then the flashlight beams of the boys
hunting them made them frenzied.

In the moving spotlights, Ruby could see the writhing snakes twisting and curling around each other in the shallow water. She sucked on a grape Popsicle just as Darryl, one of the older and meaner-looking boys who already had scraggly facial hair and a beer belly, lay down on the shore, hanging over the edge of the tire wall. His torso hovered over the water just a few feet above the viper pit. The talking and drinking ceased as Darryl scanned the water. After a few moments, he reached in and snatched a snake right out of the water. It was huge, over five feet long, and it twisted in his hand so violently that every one of the twenty or so people who were watching jumped backwards several feet.

"Oh, my God!"

"By God, he got him a serpent!"

Ruby dropped her Popsicle on the ground and jumped onto a picnic table with several other kids. She never took her eyes off Darryl and the snake.

Grasping the venomous snake just behind its head, Darryl turned around and raised it in the air. The soft lights from the pavilion shone on his bare skin and glinted in his eyes and teeth. In one moment he looked godlike, and in the next he was a demon. It was a wild fight, but the snake was slippery and strong, and it squirmed out of Darryl's hand and fell with a thud to the ground. It zagged quickly toward the water, but just as it was going over the edge of the embankment, Darryl dived and grabbed it by the tail with both hands. He brought it over his head and swung it like a lasso. He walked with it as he swung it around and around, water spraying off it and sprinkling the onlookers. He stomped over to the big wooden lifeguard chair, whipped the snake over his head a few more times, and then slammed it against the side of the stand, splattering red blood and brains onto the new paint.

A hush filled the warm, moist night air as the snake lay on the ground, more gray than blue now. After a few minutes, Ruby went over and touched the dead snake's dry, scaly body, then raced inside to tell Randy.

"Sounds like a beast to me," Randy said. He had just read *Where the Wild Things Are,* and "beast" was a new word for him.

"The snake?" Ruby asked.

Randy looked at her and shook his head. "No, the man."

Terry was very quiet that evening. He made it clear to everyone in his family that he didn't want to go to the parade with the Honors the next day. Tom agreed.

Shirl asked Aletta to go for a walk. Outside, it was quiet now. The teenage snake hunters were now off hunting girls and beer.

"I guess we're not gonna go to Minko tomorrow, Aletta," Shirl said.

"That's too bad." Aletta tried to sound casual, but uncasual tears came to her eyes. Shirl put her arm around her friend, and they started walking.

"It's not a big deal. It's just Terry needs a little while to get over it. He was scared pretty bad," she said.

"Of course he was. My God." Aletta wiped her tears away and looked out at the water. The numb emptiness inside had filled up to overflowing with dread and fear and anger. She felt hopeless and all alone, a feeling she knew well. "What in the world am I gonna do?"

Sissy was inside one of the stalls of the outdoor restroom as the women walked by. She pulled up her shorts and walked away from the lights and the noise of the dance to the big public dock where people who didn't have their own dock or boat fished and sunbathed. By the light of the moon, she saw Terry sitting at the end with his feet dangling over. She walked out and sat down next to him. They were quiet for the longest time.

"Do you hate me?" she finally asked.

"Ah, Sis, I'll never hate you," he said, and put his arm around her. "You can't help what your daddy does."

Her tears were silent and it was dark, but her shoulders shook a little under his arm, so he knew she was crying.

"I'm sorry," she sniffled. "I'm so sorry."

* * *

When they were leaving, Aletta couldn't find Jimmy anywhere, and no one remembered seeing him all night. Finally, she and Sissy found him in the back of the van, passed out. She wanted to drag him out of the van and leave him lying there on the ground but didn't want to create any more problems for the Barbers to deal with.

Sissy checked the secret compartment when her mother went to get Ruby and Randy and found the cherry vodka bottle empty.

The next morning, Jimmy wouldn't wake up, so Aletta loaded everything up—with a lot of help from Tom and Shirl—thanked her friends, and apologized for the hundredth time. She didn't want Jimmy to wake up so she'd have something *else* to apologize for, so they drove away before ten o'clock.

On the way out, she drove fast on the dirt roads to make damn sure Jimmy's precious van got dirty. She took the back way home, avoiding Minko completely. There was no way she was parading through Minko, Oklahoma, U.S. of A., with a drunken husband in the back, no matter how much her kids begged.

"I'm sorry, y'all," she said to them. "You deserve to go to the parade. It ain't fair, but we just can't."

Aletta used the driving time to think herself into a righteous anger at Jimmy. It was better than feeling sad anymore, helpless and weak. *Just so much of that can I stand*, she thought. The adrenaline pumped through her, making her body tight and her breath shallow. As they pulled into their driveway, Jimmy woke up. His hair stood at odds with his head and his eyes were bloodshot.

"We already home?" he groaned.

"Yep, we are. Happy Fourth of July. Now unload the damn van, I've done everything else." Aletta slammed the driver's-side door behind her.

Ruby was crushed about the parade, and she knew Randy was too, but the tone of her mother's voice caused the disappointment to take a backseat to a sense of dread.

"Mama, are you all right?" Ruby asked through the locked bathroom door.

"I just need a minute, Ruby," Aletta answered.

Ruby heard her dad come in the front door.

"Where do you want this stuff, Lettie?" he yelled.

Ruby felt just like she did when a spring storm closed in on the house and the claps of thunder seemed to crack so close overhead that it felt best to duck, as if they could reach through the windows and club her on the head. Unlike the storm, she knew this fear wouldn't be subdued by hiding her head under a pillow. Ruby went to the kitchen and grabbed the towels and bags off the floor where her daddy had dumped them.

"Don't worry, Dad. We'll take care of this stuff," she said. She tried to sound cheerful, to bring a little sunshine to end the rain.

But Jimmy didn't seem to notice as he walked to the back of the house.

"Help me take this stuff outside!" Ruby yelled at Randy, who was turning on the TV in the living room.

Sissy walked in from the garage.

"Daddy's back there with Mama," Ruby whispered.

They stared at each other, straining to listen. It seemed for a moment that their fear was unfounded, because everything was quiet. But then the bathroom door slammed open like a blast of thunder, and Aletta blew into the dining room where they stood waiting.

Jimmy was right behind her. "Don't walk away, Lettie. I need you to listen."

"No. I ain't listening anymore, Jimmy. This is it. I can't handle this," she raged, turning around to face him. "You have to go."

He grabbed her arm and his face turned red. "You can't say that! You can't make me leave! This is my house. I paid for it, you crazy bitch!"

Aletta tried to pull her arm away as Randy ran in from the living room.

"Stop it! Stop fighting!" he screamed.

"See what you're doin' to these kids!" Aletta gestured wildly toward them with her free hand. "If you're not gonna go, then we are!"

"The hell you are! You're not goin' anywhere!" He held both her arms now. She tried harder to pull away. He grabbed her throat.

"Stop it! Stop it, Daddy!" Sissy screamed. She knocked over a chair as she rushed toward him, but she never touched him. He was too big.

By now, Ruby had a full-blown tornado spinning inside her. Tears ran down her cheeks like rain on a windowpane.

Jimmy held Aletta's throat, his jaw clenched and the veins in his neck bulging. "You're not goin' anywhere!" he screamed again as he shook her.

Aletta grabbed for the closest thing—a half-full glass of milk on the counter. She hit Jimmy in the head with it as hard as she could.

The glass shattered, milk went everywhere, and he stumbled backward, grabbing his forehead. Blood poured between his fingers. He fell back into the door leading out to the garage, crashed through it, then slammed it behind him hard.

Aletta gasped for air and fell into a chair. She breathed hard as her children surrounded her, sobs convulsing their small bodies.

"Mama, come on, Mama, let's go! He might come back!" Ruby yelled, pulling on her mother's arm. She needed to escape before her entire world blew away.

Aletta sat in the dining room chair and sucked in air. She was terrified for her life, but she tried like hell not to cry, knowing it would panic her children and make it even harder to breathe. She was gathering herself to try to calm the kids when the pain hit her belly.

"Oh, my God!" she screamed and doubled over in the chair. The pain shot through her, hot and mean.

"Mama, what is it? What's wrong?"

Randy ran into the garage, and in the dimness he could just make out his dad taking a drink from a bottle.

"Daddy! Daddy! Mama's dying!"

Jimmy put the cap back on the bottle and stuffed it into the bottom drawer of an old chest. He ran back inside, wiping his bloody head with his T-shirt.

Aletta's voice was small and tight. "I'm having the baby."

Jimmy picked her up in one motion, and the same strength that had horrified Randy a few minutes before awed him now.

"Sissy, open this door," Jimmy said.

Sissy ran and opened the front door. She was shaking and her cheeks were striped with tear trails. "What's wrong with her, Daddy?"

"She's just having the baby. Take care of your brother and sister. I'll call you when it's over. We'll get all this worked out."

They followed him as he walked to the van. Aletta watched the eaves of the house pass above her, noticing that the green paint was cracking and peeling and thinking she'd like to paint the house in brown and beige next time. Jimmy lowered her onto the floor of the van. The only thing she remembered about that ride was staring at the red, white, and blue shag carpet, praying for God to give her strength as she felt liquid rush out from between her legs.

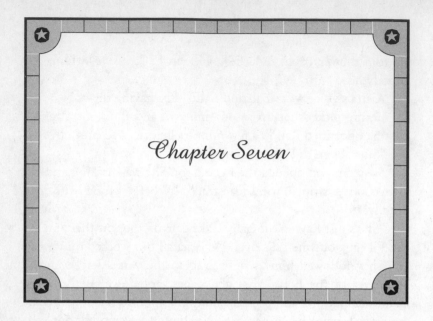

Chapter Seven

Little Aletta woke up and asked her mama if she could wear her favorite dress, the one it was easiest to run and play in, since it was the last day of school for the year. Delighted that it was finally summer, she joined the other kids at school in making it almost impossible for her teacher to keep any order at all. Mrs. Vandehay wore down by about eleven o'clock and let out for recess early, seeming as anxious for the day after the last day of school as the kids were.

Aletta played tag with her schoolmates. They ran around outside the old one-room schoolhouse with the energy of freedom, kicking up puffs of red dust and yelling just because they could.

Bobby Irvin, a blond boy with pink cheeks and big ears, raced after Aletta. She ran with all the speed her legs could find and circled around a few of the younger girls who were jumping rope. Bobby slowed down, breathing hard, and he and Aletta eyed each other through the rising and falling rope, circling slowly. Suddenly the rope stopped, and Bobby lunged for Aletta.

She screamed and backpedaled, running hard into Ralph Smart, the fifth-grade bully, knocking him to the ground. Ralph splayed out at her feet, but she stayed upright, swinging her arms in the air to avoid tripping over him. Bobby couldn't stop in time, and he tagged her with both hands, pushing her into Ralph's legs and causing her to fall on top of him. She landed right on his chest, and before she could get up, Ralph pushed Aletta off him and rolled on top of her in one motion.

"You're dead!"

"It was an accident! I'm sorry!" Aletta screamed.

His eyes were a crazy ice blue standing out against the red hot of his face. He straddled her waist and pushed her hands to the ground, grinding the backs of them into the gritty dirt and pebbles.

The images came quickly to her that first time, unexpectedly, like lightning out of a blue sky. She saw them in front of her like a movie. Ralph lying in bed, his mama throwing the covers off and yelling. His daddy pulling him out of bed by his ears. And sounds. "You're too big to wet the bed anymore, boy. For your own good." Nighttime. Ralph screaming and crying as his daddy drags him out to the barn and locks him in.

The images receded when Ralph let go of her hand and crammed his knee onto her arm to hold it down. With his free hand, he pulled her hair hard.

"Eeyow!" Aletta screamed. "Stop it, you bed wetter! I hate you!"

Ralph let go of her hair. His grip on her other hand loosened. Aletta knew she'd seen the truth by the look on his face. Before she could take advantage of his surprise, he pulled his fist back. She closed her eyes tight.

"Ralph Smart, I'm tellin' your daddy about this!" Mrs. Vandehay pulled him off Aletta by his hair.

Aletta lay on the ground, breathing heavily. It seemed that too many feelings and thoughts crowded inside her all at once. How had she seen those things about Ralph? It had been so clear, but she didn't know why. She was afraid and thrilled and confused.

"You okay, Lettie?" Bobby reached down to help her up. She knew he was just being so nice because he was afraid she'd tell on him for pushing her into Ralph, but she didn't care about that right now.

She looked up at him and took his hand but stayed sitting on the ground. He watched her as she held his gaze. Her breath left her as the images came again. This time they were weaker, but still there. Bobby was drawing on a tablet of paper alone in his room at night, then hiding the drawings under his bed. Finally, she breathed in deeply, then let him pull her up and help dust off her dress.

"You okay, Lettie?" he asked again.

"Why do you hide your drawings?" she asked.

Bobby looked like he'd just been socked in the arm. "Who told you?"

She shrugged.

"My mama says it's idle hands, but it don't hurt nobody," he said defensively, a hurt look on his face.

Aletta shrugged again. "Sure don't seem like it would."

Aletta felt shaky and a little dazed as she walked to the schoolhouse. She had a strong feeling of specialness and power, but she was also afraid of what it might mean to have something like this happen, something she'd never heard people tell of before.

"Miz Vandehay wants you, 'Letta!" called Peggy Peg Legs, a scrawny first grader, as she ran over.

Shame crawled inside Aletta and curled up like a cat in a window. She just knew Mrs. Vandehay would scold her good, as she'd done with Miss Maple, if she said something about what had happened.

"You look weird, 'Letta," Peggy said.

Biting her lip, Aletta walked past the group of kids who crowded at the door trying to hear Mrs. Vandehay and Ralph inside. She felt like crying as she closed the door behind her and waited for her eyes to adjust to the dimness of the dark wood room.

"Aletta, do you have something to say? What happened out there?" Mrs. Vandehay, hands on hips, stood over Ralph, who sat at a desk in the front row. He shot Aletta an angry look.

She figured he'd blamed her for the fight, and it made her mad all over again. She wanted to call him a bed wetter again and put him in his place.

"Me and Bobby were playin' tag is all. I accidentally ran into

Ralph, and he went crazy like he was gonna kill me. I didn't do nothin' and said I was sorry. Then . . ." Aletta stopped, remembering what she'd seen. Ralph being locked in the barn, scared and crying.

"Yes?" Mrs. Vandehay asked.

"But I'm sure he didn't mean nothin' by it," she blurted out quickly. "I ran into him real hard. I'd 'a been mad too."

Ralph's face softened a little.

"Did he hurt you?" Mrs. Vandehay asked.

Aletta rubbed the back of her left hand where a strawberry stood out red on her skin. "Not really."

As Aletta rode home on the bus that afternoon, she avoided touching the other kids. Her stomach was nervous and hurt a little, like she might be coming down with something. Ralph sat in the very back of the bus, staring out the window. She was afraid he might come and try to beat her up again, and the fear made her wish she'd gotten him in bad trouble. But as the bus approached her stop, she got up the courage to walk back near him. He looked up at her, a different shade of hurt blue in his eyes than when he'd held her down.

"I'm sorry your mama and daddy lock you in the barn," she whispered. "That ain't right."

She didn't wait for him to respond but turned and ran to the front of the bus just in time for Mr. Randall to open the door and let her out. She felt her heart beating wildly as she glanced up at the bus rumbling away. Ralph's eyes looked at her through the back window, and this time they seemed different, the blue a shade brighter than before.

★

Sissy, Randy, and Ruby sat on the floor of the living room. It was hot. A summer day like this would normally have been spent at the public swimming pool. Randy and Ruby would come home blue-skinned and starving because they'd only leave the water when the lifeguards ordered them out for adult swim.

When it was adult swim, Sissy'd get in and show off her long, even strokes, her head moving from side to side. Even though she was four years too young, she swam with the grownups because of that stroke and because she was pretty and fun. Threadbare towels wrapped around their pruney bodies, Randy and Ruby would eat their Snickers bars and Tangy Taffy and watch her with pride.

Today they leaned into her and she held them. Now she was shivering too.

"Why did Daddy choke Mama, Sissy?"

"I don't know, Randy. He was mad. He didn't want to leave."

"Maybe we should choke *him*. Then he could see how he likes it, or maybe I could hit him in the head with a baseball bat. Then he wouldn't hurt Mama no more," Ruby said, clenching her small hands into fists.

"What do y'all think we're gonna get, a baby brother or a baby sister?" asked Sissy, changing the subject.

Randy looked up into Sissy's face. "I want a baby brother."

"No way, it's gonna be a girl," Ruby said.

"I think so too. I want a baby sister." Sissy was glad to be talking about something happy, anything other than hitting her daddy in the head.

"Yoo-hoo!" They heard the screen door open. The smile on Joy's face melted when she saw them huddled together. "What happened? I saw that van take off outta here like a bottle rocket."

"Mama's gonna have the baby. Daddy took her to the hospital," Sissy said. She didn't look at Joy, afraid she'd see she had been crying.

Joy put her hands on her hips. "Then why do y'all look like somebody died?"

Randy got up and hugged Joy's legs. "Daddy choked Mama, then Mama hit him with a glass of milk. Then she had to go to the hopsital."

"It's *hospital*, Randy. Gyod," Ruby said, rolling her eyes.

Joy's face turned so red even the Merle Norman pancake makeup couldn't hide it. "You kids just stay right here. I'll be back a little later."

She stalked back over to her place and snatched up the phone. It seemed as if she were trying to squeeze the receiver in two as she dialed.

Jimmy gathered Aletta into his arms again and carried her into the main entrance of the brightly lit, bare-bones hospital that sat on the western edge of Oklahoma City, the closest one to Okay. Aletta kept her eyes closed against the pain and the sight of Jimmy above her.

He talked to her as he strained to get her inside quickly. "It'll be all right, Lettie. You're gonna be just fine."

Aletta never looked at him as a nurse came with a wheelchair and he sat her down.

As soon as she was wheeled away to Delivery, Jimmy ducked into the bathroom. He washed the blood and milk off his face, but the gash over his eye was bad. Whenever he grimaced or smiled, it started bleeding again. His shirt was sticky and bloodstained, so he took it off and stuffed it in the back pocket of his shorts. He walked into the hall trying to look nonchalant, but people stared. He already had the excuses that he would give for his battered face running through his mind. Other than that, he didn't think about the fight. He blocked it out, unable to deal with it right then.

The first nurse who came by insisted on taking him to the emergency room for stitches.

"But my wife's having a baby. I need to stay with her," he said.

"What's her name?" She took his arm and led him toward the emergency room. "I'll go check on her and let you know how she's doing, but you have to get that cut stitched up or it's gonna ruin your pretty face."

They passed by the medical offices waiting area on the way. In the corner of the waiting room, with a *Vogue* magazine on her lap, he saw Kathy Kokin looking straight at him.

It seemed to Aletta that the pain, starting between her legs and moving upward, was trying to split her in half. She thought she might've passed out for a minute there, but she was fully awake now. Unfortunately. She moved a little from side to side on the delivery table, the sharp heat in her belly not allowing for stillness.

Sweat ran from her hairline down her forehead. "Where's my shot?"

Dr. Ponder pulled his hand out from between her legs and tossed his latex glove in the trash. "You have to be dilated to four, Aletta. You're only at three." The bushy salt-and-pepper eyebrows over his green mask were his most interesting feature. When he looked at her now, those eyebrows seemed to frown. He moved to her side and pulled his mask down.

"What's this here on your neck?" he asked, pointing.

She groaned. "What? What are you talkin' about?"

"Bruises," he said.

"Well, hi there." Kathy smiled as she walked toward Jimmy, her eyes sweeping over his bare chest and muscular arms. "Looks like you lost that round."

Jimmy laughed and held the gauze the nurse had given him over the cut. "I was helping some guy push his car out of the road. He popped the clutch without telling me, and the damn thing shot forward. Door swung open and hit me a good one."

"I'll go tell Emergency you're on your way," the nurse said, and left.

"Well, otherwise, you look fine to me." Kathy looked at him sideways with a tilt of her head, and he felt a twinge in his crotch.

Jimmy put his free hand in his jeans pocket. "And you're looking beautiful as always. What're you here for?"

"Oh, just a little checkup is all."

A pudgy young nurse stepped into the waiting room. "Ms. Kokin," she said.

"That's me." Kathy smiled and walked away, her hips swaying as she went.

Jimmy watched until she disappeared behind the swinging doors, then headed toward Emergency. A few minutes later, two policemen approached the nurse who'd called Kathy in for her appointment.

"We're lookin' for Jimmy Honor, you seen him?"

"All right, Mrs. Honor, let's turn you on your side," the nurse said. She had kind eyes and a maternal way about her that Aletta was grateful for.

Aletta rolled over, and as she did, the pain seared through her again. Out of the corner of her eye, she saw a man walk up to her exposed backside with an enormous needle poised in front of his face. She wondered if it was necessary for everyone in the hospital to see her bare ass.

The nurse touched her shoulder and leg. Aletta realized that there were no images, nothing coming in. Her body must not be able to handle it right now. *Thank God,* she thought.

"Now roll up in as tight a ball as you can, hon, so he can see your backbone," the nurse said.

Aletta glanced at her and whispered, "I've been poked by too many men lately."

The nurse smiled. "I know what you mean, darlin'."

As the needle went into her spine, Aletta faded away. They could've been in a barn for all she knew. There was just the sting of the syringe in her back on top of a blur of pain in her front. But as the epidural entered her bloodstream and melted her lower body into a quiet numbness, the sterile room, with its strange pieces of equipment and shiny linoleum floor, became visible. "Ah, God," she sighed.

Jimmy stood up and shook hands with the cops. "Hey, Gary, hey, Donnie." They'd found him in the emergency waiting room.

"Hey, champ," Gary said, then lowered his voice. "We didn't expect to hear your name over the radio. Got a complaint from a neighbor." His blue uniform fit far too tightly, the buttons on his shirt straining to deny his burgeoning waistline.

"Mr. Honor, you can come in now," the receptionist called.

"Come on back," Jimmy said to the officers. "Lord knows they'll have me waiting in there for an hour." He was glad to get out of the waiting room where people could see them talking.

"I don't know what Joy's talkin' about," Jimmy said as he sat on the paper covering the examination table. "We had an argument, but don't tell me you boys don't ever argue with your wives. Women were born to nag."

They laughed a little as Donnie closed the door behind them. He was taller than Gary and looked like he might've been a football player when he was in school, a tight end maybe, with long legs and wide shoulders.

Jimmy touched the gauze over his eye. "This cut was an accident. I fell and hit my head on the table."

Gary almost always did the talking. "We know things aren't always easy in a marriage, Jimmy, but you can't touch her, all right? I personally don't believe you did, but if you did, don't do it again, okay, buddy?"

Aletta looked at the blood on the hospital bedding. She hoped her bowels hadn't moved without her knowing it. That had happened with Ruby. "Don't cut me this time, Doctor," she pleaded. "I don't have time to heal with my other kids and all."

Dr. Ponder examined between her legs. "I think you should be all right having had three already, but if it looks like you might tear, I'm gonna cut," he said. "It'll be a helluva lot worse to heal if you tear." He looked back down. "Okay, Aletta, it's time. Push as hard as you can."

"I appreciate you boys comin' by," Jimmy said as he shook hands with the policemen again.

"Hey, Jimmy, you remember that game against Okeene when you hit forty-one points?" asked Donnie.

Jimmy smiled and nodded, "Got lucky on that one."

Donnie turned to Gary, his brown eyes wide like a little boy's. "He couldn't miss. I mean *could not* miss. There was this one shot where he was on the baseline about thirty feet from the hole, falling out of bounds, and somehow he shot the ball over the backboard"—Donnie showed them how Jimmy had looked, with his leg out in front of him and hand poised above his head— "And the damn ball swished through the net. The other team just about started to cry."

The doctor walked in while Donnie was still following through on Jimmy's shot.

Gary and Jimmy laughed.

"I can't. I got nothin' left," Aletta groaned, her head thrown back on the pillow, exposing her neck and the bruises. She'd told Dr. Ponder it'd been an accident with a ski rope at the lake. She knew he probably didn't believe her, but she was too humiliated to tell the truth.

"Push one more time, really, really hard. This should do it," Dr. Ponder said, and looked at the nurse.

The nurse squeezed Aletta's hand. "You got to try. Your baby has to come out now."

Aletta took a deep breath. "Aaaahhh!" She pushed and pushed, her eyes closed, her face pinched tight. Finally there was the release, and she opened her eyes. Her scream turned into a laugh as she watched the doctor lift her squirming red baby into the air, the cord still attached to its belly.

"It's a boy!" he exclaimed.

At that moment, Jimmy was having thirteen stitches sewn over his eye.

Aletta sat up in bed, propped against several pillows, holding her baby and looking at his mottled pink skin and still-distorted features. She had the same incredible experience of intense and completely opposite emotions that she had had with her others, but this time it all seemed bigger. There was the rush of adrenaline, the feeling of awe and even euphoria as she held this miraculous, tiny being that had just pushed its way out of her body. This baby represented hope, a chance that things might finally be right.

Then came the fear, pushing the hope right down to its knees.

How could she raise four kids, let alone this one, most likely by herself, without a father? She thought about being alone, trying to make enough money, to be mother and father to her children, to have enough time for them and all their needs. She just didn't see how it was possible.

A few minutes later, Jimmy walked into the room wearing a T-shirt with the hospital's name on it. Aletta sank back against the pillows, wanting to disappear. Jimmy glanced at the nurse, who was fussing over the baby with thermometers and Vaseline as he lay on a little changing table next to Aletta's bed.

"Should I leave you alone?" the nurse asked.

"Yes. Thank you." Aletta took her baby back from the nurse and avoided looking at her husband.

Jimmy came over and looked down at the baby she held on her chest. At last she glanced up and saw that tears had pooled up in his eyes and were touching his bottom lashes. Aletta was continually surprised by his love for their children. How could all his extremes be contained in one person?

"You did great," he said. "Can I hold it?"

She offered the baby up to him, unable to deny him his own son. He was an important part of the child's life, no matter what happened. "Him," she said. "It's a boy. He looks like a little gypsy baby to me, with that dark hair."

He laughed as he took his baby. His hands looked like giant earthmovers next to the baby's tininess. He sat down, holding him gently.

Aletta watched her husband. She'd never been able to "read" Jimmy, not even a flash of information. Only her family had been beyond her abilities until she met him. She tried again to decipher the lines of his face, the way he held himself. The way his muscles rippled had made Aletta get warm between her legs the very first time she'd met him. Now he looked pale, and his eyes were ringed with red. Usually his dark suntan complemented his light brown eyes, the rich color of coffee when you've just poured in the cream.

The white bandage over his left eye made Aletta look away

again. She remembered how she had loved his thick eyebrows and his brown eyes and skin when they'd met because he looked different from most of the people in Okay—a little exotic, foreign, special. When they first started dating, his thick eyebrows had been one of the main reasons that she told her friends he looked like Omar Sharif in *Doctor Zhivago*. For a long time afterward, they teased her by calling him "Omar" when he wasn't around.

Now the slash above his eye seemed to tell of their entire relationship. She had thought she knew who Jimmy was back then, but he had changed, and now she had a vague and frightening feeling that she was living with a stranger. She didn't know him at all.

★

Sixteen-year-old Jimmy Honor strutted into the Dairy Queen, his stomach rumbling as only a teenage boy's can. He had just enough money for an ice cream cone, but he wanted more. Holding his left arm up against his chest as he'd done for the last three days, he scanned the menu board, not noticing the pretty girl with sun-streaked strawberry blond hair who walked up to take his order.

"Can I help you?" she asked. Her face flushed when he looked at her, which just made her green eyes and perfect white teeth stand out more.

He smiled at her. "Sure, you can give me two hamburgers and a Coke for the price of an ice cream cone."

"His eyes actually sparkled, like in the movies or something," she told her best friend, Connie, that evening out on the porch swing as they watched the fireflies put on a light show.

While Jimmy ate his burger, Aletta decided to wipe down some clean tables near his. "Why're you holding your arm like that?" she asked.

She'd talked Bert into one free burger, but he wouldn't let her spend her own money on a customer, no matter how cute he was.

"Broke my collarbone when my horse ran into some barbed wire hidden in the underbrush. We just moved here from over by Tecumseh. I told my dad I needed to go to the doctor, but he told me it would mend if I just held my arm right here." Jimmy held his bad arm up against his chest with his right hand.

"My goodness." Aletta was angry at Jimmy's dad, not for the last time. "It must hurt terrible."

"It did when I fell, that's for sure. I heard it crack real loud."

Aletta glanced toward the kitchen but didn't see Bert, so she slid into a chair across from Jimmy. "I can't believe your dad wouldn't take you to a doctor. What'd your mother say?"

Jimmy washed down a mouthful of food with some Coke. "She can't say anything to the old man. The real funny part is that the horse got cut up pretty good with the barbed wire, and my dad's been tending to him every day, treating him like a baby. Probably spent at least three bucks on salve and bandages."

Aletta felt sorry for Jimmy, and somehow that made her pretty sure that she loved him right then and there.

"Hold on just a minute," she said.

She went and got three clean white dishcloths from the back, tied them together, and made a sling for him. He asked her to tie it around his neck, and even though she tried to avoid it, he moved and her hands touched him. But for some reason, she didn't get the immediate images and thoughts that came up when she touched everyone else.

It was an incredible relief. Normally, she had to focus real hard on what people were saying and just let the images fade away. She never let herself pay attention to them when they came up. She hated that she had this problem and didn't want anyone in the world to know about it.

Jimmy adjusted his arm in the sling. "Hey, thanks, you're handy to have around."

Aletta heard his voice say that in her head over and over after he left, trying to decode the words to see if they meant he liked her.

When Jimmy looked up from their new baby to his wife, the guard who stood at the doorway to his heart was not prepared for the faraway sadness he saw on her face. It went straight inside him.

He stood up, cradling the baby. "I'm so sorry, Aletta. I won't ever hurt you again," he said. "I'll be right back, okay? I'm gonna go call the kids. Do you want me to call your mother?" he asked, placing the sleeping infant gently in her arms.

She took the baby and pressed him to her heart. "I guess you should."

In the van, he went directly to the secret compartment, which had been the real reason he'd bought it, even though if challenged he would have called the accuser a liar and laid him out with a right to the jaw. He took the last drink out of the bottle of Smirnoff. Vodka had been his drink of choice since he'd read on the billboards that IT'LL TAKE YOUR BREATH AWAY, and he'd found that it didn't smell on his breath like the bourbon he drank when he'd taken up the pastime a few years before.

He took another drink, then put two Certs in his mouth. Feeling the hole in his chest fill up with the warming liquid, he went back inside to call his children and his mother-in-law.

The three kids were on the bed in Sissy's room with the pink Princess phone dragged out to the middle of the floor. The glazed white four-poster bed was covered with a lacy pink-and-white bedspread worn thin from use.

"A boy. It's gonna be a boy," Randy said for the twentieth time as he lay on his tummy with his chin propped on the backs of his hands.

Ruby lay on her back, kicking her feet up above her every so often. "Nuh-uh, it'll be a girl. I wanna have a baby sister."

Sissy, arms crossed and leaning on a pillow propped against the bed's headboard, gazed at the poster of Shaun Cassidy on the wall. Just now, his smooth skin and feathered hair had no effect on her. She was old enough to be worrying.

The phone rang. Ruby and Randy bounced up to sitting positions as Sissy dived for the receiver on the floor.

"Sissy, honey, it's Dad. Your mama's just had a baby boy," Jimmy said.

Sissy looked up at the expectant, sunburned faces watching her and smiled.

"It's a boy," she said. They all cheered with such pure, child-like joy that the energy of it shot straight through the roof of their house. It flew over Okay, over the pastures and the lake on the way to Oklahoma City, over the office buildings and in through a window of Deaconess Hospital, and down into a crib that held their little brother.

The nurse saw the tiny new baby in bed number twelve wake up for a moment, move his arms and legs, grimace, crinkle his nose, and make a funny little sound before falling back to sleep. She had no idea what had just happened, but for some reason, she touched his tiny head and felt love for him and hope for his future.

Nadine was crouched on her front porch repotting a dying rose bush when the phone rang. Her generous waistline hadn't decreased any with age. "Ah, who is it?" she grumbled and stood up stiffly. Her lower back had been giving her fits lately. She pulled off a dirty glove before picking up the black phone. "Hello," she said impatiently.

"Hello, Nadine. It's Jimmy." He was always careful to be neutral with her, not too nice but not cold either. She had to be managed.

She sat down in the wingback chair next to the phone. Her house was so tidy, it looked like nobody lived there. "Hello, Jimmy."

"Aletta's just had the baby, a little boy. She wanted me to call you and let you know," Jimmy said.

Nadine sighed. "I don't know how she's gonna handle another one," she said, and sank back in the chair. "When can I come see him?"

Chapter Eight

That evening, Sissy pulled a ladder out of the garage and leaned it up against the fence next to the house. She climbed up first, pushing herself off the top of the fence onto the roof, then pulled Ruby up. Randy got to the top of the ladder, but then wouldn't budge.

"I'm gonna fall," he said, looking up at his sisters. "It's too scary. I don't wanna be scared anymore."

Sissy reached down to him, the sky a halo of pink and orange behind her. "Come on, big R, Randy-man, magic boy. You can do it."

"Come on, ya big baby," Ruby said.

"Shut up, Ruby Booby," Randy said, and reached for Sissy's hand. As soon as she grasped his hand, Sissy pulled as hard as she could, knowing this was her only chance. Randy put a foot on top of the fence, then belly flopped onto the roof.

They climbed up to the peak of the brown shingled roof and faced southeast where Annabelle Park (named after Annabelle Pappe Seery, Jeremiah's only daughter) promised the not-so-spectacular Okay fireworks display. From here, Okay was tucked away under the tops of trees that had been planted in yards for shade. Beyond Okay, there weren't any trees, just flat prairie.

The warm summer evening, heavy with humidity and leftover hurt, weighed on Sissy, and she wished she were back at the lake with the Barbers.

"I wanna do a sparkler first," Ruby said. They sat down with their knees up and their sneakers firmly planted on the downward slope of the roof.

"No," Randy said. "Black Cats."

Sissy opened the brown paper bag that held the fireworks they'd bought at Grandoak Lake. "Tonight, you can do whatever you want. It's just us."

Randy set a group of ten Black Cats onto the piece of cardboard Sissy had brought and touched the smoking punk to the fuse. *Bam, bam, bam*—the sound blasted through the air like gunshots. Sissy and Ruby jumped.

"Gosh," Ruby said.

Randy looked at the remaining Black Cats for a moment, then put them back in the bag. He pulled out a small black disk that would turn into an uncoiling snake.

Sissy, who sat between her younger siblings, put an arm around each of them. "I think it's better quiet."

"Me too," Ruby said, tracing her name in the air with the sparkler she'd just lit.

Just as the evening darkened to night, the town display burst into the sky. They sat and watched, not moving or speaking until the grand finale sent enormous streams of sparkling light into the air, then faded away. The night that was left seemed darker than usual, close and empty.

"That was nice," Sissy said.

"Yeah," Randy said.

"It wasn't so much fun this year," Ruby said. "You think that means we're growing up?"

When she got to the edge of the roof to get back down, Ruby didn't feel very grown up anymore. She was scared, and so was Randy. Sissy couldn't convince them that they could put their foot all the way down onto the fence without losing their grip and falling to their death. So they waited.

"I need to pee," Randy said, looking over the edge of the roof, but he held it until their daddy got home half an hour later.

After he got out of the van, Jimmy strode over, smiling like he'd just gone out to run an errand. He hugged Sissy, then looked up at Ruby and Randy. "Come on down," Jimmy said. He reached up his arms to Randy.

"You look like Halloween," Randy said as he traveled from the roof to the ground, eyeing his father's bandage.

"Pretty ugly, huh?" he said, then reached up for Ruby.

She looked down at her father and wanted to jump into his arms, hold him around the neck, and cry. Instead, she looked away.

"I can do it," Ruby said, and turned over on her belly.

"I can get you, Rube," Jimmy said, staying close to her. But Ruby pushed herself backwards until her foot finally, shakily, touched the top of the fence. She steadied herself, then scrambled down the ladder.

When her feet hit the ground, she ran into the house, not looking at her daddy. Jimmy stood there for a moment, hands on his hips, watching the place she'd just left.

Jimmy brought Aletta and the baby home the next day.

She was pale and looked tired, but she hugged each of the children tight, trying to let them know she was sorry about the fight they'd had to witness, since she didn't have any idea what to say or how to say it. How could she explain about people hurting each other like that, especially their mama and daddy?

Sissy held the baby first, then Aletta taught Ruby. She had to sit in a straight-backed chair and cross her legs, making sure to hold his head up with her hand. He was so little, his perfect fingers and toes with their tiny nails perfectly shaped. His black hair was soft and silky against his peach-colored skin. Ruby laughed, thinking he looked like the tiny pink pups born unexpectedly to the gerbil she'd brought home from school last year.

She was a hero returning with a great treasure when she brought Fluffy and her babies back to school. The teacher explained that it was actually because of Scruffy, the boy gerbil who'd gotten loose and squeezed into a hole in the wall he couldn't get out of. They found him when the janitor came in to track down the smell and cut open the wall. There was a lot of crying that day in class. But Mrs. Miller explained that now they had Scruffy back in a way. She gave Ruby a blue ribbon for taking such good care of the babies. Ruby came home and told Aletta she wanted to marry Rodney Bohannon and have six babies, just like Fluffy and Scruffy.

"What's his name?" Ruby whispered, looking down at her little brother.

"We think it's gonna be George Alan," Jimmy said.

"Jimmy, I told you I don't like that name. It sounds like an old man." Aletta began to pick things up off the floor but sat down wearily with a skate and two pompons in her hands. She was flat worn out. There was no way she could think about what to do with Jimmy at the moment. She just didn't have it in her.

"Well, we're not naming him Clovis, that's for damn sure," he said.

Aletta's face flushed with anger. "I never said we were."

"I don't mind George," Ruby said.

"Jimmy, let's go in the other room for a minute," Aletta said. She felt like she was talking to one of the kids when she said it, so she decided to change her tone of voice when she spoke to him again. He hated it when she mothered him. She did too.

Sissy walked back to her room and picked up the phone.

"Can I hold him for a minute, Rube?" Randy asked.

"You gotta wait 'til Mama gets back so she can teach you how," Ruby answered, even though her arms were hurting.

Aletta closed their bedroom door behind her. "Jimmy, I don't wanna fight in front of the kids. We talked about this." She'd lost the skate but still held the pompons.

"Me neither. In fact, I don't wanna fight at all, but my Grandpa George was the best man I ever knew. If our son grows up to be half of what he was, I'd be proud. You got to name the other three."

"I did not. We agreed on their names and you know it."

"Goddammit, can't we just name him George? It's not gonna kill you."

"If we do, you better stick around to be a part of his life." She said it, but it was halfhearted. She wasn't sure if she really did want him around or not.

He hugged her and kissed her neck. "I'll be here. I promise." His hand roamed down her back. "How 'bout I make you feel good? You deserve it." He moved his other hand onto what had once been her waist.

She pushed his hands off her and moved toward the door. "I've had enough action down there for a little while."

Back in the living room, she told the kids the baby's name was George. She called to Sissy, "I have to lay down. Can you change him for me? Your dad can't handle it . . . and men think they're so strong." She said the last part under her breath, but they all heard it anyway. Her resentment was as apparent as her exhaustion.

"I'll change him. I can do it, Mama," Ruby said.

"Let Sissy show you how, then bring him into my room and he can take a nap with me."

Ruby concentrated hard, her eyebrows pulled together and teeth clenched, as she unfastened the diaper pins with her little fingers. Sissy laid them aside for her, then told her to pull the diaper back and out from under the baby. Ruby tried her best not to giggle at the little wiggler or the wetness and smell of the diaper. She wanted it to seem like this was easy, but she still let Sissy wipe him down. She knew for sure she'd get squirmy from that. The toughest part was getting the pins through the cloth. Her fingers just wouldn't do it right, which made George mad. He screamed his disapproval.

"Everything okay in there?" Aletta yelled from her bedroom.

"Yes, Mama. Ruby's just not doin' the pins right," Sissy yelled back.

Finally Sissy got his diaper on and picked him up, and he quieted down. "I can't believe they named you George. Poor little thing. That's about the grossest name ever."

"I don't really like it, you know," Ruby said.

"Why'd you say you did?" Sissy asked.

"She didn't want Mama and Daddy to get in a fight," Randy said. "Can I hold him now, pleeeaase?"

Ruby was grateful to be understood and showed it by giving Randy her newly acquired expert advice on holding George. Randy took him gently and smiled at his little puckered-up face.

"We can be best friends if you want to," he whispered, then kissed the soft skin on his brother's forehead.

Aletta lay next to Jimmy on their faux oak bed looking up at the white acoustic ceiling of their small bedroom. The frosted-glass lamp had a few dead bugs silhouetted against the light.

"Back to work tomorrow," Jimmy said. "Wish I didn't have to go. I'd like to be here with y'all."

"We need every penny more than ever now. We're still behind on some bills, you know," she said.

"I'll take care of them this evening."

"I didn't ask you 'cause you and the kids were so excited about it and all, but can we afford that van, Jimmy?"

"I got a great deal on it. It's been fun, hasn't it?" He looked over at her.

"Hmmm," she said. For some reason, she didn't want him to think he'd done anything right. He had some making up to do, and she didn't want him to forget it. "Were you able to get it cleaned up yet? Sorry my water broke in there."

"Yeah, that's one way to break her in, ain't it? I guess Sissy can have her slumber party now." He took her hand just as their four kids walked in the door.

"Come on up here," Jimmy said.

"Better take your shoes off first." Aletta took the baby while Sissy kicked off her shoes and Ruby and Randy crawled between their parents. They rarely wore shoes in the summer. They all got on the bed and laughed and joked as they snuggled together. Finally everyone settled down.

Her kids' warm little bodies felt comforting to Aletta. The love she felt for them was warm inside her, like a natural hot spring. Every time she thought she didn't have any more to give, she found the spring to be deeper than she'd ever imagined possible before she had them. "You all are the best kids we could ever ask for," Aletta said.

Just then, the baby pooted a little squealer. They all looked at one another for a moment in surprise, then started laughing.

"George! It was George," Randy yelled.

"Pyoowee, stick him out the window or something," Sissy said.

"Hey, the kid's gotta do what he's gotta do," Jimmy said.

Ruby just laughed and laughed.

That night, Aletta got up at three o'clock to feed George. She sat down in the wooden chair that had seen a thousand hours of rocking babies. The little warm body snuggled against her swollen breasts, taking one of them hungrily in his mouth. She had formula sitting on the floor next to her in case she ran out of milk before he was full. With the others, she had dried up quickly, and they'd screamed with hunger. She sang him the song that had always lulled her children to sleep like magic. The sounds of the slow chair rocking and the little mouth chomping kept time.

Go tell Aunt Rhodie
Go tell Aunt Rhodie
Go tell Aunt Rhodie her old gray goose is gone
Tell her that it's gone away
Tell her that it's gone to stay
Go tell Aunt Rhodie her old gray goose is gone

When he was full, the baby fell asleep in her arms, but she kept rocking a while longer, letting the quiet wrap around them like a blanket.

When Aletta went back to bed, she had another dream about losing a child. She saw a little girl, this time about six years old, separated from her in an enormous building, which she realized was a train station. She could only see the back of the child as she walked away, and when Aletta tried to run after her, she couldn't move. She screamed "Sissy! Ruby!" but she knew the girl wasn't either of them. Then Aletta looked to her right and saw herself in a huge mirror on the wall. There was a metallic horn growing out of her forehead.

My God, she thought in the dream, *there's something wrong with me.*

The dream disturbed Aletta so much that it woke her up. *There's something wrong with me.* The thought echoed in her mind as she lay staring at the dark ceiling.

After a few minutes, she got up and went to look at her sleeping girls. Ruby slept with Sissy as often as she slept in her own bed. They were so beautiful, their faces pink, a little glisten of sweat on Sissy's forehead. As she listened to them breathe, they seemed so peaceful, so right somehow. Looking at their purity, she began to feel a tightness, a gripping in her chest. *That's how little girls are supposed to be,* she thought. She left the room and started to clean the house with a vengeance.

Jimmy got up after a while and found Aletta, still in her blue satin nightgown, bent over the bathtub, scrubbing it with Ajax.

"My God, Aletta, what are you doin'? The sun's not even up yet," he asked.

"Somebody has to do somethin' around here," she replied.

Aletta made Jimmy a piece of toast with Velveeta cheese melted on top for breakfast.

"When the hell is Eugene gonna bring back that goddamn car? He may as well pay us for it if he's just gonna keep it," Jimmy said.

"He's doin' the work for free, Jimmy. He's just tryin' to help us." She had no energy to fight with him.

"I'm gonna call him and tell him I want the car back today. That all right with you?"

"Just be nice to him. He's a good person. The kids all like him."

"What do you mean by that?"

"Nothin'. Just that the kids like to have a . . . He's just real nice to them is all."

Jimmy left ten minutes later to go to work at Southwestern Bell, a job he had to wear a suit and tie for. He hated that, and he hated having a regular job like every other guy in the world. Aletta knew that and was grateful every day he went.

Joy called after Jimmy pulled away from the house and asked Aletta to bring the baby over at one o'clock that afternoon.

"Well, you can come on over and see him any time, Joy. I was surprised you weren't over here when we pulled up yesterday," Aletta said.

"Just bring him on over at one, honey. We need to talk anyway. Without Jimmy."

"Jimmy's at work, and anyway, you know the men in this town wouldn't be caught dead going into your place."

Joy cackled. "I know. You don't think I thought of that when I named it. Keeps 'em out better'n iron bars. Only problem is, I have to beg to get a plumber over here, and you ought to see the delivery men squirm. I tell you, Lettie darlin', it's important to be in control. You gotta remember that."

At twelve-thirty, Aletta dressed the baby, who was still half asleep, in one of Randy's old pin-striped baseball outfits with a cap that had two bats and a ball on it. Although she hadn't planned on more kids, she'd never gotten rid of Randy and Ruby's baby clothes. George had been an accident, and he'd come along at the wrong time. Jimmy was already distracted, and when Aletta announced she was pregnant again, it had the effect of pushing him out the door.

As she walked over to Joy's, she noticed all the cars parked out front. *Joy is sure busy today,* she thought. She pushed the door of the salon open and found the place filled with women and gifts, a dazzling display of color wrapped in bows and dressed in flower prints. She almost started to cry. The mix of perfume, hair products, and love was so heady that she felt a little dizzy from it.

Aletta had refused to let Joy throw her a baby shower before because she was sick with embarrassment about Jimmy's absence.

When she turned down Joy's shower offer, Jimmy had only been gone for a few days. Two weeks later, Aletta was cussing herself for not allowing the shower, because she needed all the presents. She could have taken them back to Anthony's and TG&Y and gotten cash if she was lucky, or at least credit to buy shoes for her other kids. When she saw the gifts and the ladies now, she was overwhelmed with gratitude.

"Here she is, ladies. Psychic deluxe and mother of a brand-new baby boy," Joy announced. After that, there was a great deal of oohing and aahing and they all had to hold George.

"Isn't he the most precious thing? He is so adorable, Aletta, just look at those tiny hands."

"Ooh, and he smells like the brand-new baby he is, don't you, little one?"

Ruby and Randy had quietly followed Aletta into the salon and were at their favorite place, Joy's styling chair, playing with all the brushes and sprays and goops and gels. Randy found some lipstick in Joy's top drawer. Ruby took it and put some on her lips, smearing it everywhere, then Randy put some on his own lips. When Ruby found Joy's makeover kit, she and Randy went to town.

Aletta unwrapped blankets and pacifiers, bottles and rattles. It felt like a vacation from worry and bitterness to be surrounded by all these ladies, receiving gifts and compliments and blessings.

"So how're you doin' with the mind-readin', Aletta?" Iola Little asked.

Aletta didn't look up from the box she was unwrapping. "To tell the truth, I haven't even thought about it since Jimmy came home." She didn't want to encourage any further questions.

She'd been having impressions come through again when she was touched, especially now with the ladies all congratulating and patting and hugging her, but she pushed the images aside as fast as they came. She had hoped that they wouldn't come back after George's birth, since they'd disappeared during it, but she had no such luck. She was happy to have the sign put away, because now, even more than before she had George, the visions were causing her to remember the past too much.

When Aletta's mother walked in the front door, Aletta's first thought was that she looked five years older than she had six months before. Her second thought was *Oh, shit.* She could barely stand being in the same room with her mama, and she figured her mama felt pretty much the same way about her.

There was just too much between them that would never be resolved. Of course, they never said a word about their feelings. They acted like everything was just fine, neither one of them willing to bring up what stood between them as plain as a barbed-wire fence stands between a prisoner and his freedom. But, she figured, her mama felt obliged to at least see her new grandbaby, especially since it was a social occasion. It was all right if things *were* bad, just as long as they didn't *look* that way.

Randy saw his grandma and ran to her. She looked at him in horror. Aletta, who could only see his back, thought he must be bleeding.

"Good Lord above, look at this child! What are you doin' to him, Aletta?"

The entire room became silent. Randy turned around as his eyes filled with tears. He had on makeup in all the right places—baby blue eye shadow, bright red lips, pink rouge, and heavy mascara. He had put on a pair of high heels one of the women had shed near the door and then donned one of Joy's plastic capes. This *looked* real bad.

Aletta jumped up too fast and felt a wave of dizziness as she rushed to Randy. She'd given birth only a few days before.

"Hello, Mother," she said as she pushed Randy out the front door and pulled Ruby along by her shirt.

After they were gone, a few moments went by in silence until the door opened again. The ladies saw a little hand place the high heels Randy had borrowed just inside the door before disappearing again.

Back at the house, Aletta smeared cold cream on Randy's face. "Now, first of all, son, don't feel bad. You just didn't know better, but boys don't wear makeup or high heels. It's just not done. If you and Ruby are playing here at home and you want to be a clown or something, like at Halloween, you can use makeup like that, but not out in public or over at Joy's."

Randy cried, and the tears made his soft, plump cheeks wet. In the bathroom mirror, Aletta kept thinking she saw the horn she'd seen in her dream sticking out of her forehead.

Aletta had to use every bit of will, guilt, and what-will-they-think-if-I-don't-go to get herself back over to Joy's. The tightness in her chest turned to a choke hold, but when she returned, the women greeted her as if she'd just had to go Band-Aid his knee.

"I brought something for the baby, Aletta. Why don't you open it?" asked Nadine. She sipped coffee and didn't look directly at her daughter as Aletta opened the gift. It was a brown winter jumper with footies.

"Thanks, Mother. This will be great in about six months." *Just breathe,* she had to remind herself.

The party ended shortly afterwards with the ladies all giving excuses as to why they had to get home, to the store, to an appointment, anywhere but here with Aletta and her mama in the same room.

Back over at Aletta's, Nadine looked out the window at Sissy practicing her cheerleading.

"My lands, girls wear their skirts short these days. I would've never let you wear a skirt that high."

"Mama, find something good to say."

"Fine, why don't y'all come to church with me soon so we can spend some time together," she said.

Nadine had been trying to get Aletta to join the Burning Bush Battle Church for years.

"We'll see," Aletta said.

Nadine insisted on hugging and kissing all the children before she left.

She held Randy's shoulders and gazed down on him. "Remember, boys don't wear makeup, and they don't cry. It's for your own good to learn these things now."

After she left, Randy pulled a bar stool over to the fridge, climbed up, and took a gallon of Braum's butter pecan ice cream from the freezer. He went into the living room, turned on the TV, and started eating. He pretty much never stopped.

Later, Aletta ran the bath for Ruby and Randy. She'd have to wash Ruby's hair at the kitchen sink in the morning. It was too much work for tonight. As she sat on the edge of the tub watching the water pour, she remembered her mother singing to her when she was little as she gave her a bath. She wondered where that woman had gone.

Chapter Nine

"Rain on Grandma Pearl, rain on Grandpa Charlie, rain on Uncle Joey, rain on Aunt Alma," Nadine sang to her daughter.

Little Aletta sat in a washtub of deliciously warm water. Her mother poured water over her hair like a liquid hug. Her hands strong and skilled from working on a farm, she scrubbed Aletta's hair gently. The warm water soothed her, and the washcloth her mother ran over her body made goose bumps push fine blond hairs straight out from her arms.

"Mama, why do people treat their kids mean?" she asked. She'd touched both her mama and daddy's hands more than once to see if the images came, but they hadn't.

Her mother's fingers stopped caressing her scalp. "What do you mean, honey?"

"A boy at school, we were playing and all the sudden I saw his daddy hurting him 'cause he wetted the bed."

"You *saw* it?" Nadine asked and began moving her fingers again. The crease didn't leave the place between her eyebrows, though.

"In my head, I saw him and his mama and daddy. They were mean to him."

"My lands, you've got an imagination, Lettie, but maybe you should think about nicer things."

"I saw stuff about Bobby, too." Aletta was confused. No one ever talked about such things, but surely she wasn't the only one who saw things about folks when she touched them. Her mama must know about it. She knew about most everything.

Nadine's expression became stern. She stopped rubbing again. "I don't want you talkin' like this no more, Aletta, now I mean it."

That night, Aletta listened to her parents talking in their bedroom. They'd left their door open, so she could hear them.

"Maybe that's normal for a child. They have such imaginations," Clovis said.

"I don't know, but I don't think we oughta talk to anyone about it. Not even Doc Grimes," Nadine said.

"That's prob'ly for the best. It'll pass."

Aletta fell asleep thinking that maybe she was the only one like this. There must be something wrong with her, something bad enough that even the doctor mustn't know.

"Rain on Daddy, rain on Grandma Nadine, rain on Eugene, rain on Joy." Ruby was lying flat on her back on the kitchen counter with her head over the sink as her mother sang and washed. Her long thin blond hair got such rat's nests in it that Aletta washed it this way a couple times a week with Gee, Your Hair Smells Terrific shampoo, Ruby's favorite. This was something Aletta only did with Ruby, and Ruby loved that part of it and her mama singing to her. She hated the tangles, though, and having to be still, so mostly she fought it like a wildcat.

As they were finishing, the doorbell rang.

"Mama, it's the lady you read the mind of," Randy called out.

Kathy Kokin flashed through Aletta's mind, but when she went to the door, she saw Silvia with her baby and a dark man with a mustache and slicked-back hair. Aletta recognized him and smiled.

Silvia beamed. "I got him back. This is my husband, Miguel Rivera."

"Our daddy came back too," Randy said. He hadn't moved since opening the door.

"I'm very glad to hear it," Silvia said, smiling at him.

"Go on and watch your show now, Randy," Aletta said.

Miguel seemed embarrassed as he put his hand out toward Aletta.

Aletta looked at his outstretched hand, then looked him in the eye. "I'd rather not, if you don't mind," she said.

Silvia took her husband's hand in her own. "*Esta bien.* She gets the sight from touching you."

"I'm sorry. Don't just stand out there. Come on in," Aletta said.

"No, wait!" Ruby screamed and flashed by, running to the back of the house with the towel covering her naked torso.

"Oh, I was just washing her hair."

"No, we won't come in today. We don't want to interrupt, but I wanted to tell you that Miguel's brother found him in that hotel you saw." She looked at Miguel, encouraging him.

Aletta stepped outside to join them.

Miguel spoke quietly. "We needed the money because we have a son now, and I don't want Silvia to work. Some men asked me to carry some freight for them to San Antonio. I didn't know what it was, and I didn't want to know. But somebody did, and my truck was robbed the night I got down there. I knew I was in big trouble. I didn't know what to do."

"My Lord, you must've been scared outta your wits," Aletta said.

He nodded his head. "Yeah, I was so damn scared, I got drunk, but it didn't help. The men I was carrying for found me and beat me up good."

Silvia made him turn his head and show the red welt on his cheek that was turning into a scar.

"I just wanted to thank you for helping us out. I feel like I'd be dead right now if my brother had not found me."

"Oh, I forgot." Silvia gave the baby to her husband and ran

back to the car, returning with a pan full of homemade tamales. "These I made for you. Why isn't your sign up anymore?"

"These look wonderful. Thank you," Aletta said. "My husband took down the sign. He's like Miguel. He doesn't like for me to work, with the kids and all."

"But it's different. God has reached out His hand and touched you, like one of the saints. You have a gift. You help people," Silvia said.

Aletta's face turned red, and she kept her eyes on the tamales. "Thank you," she said. "For the food and for comin' over."

Jimmy drove past Kathy's enormous house on his way home, as he'd done for the past week. It was in a new subdivision called Park Avenue Estates, a mighty grand name for some oversize tract homes carved out of prairie grass and red dirt, but Jimmy was impressed. Today, Kathy happened to be outside watering her flowers. He came to a stop in the bicentennial van and leaned out of the window.

"Hey, haven't seen you in a few weeks. How was your checkup?" he called.

"Oh, it was fine." She turned and smiled. That was enough to make him get out of the van.

He had told himself he wasn't going to get out. She could get in the van of course . . . No, not really. Just a joke. *Do not get out of the van,* he told himself. Didn't help him a bit, because here he was striding over to her, wishing he'd taken his tie off and opened his shirt to show off his chest, wishing that the cut over his eye had healed, hoping he wasn't sweating through his shirt in the scorching sun.

"What about you?" she asked. "Looks like you're almost well."

"Oh, yeah. It's comin' along."

"Do you want a drink, get out of the heat? We might as well catch up on old times since you're here," she said.

He looked at the ground and hitched up his pants a little.

"Come on, I have somethin' to show you anyway." She

turned off the hose, took off her shoes at the door, and went inside. She wore tight fuchsia shorts and an unbuttoned Hawaiian print shirt that was tied at the waist.

He followed her, glancing over his shoulder as he did. The air conditioning and the smell of her rose-petals-and-jasmine perfume washed over him like a sweet, soft breeze. Her house had creamy pink carpet and dark oak furniture. It was big, expensive, quiet, clean. If he hadn't already known she didn't have any children, he would've figured it out from stepping inside this house.

"Have a seat. Whatcha drinkin'?" She went to the bar and opened a cabinet, revealing to Jimmy what seemed like a hundred bottles.

He sank down onto her couch. "What're you havin'?" he asked. He felt like he'd just walked off his daddy's farm and had no idea how to behave around somebody rich and beautiful and worldly.

"Gin and tonic," she said.

"Sounds good."

She served him his drink, then handed him a slim red hardbound book. He turned it over and read the gold lettering: OKAY HIGH SCHOOL 1956. It was her senior yearbook. She sat down close to him and turned to a picture of him as a thin, gangly freshman making a jump shot over a defender, toes pointed and elbow tucked in under the ball. He laughed loudly. Then she pointed to some writing next to the picture.

To a very pretty girl. Good luck. Jim Honor.

"Do you remember signing this?" she asked.

"I remember being nervous as hell around you," he said.

"That's sweet."

He finished his drink faster than he probably should have, but she just got up and fixed him another without stopping their conversation.

"Why didn't we ever get together in high school?" he asked.

"I was too old for you. You were a freshman when I was a senior, but you were the only freshman I had sign my yearbook, that's for sure."

He chuckled as she handed him his second drink. "That's funny, because you're sure not too old for me now."

"No, now you're too old for me," she said.

"What's that supposed to mean?"

"You've got a wife and a whole herd of children, Jimmy. That's old."

He swallowed his drink in two gulps.

"Maybe I need to prove to you how young I really am," he said, looking directly at her.

She set her glass down slowly, avoiding his eyes. She leaned back and put her hands carefully in her lap. Finally she looked up at him, her lavender eyes smoky and soft. "I'm waiting," she said.

Aletta kept hearing Silvia's voice. As she was combing Ruby's hair, putting in a load of laundry, changing the baby, or starting the Hamburger Helper, she heard it.

Touched by the hand of God. You help people.

Sissy came in the door from Angie's house.

"How's practice goin', Sis?" Aletta asked.

"Terrible." Sissy slumped onto a bar stool, her hair in ponytails and her nose in freckles.

Aletta thought she looked about seven years old. She turned her back and stirred the ground beef to hide the smile that came over her face. "What's so bad?"

"Well, the cheer's pretty good, I guess, and my routine, but I can't do a roundoff backhand spring or back flips or anything."

"I've seen you do all kinds of cartwheels and things, and since when was cheerleading about back flips anyway? When I was in school, you had to be cute and have a good personality." She tore open the flavor packet and sprinkled it over the beef. "You have both of those, honey. They'd be lucky to get you."

"You think?" Sissy asked.

"Hell, yes." Aletta was in a good mood. She felt empowered by what Silvia had said, and she wanted to pass the feeling on to Sissy.

* * *

Jimmy came in as they were eating dinner at the bar in the kitchen. "Sorry I'm late," he said. "I had to meet a customer after work. Big deal I'm trying to close."

"You musta met at a bar," Aletta sniffed.

"No, we did not meet at a bar, Aletta. We met at his house."

Randy began tracing the gold starbursts on the countertop with his eyes.

"May I be excused?" Sissy asked, "I'm not hungry anymore."

Ruby watched her parents' every move.

"No, you may not be excused. Your daddy just got home, and we're gonna have dinner together like a family," Aletta said.

"I need a shower, Lettie. Y'all go on ahead, and I'll be out in a few minutes."

The anger burst into flame inside Aletta. All she wanted was a normal life where her family not only ate together, but actually wanted to. "Great. Fine. Sissy, you go right on ahead then. Kids, why don't you go eat in front of the TV." Aletta got up and started clearing the dishes.

"All right! All right!" Jimmy stalked over to the stove and grabbed a plate. He slopped some food on it, yanked out a stool, and sat down. "I'm here. Let's just eat now, okay?"

Aletta passed Jimmy on the way back to her seat. That's when she smelled it, strong and sweet. Jasmine and rose petals. *Must be a gal works in his office,* she thought. *Must be.*

★

"Don't you think it's about time we got married?" Aletta asked, pulling back from some serious kissing. Jimmy's hand was moving up from her waist as they sat in his beat-up old pickup truck after her senior prom. "We've been going together for four years, you know. That's forever."

They were so gorgeous together that night, if they'd been sitting in a limousine in Hollywood, people would have thought for certain they were movie stars. Jimmy wore a white tux jacket with black pants and a black bow tie, setting off his greased-back jet-black hair, olive skin, and white teeth. Aletta wore a dress that looked like a glass of rosé champagne turned upside down. It was a strapless cocktail dress, shimmering soft pink, tapering down to her waist, then moving out from her body at just the right moment, falling away to just below the knee, showing off her tight calves and slim ankles.

Jimmy had been at Central State University twenty miles away in Edmond for two years now. He was on a baseball and basketball scholarship, but he had injured his Achilles tendon trying to turn a double into a triple. He had missed all but three basketball games his sophomore season, and by the time he returned, the coach's rotation was set, so he rode the bench for those. It was eating him alive. Along with his troubles at school, his mother was writing him letter after letter behind his father's back.

Dear Jimmy,

How I miss you son. Life seems to get harder and harder. Me and Stella are stuck here in this house with her asthma and all. I can't tell you how bad it's been with your Daddy either. He won't let us buy hardly nothing anymore and most times we're eating only fried potatoes unless he kills a rabbit or squirrel. When you was here, we had game most all the time. You were such a good hunter just like how good you are at everything you do. I'm so proud of you. Stella and me talk all the time about how you're going to get rich and everything will be alright. Write me soon.

God Bless,
Mama

He didn't write back. He tried, but he had nothing to say. He hated his daddy for being a miser and a bully, and he hated his mama for being so weak. He'd get a letter from her and want to hit something, but he'd go practice instead. That's what he'd always done at home when he couldn't handle it anymore. The only thing his daddy had ever done for him was to build him a basketball hoop and attach it to the dilapidated barn on the land he sharecropped.

"This is your way out, boy," was all he'd said.

Jimmy would shoot for hours out there in the dirt, his younger sister, Stella, watching him from inside the house. His older brothers had already left home, dropping out of high school and going to California together. He stayed in Oklahoma because his coaches told him he could get a full scholarship. He wanted to be the first one in his family to go to college. His mama wanted him to go, too.

She talked to him about it, how he had to make it, how he couldn't let anyone ever beat him or he'd end up like his father, a failure and poor. She made up stories to get him motivated. She'd find out who the best player was on the team Okay would play next and lie about him.

She'd say, "That Tommy Cleary from Tuttle is a rich boy, you know that? Never had to work for nothin' in his life. His daddy's got farmland he don't even know what to do with. If we lived over there, your daddy'd prob'ly be workin' his land for him."

Against Tuttle that year, he scored thirty-six points and held their best player, Tommy Cleary, to eight with his furious defense. His anger fueled him in those days. It kept him alive in his house and earned him praise on the court.

He left the anger behind when he was with Aletta Jacobs, so when she asked him to marry her, he said, "I'm thinkin' about joinin' the army to be a pilot."

There was a nagging voice in his head telling him he'd never be a starter again after his injury. He wasn't gonna stick around to see if that was true. "Would you come with me?"

"Well, yes, I will. Where we goin'?" Aletta never hesitated.

They ended up in North Carolina. He'd be a fighter pilot, and leave it all behind.

Chapter Ten

While the kids watched TV, Aletta applied her makeup, taking special care with each stroke of mascara and blush. She and Jimmy were going to a party, her first social occasion in so long she couldn't even remember the last time she'd been out. She wanted people to say to one another, "Why, that Aletta looks so good. She and Jimmy must be doing just fine now." She wasn't doing a very good job of convincing herself that they were doing just fine, so she figured her chances with friends and acquaintances was pretty bad too, but at least she could make an effort. She tried one last time without much success to get her hair to do the same thing on both sides of her head, then gave her wrists another spray of the Pavlova perfume Jimmy'd given her as a birthday present last year.

She walked into the living room but stopped before anyone noticed her. She felt her heart warming up like fresh-made rolls on Thanksgiving Day as she stood there watching her family. Sissy, her feet propped up on Randy's back as he lay on the floor watching TV, was carefully applying alternating stripes of red and white—the Okay school colors—to her toenails. Jimmy sat on the couch gently cradling George's head as he fed him his bottle, and Ruby was balanced on the back of the couch behind her dad, combing his hair.

"Y'all are the prettiest sight I think I ever did see," she said finally.

Aletta felt lighthearted as they drove to Bill and Purdie Webber's fondue party. "We just have to do this kinda thing more often, get outta the house and have some time for us without kids or responsibilities, don't you think?" she asked Jimmy as she checked her hair in the visor mirror.

Jimmy drove with one hand on the wheel. The other he put on her thigh. "I was just thinkin' the same thing, hon. I miss havin' time just for us."

Jimmy told Aletta about the heated rivalry he had going in the office with Bill Webber, a Red Sox fan. Jimmy was a Yankee fan. Aletta knew this actually meant the two men liked each other a great deal.

They arrived about an hour late at the newly-built house that had a pool out back, a wet bar in the living room, and a game room decorated with Dallas Cowboys memorabilia from floor to ceiling. Purdie was a nurse, and she and Bill only had one child, a true rarity in these parts, so their lifestyle was different from Aletta and Jimmy's.

Aletta promised herself she wouldn't say anything about Jimmy's drinking tonight. It was a party, and they were adults. He needed his time to let go, and this was a place where people were meant to drink, unlike at the lake, driving a boat.

"You all right?" Jimmy asked as he handed her a white wine spritzer.

"Go on. I'm fine," she said, knowing he wanted to go play darts with his work buddies out by the pool. She could see them through the sliding glass door and hear them whooping it up each time a dart was thrown.

Aletta walked into the kitchen to say hi to Purdie Webber, who was making another batch of cheese dip in her Crock-Pot. Purdie fancied herself a "with it" kind of person, as she'd told Aletta at a Christmas party a few years back, and tonight she wore a light blue sheer flowing number with a matching scarf wrapped around her head.

"That's a beautiful dress," Aletta said.

Purdie looked up from her task. "Oh, hi, Aletta. Thanks for comin'."

"Well, thanks for havin' us. It's awful nice to get outta the house."

Purdie cranked open a can of tomatoes. "I saw this dress on Liz Taylor when she posed with Dick Burton in *People* magazine last year. Had to get one made just like it. Do you think one can of Ro-tel tomatoes or two in the *queso*?"

"I always put in two myself."

"Livin' dangerous, aren't you?" Purdie said as she plopped in the spicy tomatoes. "By the way, I saw that sign in your yard. You have any takers on that deal?"

"Yep, had a few, but I'm just too busy with the new baby and all," she said, peering hopefully into the living room. She'd hoped people had forgotten about the sign by now. "You know what? Ray Tettleton just walked in. I'm gonna go say hi."

Ray was balding and his features were all squished together—his eyes, nose, and mouth all tightly bunched as if they didn't realize they had plenty of face to fit on. He wore a wide tie like all the men, but his sported a bald eagle with its wings spread out and a ribbon in its mouth.

What is it with these men and bald eagles, Aletta wondered. She liked Ray a lot, and as he talked to her about his insurance business, she thought how unfair it was that most of the nice guys had to be ugly. Why couldn't she just be attracted to the person's heart and mind? Why did she want a nice chest and arms and a handsome face? It wasn't only her, it was all the women she knew. She glanced over at Jimmy, who was now talking to a pretty blonde and working on another drink.

She watched as Ralph Lawless walked up to Jimmy and shook his hand. He was a vice president in the company, about fifty-five, beer belly, red face, no neck, toupee. The blonde was his wife. Aletta corrected herself on her earlier conclusion about men. Unless they're rich, of course, then they don't have to be handsome at all. This made her think about Kathy Kokin for a moment, but she took another quick sip of her spritzer and turned her attention back to Ray.

Betty and Frank Conway walked in the front door a few minutes later, and the moment Frank saw Aletta, he whispered something to his wife and headed straight toward her.

"Hi, Frank. I met your son the other day at the IGA," Aletta said.

"Can I have a word with you?" he asked, and glanced at Ray.

"All righty," she said, her heart suddenly pounding. She felt like she must've done something wrong.

They walked down the hall until the safety of the party seemed a distant hum.

"My son Rusty says you told him he's gonna be a goddamn rock star," Frank said, glaring down at Aletta. He was tall, about the same height as Jimmy.

Aletta pushed her hair behind her ears. She'd tried to get it to do like Mary Tyler Moore's, but it was so straight it would barely hold a curl. "I talked to him, but I didn't . . ."

"He's dressing like a fairy and growing his hair out. He plays that damn guitar day and night, his grades are going to hell, and he's about to lose his job."

"I told him to keep practicing his guitar. That's all I said, Frank," she said. "Maybe I should talk to him again."

"Maybe you should. He sure as hell seems to listen to you. He thinks you're some kind of psychic because of that sign you put up. That sign's your business, Aletta, but talkin' to my son ain't."

Aletta saw Betty hovering at the end of the hall watching them. "I'm sorry, Frank," she said. "I didn't know he was gonna take it so seriously. I wouldn't have ever said anything."

"He'll be at work tomorrow . . . I hope," he said. "Maybe you can talk some sense into him." He turned to walk away.

"Frank, he's not gonna be a rock and roll star, but the music'll be good for him," she said before she could catch herself. Frank looked blankly at her for a moment, then walked down the hall to his wife.

Aletta walked back into the living room, but she felt like she wanted to hide. It mattered to her if people liked her or not, and it was pretty darn obvious what Frank Conway thought.

Jimmy walked over to her and gave her a sweet kiss on the lips, but he already smelled like booze.

"Hey, darlin', I been talkin' to Ralph about an opening at work. I'd be a manager, make more money. It sounds good," he said, his words slurring slightly.

Aletta looked toward the door as Eugene walked in with mousy Patty Simpson. He saw Aletta and started to smile and wave, but looked away when he saw Jimmy.

"Eugene Kirshka," Jimmy said, following Aletta's gaze. "I never talked to him about that Chevy."

Aletta put her hand on Jimmy's face so he would look at her. "Please don't talk to him about the car tonight, Jimmy. Promise me. This is not the time or the place."

"Fine, fine. I just haven't seen the s.o.b. in a while," he said, and walked toward Eugene.

"So when am I gonna get my car back, mister?" Jimmy asked as he shook hands with Eugene.

"Soon as you like," Eugene said. "She ain't fixed yet, though."

"She *isn't* fixed yet, you old farm boy." Jimmy clapped Eugene on the back.

Eugene laughed. "You're the damn farm boy, Honor. I grew up in town, even though it was only fifty people."

As soon as Aletta saw Eugene laugh, she went to find the restroom. Betty Conway was waiting for her when she came out.

"Hi, Betty," Aletta said, trying to slip by without having to talk to her. She'd had enough scolding for one night.

"Aletta, kin I tawk to you fer jist a minit," Betty said with a serious twang. Aletta knew she sounded just like her. It proved to her once again that a slow way of talking doesn't mean a slow mind. Betty Conway was sharp as a fillet knife and a member of the Okay Town Council.

"Betty, I'm gonna go talk to Rusty tomorrow at the IGA. Frank told me what was goin' on, so I'll get it straightened out."

"It's not about that," Betty whispered, glancing down the hall, her pink eye shadow glistening in the dim light. Betty wasn't a pretty woman—her hazel eyes were too far apart and her nose was tilted up a little so you could see her nostrils—but she knew how to put herself together. "It's about my dad," she said hoarsely.

"What about him?" Aletta asked.

Tears began to form in Betty's eyes and her chin quivered. "He died about two months ago," she said.

"Well, I'm real sorry to hear that." Aletta tried to sound sympathetic and to hide her surprise that Betty was crying in front of her in the hallway of a party.

"I—I need your help," Betty sniffled.

Aletta looked at her like she was speaking a language never heard of in Oklahoma, until she finally understood what Betty meant. She wanted Aletta to give her a reading. "Oh, no. No, ma'am. I just got my butt chewed out by your husband. He'd kill us both."

"But I've seen him in my bedroom at night," Betty said.

"Yes, my point exactly, Betty. You sleep with him," Aletta said.

Betty waved a hand in front of her face. "Not Frank! My father. I've seen him standing by my bed, and he's trying to tell me somethin' but I can't hear what he's saying."

Aletta turned and walked a few steps down the hall, then turned back around biting her thumbnail. "You swear about this? You're not just trying to get back at me over Rusty?"

"I need your help, Aletta." Betty sounded desperate and afraid.

Aletta bit a piece of her nail off. "Damn." She didn't like this, not at all. At a party, with Frank's wife, trying to talk to spirits. She liked the last part least of all.

"Please," Betty whispered. "You know I got two feet on the ground and my head on straight, Aletta. I wouldn't ask . . ."

"Shitfire," Aletta said finally, and led Betty down the hall. She couldn't stand to see Betty, or anybody for that matter, look so sad. At the first door she came to, she peeked into the game room, but jumped back when she saw Roger Staubach staring at her.

"What's wrong?" Betty whispered nervously.

"There's somebody in there," Aletta said.

Betty looked inside and saw the life-size cardboard cutout. "Don't scare me like that," she said, catching up to Aletta, who was already standing in front of another door.

Aletta gently turned the doorknob and looked inside. It seemed to be a guest room because it didn't look to her like anything people actually lived in. It was way too neat. As she entered the dark room with Betty on her heels, she had a weird sensation— a chill on her arms and a strong desire to leave. The only thing that made her stay was the look she saw on Betty's face when she turned on the bedside lamp.

Aletta sat down on the edge of the bed and patted the spot next to her for Betty to sit down. "I'll be honest with you, hon. I haven't talked to spirits since I was real little, so I have no idea if this is gonna work."

Betty nodded. "I understand," she said, her voice barely even a whisper now.

"You ready?"

Betty nodded and wiped the tears off her cheeks.

Aletta took Betty's hands and closed her eyes. As she prayed, talking to God like He was right there in the room with them, she felt a sense of determined calm come over her. She opened her eyes and smiled warmly at Betty. "Why don't we just take a deep breath and relax a little bit."

"That sounds like a good idea," Betty said.

They breathed deeply, and Aletta felt Betty's tight grip on her hand loosen and saw her shoulders relax a little. She had a sense she had to be strong for Betty, that they couldn't both be scared.

I can do this, Aletta thought. The words were simple, but they cleared her mind and strengthened her resolve. She closed her eyes again and focused on the images that were coming in. They were like shadows at first but became clearer after just a few moments. A child with long brown hair, the blue of her dress, playing by herself with a doll, dressing it, combing its hair.

The little girl spoke to the doll: "You're the prettiest girl in school. Let's get you dressed to go to the picture show in town and show off your new dress."

A young man, maybe nineteen or twenty, entered the room and sat down to watch. Aletta's body flinched when he walked in. He smiled at the little girl and she smiled back.

"What is it?" Betty asked, but Aletta didn't hear her.

She heard the man talking to the little girl. "Why don't you come over here and show me your doll?"

The little girl walked over to him and he pulled her up on his lap.

He began whispering to her, "You're the pretty one, prettier than your doll even," he said, and kissed her neck.

The vision faded away and Aletta heard crying. "Tell her I'm sorry," a man's tortured voice said.

"What's your father's name?" Aletta asked Betty.

"Orel. It's Orel. Can you see him?"

"Is that you, Orel?" Aletta asked. She didn't like this, but she knew she couldn't leave now.

"Yes. I'm so sorry," he sobbed.

"I can hear him. He says he's sorry."

"Sorry? What for? What's he sorry for?" Betty asked.

Suddenly Aletta saw the young man and the little girl in the chair again.

"This is real fun, but don't tell no one. This is just between you and me 'cause you'll get in bad trouble if you tell," he said, pulling up the little girl's dress, the doll falling to the floor.

Aletta heard Orel almost wailing now. She thought for sure everyone in the house must hear it too.

"Did he try to . . . Did he?" Aletta couldn't say it. She wanted to run out of the room, but it felt like she was being held in place, like someone was holding on to her.

"Did he what? What do you see, Aletta?" Betty sounded scared.

"I see a man and a little girl. He's trying to . . . Did your daddy rape you when you was little, Betty?" asked Aletta finally, opening her eyes, not wanting to see any more.

Betty's face transformed into a mask of pain. She collapsed backwards on the bed and turned over on her stomach. She cried huge sobs into the bedspread, and her hands clawed at it as if she were trying to dig a hole.

Aletta didn't know what to do. She was afraid she'd gotten Betty into something she didn't know how to get her out of. "I'm so sorry," she said, almost crying herself from seeing someone hurt so bad. "I'm so sorry."

"It wasn't my daddy!" Betty finally said. "It wasn't my daddy!"

Aletta gave her a pillow off the bed and patted her back. "I'm sorry, honey. You got to be quiet."

Betty put her face in the pillow, muffling her sobs.

"Maybe I was mistaken, then," Aletta said.

"It was my Uncle Walt, my daddy's brother, when I was seven." Betty put her face back in the pillow and her shoulders shook. Her yellow pumps fell off her feet, which dangled over the edge of the bed, and onto the ground one at a time.

Aletta searched Betty's purse and found some tissues at the bottom. She started to feel panicky.

"Just let her cry," she heard Orel say, and now she saw a faint outline of him standing in front of his daughter, looking down at her. He was a young man, maybe twenty-five. Aletta had never understood her gift, but seeing the soft, shadowy image of a young man who had died months ago well into old age standing there in the room with her, it was more of a mystery than it had ever been before. All she could do now was trust it, to know that something bigger than herself was happening and just to be there for it to reveal itself. *It's not me,* she thought. *It's just happening through me.*

"She's held it in for so long." Orel's voice was almost a whisper now. "She told me afterwards, but I wouldn't believe her. I didn't want to believe my brother could do that. I told her she was imagining things and never to tell anyone else, especially her mama and her grandparents." He paused for a few moments, his lips trembling, then said, "I was supposed to protect her."

Aletta felt the sadness and suffering fill the room, but somehow she knew she needed to just keep loving Orel and Betty and even Orel's brother Walt.

"Why is he sorry?" Betty asked into the pillow after a few minutes.

"Because he couldn't believe you when you told him, and he couldn't protect you. He loves you so much," Aletta said, tears running down her face. She couldn't hold them back any longer.

Aletta wiped the tears away with the back of her hand and was enormously relieved to see Betty stop crying and raise her head. A faint smile crossed Betty's face, and she blew her nose in the tissues Aletta had given her.

"Is that really what he said?" she asked.

Aletta pointed to Orel. "Yes, he's standing right in front of you."

Betty looked at Aletta with an expression of disbelief mixed with hope. It was a funny expression, and Aletta smiled. She reached out her hand. "Dad?"

Aletta saw him put his hand out, but the instant his hand touched his daughter's, he vanished.

Betty gasped and sat up straight.

After a few moments, she grinned at Aletta. "He went right through me. I felt him. I felt his love for me." She put her head in her hands and cried. "Thank you," she said. "Thank you."

Aletta thought Orel was gone, but then she heard him say, "There's someone who wants to speak to you."

Aletta felt a fear rise up in her that propelled her off the bed. She didn't want to hear it. She couldn't handle it right now.

"I have to go now," she said to Betty. "Are you all right?"

"I think so. Could you tell Frank to come back here, please?" Betty sounded completely exhausted. "Don't worry. I'll just say I'm still upset about my dad's death and I need to go home, I promise."

Aletta opened the door and slid into the hall. She went to the bathroom to check her makeup and wash her hands. She felt disoriented, coming from what she'd just been through back to the party with people everywhere.

In the brightness of the living room, Aletta tried to keep a smile on her face. She found Frank and quietly told him his wife's whereabouts.

Eugene walked over to her. "Hi, Aletta, how ya' doin'? Haven't seen much of you."

"Oh, pretty good, I guess, how 'bout you?" she said, trying to compose herself. "Do you mind if we sit down a spell? I really just need to sit down."

"Not at all," he said. They sat down on the love seat in front of the empty fireplace made out of lava rocks. "I see Jimmy's come back. How's it goin'?"

"Now there's a question," she said. She liked Eugene, but she was exhausted and just wanted to go home and go to bed. She had to rest a few minutes first, though.

"I saw you took the sign outta the yard," he said. "I figured you'd do good with it."

"Yeah, he took it down. . . . You know," she said. "I married him. What can I say?"

Jimmy walked into the living room from the backyard and saw them.

"Hey there, you flirtin' with my wife again?" he said to Eugene as he crossed the room. It came out way too loud, and there was a hush in the room for a moment.

"We're just talkin'," Eugene said.

"We should get home to the kids, Jimmy. You ready?" Aletta stood up, looking at Jimmy, her eyes pleading with him.

He ignored her. "But I know what you're thinkin'. You rednecks are all alike. Fuckin' and drinkin' beer's about all you can fit into that tiny little brain," he said, and tapped Eugene on the head with his forefinger. "Instincts," he laughed. "Like a dog."

Eugene stood up. He was a good-size man, but not as big as Jimmy.

"You're drunk, Honor," he said, and turned to leave.

"You're an asshole," Jimmy said, pushing him hard in the back.

"Jimmy, stop it!" Aletta screamed.

Eugene flailed forward, almost falling, but he pushed off from the coffee table and in one motion turned and threw a big round-house right at Jimmy. Jimmy stepped back, avoiding the punch, then cocked back his fist, but Bill Webber grabbed his arm before he could let fly.

"That's enough, Honor," he said.

Eugene ran at Jimmy headfirst and tackled him to the ground, bringing Bill down with them. Bill scrambled out of the way as Eugene and Jimmy rolled over and over on the floor. Aletta watched with her hands over her mouth. She knew if she screamed, she might never stop.

Ruby lay half awake in the darkness, her mind vigilantly awaiting any movement in the air or sound in the silence. When she heard her parents stumble through the front door, her father slurring and swearing, she was instantly alert. Her body rigid with fear, she tried to breathe more quietly so she could hear everything—maybe something in her daddy's voice that would let her know his fists were about to fly, or something crashing to the ground telling of a troubling, hateful dance between her parents, or even the words her mama might say that would surely send her daddy over the edge.

Ruby heard her father's voice rise for a moment before it was muffled as he went into their bedroom. She pulled her covers off and waited, her head cocked to one side. A few minutes later, she heard her mama go into the bathroom and open the window. She smelled cigarette smoke and knew the party hadn't gone well.

Chapter Eleven

Little Aletta walked the mile home from playing at her friend Helen's an hour later than her mama had told her to, so by the time she got there, she was afraid of getting in trouble and deciding which story to tell as an excuse. She walked through the gate and saw that the front door of the house was open, which was odd because her mother hated the flies. Walking past the enormous oak tree that shaded the entire farmhouse, she saw a wooden barrel overturned and could smell the strongly sweet and pungent odor of something spilled out on the ground.

Loud and angry shouting from inside the house startled her, and she ran up the porch steps and into the house. Her daddy and Johnny Redding stood across the kitchen table from each other. They didn't see her, so she stepped back out of the kitchen and peeked around the door at them.

"What I'm tellin' you is you're not workin' for me anymore 'cause you can't control your drinkin'!" Clovis yelled.

"Goddammit Clovis, I been with you more'n five years!" Johnny slurred. He held onto the back of a chair to steady himself.

"I done warned you twice already, and now I find a barrel a' whisky buried on my property and you drivin' my tractor, taking a goddamn drink ever' time you go 'round the field!"

Aletta had never heard her daddy so mad. She wished he would be nicer to Johnny. It sounded to her like he was real sorry.

"I won't do it again. I promise," Johnny said like it was final, like the discussion was over.

"Where's the still?" Clovis asked evenly.

"What still? I dunno."

"The hell you don't! Where's the still you got that mash from out there?"

Johnny ran his hand through his hair before he answered. "Do I got my job?"

"No sir, you ain't got your job. I won't have a drunk workin' for me," Clovis said.

Without warning, Johnny took a swing at Clovis from across the table and nailed him in the jaw.

"Daddy!" Aletta screamed.

Nadine ran down the stairs from where Clovis had sent her so he could talk to Johnny man to man.

Clovis fell backwards into a wall, then rubbed his jaw. "You come outside, Johnny. We ain't gonna do this in front a' my wife and child."

"There she is," Johnny said, looking at Aletta, his eyes wild now. To Aletta they looked how a horse's did when it was scared by a snake. "She's the one told you where the barrel was, ain't she? She's a little witch, told me she sees people at night in her room. They ghosts, ain't they, Lettie?" He stumbled toward her, knocking a chair out of the way.

Aletta didn't move. She could only stare up at him, terrified by what he'd said as much as him coming at her. Just as he reached her, Clovis stepped forward and punched him in the side of the head, then grabbed Johnny by the shirt and hair and dragged him outside.

"Nadine, call Sheriff Lloyd!" he yelled.

Johnny bucked like a wild bronco trying to throw Clovis off as they reached the porch, causing them to tumble down the porch steps and roll over and over in the dirt. They took swings at each other when one of them could get a free arm, but it was nothing like in the Westerns Aletta saw at the picture show where they hit each other one at a time, standing up. Aletta always rooted for the good guy. She knew her daddy was the good guy, but she didn't want him to win. She just wanted them to stop fighting. Covering her mouth with her hands, she held back the scream that burned in her throat.

Her mama pushed Aletta out of the way as she walked out onto the porch, carrying a shotgun that looked more like a cannon in her small hands. She cocked the gun, pulling the wooden part of the barrel back toward her and pushing it forward again. She pointed it up into the oak tree and pulled the trigger. The blast stopped Johnny and Clovis midswing, and the kick from the gun knocked Nadine right onto her rear end. The blast echoed eerily as a flock of crows flew out of the tree.

It was several seconds before the dead crow dropped on the ground with a thud, right in front of her daddy and Johnny.

Nadine pushed herself to her feet and just about ran Johnny through with her eyes as she pointed the gun at him. She glanced at the dead crow first, then said, "You're next, mister."

That night, Aletta went to sleep later than usual and awoke in the middle of the night. A young woman with beautiful skin, darker than Aletta's but lighter than Miss Maple's, sat on the bed next to her, looking at her with eyes as sad as they were brown. Aletta drew in her breath and pulled the quilt closer to her. This was the first time she'd felt a little frightened by any of her visitors. She hadn't had any for a long time and was starting to hope they wouldn't return. But Isabella was lovely with her long black hair, and she was nice to Aletta. She wanted to know what Aletta thought and how she felt. Another thing that made her different was that Isabella never moved her lips to speak, but Aletta could hear her as clear as she could her daddy when he tucked her into bed. She asked about Isabella too, but Aletta went ahead and moved her lips.

"Where do you live?" she asked, pushing herself up on her pillow.

"I lived in Italy a long time ago," Isabella said, then paused for a moment before continuing. "It was a time when everyone was frightened. People were being hurt very badly because they were different from the people in power. I got hurt then. Many of us did. That's why I came tonight, to tell you that you are a precious girl. Don't believe it if anybody says bad things about you."

"Like Johnny?" Aletta asked.

Isabella nodded and placed her small hands in her lap. "Yes."

Now Aletta was grateful that Isabella had come. Her parents had talked about the fight with Johnny throughout that evening. Clovis had laughed and called Nadine "Calamity Jane," but they pretended like Johnny had never mentioned Aletta. It was like that part had never happened.

With Isabella watching over her, sleep came easily. When she opened her eyes, the sun was shining in her window and Isabella was gone.

★

Aletta lay in bed listening to Jimmy snore. She replayed the events of the evening in her head—Betty, the party, Eugene. She worried that Eugene must despise her now, or at least not respect her. Hell, she didn't even respect herself.

She couldn't get Betty's daddy's voice out of her head. He'd said someone wanted to speak with her, but she couldn't stay in the room. She had a sense of who it would be.

Finally, dozing off at four in the morning, she had a dream. A young woman with dark eyes and olive skin was walking down a dark stairwell that smelled of rotting wood and mildew. She entered a small underground room lit with candles where other women were waiting. The fear felt like a plague that hovered about them. Aletta didn't know why the women were so scared. When she woke up, she could only remember the woman walking down the steps, but the anxious, clammy feeling of fear lay upon her like a heavy blanket.

Aletta groaned and rolled over, expecting to see Jimmy still

passed out, but he wasn't there. She got up and saw Randy standing in the carpeted hallway in his Scooby-Doo pajamas, listening
to something. Sissy appeared holding George who was whimpering
with hunger. As Aletta went to get the baby, she heard what they
heard—Jimmy puking in the bathroom.

"You kids get dressed. Your daddy isn't feeling very good, and
I want to leave him alone for a while," she said, herding them out
of the hallway.

Half an hour later, she piled them into the van without speaking to her husband. Big gray clouds with black bellies had rolled
in since last night. As she drove, Aletta decided she felt just about
like the sky looked, about ready to bust open and cry.

At the Hilltop Diner, they sat in a red vinyl booth patched with
duct tape. Aletta told the kids to order whatever they wanted. Her
nervous stomach wouldn't let her eat, so she just held George, kissing him and smelling his hair. She noticed the signs that were taped
to the walls of the diner. One of them said: DO YOU WANT TO TALK TO
THE MAN IN CHARGE OR THE WOMAN WHO KNOWS WHAT'S GOING ON?

Another hung near the kitchen: WANTED: A GOOD WOMAN WHO
CAN COOK, SEW, CLEAN, AND DIG WORMS. MUST HAVE BOAT AND MO-
TOR. PLEASE SEND PICTURE OF BOAT AND MOTOR.

Usually, Aletta smiled at the jokes, but today they pissed her
off. She was tired of men, at least her man, getting an easy ride
just because he was a guy.

"I'll be back," she said. "I'm gonna walk over to Eugene's for just
a sec. Y'all finish your breakfast. And thanks for bein' so good today.
I really need it." She put George back in his infant seat—the same
one she'd used since Ruby was born—and carried him with her.

She figured Eugene probably wouldn't be there after last night,
but the garage was open, and he was bent over the engine of a
black Nova SS.

She shifted George to her other hand and looked at the wall
calendar that showed a picture of a woman in a bikini holding a
wrench, her long blond hair blowing back and her lips pursed.
"Looks like rain," she said quietly.

He turned around and saw her. "Yeah, sure does," he said, and wiped his hands on a red shop towel. He didn't look like he'd been in a fight. Frank and Bill and Ray had broken it up before any blood spilled.

"I just wanted to come over and make sure you're all right," she said. She felt humiliated and exposed standing there in front of him.

"I'm okay." His smile was sad. "What about you?"

She chuckled and shrugged. "Me? Yeah, sure."

He paused for a moment, and it seemed he was looking right through her. "Aletta . . ."

"You know," she said quickly to stop him. She didn't handle tenderness very well. "I'm real sorry about all that last night. He didn't mean nothin' by it. He just had too much to drink. You know that, right?"

"I know you ain't him. I know you're in a real tough situation, and I don't hold you responsible for what he does." He took a couple of steps toward her, then stopped.

She just looked at him, not sure what to say next, how to respond to such honesty. "Thanks. I appreciate that. I really do," she said finally, and turned to walk away.

"I also know you don't have to put up with that. I know you got a choice," he said to her back, but she didn't turn around. She just waved, walking as fast as she could back to the diner. She was unable to keep the shame and regret inside her any longer, and it was pushing its way out her eyes.

Aletta drove to the IGA, clicking her wedding ring on the steering wheel, mad as hell at herself for saying anything to Rusty Conway in the first place. It was like something had compelled her to touch his shoulder that day and tell him to play his guitar. "Big mouth," she said under her breath.

George began to cry as they pulled up and wouldn't quiet down unless Aletta held him, so she put him over her shoulder but made the other kids stay in the van. The cloud cover made it bearable outside. Inside the store, she scanned the checkout stands for Rusty. *God, please don't make me have to talk to anybody,* she thought. As she stood there searching, bouncing a little with George and patting him on the back, Rusty walked in the door right behind her.

"Hi," he said, smiling. "I guess you had the baby."

"Oh, hi." She turned around, noticing how much longer Rusty's hair had grown. "This is George."

"George?" He laughed a little and touched the baby's soft hair. "He's cute."

"Rusty, I need to talk to you for a minute." Aletta glanced around the store.

Rusty's voice lowered. "Mr. Snyder gets mad if I just talk to people without working. Do you need any groceries? I'll take them out to your car for you."

"Sure, I could use a few things," she said.

Rusty took a shopping cart from its place in the line and turned it over to her.

"I'll make sure and bag you," he said.

Aletta walked quickly through the store, grabbing things, wondering how she'd gotten herself into this mess. She got in line with a jar of pickles, a jar of peanut butter, a loaf of bread, two cans of Campbell's soup, and a ladle. She'd been wanting a ladle since Sissy had melted the last one months ago by leaving it on the stove. She hoped she had enough stuff to require a carryout.

"Rusty, I talked to your mom and dad," she said as they walked to the van. "They're concerned that you took what I said about your guitar-playing to mean you shouldn't do anything else."

Rusty shifted the bag from one arm to the other. "It's all I wanna do. I mean, I don't care about anything else. I'm gonna be in a band."

"Rusty, I said you should keep playing your guitar. It'll be a good thing for you, but you're not gonna be a rock and roll star." Rusty looked so sad, Aletta almost took it all back.

"I know what you said. But I also know what I feel," he said, and patted his chest. "I got a fire that burns inside me."

They talked in front of the van, the windshield glaring in the sun.

They couldn't see inside, but Sissy could see them. She'd seen Rusty before in school. He'd grown his yellow-blond hair down to his shoulders and it feathered back around his face. She saw the passion in his eyes as he talked to her mother, and a minute later found herself standing next to them.

"You want me to take that?" she asked him.

"Oh, sure," he said, handing her the bag of groceries.

"Rusty, this is my daughter Sissy who's gettin' back in the van now," Aletta said.

"I've seen you around," he said. "You're gonna be a sophomore, aren't you? I'll be a junior."

Sissy smiled. "I'm tryin' out for cheerleader."

"Sissy, can you wait in the car for just a minute?" asked Aletta, giving her daughter a look that said *now*.

Sissy got back in the van and fell against the seat. "You're so immature," she said aloud, then mimicked herself. " 'I'm tryin' out for cheerleader.' Ugh!"

Outside, Aletta pleaded, "So please tell me you're gonna stay in school and keep your job here. Your parents are really worried about you."

Rusty rolled his eyes and groaned. "It's my life."

Aletta put her hands on his shoulders and looked him in the eye. "I can see this for you, Rusty. Stay in school and mind your dad. It's for your best. It's important for your music. Believe me," she said. "I've seen what's possible for your future. It depends on your choices, though. You need to stay in school." She was lying like a bad politician. It didn't matter a hill of beans if he finished high school for what she'd seen in his future.

His shoulders slumped as he gave in to her. "Okay," he said.

"Good." She smiled and touched his cheek. "That's great. You'll be glad, I promise you." Aletta was relieved. At least one thing had worked out today.

Sissy grilled Aletta about Rusty as they drove home. "What's his last name again?" she asked.

"Conway," Aletta said, her stomach tightening in knots as

she saw the '57 Chevy sitting in the driveway and Eugene's truck gone.

Jimmy was in the backyard mowing the grass when they arrived. When he finished, he came in shirtless and sweating. "I wanted to finish the yard before it rained," he said, and tried to kiss Aletta as she put George down for a nap.

"Stop it." She walked away from him, into the kitchen. Ruby and Randy sat at the dining room table, crayon box open, working on coloring books, and Sissy was at the bar, talking on the phone. "I want you kids to go out and play now. Your daddy and me need to talk," Aletta said.

"Hold on," Sissy said into the phone, then held it out from her ear. "Mom, I don't 'play' anymore." She rolled her eyes.

Aletta turned to her daughter, her face suddenly reddening. "Then go practice, and do it now!" she yelled. "I got no patience for your flip lips!"

"Gyod, I didn't even *say* anything," Sissy whined.

Aletta grabbed the phone out of her hand and slammed it on the receiver. "Don't talk back to me, young lady." She grabbed Sissy's arm and led her to the door.

"Lettie, it's all right, she's leavin'," Jimmy said. He had followed her into the kitchen and stood at the fridge drinking orange juice out of the carton.

Aletta let go of Sissy and turned around. She started screaming. "Are you talkin' to me?! You who never have to discipline these kids let alone change a dirty diaper or make a school lunch?" She slammed her hand down on the dining room table. "You who were pukin' your guts up this morning from gettin' sorry-ass drunk and tryin' to beat up on poor Eugene? You who've run around on me since North Carolina?!"

Jimmy still held the juice with one hand and the refrigerator door open with the other. He didn't move. Neither did Ruby or Randy or Sissy.

The veins in Aletta's neck bulged, and she pointed a finger at Jimmy. All the fight she had in her was right at the surface. It was a hard layer, but underneath was something rich and important. "Yes, oh, yessir, I knew all about that. I ain't stupid, Jimmy Honor, and I don't want you tellin' me what to do no more. Not one more minute. I want you *out* of here!"

So much adrenaline pumped through Aletta that she slammed out the back door and was on her knees in her little garden stabbing the ground with a hand spade before the refrigerator light went off. The first heavy drops of rain landed on her hair and ran down her arms, but she just kept digging into the hard layer of dirt on top to expose the soft, rich earth underneath.

★

Shortly after their wedding, Jimmy and Aletta left for North Carolina in an old Ford Fairlane that Aletta had begged off her mother. He was excited as a little boy, even talking about becoming an astronaut one day. Soon after they arrived at Fort Gibson, however, the commanding officer told the twelve men who were there for pilot training that they were only going to be able to select two of them. They would put them through some testing and see who was most qualified.

Jimmy paced through their tiny house on base. "They promised us, Lettie, and now they won't even tell us why they're only takin' two. I guarantee you one thing, it ain't gonna be a sharecropper's son from Oklahoma they take."

He was told after the physical exam that he had a mildly irregular heartbeat that would disqualify him from being a fighter pilot. They'd let him serve for six months and give him an honorable discharge. He moped around after that, almost inconsolable.

Aletta wanted to make him feel better, but after a few days, she started nagging at him. "I just don't understand why you can't get over it, Jimmy. I mean, life does go on," she said, standing over him, hands on her hips. "Get up and do something." She was in a new place with strangers all around, and *she* wasn't complaining.

He went out with the guys to watch the World Series at a bar one night. At midnight she went to bed and stared at the ceiling, waiting for the sound of his key in the front door. When he finally showed up, loud and drunk at four o'clock in the morning, she was just so glad he wasn't dead, she didn't say a thing. He'd never been drunk around her, so she could forgive that. But when he took off his coat, she saw that his shirt was buttoned up wrong and his fly wasn't zipped.

She went back to bed crying. By the next morning, she'd gone through a million scenarios of how to handle it. She decided not to make a fuss or mention the zipper or the shirt. She figured they'd move back to Oklahoma, he'd get over this pilot thing, and everything would be fine. Three days later, she woke up nauseated and vomiting. She needed him worse than ever.

They moved back home pretty much the same as they'd departed, except for Aletta's swollen belly and Jimmy's damaged dreams.

Because of the baby, Jimmy had to get a job right away selling cars. His mother, who had never touched a drop of booze in her life, suddenly began drinking and drank so much so fast that she died of cirrhosis in less than five years. They bought a house, and he moved to a sales job at Southwestern Bell. In the meantime, Sissy and Ruby were born.

Jimmy would go to work, not liking or disliking it much one way or the other. On the weekends, he'd watch baseball and basketball games on TV, then he'd go out in the driveway and shoot baskets for hours. Occasionally, Aletta could hear him counting down like it was the end of the game, then he'd throw his hands up in the air if he'd hit the last-second shot. He joined a softball league one summer and crushed the ball every time he got up to bat, but when he tore a hamstring chasing down a fly ball, he limped off the field and never went back.

"I'm gettin' old," he told Aletta that night as they lay in bed. "I never made nothin' of myself. At least my mama's not here to see it."

"But you're a husband and a father. That counts for a whole

lot," Aletta said, stroking his hair. He just closed his eyes and nodded slightly, but the anxious feeling inside Aletta didn't let up a bit.

Jimmy had kept the demons that had served him on the basketball court and the baseball field at bay for the most part up until then, but after that, Aletta saw he was changing. He started to drink to loosen up, and she knew it was like pouring gasoline on a flame, because, like his mama, he had an allergy to the drink.

Chapter Twelve

For Sissy's slumber party, she and Angie decided that since they had the van as bait, they'd invite two popular junior cheerleaders instead of their usual friends. Jill Dwight and Mary Lou Rudolph arrived just as the shimmery orange sun melted into the fields that stretched out west of Okay.

Everything inside the house was quiet, and Sissy prayed to Jesus that her mama and daddy wouldn't fight tonight. They had been fine since her mama had ripped into him.

They opened up all the van doors and sat inside listening to the radio.

"Shaun is so much cuter than Parker," Mary Lou argued.

Jill fell back on the blue vinyl seat. "How can you say that? Parker Stevenson's a man. Shaun Cassidy looks like a little boy."

Sissy and Angie kept their mouths shut, not wanting to disagree with either of them. Of course, they were Shaun Cassidy girls all the way.

Aletta and Ruby brought out hamburgers and Cokes. "Here y'all go," Aletta said. "I hope you're hungry."

"Can I eat out here, Mama?" Ruby asked.

Sissy shot Aletta a look.

"No, you can eat inside. These girls are havin' a private party. Isn't *Happy Days* on tonight?"

"Who cares about stupid old *Happy Days*." Ruby sulked.

Just after nine, when the last pink of the day was fading away, Rusty Conway rode up on his Suzuki 125 Enduro motorcycle, his blond hair wind-blown from the ride.

"Rusty, is that you?" Jill Dwight squinted through the darkness. Sissy, sitting behind the wheel changing the radio station, felt her face flush when she heard his name.

"That's the guy I told you about at the IGA," she whispered to Angie.

Angie pulled her head in from the passenger's side window after taking a look.

"I've seen him. He's a fox," she whispered back. "Go say hi."

Jill and Mary Lou were already out talking to him by the time she got there.

"Hi," she said.

"Hi," he said, smiling, his hands rubbing the denim on the tops of his thighs.

"Did my mama tell you I was havin' a slumber party?" Sissy asked.

"Nope. Just came by to see if you wanted to go for a ride."

Sissy hesitated for a moment, making sure she'd heard him right. He was talking to her, wasn't he? "Oh, I'd love to, but Mama'd kill me and I'm kinda havin' this party," she said, but inside there were wings starting to grow on her heart.

The other girls teased her and told her she should go.

"If you won't go, I will," Jill said, but Rusty ignored her, kick-started the bike, and waved as he rode away.

My God, he just turned down a cheerleader, Sissy thought. To her, a guy turning down a chance to hang out with a cheerleader and possibly be her boyfriend was about as likely as her going all the way with Barry Sneedlever, the thirteen-year-old boy who lived on the street behind them and dressed up like Mr. Spock on the weekends, greeting everyone with his fingers split open in a V.

Barry had asked her to go to an evening of square dancing

with his parents at the Polka Palace one time, and when she was polite and made up an excuse, it made him think he had a chance. Finally, she was forced to tell him he was queerbait and she'd never go out with him in a million years.

The girls hid around the side of the house and smoked the Pall Malls that Angie had stolen from her mother.

Joy walked out just after they lit up.

"Hi, girls," she said as she approached them, her hips swaying as they always did. They all threw their cigarettes down and stammered out hellos.

"Don't mind me." Joy lit a long cigarette with her slim gold Colibri lighter. "I just didn't feel like smokin' alone. What're you girls up to, other than sneakin' a smoke?"

"This is the first time I ever tried it, Joy, I swear," Sissy said.

"I was about your age first time I tried. Wisht I'd never started. But I won't tell on you, hon. I ain't that old or mean quite yet," she said.

They picked up the cigarettes and lit back up.

"What do you think I should do with my hair for the tryouts, Joy?" Mary Lou asked.

That question was the beginning of an evening in the salon. For hours, it was a frenzy of femme. Joy finally left them and went to bed, allowing them to continue curling, ratting, spraying, pinning, glossing, and painting. Hair, nails, skin, eyes, lips.

Randy would love this, Sissy thought to herself.

Around three o'clock in the morning, they were back in the van daring one another to go streaking.

"I'll do it if you do it," Jill said.

"I'll do it, but you have to do it first," Sissy answered.

"I'll do it, but first I want to show y'all this," Mary Lou said, peeling the paper off the cigarette butts they'd smoked. "I'll try it on you, Sissy, since Rusty's your new boyfriend. Make a fist, but not too tight."

"He's not my boyfriend," Sissy said as Mary Lou stuffed three peeled and shredded cigarette butts into Sissy's hand.

"But you want him to be, don't you?" Angie asked.

"I don't know. Maybe."

"Well, we all know what's gonna happen. He's gonna stick his thing inside the hole—Mary Lou pushed her finger in and out of Sissy's fist, then she took a bottle of fingernail polish remover borrowed from Joy and poured a capful in on top of the butts.

"—and this is what you get!" She opened Sissy's hand, and inside was a mess of white goo.

"Oh, gross, it's semen!" Jill shouted, laughing.

"That's disgusting!" Angie said.

"I'm gonna throw up," Sissy said, holding her dripping hand out the van door like she'd just pulled it out of George's dirty diaper.

Mary Lou laughed with delight. Minutes later, she was stripped naked, racing as fast as she could down the middle of Main Street, her breast buds flying up and down to the rhythm of her strides.

The rest of them followed her, tearing off their clothes and sprinting down the street, their young bodies daring the night air or any roaming police officer to stop them. Sissy ran faster than she thought she could, the fear and excitement propelling her forward, feet slapping the pavement, breathing *in out in out*. Light-headed from the rush of absolute freedom, she stopped in the middle of the street at the corner of Elm and Main. She raised her bare arms to the sky for a moment, and it seemed to her that the nearby stars were like jewels to be worn by courageous young princesses.

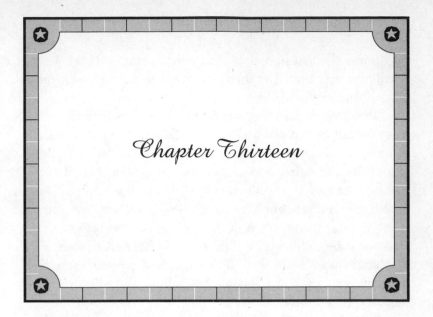

Chapter Thirteen

After Aletta's explosion, she thought maybe Jimmy was really changing this time. He was on his best behavior for weeks and even went to the First Christian Church with her and the kids. It was a short brown brick building at the corner of Elm and Fifth. It looked puny and a bit sad compared to, say, the Burning Bush or the Jesus Is Lord with their massive new buildings and their huge congregations. No doubt First was quieter than those churches, like a shy little sister compared to her popular big brother, but its followers were no less devoted to God.

During the service, Ruby and Randy squirmed in the wooden pews until Aletta pinched their arms and dug a stick of fuzzy Wrigley's out of her purse, tore it in half, and gave them each a piece. It tasted like lipstick and metal and perfume, and they smacked it and made faces at each other. She knew it had been a mistake to let them come to "big church" instead of going to Sunday school, but they'd said they wanted to be with the family.

Pastor Mueller was a round man with no hair except over his ears and around the back of his head. The dome of his head seemed to weigh down the rest of his face that was small in comparison. Aletta knew it wasn't his looks that had gotten him the job.

Jimmy thought he was fat and boring, but Aletta felt he was intelligent and kind. The theme of the sermon was faith, and he read a passage that she loved.

"In Matthew six, verse twenty-five, Jesus says 'Therefore I tell you, do not be anxious about your life, what you shall wear or what you shall drink, nor about your body, what you shall put on. Is not life more than food, and the body more than clothing? Look at the birds of the air: they neither sow nor reap nor gather into barns, and yet your heavenly Father feeds them. Are you not of more value than they? And which of you by being anxious can add one cubit to his span of life? And why are you anxious about clothing? Consider the lilies of the field, how they grow; they neither toil nor spin; yet I tell you, even Solomon in all his glory was not arrayed like one of these.'"

Aletta looked over at Sissy, who was anxious about her clothing every day, especially school days.

Sissy smiled and mouthed "Who, me?"

Aletta nodded her head and gave her a pat on the thigh.

After the service, Aletta put George over her shoulder, his favorite place to be, it seemed, and sought out newcomers to the church. She introduced herself to the Tittles, a young couple with two little boys, making sure to shake hands with both husband and wife.

After some talk about the heat, she said, "Pastor Mueller wanted me to let y'all know that you can feel safe leavin' your boys in Sunday school while you're in service. You don't have to worry about that at all. We got some of the best teachers around. Mrs. Gray's taught third grade at Pappe Elementary for eighteen years, in fact, so we're lucky to have her every Sunday with our kids."

Mr. and Mrs. Tittle looked at each other for a moment with raised eyebrows before he replied, "Well, that's a real relief. That's just what we were talkin' about on the drive over here."

Aletta allowed herself this use of her gift because it was for the church, but when she finished, she had to admit she missed reading people a little bit. She still didn't want all that went with it, though. *Not one bit,* she thought.

She took her sweet time drinking coffee in the Fellowship Hall even though George was drooling on her neck. Jimmy stood in a corner, his suit jacket in hand, leaning against the wall and looking at his feet. She knew he was uncomfortable, and she couldn't help but enjoy it. She felt he had some paying back to do.

The next day, Jimmy called at six in the evening. "Hon, I have a late meeting. This project we're workin' on is a doozy. I just hate not gettin' to come home, but I'll be there as soon as I can," he said cheerily. He got home after ten.

After he called to tell her he'd be late on Thursday, the fourth night in a row, she went for a drive. She took George because she knew she wouldn't do anything crazy with him there. She told the kids she was going to the store and wouldn't let them come along.

She drove across Main to the other side of the tracks first, someplace she knew Jimmy wouldn't be. It was humid out, the kind of moist that gets under your clothes in just a couple of minutes. The full moon looked flat and ghostly pale in the light evening sky. It tempted her to point the Pink Pumpkin toward it and keep driving until she got there. Instead, she turned back onto Main Street and drove past Eugene's shop. He was getting into his car as she pulled up.

"Thanks for bringin' back the car. It's drivin' real good," she called to him from the road.

"You bet. Everything all right? How're the kids?" he asked, walking over and putting his hands on the top of the door, bending near her.

She looked up at him, her hands still tight on the wheel. It felt so fake to make small talk, but there wasn't much else to say, nothing that would help anyway. "They're fine. They keep askin' when you're comin' over to play saloon with 'em again."

"Tell 'em I said howdy," he said.

"I will." She knew full well she wouldn't say a thing, in case it got back to Jimmy. "You have a good evenin', Eugene. Thanks again."

It took every bit of willpower she could muster to turn down Holly Street, the way to Kathy Kokin's house. As she got closer, her chest began to tighten, and she took long, deep breaths. George started whimpering.

"It's okay, baby. Shhh, shhh, it's okay," Aletta said.

She drove past Kathy's huge stone-and-wood house and saw the lights on. About half a block away, she turned into a cul-de-sac and there sat the van, about as inconspicuous as Evel Knievel at the Grand Canyon. Aletta stopped the car next to the van and put it in park. She stared up at the moon before putting her head on the huge steering wheel. She cried hard tears that were just symbols of harder feelings. George joined in the crying, so Aletta picked him up and held him to her.

"Shhh, baby, shhhh. It's gonna be all right," she said. She was saying it as much to herself as to her baby.

The next day, while Jimmy was in the shower, Aletta took George from his cradle and went back to bed with him. She stayed there until after Jimmy left for work even though there were six loads of laundry to do, Ruby had to get her allergy shot, and George was crying to be fed. When she was sure Jimmy was gone, she fed George his bottle while she dumped the contents of her broken heart onto Shirl.

"You gotta get the hell away from that son of a bitch, Lettie. You don't deserve this." Shirl's voice quivered with anger through the phone line.

"I'm so nervous, Shirl. I'm sittin' here and my hands are shakin' like a leaf," Aletta said. "I can barely hold George's bottle for him."

Aletta called Joy, and she came over as soon as she had a break. "Kathy Kokin? Oh, that harlot, that hussy, that slut," Joy whispered.

Ruby stood in the hallway and listened. As her mother and Joy spoke, she slid slowly down the wall until she was sitting on the carpet.

Aletta paced her kitchen from stove to fridge and back, over and over. She was furious with Jimmy, but she wanted to scratch that snooty tramp's eyes out. "She's had an eye on him since I can remember."

"He's gone beyond this time." Joy sat at the bar watching Aletta wear a path in the linoleum. "You gotta move on, girl. I don't care if it harelips the governor. I know it's hard, but Jimmy ain't changin' his ways, and you can't force him."

"How do I do it, though?" Aletta finally stopped and looked at Joy. "I don't know how to get him out."

She was scared, and the fear felt similar to being afraid of the dark when she was four years old. It was both the unknown and what she did know about it that frightened her. The unknown was the distinct possibility of a bogeyman under the bed or a monster in the closet, while outside were the definite problems of howling coyotes and scary noises and sometimes thunder or even tornadoes. Now the unknown was how Jimmy would react and what he might do, while what she knew for sure was that going back to taking care of everything by herself again seemed damn near impossible. When she was a kid, she had just stayed in bed under the covers or gone in with her parents, but now she had to face the monster in the closet alone.

She and Joy decided she should call Jimmy at work and tell him not to come home. Her hand shook so badly as she dialed her rotary phone that she was surprised when the call went through.

"Jimmy, it's me."

Joy stood at the other end of the bar, watching.

"No, I need to talk to you *now*," Aletta said, winding the long cord around her quivering hand. She took a deep breath and closed her eyes. "I know you're havin' an affair, and I don't want you comin' home tonight or ever again."

Joy thrust her fists up in the air and whispered, "Yes!"

Aletta frowned. "No, I don't wanna talk about it tonight. There ain't nothin' to say."

She paused for a moment, listening, her eyebrows knitted together. Without saying anything else, she hung up the phone.

"Well?" Joy asked.

Aletta fell onto a bar stool. "He couldn't yell 'cause he was at work. But he says he's comin' home tonight just like always and we'll talk then."

"Well, I'll be a thin-whiskered Jew. What in hell could he have to say? You caught him practically with his pants around his ankles."

Around six o'clock, Aletta's intestines started imitating an accordion, and she was in the bathroom every half hour until Jimmy drove up in the van at eight.

He walked in holding his jacket and loosening his tie. Aletta sat on a chair at the dining room table, the same table where she'd painted her sign. She kept very still, her hands in her lap, as he came and stood over her.

Ruby and Randy and Sissy gathered in the entryway to listen. Ruby had told them what she'd overheard earlier.

"We're just friends, Aletta," Jimmy said with a sigh. "I been goin' over there just to talk. Her husband died and she hasn't had anyone to talk to."

Aletta covered her ears with her hands and closed her eyes. "Please go, Jimmy. Don't do this."

Even though she couldn't see them, Aletta could hear her kids' breathing and knew they were there. She told herself she should send them to a friend's, but she was too scared.

"Just go, Jimmy," she said again. "These children have had enough."

"I'm tryin' to talk to you," he said through gritted teeth. He pulled her hands from her ears, holding her wrists tight.

Sissy peered around the wall into the dining room, and when she saw him touch her, she screamed, "Daddy, don't hurt Mama!"

Ruby ran out the door and over to Joy's. She pounded on the door, and Earl answered.

"Daddy's beatin' up on Mama again," she yelled.

"Oh, Lord," he said, his jowly face creased with concern as he tucked in his T-shirt.

"What is it?" Joy came to the door holding a wooden spoon in one hand. Ruby could smell the beef stew and hear the TV. She wished she could just go in there where there were no crazy people and no other kids and fill up on stew and Coca-Cola and attention.

"Shouldn't we call the police?" Earl asked.

"She could be dead by then," Joy said, and pushed her way out the door. "They didn't do crap the last time I called." She stopped and looked at Earl, who was on her heels. "Do you think you oughta take the shotgun?"

Earl shook his head. "I don't wanna make things worse than they already damn well are."

Joy's words echoed in Ruby's head. *She could be dead.*

Joy pushed the doorbell as they walked into the house.

Jimmy stood over Aletta, sweating and clenching his fists. "Get the hell out of my house!" he yelled when he saw them. "This ain't your business!"

Joy stood behind Earl and pointed at Jimmy over his shoulder. "You bastard! You get outta here and stop torturin' your wife and kids! You're crazy!"

"Joy, let me handle this, and I mean it now," Earl said in a strong, deep voice.

Aletta looked up, surprised at him. Earlier in the day, she'd been so mad, but now she had no more fight. She was just trying to get through this without Jimmy hurting her too bad. She never expected anyone to stand up to him, and certainly not Earl.

Earl went on, "Jimmy, you get the hell on outta here and don't never touch Aletta again or I'm gonna kill you personally. I don't care if I go to jail for the rest a' my life or if they fry me in the chair. I won't put up with this for no reason you can come up with."

A smile stole over Jimmy's face. "Earl, come on now . . ."

"No sir, I won't come anywhere. I mean what I said, and I want you outta here right now." Earl crossed his arms on top of his round belly as a drop of sweat coursed down one side of his face.

It seemed like half an hour that Jimmy and Earl stood there— Jimmy standing in front of Aletta and Earl in front of Joy. The only thing that broke the silence was Randy and Ruby's crying and sniffles. Aletta felt like her heart didn't beat the whole time. *Go,* she thought over and over. *Please go.*

"Well, let me get some clothes, at least," Jimmy said finally. He sounded like he'd decided to go get an ice cream cone, he was so casual about it.

He went into their bedroom and packed a duffel bag. When he came out, he picked his suit jacket up off the ground and walked to the door.

Again, Aletta held her breath. She didn't look at him straight on, in case eye contact would set him off again, but she watched his pant legs closely, willing them out the door.

"I'll be talkin' to y'all real soon," he said to the kids, then walked out the door, slamming it hard behind him.

Finally Aletta let out the breath she'd held in for so long. It didn't mean he was gone for good, but they'd made it through tonight, and that was the most she could've hoped for under the circumstances. Aletta let all her kids stay in her bed, but not one of them slept much that night except for Jimmy, who went to Kathy's, got drunk, and passed out.

The next morning, Aletta was worried sick about everything—Ruby's asthma, the kids' mental health, Joy and Earl, Jimmy coming back and killing her—but mainly she was worried about money. She knew Jimmy wouldn't give her any willingly, and she had no idea how much was in their checking account anymore. She thought of Pastor Mueller's Bible reading, "And which of you by being anxious can add one cubit to his span of life?" She thought that's sure as hell what's happening. *I'm aging a year for every minute of this day.*

Aletta drove to the Bank of Okay, a self-important establishment in spite of its small size, its location in this one-light town, or its average account balance of four hundred bucks. She walked in to refrigerator-like air conditioning, wall-to-wall carpet, and the hush-hush of negotiations between men and their money. In an overly nice tone of voice, she asked the teller for her account balance. The teller, a young girl with a shiny face and a mouthful of braces, wrote on a piece of paper and showed Aletta: $135.23.

"Are there any other accounts in Mr. and Mrs. James Honor's name?" asked Aletta. Surely this wasn't all there was. The teller looked at her funny.

"My husband usually takes care of the finances, but he's ill right now." Aletta smiled, but inside she was mad at herself for caring what this high school kid with a part-time job thought.

"No ma'am, I don't see any other accounts," the girl said.

"Are you sure?" asked Aletta, trying not to cry. Jimmy must've been putting money somewhere else.

"I'm sorry," the teller said.

"I'll just withdraw some from the checking, then."

"How much would you like?"

Aletta paused and thought about groceries, mortgage payments, possible jobs, and baby-sitters. Her thoughts flew by until she saw an image of Kathy Kokin standing in her living room looking down at the ten-dollar bill. A cold chill tickled her scalp and neck.

"Mrs. Honor, how much would you like to withdraw?" the teller asked again, glancing at the people waiting behind a red velvet rope for service.

"What's the minimum you need to keep the account open?" Aletta asked finally.

"Fifteen dollars."

"Oh, hell, give me all of it, and I want to open a separate account. Also, what type of loans do you give out?"

Her hands shook as she sat at an empty desk filling out the applications. She forced herself to answer the questions as best she could, even though all she wanted to do was run out of the quiet, civilized bank and scream. She wasn't sure if they'd even give her a checking account.

She wrote in her sprawling handwriting in the margin at the bottom of the loan application: *My husband and me are just separated and I have four kids to take care of. I need this loan of $500 to get me on* *my feet so* . . . At this point she ran out of room on the bottom, so she started writing up the side: *I can get my baby a sitter while my other kids are at school and I'm working. Thank you a million* . . . That took up the side of the page, so she wound the words up across the top: *and I promise I'll pay you back. Aletta Honor.*

She waited until Donald Hulnick Jr. came out from the back. He was the twenty-three-year-old assistant branch manager, scrubbed clean with a fresh haircut and a pressed suit.

"Good morning, Mrs. Honor," he said, taking her hand in his.

She half smiled but wouldn't look at him directly. "Hi, Don. I thought you were still at Oklahoma State."

"Graduated in May. This is my first job since I got out. Majored in finance, so it worked out pretty good," he said as he escorted her to his desk and sat her down.

"Bet your dad's proud," she said. Donald Sr. owned the local State Farm insurance agency.

"He wouldn't say it to me, but mom says he tells her." Don took the loan application from her and read the bottom, then up the side, finally turning the page upside down to read the top. He smiled when he looked up, but the smile had pity in it.

Aletta shifted uneasily in her chair. She felt small and weak, like her life had been a series of failures leading her to this chair, sitting in front of this smug, set-for-life young man, begging for some of his good fortune.

"Well, the new checking account won't be a problem, but you will need to leave at least fifteen dollars in the old one. We'll need your husband's approval to close that one, of course," he said, glancing toward the door.

That way he didn't have to look at her, she figured. It was all so embarrassing, even if it wasn't you it was happening to.

Donald studied the documents. "I can get you some temporary checks and get another signature card for you to fill out. The loan'll take a few days to process. I'll have to pass it on to my underwriter, and we'll let you know."

When she got home, Aletta opened the garage door and dug

her sign out from where Jimmy had hidden it behind a bicycle, a twin mattress, and some Christmas decorations.

Grabbing a hand shovel, she walked out to the yard, got on her knees in the scorching sun, and started digging. She dug with all her strength, tossing the red dirt over her shoulder, her hands covered in it. Sweat dripped down her forehead and onto the earth.

She wanted to dig a hole big enough and deep enough to crawl into. She could pull the cool earth on top of her like a blanket and go to sleep. She could bury herself and leave the past underground, wake up a different person, someone free.

Instead, she planted the sign, staking a claim on the past to pay for the future. Burying the post deep in the ground, she packed the dirt around it and made it sturdy. She stood up, wiped her forehead with the back of her hand, and read the sign.

ALETTA HONOR
PSYCHIC READER
DROP-INS WELCOME
9am to 6pm

"God," she said, looking up to the sky. Her voice sounded strange to her, so she said it again.

"God." She felt her windpipe move when she said it because her head was thrown back and her skin was taut against her throat. She opened her eyes, and the brightness of the sun and sky filled up her vision so she was blinded by it.

"God," she whispered and felt like she might lift right up out of her body with the taut skin and the moving windpipe and the sweat and the exhaustion. Her body and the ground under her feet and the dirt on her hands seemed strange to her, foreign somehow, and she felt herself moving away up into the brightness and the blue.

A car horn blared and the driver yelled something that Aletta couldn't understand. She opened her eyes and leaned a hand on the sign.

Sissy opened the front door, "Mama, George won't stop cryin'!" she yelled. "You didn't put that sign back up, did you?"

The next day, Aletta walked into the one-story brown building next to City Hall with George, Ruby, and Randy. Sissy's cheerleading tryouts were in a few days, and she was "completely unavailable until afterwards." The hallway smelled like stale cigarettes and burned coffee.

In front of a door marked DOUGLAS RAMEY, ATTORNEY AT LAW, Aletta looked down at her two middle children as she held George on her shoulder. She touched each of them on top of the head. "Y'all be polite and quiet in here, you hear me? Mama can't handle any acting-up right now."

They nodded, and she was hopeful.

Ramey's secretary, Dottie Garstin, greeted them when they entered the small office. "There's that sweet little one," Dottie sighed, taking the baby from Aletta.

Dottie had been at George's baby shower, and she watched the kids now while Aletta went in to see her boss.

"So how does it work?" Aletta asked the thin, balding lawyer after shaking his hand. She wanted to act tough, so she wouldn't get ripped off, and to ask enough questions to know what the hell was going on. Ramey wore a tie but no jacket, and his shirtsleeves were rolled up. Aletta relaxed just a little.

"Please sit down," he said, then replied, "First we file for divorce, then we try to get you alimony and child support."

"What if he doesn't pay?"

"If he stays in Oklahoma, law enforcement can track him down and take him to jail. If he leaves the state, things get tougher, because it's hard to get the law in other states to enforce a judgment in Oklahoma," he said, his palms facing upward. "It's a matter of logistics, really, not jurisdiction."

"He, um, he's a little bit outta control." She laughed nervously and dug in her purse for a tissue.

"It'd be better if you were more specific, Mrs. Honor. I know this is difficult."

She wiped her nose and looked out the window onto Main Street. "Well, specifically, he's been usin' me as a punchin' bag."

Ramey took off his glasses and set them on the desk. He looked at her intently. "We'll get a restraining order filed by tomorrow. He won't be permitted to come within fifty yards of you," he said. "It'll take a few days, maybe a week, to get him served, so until then, just be careful."

"How much will all this cost?" she asked and cleared her throat, trying to pull the tears back in. *Tears are not tough,* she thought.

"I'm sixty-five an hour. It'll take six or eight hours to do everything we've talked about."

"You gonna make me get out my calculator?"

Ramey smiled. "I'd plan on about five hundred bucks. Right now, I need a hundred and thirty just to get things started."

She looked out the window again before she spoke. "If I pay you that, it gets you started, but then I got no idea how I'm gonna get you finished."

He followed her gaze out the window to the Pink Pumpkin parked outside.

"I saw you drive up in that Chevy. It's a beauty. What is it, a '57?" he asked.

She drove straight from the lawyer's office to Billy Bob Cooper's used car lot just outside of town. After two and half grueling hours of bad coffee, talking to three different managers, and test-driving four cars, she was about to give up.

Finally, Aletta gathered her things. "I gotta take these kids to get some lunch or all hell's gonna break loose," she said.

"Now, Mrs. Honor, that Chevy must be costin' you a fortune in gas," Hank, the salesman with the Oklahoma State Cowboys belt buckle and the pointy cowboy boots, said for the tenth time.

"I ain't takin' no eighteen hundred dollars for that car. No way, no how. That's the only thing I ever owned all by myself, and I'm not just giving it away." She picked George up off the floor where he was lying on a blanket.

"All right, all right, I'll give you two thousand for it," he said.

"Twenty-two hundred, and you're gettin' a steal."

They drove away in a tiny yellow '71 Datsun F10 station wagon with 86,000 miles on it. She'd gotten it for eight hundred and sixty-eight dollars.

"It looks like a pig snout, Mama," Randy whined. "I like the Pink Pumpkin."

Ruby laughed, "It does look like a pig snout. We're ridin' around inside the snout of a pig."

Aletta ground the stick into third gear. "Y'all better be happy we got a car to ride around in at all. Your daddy left us with nothin', and I don't know how I'm even gonna keep shoes on your feet." A frown creased her forehead. She felt mad at God and the whole world, so she decided to splurge and go to the Hilltop for lunch.

After they ordered from Kitty, the woman who really knew what was going on, Aletta took George into the bathroom to change him. After she wrestled a new diaper onto him, she washed her hands and read the sign over the sink.

Dear God,
So far today God, I've done alright.
I haven't gossiped, haven't lost my temper,
haven't been greedy, grumpy, nasty, selfish,
or over-indulgent. I'm really glad about that
God, but in a few minutes, I'm going to get out
of bed and from then on I'm probably going to
need a lot more help. Thank you.
In Jesus' name. Amen.

"Amen," she said.

She walked back to Ruby and Randy sitting at the booth eating quietly. "I'm sorry for getting mad," she said as she slid in next to Ruby. "Y'all have been so good. It's been a hard day for me, and I'm not even a kid. I can imagine it's been even tougher on you."

* * *

Over the next several days, Aletta only had a few customers. It was easier having the sign out this time, since she'd already gone through it once. This whole business wasn't what she wanted for her life, but it was better than being in the poorhouse. Only not many folks were coming by. She figured they must be scared for some reason, or more likely they didn't believe she could do what she said. Most folks knew she was in a bad way.

One of the people who did come was a woman in her sixties. Geraldine was from Seminole and wore old-lady shoes, but she had long auburn hair that fell down past her shoulders.

"I don't really believe in this, you know, but I'm at my wit's end. Sally's my best friend for three years now, and I'd do anything to find her," Geraldine said, sitting stiffly on Aletta's couch.

Aletta told Geraldine that Sally, her cocker spaniel, was in an old barn down the road from her house, nursing a litter of puppies.

"But I had that dog fixed!" Geraldine exclaimed, her eyes as big as quarters, then they got narrow. "You must be wrong about this one, 'cause there ain't no way unless she's havin' the Christ child or somethin'."

"Just go look," Aletta said. She didn't have any control over what came through. All she did was report it. Sometimes, though, she *felt* things more, and when that was the case, she was pretty confident she was right. This was one of those times.

"I will, but if you're wrong, do I get my money back?"

Aletta smiled patiently. " 'Course you do."

Chapter Fourteen

Aletta smoked cigarette after cigarette in the bathroom. Her worrying felt out of control. She thought several times about calling Dr. Lowrey to try to get some pills for her nerves but was afraid she might get hooked on them. She also didn't want Jimmy to have any ammunition against her when they went to court, since she'd have to buy them on his insurance. She wondered when Jimmy would be served with the divorce papers and the restraining order.

One morning a week or so after she put the sign back out, twelve loud, rumbling motorcycles blasting down Highway 66 suddenly turned and parked in front of the house. The roar drew Randy to the open window in the living room. After they turned off their bikes, Randy could hear them, their voices almost as loud as their motors.

"Iron, you're not gonna see a psychic, are you?" a man bellowed. "Man, you gotta be kiddin'!"

"That's a fake, Iron. It's a scam, man."

A tall, thin man with a pockmarked face and a ponytail climbed the steps to Aletta's front door. He stuck his middle finger in the air at his buddies with one hand and knocked with the other.

Randy opened the door, his mouth hanging open. "Ain't you gonna say trick or treat?"

"Very funny, kid. I came about the sign out front." The man jerked a thumb over his shoulder.

"Mama!" Randy called, never taking his eyes off the man with the bandanna tied over his head. The road dirt on his face and clothes made Randy want to ask him if he ever got to take a bath. When Aletta didn't come, Randy pushed the door closed in his face and ran back to get Aletta, who had just finished changing George.

"Mama, there's a hippie outside!"

She put George in his playpen and went to the door.

"May I help you?" Aletta glanced past the tall man to the gang outside.

"You a psychic, lady? I mean a real one, 'cause I ain't payin' you shit if you're a fake," he grumbled.

"That's what everyone says, and some figure out how to say it without cussin'. Can you imagine?" Aletta was surprised at herself. This man was probably a Hell's Angel or something. She stood there hesitating, trying to think of a good enough reason to run him off. But the sign was out, big as June, and she figured it'd probably be less dangerous to give him what he wanted than to make him mad by turning him away.

Anyway, the truth was she needed the money, wherever it came from.

"Come on in," she said, "but mind your manners."

She sat him down on the couch and just looked at him before beginning, unsure if she should touch him. He wore a denim shirt with the sleeves cut off and embroidery on the shoulders, and his black leather pants were filthy. His eyes were green, an unusual soft shade that Aletta didn't think she'd ever seen before. It seemed that he'd built up layers of toughness and meanness from the inside out, but his eyes had somehow been unaffected.

When he shifted his gaze from hers, Aletta felt she could begin. "I gotta hold your hand, and I always pray first," she said.

The wave came over her less intensely this time. She'd been practicing keeping it down since she'd been shaking so many hands lately, what with the bank and the lawyer and the car dealer and all.

"What's your name, by the way?" she asked, opening her eyes for a moment.

"They call me Iron Ass 'cause I've done more cross-country trips than anyone else I know. Iron for short is all right. That way we don't cuss in your nice little house." He grinned at her wryly.

She closed her eyes again. A single word was all she got. "What would you like to talk about today, Michael?" she asked.

She opened her eyes slowly and he stared at her until she could see moisture gathering in his eyes. His shoulders slumped a little, and he leaned back against the couch. It was like he'd been right on the edge of giving in to some sorrow he was carrying, and it only took a light touch to push him over.

"I thought I wanted to know about my old lady," he said, looking down.

She could smell him, gritty and pungent like the road, with tobacco and yesterday's whisky mixed in.

"To find out if she was cheatin' on me, but that's just bullshit 'cause I know she is. I just haven't wanted to admit it. But to tell you the truth, if I was her, I'd cheat on me too. I'm kind of a bastard."

"You'd like to talk about your mama, then?" Aletta asked. She hadn't gotten this like she normally did, in images and words. It was subtler than that, just a feeling.

He looked at her again, unable to speak, his clear green eyes welling up.

Aletta figured out what he smelled like and she smiled. He smelled like the gypsies, just like them.

"I miss her," he blurted out, and quickly wiped his eyes with a thumb and forefinger.

"She loves you, Michael. She loves you so much. I can hear that crystal-clear," Aletta said. She couldn't hear anything, actually. She'd only gotten the one word "Michael." With her luck, she thought nervously, she was probably losing her gift just when she actually needed it. But she couldn't tell that to this crying Hell's Angel, not when his heart was at stake.

"She said that? Even after all the shit I've . . ." He broke down then and cried like a baby.

Aletta thought about Betty crying so hard that night at the party. She wished she had given her a hug. All her upbringing and good sense told her not to this time, but she went ahead and put her arms around Iron Ass anyway.

"She loves you no matter what. You're her darling Michael and there's nothing you could do to make her not love you," Aletta said. She felt that floating feeling again, like yesterday after she put the sign back up, and it seemed she expanded into something bigger than just herself again, like she had done with Betty.

Outside, as the Reverend Glendon Taylor, pastor of the Burning Bush Battle Church, drove by in his white Chrysler Town Car, he took a good look at the gang of bikers drinking out of paper bags and passing what looked like a marijuana cigarette back and forth. He decided to park across the street and watch from a safe distance.

After a few minutes, a patrol car turned the corner onto Main. The bikers quickly hid the bags and the joint. Taylor opened his car door to go tell the policemen about the drinking and drugs. He got one foot on the pavement before he decided to stay where he was.

The lights on top of the patrol car started flashing as it came to a stop. "What you boys up to?" Gary asked as he stepped from behind the wheel.

"Just enjoyin' the day," one of the bikers answered. "Little hot, though."

"That's not regulation parking on a business street," Donnie said as he slammed the passenger's side door and walked over to them, one hand hovering near his revolver.

"Is that what this is, a business street?" A biker with a huge belly and a fringed leather vest said, looking around. "Don't look like there's anything goin' on to me."

There was a growing crowd of people watching from storefronts and parked cars, and if Joy hadn't been in the application part of a dye job, she'd have called over to Aletta's to tell her.

Inside, Michael still had his head on Aletta's shoulder.

"Is she . . . at peace?" he asked, his voice quiet now.

"She is, and she watches over you all the time."

"She used to hold my hand and pray with me, just like you did," he said.

"She still prays for you. She prays that you'll open your heart again and not be so angry. She prays you'll start to see how good you are inside." Aletta patted his back. "She knows you're just about to bust wide open."

After she held him and talked to him a few more minutes, his crying died down.

"I gotta go soon. They'll be knockin' down the door." He sat up and wiped his eyes again. "Will you do me a favor? I need something out of my saddlebag."

Ruby pedaled up on her too-small bike from her friend Tammy's house a few blocks away. Her heart stopped when she saw the police car. Joy's words rang an alarm in her head. *She might be dead.* Then she saw the motorcycle gang beyond the car, moving their motorcycles back and forth under the direction of the cops, not trying very hard to get them lined up right.

Ruby walked up to the blond policeman. "Excuse me, sir, I live here. What's happening?" she asked.

Aletta opened the front door, and her face lost all its color.

The police lights were flashing, cars were backed up in a traffic jam on both sides of Main Street, and people were standing watching the hubbub.

"Hey, are you the psychic lady?" one of the bikers yelled. "Where's Iron Ass?"

"He's using the men's room," she said. "Ruby, you get on inside."

Ruby moved about two steps toward the door.

"These friends a' yours?" Officer Donnic called to Aletta.

She walked evenly down the porch steps and noticed Reverend Taylor sitting in his car across the street. She got close enough to Donnie to speak in his ear. "They'll be leavin' in just a minute. How 'bout just movin' on?"

He leaned down toward Aletta as he spoke. His mirrored sunglasses reflected her twice. "We're enforcing the law here. What the hell're you doin' messin' around with the likes a' them anyway?"

"Enforcing the law?" Spittle flew from Aletta's mouth. She looked around at the people watching her, then lowered her voice. "Just like you enforced the law protectin' pregnant women from gettin' beat on by their husbands? You walked away then, and you can sure as hell walk away now." She looked up at him defiantly, and they stared at each other for a moment. She couldn't see his eyes, but she held the stare anyway.

"Mama, Ruby's havin' her asthma," Randy said, tugging on her arm.

Aletta turned to Ruby. "Honey?"

"It's not that bad, Mama," Ruby said, taking a deep breath.

"What are you kids doin' out here?" Aletta asked.

"That hippie man said to come out and tell you hurry up," Randy said.

Aletta rolled her eyes and hurried to the empty motorcycle. She grabbed the saddlebag off the seat.

"Hey, what the hell're you doin', lady?" a biker with huge sideburns and bad teeth asked.

"You want a ride, baby?" another one said. "You don't have to read my mind to know what I want."

As she turned, she saw Gary and Donnie getting into their car. The flashers stopped, and they drove away. *Thank you, Jesus,* she thought.

She took Randy and Ruby inside where Michael was waiting at the door.

He grabbed the saddlebags. "What took so long?"

"Your friends attracted a crowd outside." She went to the kitchen cabinet and searched for the medicine bottle. "Honey, sit down and just relax," she said to Ruby.

Michael took his sunglasses out of his bag and put them on.

He took off his bandanna, smoothed his hair back, then put it back on his head.

"What do you think?" he asked Aletta as she gave Ruby a Tedral.

"I think you're just a big sweetheart inside," she said.

"Come on," he said, exasperated but smiling in spite of himself.

"But you look mean as a snake."

"Good." He pulled out his wallet. It was embroidered with a bald eagle and attached to a chain on his belt. He held out a twenty-dollar bill.

She looked up at the twenty as she knelt next to Ruby. "I don't have any change."

"Don't want any." He extended the bill closer toward her.

She paused for a moment before taking it. "I can't tell you how much this helps us right now." Ruby's breathing was calming down, so Aletta walked him to the door. "Can I ask you a question? What is it with men and eagles?"

"Freedom, baby, freedom," he said, stepping outside.

"Do you have to be a son of a bitch to have freedom?"

He smiled. "I've always thought so, but I guess we'll see."

"Will you come back some day and let me know what you find out? Maybe without your friends next time?"

"You bet," he said.

Aletta watched him saunter across the yard and realized she'd just been paid more than she ever had before for a reading, and she had gotten almost no psychic information. When the bikers started their engines, it shook the house under Aletta's feet. For just a moment, she had an overwhelming desire to run out and ride off with them.

"Freedom," she whispered to herself, then went back inside to check on Ruby.

Chapter Fifteen

Every spring after the first heavy rain, Clovis went down to the creek and seined for crawdads to use as bait for catching catfish in the river near Mackey's Bridge. Aletta was nine now, and this year they had finally convinced Nadine that she was big enough to go along without getting swept down the creek.

That morning, Nadine fixed a big breakfast of eggs and sausage and biscuits and gravy. Aletta was so excited she didn't want to eat, but Clovis said if she was his helper now, she needed a full belly.

Her mama saw them to the door and looked at Clovis. "She ain't a boy, you know," she said.

"We all know she ain't a boy, and seining for crawdaddies won't make her one neither," Clovis said.

Aletta wanted to change the subject. "I'm real glad we're gonna get to see Uncle Joey, since he didn't make it for Christmas this year."

"What're you talkin' about, Lettie honey? Joey's up in Kansas," Nadine said, looking at Clovis for a clue.

He just shrugged. "Okay, darlin', let's go find us some Cajun lobsters."

The sun shone bright like it was polishing the earth after the rain cleaned it off. As they walked with the seine down the dirt road still pocked with mud puddles, she felt proud to be walking with her daddy heading out on a job. She wished somebody would pass by so they'd see her and know how important she was to him.

He stopped beside the tree-lined creek at a short muddy trail leading down into the water. He held the trunks of the trees for balance as he slipped down the trail and waded into the red-brown water up to his knees. Taking her little hand, he steadied her uncertain steps until she too stepped into the cold water, and it lapped at her thighs.

"Okay, I'm gonna stand right here in the middle," he said as he unrolled the net and gave her one end, "and you walk around me in a circle, dragging that net along the bottom."

She pushed her pole into the muddy creekbed and put one foot in front of the other. With each step, the mud squished up around her boot and she had to pull hard to get it out. She made it halfway around him when her foot caught on a submerged tree branch and she tumbled face-first into the creek. The water soaked her old dress, leaving it tinted like rust.

"That's all right." Clovis laughed. The water made his overalls cling to his legs from the knees down. "Happens to the best of us."

Aletta went around him twice more before he said to pull the net up to see what they got. The brown, bug-eyed crawdads flipped their tails and jumped around on the net.

"Hey, that's a good take for one pass," Clovis said.

"Twelve, Daddy. I think there's twelve," Aletta said excitedly.

Clovis started grabbing them and putting them in a bait pail that hung on his belt.

Aletta tentatively put her hand out and touched one of the smaller ones. It flip-flopped on the net, and she screamed and pulled her hand away.

"I'll get it, Lettie. Don't worry about it," Clovis said.

Aletta took a deep breath, then reached out and grabbed the crawdad, fast and sure, and handed it to her father.

He smiled at her but kept the laugh to himself. "Thanks. You're one heck of a helper."

They caught fifty-six crawdads, and Clovis decided that was enough.

On the walk home, they saw a big old truck sitting on the side of the road. It had a huge homemade wooden camper fixed to its bed. There were pots and pans and clothes hanging off it and a couple of scroungy dogs roaming nearby.

"Gypsies," Clovis said.

"Where do they come from, Daddy?" Aletta asked. She was fascinated with the gypsies whenever she saw them. Seemed like they just went wherever they wanted and led such a life of adventure, like Huck Finn and Tom Sawyer.

"The Old Country, mostly. We always just called them Bohemians. They don't seem to come from anywhere. Don't belong nowhere neither. Just roam around." He swung the pail filled with crawdads a little as he walked, making sure to stay on the other side of the road from the truck.

When they got home, Aletta changed her clothes, ate lunch, helped clean the dishes, and then ran outside as soon as her mama would let her.

"I don't wanna see you near that old well, now, Lettie," Nadine called as Aletta raced down the front steps. They didn't use the well anymore now that they had running water, but Nadine didn't want to fill it in. Just in case, she said, not fully believing in the long-term dependability of modern plumbing. So every time Aletta went out to play, Nadine told her to stay away from the well.

Aletta's mind was as far from the well as it could be. She went straight back to see if she could see any gypsies. She approached the gypsy truck and watched it from behind a tree for a few minutes before slowly moving closer, her heart whirring like a threshing machine inside her chest. When the two big black dogs saw her, they barked at her fiercely, but she knew how to handle dogs that chased and barked. Every farm in the county had them. She took the bacon strips out of her dress pocket and held out one in each hand.

She approached the back of the truck, the dogs wagging their tails beside her. The two-part door on the back of the plywood camper was closed on the bottom, but open on top. She jumped up, springing from her toes like a jack-in-the-box to try and peek inside, but it was too dark to see anything. The smell was strong, like tobacco and food and the outdoors, and a little like the creek she'd just climbed out of.

She was sure the gypsies were gone, off in the field working for the day. That's why they came around, to get work for a day or three so they could keep moving. She climbed up on the back step to get a better look. After adjusting to the darkness, her eyes scanned the ceiling of the musty-smelling camper where more dishes and utensils hung. As she strained to see what was in the crates full of junk on the floor, her eyes became huge and she gasped. One of the crates held old engine parts, but on top of the dirty metal was a huge green bug with long antennae, frozen inside a piece of glass.

When she realized it was dead, she scanned the ceiling and saw bamboo fishing poles hanging from it. Farther in back, there were homemade cots on both sides. The beds were rumpled with unmade blankets and pillows.

As she stared, she could've sworn she saw a rumple on one side move. She gasped again and took a step backwards, stumbling off the step and down into the mud. She sat there for a moment, her heart beating faster than ever. But she was too curious to leave, so she convinced herself that it must have been a cat or a puppy.

Slowly she climbed back up on the step but stayed in a crouching position, so when she peered over the half-door of the camper, all that showed was her head. As soon as she looked at the cot again, something on it glinted and caught the light from outside. Someone was looking right at her. She could see the whites of their eyes. Aletta almost screamed, but she held onto the door and didn't move. After a few moments more, she could make out the face.

It was an old woman. She looked ancient, with long creases lining her face like the rows in a cornfield. Her body barely caused the blanket to rise off the bed. Aletta saw the woman's bony hand come out from under the old brown blanket. The hand held something, a round object that seemed to glow in the darkness. After a moment, she shifted it from her palm to her fingertips and held it out farther toward Aletta.

It was a crystal ball, a small one.

Aletta couldn't take her eyes from the woman or the beautiful ball she held out so invitingly. Aletta slowly stood up and opened the door to the camper. She stepped inside and walked slowly to the feeble old woman whose hazy brown eyes remained as steady on Aletta as Aletta's were on her. They seemed like kind eyes, so Aletta moved closer. She stared at the woman's silver-white hair that lay around her face on the dingy pillow. It looked like it would be silky and soft to touch.

Aletta stopped, but the woman beckoned her closer with the hand that held the ball. Aletta glanced back out the door of the camper before she stepped closer.

When she got near enough, the old gypsy pushed the ball into her hand. Aletta looked at it, trying to see how it glowed. *Must be catching the sun,* she thought. The ball was smooth and cool and heavy. She turned it, feeling its perfect roundness in her palm.

She felt strange as she stood there, kind of like she was floating, a swelling feeling in her chest. Smiling, she held the ball out to give it back to the old woman. But the woman pointed a crooked finger at Aletta, pulled her hand back under the blanket, and smiled back at her. There wasn't a tooth in her head.

Outside, the dogs started barking happily. Aletta jumped. She could hear people talking. She ran out of the camper and down the step. She raced up the road until she came to a big enough tree to hide behind.

From there she watched, clutching the ball in her hand, as a man, a woman with a baby, a teenage boy, and a girl about Aletta's age walked around the truck to the camper. They were all black-haired with olive skin and bushy eyebrows. The man took the baby from the mother and held him up above his head for a moment, then kissed his forehead and handed him back. Even the baby had a shock of black hair.

They loaded into the truck, the man and boy climbing into the front seats, the mother and girl in the camper. The engine started up with a roar and suddenly they were gone, the truck rumbling down the road, only a fading sound in the distance.

As she walked home, Aletta thought about the old gypsy woman. It seemed she wanted her to have the ball for some reason. Aletta was delighted with her gift. She decided it looked like a perfect snowball captured in stone.

"Aletta Marie, how is it possible for a little girl to find her way into the mud all the time?" scolded Nadine as Aletta walked inside.

"I saw some gypsies, Mama," Aletta said as Nadine pulled her dress over her head.

"I've told you to stay away from them. Things disappear every time they come 'round," Nadine said.

"But an old lady gypsy gave this to me. Ain't it the prettiest thing you ever seen?" Aletta showed the stone snowball to her mother.

"It must be pure crystal. I wonder how they made it like this," Nadine said, turning the ball over in her hands. "Why'd she give it to you?"

"I don't know. She didn't say anything, just held it out to me, and when I tried to give it back, she wouldn't take it."

"You didn't get inside one a' their trucks, did you?" Nadine asked, her fists on her hips.

Aletta stood in her underdrawers and old shoes. "No, ma'am. She was standin' outside, and all the other people were gone."

When Clovis got home, Nadine showed him the ball.

"Yep, pure crystal's what it is. Bet it's worth somethin', too," he said.

"Can I keep it, Daddy? Please?" asked Aletta from the stairs.

"Don't see why not. If it was given to you, it's yours," he said. She ran down the stairs, hugged his waist, and took the ball from his hand.

"I don't recall seein' a old lady when we was comin' back from seining today. Just make sure you don't go inside them gypsy trucks no matter what. Okay, Lettie?" He looked at her with eyes that seemed to see everything.

"Yes, Daddy," she said, and ran back up the stairs so he couldn't see her face burning red. For some reason, it was harder to lie to her daddy.

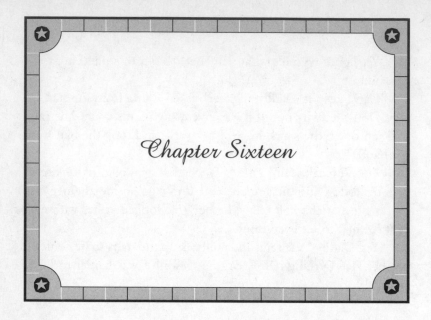

Chapter Sixteen

On Monday, when the salon was closed, Aletta took a home-made chocolate cake to Joy and Earl, scolding herself that she hadn't done it before. She felt embarrassed about them having to get in the middle of her mess, but they said all the right things, somehow making her feel like it was no big deal to threaten a man beating up on his wife. She walked back home, took the mail out of the box, and tore open a letter from the Okay National Bank.

Dear Mrs. Honor,

Thank you for your personal loan application. At this time, we are unable to fund the loan due to the reasons cited below....

She wadded the letter in her hand and wondered if her new checking account was overdrawn yet. She opened the gas bill, the phone bill, and a bill from her lawyer. She saved for last the no-tice from the county courthouse which told her that Jimmy had been served with divorce papers and a restraining order that said he wasn't supposed to come within fifty yards of her.

As she stood on the porch reading, she saw the bicentennial

van driving toward her. She tossed the restraining order into the air and let it flutter to the ground. It had obviously had a big effect on him. Fear and anger joined her like old familiars and waited for him to arrive.

Inside, Ruby stood at the living room window holding George and watching her father get out of the van. She felt ashamed but didn't know why. He walked up to her mother, his face and eyes red. They talked for a minute, and Ruby saw her mother gesturing. She knew she was yelling even though she couldn't see her face or hear her.

Her daddy took a few steps toward the house, but Aletta got in front of him and pushed on his chest. Ruby went to the front door, ready to go out and defend her mother.

The storm began raging inside her again. She had no idea how she could make her father stop doing anything he wanted to do. She just knew she'd have to try, and it scared her.

As she opened the front door, George let out a cry. Both her parents turned around, their arms and anger still entangled.

"Please, Jimmy!" Ruby heard her mother say. "You can see the kids, but we have to plan it beforehand. You can't just come over here. They've gone through too much."

"This is my house! I want to see my kids! Ruby, come here with your brother," he called to her.

She wanted to run or scream, but she walked over to her daddy and let him kiss her on the cheek.

Her mama stood with her hands on her hips, her hair whipping around in the wind and her lips sealed together over clenched teeth. She was so angry that Ruby felt it in her own body.

"You still my girl?" Jimmy asked Ruby as he stroked her hair. She could see the tears in his eyes.

"Yeah," she said.

He took George from her and kissed him on his soft black hair.

"Give me that baby and leave or I'm calling the police," Aletta said, pulling at George.

Ruby felt angry with her mother. Why couldn't she just be

nice to him? Maybe he would change if she wouldn't gripe at him all the time. He was crying, wasn't he?

Ruby knew he couldn't turn his back on them. They loved each other.

George started crying. "I think he's wet," Ruby said.

Jimmy allowed Aletta to take him.

"I knew that would do it." Aletta rolled her eyes and gently pushed Ruby along with her as she walked inside. "I gotta have some money, Jimmy," she said without turning around.

Ruby glanced back at her daddy standing there in the yard, his arms limp at his sides, the expression on his face sad and pitiful.

"I'm sorry you had to go through that, Ruby," Aletta said when they got inside. She sat down on a bar stool and closed her eyes, holding the baby to her chest.

"Is George all right?" Ruby asked, not knowing what else to say.

"He's not a George, some old man with gray hair and a belly. He's my little gypsy baby. Aren't you, little baby? I'm gonna call him Gyp from now on," Aletta said, rocking him back and forth. "Come on, Gyp, let's get you changed."

★

Just a few days after the old gypsy woman gave her the crystal snowball, Clovis asked Aletta if she'd like to ride with him in the fields. It was the tenth of May, cotton planting day, so Lute and Pete and some other farmhands Aletta had never seen before ate breakfast with them.

"Johnny's back in town. He was askin' about y'all," Lute said, his mouth full of biscuit.

Nadine stood at the sink scrubbing a big black skillet. She froze but didn't turn around or say a word. Clovis glanced toward Nadine, then just grunted in response. Aletta wanted to hear about Johnny, curious to know what he was doing now, but she knew that her parents didn't want to talk about it, so she kept still.

She helped her mama clean up the dishes while the men got the equipment ready, then she ran outside and scrambled up onto the big green tractor next to her daddy. The tractor reminded Aletta of the huge green bug in the gypsy truck as it crawled over the freshly turned rows of velvety red earth. The cotton field was the biggest on the farm, and even riding way above the ground she couldn't see all of it at one time. She and her daddy had a game of seeing who could spot the most rabbits, coyotes, squirrels, raccoons, and deer scurrying out of their way or hiding in the trees that lined the creek. Her daddy pointed out the birds flying overhead—hawks, geese, mallards, scissortail flycatchers, buzzards. Sometimes they'd see a wild turkey or a pheasant or a covey of quail, and he'd say he wished he had his shotgun.

"Daddy, tell me a story," Aletta said. She loved to hear his stories.

Clovis looked over his shoulder at the seed spilling out. "I ever tell you the one 'bout my daddy in the storm?" he asked.

"Tell it again. Tell it again."

"Well, I was just a little boy that winter, and we were in the middle of a three day snowstorm I haven't seen the likes of since. After the second day, we ran clean out of food and Daddy had to take the horses and wagon to town to get us some more." Clovis turned around in his seat, satisfied that the planter was working right.

"My daddy made it to town, but on the way back it started snowing so hard he couldn't see two feet in front of him. His hands and feet were frostbit, and he wasn't sure which way he was going. He was completely lost. So he climbed off the wagon and got behind it, hoping just to get out of the driving snow for a minute."

"What'd he do, Daddy?" Aletta asked.

"Well, he stood there thinking he was about to die when his horses started moving. Not knowing what else to do, he grabbed onto the back of the wagon and walked behind. After about half an hour of just trying to stay on his feet, he felt the old wagon come to a stop." Clovis paused a moment for effect.

"With all the strength he had left, he walked around it and up to his horses, keeping a hand on the wagon all the time. If he let go, he thought he might not be able to find it again. The horses stamped the ground and shook their heads up and down until he looked up. Just a few feet away, he made out something glowing through the blizzard. It was the window to our house where I was sitting waiting for him."

Aletta smiled. "Them horses saved his life, didn't they?"

"They sure did. Sometimes animals are smarter than we are, that's for sure."

Clovis and Aletta had been out for an hour or so, going up and down the rows, letting the planter spill cottonseed out behind them. He told her that tomorrow he'd drive to African Town outside Oklahoma City and pick up a truckload of workers to spread by hand the seed that they were dropping today.

"What's that one, Daddy?" Aletta asked, pointing to a bird in the distant sky.

Clovis looked at it for several moments before he told her it wasn't a bird at all. It was an airplane. They watched the small biplane buzz over their heads, then circle back around and start descending.

"Where the hell is that thing goin'?" Clovis asked. It looked like it was headed straight toward his house.

He turned the tractor toward home. He and Aletta pulled up just in time to see Nadine, still in her apron, standing on the porch laughing with her brother—a suntanned, smiling Joey Halbert.

He'd landed his plane on the road out front and pulled it up to the house. As soon as Clovis stopped the tractor, Aletta, who was as excited to see an airplane close up as she was to see her handsome uncle again, jumped down and ran to Joey. He picked her up and swung her around as they hugged and laughed.

★

In the bathroom, Sissy checked her face for blemishes, oblivious to her parents' latest fight. The bathroom was her refuge in a houseful of people, because it had the only door that locked. The day for cheerleading tryouts had finally arrived, so she was spending more time hiding away than usual.

She just knew she'd get a zit right before tryouts, but when she looked in the mirror, she was almost pleased with what she saw, except for the freckles on her nose. She stood up on the edge of the bathtub so she could get a full view of her naked body in the mirror. Her breasts were getting bigger and her tummy was flat, but her thighs were becoming a concern. They definitely looked too big. She raised her hands over her head in a cheerleader V and whispered, "Go, fight, win tonight." Smiling her perkiest smile, she held the pose for a moment. Turning around, she looked at her butt and decided it didn't look any bigger since yesterday. She dipped a toe in the hot bath water to test it.

As she stepped down into the tub, Randy burst out from under the sink and yelled "Surprise!"

"Eeeeyyaaaah!!!" Sissy screamed so loud, Randy had to cover his ears. Her foot slipped on the bottom of the bathtub and she fell backwards, arms and legs flailing like a spider on its back. Water splashed out all over Randy and onto the floor.

"Get out! Get out of here!" she shrieked, covering her breasts with her arms.

He ran out of the bathroom and right into Aletta, who grabbed his ear hard, not a doubt in her mind he'd done something wrong.

"What the hell's goin' on in there?" she demanded, holding Gyp with her other arm.

"He's a little creep! Creep! Creep! Creep!" Sissy yelled from inside.

"I just wanted to surprise her," Randy said, tears coming into his eyes.

"He was watching me! I never have any privacy!"

The ugly blue-and-green upper-thigh bruise Sissy got from falling onto the edge of the bathtub wasn't that bad compared to the bruise on her ego. Aletta helped her with her makeup and hair, giving her attention and assuring her that someday she'd look back on this and laugh. Sissy felt a little better by the time she left, knowing that Randy had been grounded for a week.

"You look beautiful," Aletta said as she fussed with her daughter's hair one last time. Angie's mom honked in the driveway. "We'll be cheering for you."

There were thirty-three girls in the high school gym trying out to be cheerleaders for the Okay Millers. Six would make it for the junior high and six for the high school. The ones who were already cheerleaders, like Mary Lou and Jill, walked around brimming with confidence and laughing with one another in little groups.

Some of the girls' mothers kept straightening their skirts or messing with their hair. Sissy felt embarrassed for them. She wanted everyone to think that this was all no big deal to her. Finally, Mrs. Stolsteimer, the cheerleading coach, gave each of the girls a number on a piece of paper. Sissy got number twelve.

The week before, she and Angie had washed Angie's little tiger-striped kitten in the bathtub. It became a thing possessed as they lowered it into the water. After its body was submerged, the bony little animal screeched away from them. They had to chase it around every inch of that bathroom, up walls and inside cabinets, before they caught it. Sissy felt like that kitten was inside her stomach right now, claws out and crazy. Then she looked up and saw Rusty Conway sitting at the top of the bleachers, and she excused herself to go to the bathroom.

Most of the girls were clumsy and awkward, but a few could do not just cartwheels, but back handsprings and flips. They were the ones whose mothers drove them to the city for gymnastics lessons three times a week like Sissy had asked her mama to.

Her mother told her they'd see, but they never talked about it again. Sissy knew there were just too many kids to keep up with.

Sissy figured the girls who could do gymnastics would make it, and that guess was confirmed when she saw the three ladies who were judging nodding their heads and smiling after they were finished. Sissy hoped that because of her personality and looks, she still had a chance. When it came to her turn, Angie, who had number seventeen, hugged her.

Sissy walked to the middle of the gym floor in her red pleated miniskirt, red Keds, and Okay Millers T-shirt. She glanced up at Rusty as she smiled her biggest smile and began shaking her pompons and yelling out her cheer. She had chosen a response cheer where the audience yells back to show how she would get the fans involved in team spirit, but since there were no fans, she did both parts:

When I say go, You say fight. Go Fight Go Fight. When I say win, You say tonight. Win Tonight Win Tonight.

Sissy punched her pompons up and down, jumping and moving to each word, making sure her smile was cranked as wide as it would go.

When I say boogie, You say down. Boogie Down Boogie Down. When I say all, You say right. All Right All Right. Go, Fight, Win Tonight, Boogie Down, All Right All Right. Go, Fight, Win Tonight, Boogie Down, All Right All Right.

She punched the pompons down, then up in a V, and circled them in front of her. She shook her skirt by twisting her hips, making the pleats fly out around her, as one hand was poised in the air and the other sat on her hip. Her face glowed with hope and fear and physical exertion.

She took a deep breath, tossed her pompons to the side, and went heels over head into a cartwheel, then a roundoff. She paused for a moment before the walkover, her hardest move. She put both hands on the ground in front of her and kicked her left foot up, then her right. She was supposed to go over into a full backbend and then stand up again, but her left foot came down a bit to the side and as her weight shifted, it slipped out from under her and she fell flat on her back with a *humph*.

She lay there for just a second with the breath knocked out of her before scrambling quickly to her feet. She put her arms over her head in a V and smiled weakly.

Refusing to cry, she waited for the rest of the girls to finish, making herself believe that she still had a chance and that if Angie made it and she didn't, it would be okay.

She glanced over her shoulder to look for Rusty, but he was gone. Finally everyone was finished, and they waited for Mrs. Stolsteimer to announce the winners. As she called out each name, there were gasps and screams of delight, but Sissy didn't make it and neither did Angie.

Ruby and Randy were up on chairs in the living room, using candlesticks for microphones, belting out "Jeremiah Was a Bullfrog" when Sissy burst through the front door, crying her eyes out. She ran to her room and slammed the door. Aletta tried to talk to her, but Sissy wasn't coming out for anything. After an hour, Ruby knocked on the door.

"Go away," Sissy sobbed.

Ruby walked in anyway.

"It's no big deal, Sis. It's just dumb old cheerleading," she said almost in a whisper. She'd never seen anyone cry for this long, and that was saying something.

"It wasn't dumb to me. You'll understand some day," Sissy wailed. But Ruby knew she'd never understand caring so much about standing on the sidelines. She wanted to be in the game.

After another solid hour of crying, Randy entered Sissy's room. He stood for several minutes just watching her lie on the bed bawling. When she didn't kick him out, he crawled up on the bed, lay down beside her, and started crying too.

"I'm sorry," he said.

"It's not your fault," she sniffled.

"I'm sorry anyway Sissy. Sorry it hurts." He put his arm around her, and they lay there crying together until they fell asleep.

That evening, Rusty drove up on his motorcycle and came to the door asking for Sissy. Hunger had just forced her out of her room, but when she saw him drive up, she ran back in and closed the door so he wouldn't see her like that.

"Why don't you come back another time, Rusty? She's had a rough day," Aletta told him.

* * *

A few days later, after Aletta finally convinced Sissy that she absolutely had to attend high school, they all piled in the Pig Snout and went shopping for school clothes. That was always a challenge anyway, but today they had to shop at secondhand stores.

Whenever Aletta thought they'd found a cute outfit that was in decent shape for Sissy or Ruby or Randy, they'd hate it. They wanted things that she thought looked cheap or downright humiliating. Sissy's newfound desire for tube tops fit into both categories.

"No girl of mine is wearing one of those," Aletta said, looking at the strip of stretchy material encircling her daughter's breasts.

"But Mama, everybody's wearin' them! I swear to Jesus I'll only wear them under other blouses," Sissy begged. By the end of the day, she got two, peach and bright yellow.

All three of them wanted bell-bottoms and hip-huggers. Aletta thought they looked silly, but if she didn't agree to some of the things they wanted, she would have no bargaining power to get them into the darling little things they sneered at.

After the secondhand stores, they made a special trip to Harold's Shoes in the city, the only place in all of Oklahoma that Aletta could find shoes that fit Randy. He wore a quadruple E width and was extremely particular about how they fit. She had had several complaints from his teachers last year that he wouldn't keep his shoes on.

He was also harder on shoes than anyone she'd ever seen, grown up or not, so she spent thirty-three precious dollars on a sturdy pair of Earth shoes one size too long and hoped they'd last a year.

She bought Sissy and Ruby mood rings and Randy a pet rock at the gag gift store next door. On the way home, packed tightly into the small car, they sang songs from Sunday school.

By the time Aletta answered the phone and heard her mother's voice on the other end, she was too worn out to argue.

"You said I should be more involved with the kids," Nadine said sweetly. "They can spend the night Saturday, then get up and

go to church with me in the morning to see this wonderful play.
You can meet us there."

"What kind of play?" Aletta asked, holding the phone up to
her ear with her shoulder while she unpacked the clothes. She was
always a little suspicious when it came to her mama's religious be-
liefs. There had been too much pain from having them directed at
her in the past.

Her mother sounded more patient than usual. "It's a play
about the Lord, Lettie. It's church."

"Are you sure you want to take the baby?"

"Just give me plenty of diapers and formula. I've taken care of
babies in my life, you know," Nadine said.

The thought of an entire evening by herself without the kids
opened up before her like a field of sweet wildflowers blossoming
in the sunshine. She told her mother she'd drop the kids off at
five on Saturday.

Outside, Aletta heard the whine of a small engine and looked
out the window to see Sissy's chestnut hair flying out behind her
as she rode off on the back of Rusty Conway's motorcycle.

The phone rang again. It was Jimmy. He was drunk.

"What're you doin'?" he asked.

"Well, right now I'm tryin' to figure out what I'm gonna spank
your daughter with when she gets home from goin' off on a motorcycle with some boy 'cause she don't have a daddy around to discipline her. Why the hell do you wanna know?"

"I ain't gonna let you have a divorce, you know. I decided,"
he slurred.

"Oh, you did? Did you decide that layin' in bed with your
girlfriend one night?" Her knuckles were white as she clenched the
phone.

"I'm comin' over. You better watch out," he said.

She slammed down the phone. She didn't even see Ruby
standing right next to her with eyes huge and afraid.

"Was that Daddy?" Ruby asked.

"Yes, that was your daddy. God help us all," Aletta said, and
went into the bathroom for a smoke.

* * *

Rusty drove fast out a country road, flying past fields and farms. It amazed Sissy that the cattle could be so calm during the most exciting moment of her life. She felt that the sun, which hung low in front of them, was a spotlight shining on her and Rusty because they were special, their hearts beating to a different rhythm than everything else around them.

He drove a little recklessly so he could show off and so she'd have to hold him tighter around his waist. He waved at every car they passed as if he were lord of the road.

She loved that.

Finally he pulled back onto Main Street, then onto the gravel in front of the huge flour mills that looked like three giant metal batteries standing side by side. They reached at least ten stories into the sky. Okay's Best Flour was still visible across the front, but the letters were faded and worn now after years of neglect. They got off the bike, and Sissy tried to smooth her hair down and make sure it was parted right. She wore it parted down the middle, like most of the girls she knew.

"What're we doin' here?" she asked. All the kids in Okay had been warned not to go near the mills because people had fallen off them and died.

"I just like it," he said. "Come on."

They walked around the side and saw a small metal sign that read BUILT IN 1916 BY OHLMEYER AND CRAFT, CHICAGO, ILLINOIS. COMMISSIONED BY J.T. PAPPE.

"My daddy told me this mill was the biggest thing around for a long time. Everybody either worked here or brought their grain here to sell," Rusty said.

"Why'd it close down?" She touched the metal exterior of the building expecting it to be cool, but it was warm like the evening.

"He says it's outdated. Now there's a lot cheaper and easier ways to mill flour."

Sissy had never been this close to the mill before even though she'd passed by it a million times. Standing there, she felt the history of the place. They turned the corner and went around back. Rusty pointed to a platform where a vehicle obviously went.

"This is where they'd pull up with a truckful of wheat and get weighed. It's a huge scale. After that, they'd pull in there," he said, pointing now to an overhang that jutted out the side of the huge structure with padlocked doors under it. "That's where they'd dump the wheat, and it'd be hauled inside the mill. Then they'd pull out onto the platform scales on the other side and get the truck weighed again empty. That's how they knew how much the wheat weighed alone. They'd get paid right then and there."

"That's cool," Sissy said, smiling. It was so simple, but ingenious.

Rusty grabbed a huge piece of thick plywood that was lying on the ground and dragged it to the side of the mill just below the steel ladder high above their heads that led all the way to the top. He propped the plywood against the building and steadied it, then tested it under his feet before climbing.

"Come on," he said, and reached his hand out to Sissy.

She hesitated only a moment before taking his hand. She walked up the plywood sheet in front of him, her feet pointed outward, until she got high enough to grab onto the bottom of the ladder.

"You got it?" he asked, looking up at her.

"Yeah," she whispered.

He took her waist in his hands and pushed her up. She pulled with all her strength until she was far enough up the ladder to get a foot on the bottom rung.

"That a girl," he said, and smiled.

She climbed up several rungs so he would have enough room to get on. Looking around, she felt an exhilaration and a power in her body she'd never experienced before.

"Come on. Let's go," she whispered.

He swung himself up, and she saw the muscles in his arms as he did. She wanted to touch his hair as he stood below her.

"Hold on tight and don't look down," he said.

The ladder rungs felt rough under Sissy's hands as she climbed into the sky on this sultry summer evening. She thought for sure they could be seen by all of Okay and there'd be people swarming below them any minute. It made her feel good somehow, knowing for certain that if they were seen, there would be hundreds of people who would be worried for them.

But she didn't want to be seen at all, except by the boy who was encouraging her on from below. Out of breath, they finally reached the last rung and climbed onto the small platform with handrails on three sides at the top of the ladder.

Sissy made sure Rusty was safely next to her, and then she looked out. The vastness of the space around and underneath surprised her and made her feel off balance for a moment. She grabbed tightly onto the handrail until she could adjust. In the soft evening sun, the land looked like a patchwork of quilted velvet stretching out forever on all sides. Her excitement and fear escaped in a laugh.

"What do you think?" Rusty asked, looking around proudly.

"It's so amazing. I've never been up this high in my whole life," she said, her voice sounding small because of the vastness of space around her.

"Sometimes when I'm up here I feel like I could just take off and fly, just soar around like a big hawk in the sky," he said, and paused for just a moment before he started to sing. *"Sometimes, from way up here, I could just take off and fly, Soaring around like an eagle way up in the sky."*

"That's beautiful," Sissy said, and she meant it. He had a deep, smooth singing voice. "Sounds like a country song."

"Nah, I like rock 'n' roll," he said, and they stood there looking down at the tiny houses of Okay. Sissy was trying to pick hers out at the other end of town when Rusty leaned over and kissed her. It was a soft kiss and his tongue barely went inside her lips. His mouth was pillowy against hers, and the warm wetness of his tongue tasted sweet. She couldn't believe how different it felt from kissing Terry.

"Come on," he said afterwards. "We better get you home to your mama."

"Okay," she said.

"Sure is." He smiled, and started down the ladder.

All she could think as she floated down the ladder was *Wow, oh my God, wow, oh my God.* She couldn't wait to tell Angie, and she couldn't wait to kiss him again. She had no idea how she got off that ladder and back down to the ground, but she did and was inside her house being screamed at by her mother before the tingle of that one kiss wore off.

She was grounded for a week which only lasted two days because Aletta didn't have the energy to stay on top of the blooming sexuality that was driving her firstborn out of the house and onto the back of a boy's motorcycle.

Chapter Seventeen

Aletta pulled up to her mama's at exactly five o'clock. It was the first time she'd been on time for anything in weeks. It had taken her hours to pack everything for the kids, and they could barely fit in the Pig Snout, sitting with bags piled on their laps.

Nadine's little yellow house sat on a street that had seen some wear. Aletta knew it drove her mama crazy that there were boats in yards and broken washing machines sitting next to her neighbors' run-down houses, so Nadine kept her house especially neat and pretty to give them an example of what was proper.

Even though her folks had come over in the land rush and lived in a dugout underground while they built their house on their free farmland, her mama had always had an aristocratic air about her, in the way she carried herself and how she dressed and most definitely how she kept her house.

It always felt strange to Aletta to walk into that house, because it was so familiar on the one hand and so unwelcoming on the other. "Here's Gyp's bottles and diapers, Mama," she said, walking down the hallway of her mother's tidy but cramped little house. There were little antique figurines, glass eggs, collector's plates, and decorative crosses on every wall and inside glass-enclosed cases everywhere she turned.

She walked to the guest room and stopped, taking a breath before stepping inside. This room affected her more now than it usually did. Almost everything in it was from her childhood bedroom on the farm. The bed, bedspread, toybox, dresser, even the old rocking horse her daddy had made for her fifth birthday. The only additions were several crosses on the walls and a picture of Jesus hanging on the cross, sad and skinny, above the bed, with the Lord's Prayer engraved next to it.

"My Lord, Mama," she said to choke back the feelings. "Why do you still keep all this stuff?"

"Reminds me of the best time of my life, when you were just a baby and your daddy was alive," Nadine said, walking in with a grocery bag full of Randy's clothes.

"Too bad babies have to grow up, ain't it?" Aletta asked. Almost everything her mama said these days got right in under her skin.

Nadine ignored her and took Randy's church clothes out of the bag and laid them out on the bed. "These are nice shoes. You get Jimmy to pay for these?" she asked.

"He hasn't given me a penny. I been makin' it myself," Aletta answered, her face flushing hot.

"Well, I better check the roast in the oven and make sure George is bein' looked after. You wanna stay for dinner?" Nadine smiled weakly at her daughter, then walked out of the room before she could answer.

Aletta went to the dresser and opened the top drawer, half expecting to see the crystal snowball inside where she'd always kept it, but of course it wasn't there.

In the back of the drawer she saw the edge of a stiff piece of paper and pulled it out. It was a picture that she'd taken with Joey's camera a few months after he'd arrived from Kansas. The sepia tone and worn edges of the photo made it look like a relic from a hundred years ago. It felt like that long ago to Aletta.

Her mama, daddy, and uncle stood in front of the old oak

tree in the yard. Nadine was smiling but stood a little stiffly between her open-faced husband and her confident, relaxed brother.

The picture seemed to burn Aletta's fingers as she held it. She dropped it back into the drawer, but then picked it back up and put it in the pocket of her shorts.

After several good-bye kisses and hugs and pleadings from the kids for her to stay, Aletta got into her car. She turned the AM radio to WKY. "Rhinestone Cowboy" played through the tinny speakers, so she twisted the dial, but the farm report was all she could find, so she switched it off.

As she turned onto Kathy Kokin's street, she wondered why she was doing it. There in the street sat the bicentennial van, and there in her chest sat her hurt and angry heart. She turned into the driveway and honked, but then backed out quickly and drove home.

At home, the silence she'd longed for made her feel crazy because she could hear her thoughts so clearly. To fill the void, she got busy and cleaned the house. As long as she was working, she couldn't feel that screwed up. Within an hour and a half, she had two loads of laundry going, the kitchen floor mopped, the vacuum run, the bathroom scrubbed, and everything dusted and was moving into the closets, pulling out old clothes and shoes. She was deep into her own closet in the back of the house when she thought she heard the doorbell ring. She pulled herself out and heard the ring again.

Aletta pushed her hair away from her forehead with the back of her hand as she opened the door. A bald man who wore white robes to the ground and had sparkling blue eyes behind little round glasses stood smiling at her. Hopeful. Expectant.

There's a nutcase at my door was her distinct thought. She stood for a few moments trying to think of an excuse to turn him away.

"Aletta," he said, his tone familiar.

"Yes, that's me," she answered.

He grinned at her. "You don't know who I am?"

Aletta looked harder for a sign, a glimpse of recognition, but she couldn't get past the baldness and the robes. Nothing came until he smiled wider, and his eyes turned into little upside-down crescent moons.

"Oh my Lord a mercy. Jerry? Jerry Baker, is that you?" she asked. "You're bald!"

"That's true," he said, and laughed.

"Well, for cryin' out loud, come on in," she said, and opened the screen door. She was glad to see him but unsure how she should treat him. Had he gone crazy? "Last time I saw you, you had as much hair as me." She hugged him and led him to the dining room table. "I'm sorry, I look a mess. I've just been cleaning the house."

They sat down at the table and looked at each other. When she knew him in school, his skin was bad, but now it was clear and smooth. His face was much thinner now, making his jawline and cheekbones stand out where they hadn't before.

"Jerry Baker. My lands, I can't believe it's you," Aletta said.

"I have a new name. Shanti," he said, and pushed his glasses up on his nose.

Yep, he'd gone crazy.

"How have you been, Aletta? It's good to see you," he said warmly.

"Oh, boy. I wouldn't even know where to begin, and who cares? I've just been here in Okay. You went to college after high school, didn't you?" Aletta asked.

He nodded. "University of Michigan."

"And how did all this come about?" She waved a hand at his robe. He didn't look crazy out of his eyes, she had to admit. He looked, what was it? Peaceful, she decided.

"I studied philosophy until I met my master Ananda Maharishi. He was on a speaking tour and came to the university. It changed my life. I quit school and went to live in his ashram for five years."

Aletta started to giggle. She covered her mouth with her hands, but the laughter spilled out anyway.

Jerry smiled and his eyes again turned into little crescent moons.

"I don't have any idea what you're talkin' about," she said through her laughter.

"What part don't you understand?" he asked.

"I'm sorry Jerry, I mean Shanti. I don't know why things make me laugh sometimes."

"I assume you understand studying philosophy in college?" he asked. He could have been talking to a ten-year-old.

"Yes, yes. I understand that part," she said.

He took off his glasses and cleaned them with the hem of his robe. "Ananda Maharishi is a spiritual master from India. He has students throughout the world. Well, not in Okay, of course. I went to his ashram, which is a kind of spiritual retreat where he lives and teaches. I lived there, studying and meditating under his instruction, for five years."

"What an exotic life you've been living," Aletta said.

"I would've thought you knew a little about such things," he said, putting his glasses back on.

Aletta shifted in her chair. "I moved to North Carolina with Jimmy for a few months, but other than that, I haven't been any-where, let alone India."

"How is Jimmy?" he asked.

"Hell if I know. We're gettin' a divorce," she said. "Did you know I have four kids? They're with their grandma."

His smile was kind. "My mother said you had children. That's wonderful."

"I see your mama at the store and whatnot every once in awhile. She never said anything about you goin' to India."

"I'm sure she didn't," he said and looked out the window.

She glanced at the window, then realized he was looking for the same thing from his mama she was looking for from hers, but he wouldn't find it out there. "How often do you get back home?"

"This is the first time in two years. I live in San Francisco now, but I still don't get back that often. It's hard on them. They don't really accept me like this."

"Well, it's sure different than what people are used to around here, I guess."

"I would think you could relate to that," he said, looking at her intently.

She paused, not understanding what he meant for a moment. "Oh, you mean the sign out front."

He nodded. "What is it that you do?"

"I can tell things about people is all. Don't even know where it came from. Always felt more like a curse than anything, really."

His eyebrows rose slightly, a question forming before he even asked it. "A curse? How so?"

"Well, not really a curse. I don't know." Aletta popped out of her chair and pushed her hair behind her ear. "You know, I am so filthy, I really need to take a bath," then, before she could think, "You wanna stay for dinner or something?" She regretted saying it immediately.

He smiled, surprised. "Sure, that'd be great. I'll cook some curry if you want me to."

"Sounds good," Aletta said, pretending to know what he meant.

"I'll go get supplies while you're in the bath. It's good to see you, Aletta." He stood up and hugged her. His robes smelled smoky and floral.

"What's that smell?" she asked.

"Incense, from India," he said.

"Oh, well, it's real nice."

Aletta walked down the hall to the bathroom rolling her eyes. Now her entire evening was going to be spent talking to some weirdo who wouldn't even have come by if it weren't for the damn sign making him think they were the same kind of crazy breed.

Maybe we are, Aletta thought as she got undressed and ran water in the tub. She felt in her shorts pocket and pulled out the picture of her parents and her uncle. This time it caught her off guard, in her own house, standing naked and alone. She was there in an instant, holding the camera, standing on the front porch steps to get a better angle.

★

"Smile, y'all," Aletta called, and snapped the picture. It was Sunday afternoon and Joey had only been with them a couple of months. He was helping out on the farm while he drove Clovis's pickup to all the farms in the county to let them know he was in the business of spraying fields in his airplane, expert, on time, and guaranteed.

On Friday after school just two days before, he'd taken Aletta into Okay. He bought her an ice cream cone at the Dairy Queen and then drove to the flour mills.

"Men who work the mills know all the farmers in these parts. Won't hurt a bit to make their acquaintance," he said.

"You gonna stay on with us, Uncle Joey? I know that's what Mama wants." Aletta licked the melting ice cream as they drove through town. Town consisted of a few stores and the mills on Main Street with the townfolks' houses spreading out beyond.

"I dunno, darlin'. Only thing I do know is I ain't gonna be a burden on anybody."

"You ain't a burden. You ever see a Gary Cooper movie where he was a burden?" Aletta was convinced Joey looked just like Gary Cooper, with his blue eyes, square jaw, and creases in his cheeks when he smiled.

Joey's creases were showing now. "You know how to be very convincin', that's for sure."

Joey stopped at the enormous mill and hopped out. He told Aletta to stay near the truck, this wasn't any place for youngsters. She climbed into the back of the truck so she could see better.

Joey walked to the weigh-in area and shook hands with two

or three men. He smiled and laughed and clapped the shoulder of a stocky man wearing suspenders and a straw hat as he shook his hand.

Aletta understood that meant Joey knew the man in the hat from when he'd lived here as a boy. The man took out a pouch of Redman tobacco and each of them took a wad and stuffed it in his mouth. They chewed and spit and talked for several minutes, and then he took Joey inside.

Joey looked over to Aletta before he went in and waved at her. Her chest swelled up like a balloon, she was so proud of him. On the way home, he let her sit on his lap and steer the truck while he worked the pedals.

That Sunday evening, after taking pictures, they sat down to a supper of roast beef with potatoes and carrots. They held hands as her mama said grace.

"Dear Heavenly Father, we ask for Thy blessing upon this meal and upon Thy servants who are grateful to receive it. We also give eternal thanks for the gift of our loved ones here in our presence. In Jesus' name we pray. Amen."

She looked up and Aletta was surprised to see that her mother's eyes were moist. She'd never seen her cry. Her daddy cleared his throat but stayed quiet.

"Clove, I forgot to tell you," Joey said, passing him the potatoes, "Hank Stenstrom over at the mill said he thought you'd be interested to know that Johnny Redding's back in town."

Her mama set her tea glass down hard on the table.

"That's what Pete told me," Clovis said. "I didn't wanna discuss it with him, though, afraid it'd get back to Johnny."

"How long?" Nadine asked.

"Few weeks. I guess he moved to Wyoming to work the fields, but he said one winter up there was enough for him."

"He still drinkin'?" Clovis asked in his slow drawl.

"Hank didn't say. Said he came around lookin' for a job at the mill, but the foreman wouldn't hire him on account of you bein' one of their best suppliers."

Clovis looked down at his plate. Aletta listened, wanting to hear every word about Johnny.

"Serves him right, Clovis. Don't get soft on him. He tried to. . . ." Nadine glanced over at Aletta, then wiped her mouth with her napkin. "We oughta not talk about it no more."

"I'm sorry, Nadine. I shouldn't of brought it up at dinner," Joey said.

"Oh, it ain't your fault," she said.

"She's right, Joe. Don't even think about it," Clovis said, then paused before adding, "By the way, you comfortable up in that room?"

"Sure. It's a lot nicer'n what I was livin' in up in Dodge City. It was a shack, I tell you. I was savin' every penny to buy the airplane."

"Think you'd wanna stay on with us? I could sure use the help 'round here."

Aletta started jumping up and down in her seat, forgetting all about Johnny Redding, until she jumped right out of it and ran to Joey. "Please, please, please stay!"

Joey blushed red and smiled sheepishly. "Only if you're sure, Clovis."

"I'm sure," Clovis said. He sounded almost gruff, but Aletta knew it was because he didn't want to get emotional.

Nadine got up and gave Clovis a kiss on the cheek and hugged Joey. "This calls for a celebration. I just happened to make a chocolate cake."

That night, after her daddy tucked her in, Joey came in to say good night too.

"You playing with that gypsy ball again?" he asked.

"I like the way it feels," she said, rolling it up and down the covers on her belly.

"I'm glad we're good friends," he said.

"Me too. . . . Um, I wanted to ask you something, but I'm kinda embarrassed," she said.

"Better just go ahead and jump is what I always say," he smiled.

"Can I pretend you're my big brother now?" she asked.

" 'Course you can, but only if you'll be my little sister," he said, and kissed her forehead. "That all right with you?"

She nodded her head.

He turned around in the doorway before leaving. "G'night, Sissy. Sweet dreams."

★

Aletta was sitting at the bar in the kitchen drinking iced tea when Jerry came back carrying two bags of groceries. Now she didn't care if he was a kook. She knew from his eyes that he was harmless, and she was just glad to have someone there, somebody to talk to. She liked hearing about his life, so different from hers. It was like reading a book and escaping into another world.

"I brought a few things from California you can't find out here—curry powder, coconut milk, tofu," he said as he set the bags on the Formica. "You mind if I just make myself at home?"

She started to get up and help but sat back down where she really wanted to be. "Sure, go right ahead. It'll be interestin' to have a man cook for me."

He opened a bottle of cheap white wine and poured them each a glass.

They chatted about old times as he cooked, chopping vegetables, potatoes, and whitish stuff that looked like colorless Jell-O to Aletta.

"I used to have a crush on you, you know, when we were freshmen," he said.

She smiled. "I didn't know that. You never told me that."

He turned to her. "I never had the courage. I was too shy."

"Then you started going out with Nancy. You were crazy about her."

"I really was," he said, and scraped onions off the wooden cutting board and into a skillet.

Aletta watched him. He could really cook. "She's married now, livin' in Dallas, has a bunch of kids," she said.

"My mom keeps me completely informed. She thinks memories of Nancy will turn me around." The onions started to come alive in the pan.

Aletta sipped her wine. "Do you still go out with women?"

"Not since college. I'm open to it now if it happens, but as my master says, relationship is a fierce yoga," he said.

"It's fierce all right. There ain't no doubt about that." She began to feel the warmth of the wine in her belly.

They ate and talked about India and her kids and Jimmy Carter. Aletta loved the curried potatoes and peas with basmati rice, but the tofu had a little too strange a texture for her. They finished off the bottle of wine, and she felt . . . what was it? *Real close to happy,* she thought.

"All right, Jerry Shanti, what's up with the outfit? I can't wait any longer," she said, emboldened by the wine.

"You've been holding back, have you?" he asked. "The robes and shaved head are signs of renunciation of the world, of worldly things."

"Wine is a worldly thing, ain't it?" she asked, holding up her glass.

"So I'm loosening up a little." He chuckled.

"Maybe you oughta loosen up even more."

"Oh, here we go," he said, waving his hand in the air.

Aletta swiveled on her bar stool so she faced him directly. "What do you mean?"

"Why do all you people have to tell everyone else how they're supposed to be?" There was an edge in his voice.

Aletta stared at him for a moment. She didn't know him well enough to want to get into anything, and she was having a good time. Why screw it up? "You're right. Do as you please," she said, and got up to clear the dishes.

He picked up his plate and followed her to the sink. "Now I have a question for you. How long have you been psychic, and why didn't I know about it?"

"Since I was a little kid, a long time," she said.

"And?"

"And what?" She rinsed her plate under the water.

"I heard things about you. Some of the kids would say that you used to be a witch but you'd been saved or some nonsense." He took the plate from her. "I'll do these. Just relax. You said it was a curse, your ability?"

"Yes, I did, didn't I?" she said.

They looked at each other, the water running, the mini-grandfather clock ticking.

"I always wanted to ask you what happened to your daddy," he said softly.

Aletta set down the cutting board and the skillet she'd just picked up. The darkness closed in on her. "I gotta use the restroom."

"I didn't mean to . . ." he began, but she waved her hand and walked out of the room.

She stared into the mirror. Her breathing sounded like a question. Why? She inhaled. Why? Her chest rose as she watched herself. Why? The bathroom seemed to get smaller around her, and her breathing got faster.

A few minutes later, she peeked into the doorway of the kitchen at Jerry. "Can we go somewhere else? I need to get outta here for a little while."

"Where do you want to go?" he asked, wiping his hands on a towel.

"Outside somewhere. No walls in sight."

"You think we could get onto the old Crowley place? I used to love it out there."

He drove the Pig Snout out of town, speeding south, and turned onto a flat dirt road. It was after nine o'clock now, and the headlights cut a path through the moonlit darkness that enveloped miles of farmland on both sides of the road. Just being out of the house doing something with the warm night air blowing through the open car window helped Aletta relax a little.

Both she and Jerry had traveled this road many times as

teenagers on their way out to the bonfire parties at the Crowley place. Mr. Crowley, an Okay alum and a big supporter of the basketball, football, and baseball teams, never cared as long as there was no trash left and no fire still burning. Every Thanksgiving the Crowleys hosted a huge weenie roast and hayrack ride. The kids came from all over the county to attend.

The sound of the tires on the familiar gravelly road was like an old friend to Aletta. She'd driven on dirt her whole life, and the sound of it was like a forgotten scent that created a feeling of time already passed.

On the left, a grove of trees stood out against the inky blue sky. Jerry slowed down and turned onto a lane that led through the trees to the clearing where they used to gather. He stopped at a gated fence. "I'll get it," he said, but Aletta hopped out of the car.

She walked to the gate and pulled the wire loop off the fence post. She pulled the big gate out of the way and got back in the car.

"There's a good-size mud puddle on the other side, but go on through. We'll make it," Aletta said, breathing from the exertion. Just ahead of them, the circular clearing in the thicket of trees seemed to beckon her. It was lit up by the soft glow of the moon. The tops of the trees were silhouetted regally against the starry night sky.

Jerry put the car in first gear and gunned it. Just as the tires hit the mud, he shifted to second. The wheels spun for a few seconds but then gained some purchase on the other side, and they catapulted into the clearing.

"Ride 'em, cowboy!" Aletta cried.

"Yeehaw!" he shouted.

He stopped the car near the center of the clearing where a fire pit still scarred the ground.

"Watch for cow patties," Aletta said as she unloaded the blanket from the hatchback.

They gathered fallen wood and piled it into the fire pit on top of the old newspapers they'd brought. In the darkness and the silence, it seemed to Aletta that every footstep and each breath lingered in the air before fading into the next.

"I have to tell you, boots and jeans would work a hell of a lot better right now," Jerry said as he dropped branches onto the pile, trying to keep his sandals on his feet. His robes were getting filthy at the bottom from dragging through the mud and dirt.

Aletta lit the crumpled newspapers and the fire caught quickly, crackling and sparking. The scent of the wood, the big sky, and the simple act of starting a fire made her smile.

They sat down on the shabby bedspread Aletta had remembered at the last second. She lay back, using her hands as a pillow, and watched the fireflies blink on and off in the darkness of the trees.

Jerry sat with his arms resting on the tops of his bent knees. "The universe is such mystery. How improbable is it that there are insects that can light up like a lantern in the night?"

"About as improbable as you sittin' by the fire at Crowley's, bald and wearing Jesus robes, renouncing the world," she said.

He chuckled and lay back. "What about you, a psychic in Okay?"

"Yep," she said.

He turned over on his side and looked at her.

"Are you really psychic?" he asked. "I mean, how much do you know?"

"You won't leave this alone, will you?" she asked, turning her head toward him.

"Darlin', this is the most exciting thing Okay has to offer."

She smiled. "So you want me to prove myself. What a big surprise."

"I believe you, but it's just that my master knew a lot. It was like he could see people's souls more clearly than their bodies, but he'd practiced meditation for decades," he said.

She shrugged. "You got me. I don't understand it, but I do know you're gonna meet someone, a woman, soon."

"Really?" He sat back up.

"Shelly, Sherry, something like that. You're gonna marry her and have a daughter."

"But I never thought I'd have children, ever," he said.

"Sometimes I'm wrong," she shrugged again. "And no more robes, either, by the way."

"Now you're teasing me," he said. "You hate my robe."

"And you're gonna move back to Okay and become an accountant and a member of the Chamber of Commerce," she said, a smile stealing across her face.

"Please." He rolled his eyes.

"Everything I told you except the last part," she said. "That's why I asked you about wearing the robes. I know it pissed you off."

He picked up a twig and tossed it into the fire. "I wasn't pissed off. I just feel like people get in each other's business way too much here."

She turned on her side and propped her head up with her hand. "You were kinda pissed, Jerry, but it's fine. You don't have to be perfect just because you lived in an assram."

"It's an *ashram,* not an *assram.* Please, I have enough trouble without living in an *assram*," he laughed.

Aletta gazed into the flames quietly for a while. When she reached into her back pocket and took out the picture, it was without much thought, really. Just something she wanted to do. She handed it to him without saying anything.

He turned from the fire and held it up so he could see the faded photo in the flickering light.

"Your mom and dad?" he asked.

"And my uncle Joe. He's the one on the right," she said.

"That's your old farm?"

"Yeah," Aletta whispered.

Jerry looked at her. "What happened to your daddy, Aletta? I'll just listen."

She sat up and crossed her legs. He put his arm around her

and they looked at the fire together. After several moments, Aletta got up and threw some more wood on. She picked up a long stick and pushed at the burning limbs.

"My uncle Joey came to live with us, you know. Came down from Kansas."

As she stirred the fire, sparks shot upward in front of her, defying gravity, blinking in the night. Both their heads tilted up to follow the ascent.

Chapter Eighteen

Patches of spring snow melted on the ground in the warm sun as Aletta walked home from school. She couldn't wait to get there because Joey had bought a guitar and was teaching her how to play. He'd been living with them close to a year now. Almost every night after dinner, they'd sit and listen to him play and sing. It was one of the only times her mama stopped working and sat down. To Nadine, if you were working, you were worth something, but Joey could get her to not give a hoot for a spell.

"Play 'Blue Eyes Cryin' in the Rain,' Joey. You sing it so good," she'd say, taking off her apron. It was her favorite song. He'd croon, and she'd hold onto Clovis's arm.

"In the twilight glow I see you, Blue eyes cryin' in the rain. . . ." After Joey sang it one evening, she leaned over and kissed Clovis right on the mouth for a long time. It was the only time Aletta ever saw her parents kiss on the lips.

Joey had easily fit into their lives. His field spraying business was doing very well, and she knew he had money to buy his own property, but she'd heard him tell her mama how much he liked feeling part of a family.

Every once in a while he'd ask her daddy if he was wearing out his welcome. Clovis would clap him on the back and tell him he'd be pleased if he stayed on.

"You're like a son to me now," her daddy said one night. He was fourteen years older than Joey.

When Joey took Aletta out to hunt and fish and ride horses, Nadine never told him those things were for boys like she did with Clovis.

Joey played for the local Elks baseball team, and all through the summer they'd go out and watch him. He wouldn't join the Elks because he told Aletta he didn't agree with all their politics, which she didn't understand at all, but they let him play anyway because he was by far the best player on the team. He pitched or played shortstop and hit those paunchy ex-athlete pitchers from the other Elks teams at about a .600 clip.

Aletta would sit in the stands and watch all the young women point and giggle and cheer when he did anything. When her daddy let her, she'd go talk to him through the fence as he sat in the dugout so those giggling women would know he belonged to her and her family.

After one of his games, as Aletta, her parents, and Joey walked out to the truck, they saw Johnny Redding leaning against a fence. He looked older and skinnier, his skin slack on his body and stubbly face.

"Johnny," Clovis said, and nodded toward him.

Nadine kept her head high and looked away.

"Clovis," Johnny said, swaying as he shifted his weight. "Still ruler of the free world?" He spit a stream of tobacco near her daddy's feet.

Joey turned on him, but Clovis put a hand on his shoulder and led him away.

"He's still a pitiful drunk," Nadine said as they drove home. Aletta sat on Joey's lap in the truck while Clovis drove and her mama straddled the stick shift, the sound of the wheels on the dirt road humming underneath them.

"Drunk or not, he better watch himself or somebody's gonna have to teach him a lesson," Joey said.

"He's had a hard life. Just stay out of his way, now, Joe. No need to beat a man who's beat already," Clovis said.

Aletta felt frightened as she rested her head on her mother's shoulder, but she didn't know why, so she nuzzled her face into her mama's neck, and Nadine patted her head. That made her feel better.

That evening, Joey came into her room to say good night.

"Isabella came again last night," she said, the homemade quilt pulled up around her neck.

Joey sat down on the edge of the bed. "She did? What'd she say this time?"

Aletta shook her head a little. "Nothin' at all. I just woke up and she was there. She just sat right where you are and watched over me 'til I fell back asleep."

"That was nice of her," he said, but he didn't smile. It seemed like he never smiled when she talked about her visitors.

"It was nice," she said, and yawned.

"You're still not tellin' anyone but me about your visits, are you, Sissy? It's just our secret, right?"

"Right," she said, but she felt funny inside, like she was doing something wrong.

"G'night," he said, and kissed her forehead. "Sweet dreams."

They didn't see Johnny again for almost a year, until the next spring. Aletta overheard little bits about him sometimes from the farmhands or her parents talking. Pete said he was still looking for a job, but for the most part Aletta forgot all about him.

She'd begun to avoid touching people outside her family, because sometimes she'd see something about them like she had that day at school with Ralph Smart. It was usually private stuff that she didn't feel she could share with anyone because they always acted so strange, so she just decided it was best not to try.

That warm, sunny March day, Aletta had just turned eleven years old when she started home from school after a huge spring snowstorm two days before. The snow, which had been piled in drifts almost as tall as her, had melted for the most part, so the dirt road was now muddier than she'd ever seen it. She plodded along the road, bare brown trees lining its sides—until she saw a cottontail rabbit scurry over some melting snow and nibble on a patch of fresh new grass. She followed it to the edge of the road and felt her feet sink into the soft ground. It was so cute, watching her warily as it nibbled away, unwilling to lose such delicious food because it was frightened by her standing there. She wanted to pet it, but she knew it was too fast.

When she tried to start walking again, she couldn't move. The muddy red clay had swallowed her galoshes up to the ankles. As she struggled, one foot came clean out of her stuck galoshes. She was wearing the shoes she'd picked out of the Sears catalogue for Christmas, so she put her foot back in the boot and started to pull again, this time tugging on the boot with her hands.

She stood there yanking and pulling for several minutes until sweat was beading on her forehead. She got her right foot loose and stepped forward, but by the time she'd gotten the left one free, the right one was stuck again.

Half an hour and about ten feet later, she was grateful to hear a truck coming up the road behind her. She couldn't see who it was in the glare of the sun on the windshield, and the rusted, beat-up old truck didn't look familiar.

"You need a ride, little lady? Looks like you're in quite a pickle," a man said from inside.

She opened the door and hopped into the front seat, leaving her galoshes stuck in the road. As she slammed the door, she looked over to see Johnny Redding grinning at her with a mouth full of tobacco-stained teeth.

She wanted to open the door and jump right back out, but before she could, he put the truck in gear and spun forward in the mud.

"You remember me, don't you?" he said, one hand casually

resting on top of the steering wheel. She hadn't noticed the pint of whisky tucked between his legs until he took a big drink from it. His eyebrows were bushy, with long hairs sticking crazily out of them at odd angles.

"Yes," she said. Her voice quivered slightly. She knew her mama would throw a fit to tame the devil over this.

"Who am I?" he asked. The truck spun out a little in the rear, and Johnny spilled whisky on himself as he grabbed the wheel to keep the truck on the road. "Goddammit!" he yelled.

Aletta kept quiet, praying he was going to turn on the next road, the one to her house. She could barely see over the dashboard of the truck, so she strained her neck, keeping an eye on the intersection.

"Well?" He wiped his mouth with the back of his hand. "You said you remember me. You know my name?"

"Johnny," Aletta said then pointed. "That's my road there."

"What? Don't you wanna go on a drive with your old uncle Johnny? It's such a beautiful day and all," he said. "Sun shinin' and birds chirpin' and all." He took another drink as he put the truck in third and sped past the turn.

They fishtailed down the road, and Aletta breathed in deeply, grasping the door handle.

Johnny laughed. "You a little scaredy-cat, ain't you? You was a lot braver when you tattled on me to your big daddy and your snooty mama," he said.

"I didn't tattle on you. I wanna go home," she pleaded. She was really scared now. Where was he taking her? What should she do?

He looked over at her and glared. "I remember them things you told me 'bout seein' ghosts and stuff like that. You a little witch girl, ain't you?"

Aletta could see that the truck was veering toward a ditch, and it must've been the look on her face that caused him to look back at the road just in time to yank the wheel straight. That made the truck spin across the road and slide to a stop sideways.

Aletta grabbed for the door handle that was actually a pair of vise grips, but Johnny reached across her and held it shut as he pulled away. She smelled the booze and chewing tobacco on him. He was so close.

"Now that wouldn't be right. I gotta repay your daddy for helpin' me out so much after so many years of workin' my ass off for him. You gotta let me give you a ride, little witch girl," he said, and took another pull on the bottle.

"I ain't a witch. My daddy's gonna hurt you for this," she said.

He tucked the whisky back between his legs, reached over, and grabbed her shoulder hard. His face was red with anger.

"You don't think he already has?!" Spit flew out of his mouth as he yelled.

She saw the vision flash in front of her when he touched her. Johnny was in handcuffs, being escorted on either side of him by two policemen. He was going to kill her!

He'd grabbed her with his right hand so hard that he'd yanked the steering wheel across him with his left. The truck veered violently across the road.

Aletta screamed.

Johnny tried to pull the truck back straight, but this time they flew nose-first into the ditch on the side of the road. A farmer had dumped rotten hay there, so when the truck hit, it didn't slam into the ground but plunged deep into the soaked hay. Aletta put her left hand on the dash to brace herself when she saw they were going to crash, so the force of the blow moved up through her arm and snapped her collarbone like a dry twig. Her head hit hard on something, and everything went black.

Aletta woke up soaking wet, lying on the soggy old hay. She couldn't see very well, but she felt someone softly pulling at her good arm, encouraging her to get up. The pain in her shoulder was mean and stabbed at her, shooting down her arm and up her neck. Finally, with the assistance of whoever was tugging at her, she pulled herself up.

She looked around to see who had been helping her, but there was no one around, not even Johnny Redding. She climbed out of the ditch, covered with wet hay and mud, and stumbled back down the road toward home.

Her whole body shivered. The sun was sinking quickly on the horizon. Her head buzzed like Joey's airplane was flying inside it. She felt more tired than she'd ever been in her whole life and decided to just lie down for a few minutes.

But then she heard a whisper in her ear. "Look there," the voice said.

She looked up and saw a light flicker on in the distance. It was coming from inside a falling-down one-room sharecropper's place that had been empty since the land was sold to Milt and Evie Rumph several years ago. They didn't need sharecroppers since they had nine children to work the land.

She pulled her feet, one after the other, through the snow and mud to the open door of the shack. There was a fire just starting to catch inside the hearth. She tried to get her foot over the doorsill, but it was too high, and she stumbled into the room and fell onto the dirt floor with a thunk.

"Aye God!" a woman screamed and grabbed the toddler who was trying to stand up against a wall. A dark-skinned man with long hair rushed to Aletta and turned her on her back.

"It's a ghost!" the woman gasped. She was lighter-skinned than the man, and her jet-black hair went down to her waist. Aletta knew, even through the fog in her head, that they were gypsies.

✪

"That's when I passed out," Aletta said to Jerry as they sat by the fire. She stirred the fire again to coax out some more heat.

"My God," Jerry said after several moments. "That must've been scary as hell."

She nodded and looked at him. "I'm getting chilly. Are you ready to go?"

"No way," he said getting up. "I'll get some more wood for the fire. I want to hear the rest."

She watched the embers as he gathered more wood. She felt numb, but underneath the numbness was an opening. She didn't know what lay in there.

Jerry came back with an armful of limbs and branches and threw half of them on the hot embers. "You look beautiful right now. You know that?" He sat back down next to her.

She took his hand and smiled a little sadly. "You're very sweet."

"I'm ready," he said.

"You know this is the first time I ever told this whole damn thing to anyone? Do you think that's crazy?"

He enveloped her hand in both of his. "You must've told the police after it happened."

"I told 'em about the wreck and all, but I mean the whole story. I couldn't tell 'em that because it hadn't happened yet."

★

"Help!"

Nadine thought she heard a man's voice off in the distance outside, and her stomach flipped over. Clovis had just left to go out looking for Aletta since it was now after dark. Nadine and Joey waited for her in the house.

The sound of Joey's boots pacing on the wood floor muffled the cry, but he heard something too and stopped.

"Help!"

This time it was clearer, and they were at the door and out on the porch together a few seconds later.

"Hello!" Joey called out into the darkness.

Just then, a gypsy man with hair to his shoulders appeared in the glow of the porch light, breathing heavily.

"It's a girl!" he cried, and bent over, resting his hands on his knees. He'd run a long way, but theirs had been the closest house he could find. "She's hurt!"

Nadine and Joey jumped into Clovis's work truck without saying a word to each other. The gypsy climbed in back and Joey sped out onto the road.

Nadine shook uncontrollably.

At the intersection, they saw Clovis in the pickup coming from the direction of the school. Joey honked and honked but didn't slow down as he turned toward the shack, the gypsy holding on with all his might in back as the truck skidded around the corner. They slid to a stop in the mud with Clovis close behind.

The gypsy woman sat on the dirt floor with Aletta's head in her lap, stroking her hair, when they burst through the doorway.

Clovis swept Aletta up and ran her out to his truck. She groaned and opened her eyes a little from the movement.

"Follow us," Clovis said to Joey, panic on his face. Nadine climbed in and Clovis laid their daughter gently on her lap.

"Mama," Aletta whispered groggily. "I'm sorry. I ruined my new shoes."

She went unconscious again as they raced to Deaconess Hospital forty minutes away.

"What could've happened? What could've happened?" Nadine asked again and again, her trembling hand stroking her daughter's matted blond hair.

Aletta opened her eyes, but the glare of the lights blinded her. Her head and shoulder hurt more than the rest of her body, which hurt a lot too. She heard her parents and Joey in the room, but when she tried to look again, she could see only their outlines against the glare.

"It's so bright, Mama," Aletta said. "I can't see so good."

Her daddy and Joey moved to her and greeted her loudly, but Aletta still heard her mama's intake of breath, then her shoes on the floor as she ran down the hall.

Moments later, she came back with a gray-haired doctor with no lips and a pointy chin. He came over and put his hand on Aletta's arm.

"I'm Dr. Foster. I'm going to check your eyes, all right?" He shone a light into each of Aletta's eyes, and asked her to look left, right, up, down.

"As I thought," he said afterwards, "she's had a pretty bad concussion to the head. One of the standard symptoms is a sensitivity to light. That normally goes away within two to three weeks, if not sooner. We'll keep an eye on her."

"Doctor? What's a concussion mean?" Nadine asked, kneading the handkerchief she held in her hands.

"It means she bonked her head," he said, smiling.

Aletta stayed in the hospital for two days. She told them about Johnny, and Clovis almost let Joey talk him into going to find him themselves. Instead, he called the sheriff, who picked Johnny up at the Red Dog Saloon just outside of town the next day.

He was banged up and bruised and said he thought he had a broken rib because he couldn't breathe without it hurting like hell, but he was standing and drinking. He'd had some of his drinking buddies go out and pull his truck out of the ditch for him. It was still running somehow.

When they thought she was asleep, Aletta heard her mama and daddy talking about how it was a miracle she'd gone off the road just where the hay was dumped.

The doctor told them that that and the gypsies most likely saved her life. As soon as they had a chance, Clovis and Joey drove out to the shack to thank the gypsies, but there wasn't a sign they'd ever even been there.

Clovis went to the sheriff's office to see Johnny alone. Joey wanted to come, but Clovis knew there'd be nothing but trouble, so he refused.

"We've charged him with kidnapping and drunk driving, but he says your girl was stuck in the mud, and he was just tryin' to do a good deed and give her a ride home," Sheriff Calmus, a man who looked tougher than he was, said.

Clovis sat at his desk in his overalls, sipping coffee from a tin cup.

Sheriff Calmus rolled his eyes a little. "He swears he wasn't drinkin'. Says they just slid off the road 'cause of the mud."

Clovis put down the cup and looked hard at the sheriff. "He's lying."

Calmus lifted his palms to the ceiling. "I believe you, but that's gonna be up to the judge, Clovis."

Johnny's lawyer was a smart young man in his first year as public defender with his eyes on much greater things. During the trial, he explained that Johnny had accidentally missed the turn to the Jacobs place and was looking for somewhere to turn around where he wouldn't get stuck when he lost control of the truck because of the treacherous roads.

There was no way to prove he'd been drinking or that he'd touched the girl. Clovis Jacobs was out to ruin his life and had already shut down any opportunity for employment in the entire county for him. Mr. Redding was actually a good Samaritan with some bad luck on some very slippery roads, and we've all had that experience, haven't we?

Her lawyer, an older man who seemed a little unsure of himself, called Aletta to the stand to testify against Johnny. Her daddy told her to just tell the truth, but she was nervous just the same. All these big people watching her and listening to everything she said, and that lady writing it all down on that machine. It was scary.

"Can you tell us what happened the day of the wreck, Miss Honor?" the lawyer asked. His voice sounded kind, so she felt a little better.

She told the whole story just like she remembered, all except the vision she'd had, of course. Then Johnny's lawyer got up to ask her questions.

He asked her about getting stuck in the mud and said that must've been scary, standing out there all alone like that.

"It wasn't so bad," Aletta replied. "There was rabbits comin' out and hoppin' over the snow, so they kept me company."

Everyone in the courtroom smiled and Uncle Joey laughed, and that calmed Aletta down more. She told again how Johnny picked her up and was drinking and mean and how he grabbed her and they crashed.

When she finished, the lawyer took off his jacket and rolled up his shirtsleeves. "You remember how you swore you'd tell the truth, don't you, sweetheart?" he asked, his voice gentle.

Aletta shifted in the chair and glanced at the silver-haired judge. He had hair growing out of his nose. She almost smiled until she remembered the question. "Yes, sir," she said.

The lawyer bent close and looked at her with his cloudy blue eyes. "Is it true you see dead people in your room at night?"

The courtroom stirred and she saw the dark looks on the faces of her parents.

Joey put his hands to his lips like he was starting to pray.

The assistant district attorney slammed his hand on the table where he sat next to her daddy. "Objection!" he yelled.

"Trying to establish credibility of the witness's testimony, Your Honor," the defender said.

"It's a strange question, but you must have some reason for it. I'll allow it," the judge said, and looked back at Aletta expectantly. She tried hard to understand what the man meant about credibility, but she didn't know that word.

"Answer the question, please, Miss Jacobs," the judge said.

He seemed so stern, and she was scared again, really scared. If she lied, she'd probably go to jail. Her daddy told her to tell the truth. What was wrong with it, anyway?

"They're my friends," Aletta said finally.

"Who're your friends?" the lawyer asked, his voice still calm and friendly.

"They visit me at night, but they're real nice. They just like to talk mostly. Miss Maple tells me about her children. She had fourteen," Aletta answered. They had to know it was true.

"And these people are dead? They're ghosts?"

"I guess so. I don't know where they come from." Aletta shrugged.

Nadine started to cry.

Aletta felt her stomach turn on her. She wished she'd lied to the man, even if it meant she'd sinned against Jesus, let alone broke the law.

It took three weeks to get to trial and one day for the trial itself. Johnny Redding was out free and clear within a month of the crash.

* * *

The farmhouse was quiet for weeks after the trial. Nadine hardly spoke, and none of them talked about Aletta's testimony.

Aletta felt she'd done something terribly wrong but didn't know how to make up for it. She knew for certain she didn't want any more visitors, though.

One Sunday, Nadine didn't want to go to church, so Uncle Joey took Aletta with him to look at a used Ford truck Milt Rumph had for sale.

"Can't be relyin' on that old work truck no more. It's broke down most the time, and I got responsibilities now," he said.

They pulled onto the Rumph homestead, which everyone knew Evie Bowden Rumph's family had claimed in the land rush. Aletta thought the big two-story farmhouse looked tired and run-down, just like Mrs. Rumph. Old, rusted farm equipment lay around looking like carcasses that had fallen down dead and had never been moved. Children ran around everywhere.

"Go on and play with the kids, but no horseplay. Your bone's still healin'," Joey said as he turned off the old truck.

As soon as she saw Joey shake hands with Mr. Rumph, she took her sling off, left it on the ground near a water trough, and ran to the barn. Her shoulder barely hurt anymore, and she wanted to play after being cooped up in the house for so long.

Six or seven children ran around shooting at one another with homemade wooden guns. They all had yellow hair and wore threadbare clothes that had been handed down from one to the next. Their faces and hands were smeared with grime. Aletta knew her mama would never let her stay that dirty.

"Hey, it's Aletta," yelled seven-year-old Imajean.

"Whatcha playin'?" Aletta asked.

"Cowboys and Indians," she answered.

"Can I play?"

Curtis stepped toward her. At twelve, he was the oldest, and he was tough. Aletta didn't like him.

"No," he said. "You're a witch. You see ghosts."

"I'm not a witch!" Aletta yelled.

"Yeah, let her play! She can be the Indian! Nobody else wants to be!" his younger brother Bucky screamed at the top of his lungs. He seemed like a wild animal to Aletta. Unlike Curtis, whose hair was buzzed into a crew cut, Bucky's hair was a shaggy mess.

Curtis's eyes lit up at this idea. "You better run, Indian!" he yelled at her. His face looked so mean that she decided to do what he said.

Aletta ran outside looking for Joey, but the pack of kids was right on her heels. She raced past the truck to the other side of the house where she'd seen him and Mr. Rumph go, but there was nobody there. She became terrified then and felt as if she were running for her life.

"Get her!"

"Grab her hair, Curtis!"

They were gaining ground, their feet pounding the dirt as they raced after her. As she turned to the back of the house, the Rumphs' German shepherd started barking and chasing her too.

As she fled, her heart beating wildly, she thought for a split second about Isabella. Finally Curtis caught her and grabbed her from behind, and she fell onto the ground.

"Take the Indian witch to the barn," he said in a deep voice, holding her to the ground.

Aletta looked at Imajean, hoping she'd help her, but she just grabbed Aletta's arm and helped pull her to her feet. "Indian witch, Indian witch," Imajean chanted with her siblings.

In the barn, Curtis held her while Bucky tied rope around her wrists and ankles.

"This is a dangerous Indian, cowboys and cowgirls. Be careful," Curtis said.

Aletta refused to cry, but inside she was dying and her shoulder hurt bad, especially when they pulled her hands behind her back to tie them. After fighting about how they were going to punish the Indian witch, they decided that she should be pushed from the loft onto the hay below, but then there was the matter of getting her up there with her hands and feet tied.

As they haggled about how to do that, Mr. Rumph and Joey walked into the barn. Joey's expression went from dark to enraged.

He covered the ground between him and Aletta in three strides. "What the hell're you doing?! Get your hands off her!"

"You said she's a witch, Daddy!" Bucky yelled.

"Shut up!" Aletta screamed. "I am not!"

Joey took his pocketknife out of his jeans and cut the rope that bound her hands together. He escorted Aletta out of the barn, not even glancing at Milt Rumph. He didn't say a word to her as the truck screamed down the dirt road, dust flying out behind them in a cloud.

Aletta thought he might be mad at her.

He jerked the truck to a stop and ran up the steps into the house.

Aletta ran after him, scared.

Inside, he faced Clovis and Nadine, who sat on the couch drinking coffee. He was breathing hard and the veins stood out in his neck.

"Rumph told me Johnny's braggin' to everyone about how he beat Clovis Jacobs and his . . ." he stopped and glanced at Aletta, "daughter. Then I go to find her, and all those Rumph brats have her tied up calling her a witch."

Clovis stood up, the muscles in his jaw working fast. "Tied up?" he asked so quietly that it was only by reading his lips Aletta knew what he said.

Joey set his feet wider apart. "I'm goin' to find Johnny, Clovis."

Nadine stood up and looked at Clovis. "Back when my daddy settled this land, there wasn't no law, so the men'd go and enforce justice. They had to." Her eyes were narrow and hard.

Clovis bent his head and hooked his thumbs in the loops of his overalls. The room was quiet except for the ticking of the old grandfather clock. Finally he sighed and walked to the door.

"Let's go get him," he said, taking his hat off the hook.

"Daddy!" Aletta pleaded as the men walked onto the porch. "I don't want you to go!"

He turned to her before getting into the truck. "Don't worry, Lettie. We'll be back."

Joey got in the truck and slammed the door. His mouth was set in anger, but she could still see the love for her in his eyes when he looked back. Aletta turned to her mother as they drove away, but Nadine was already inside the house.

★

Tears streamed down Aletta's face and glinted in the light of the fire as she told Jerry how Clovis and Joey had driven to two other beer joints on the way to the Red Dog Saloon, but they found Johnny at his favorite.

He was in a dangerous part of the day. He'd had enough booze to make him full of the false courage and rage that came as part of his addiction to the drink, but not so far gone yet that he couldn't cause trouble.

Joey and Clovis walked into the bar and told him to come outside.

Johnny laughed. "That's just like you, Jacobs, but you forgot one thing. You ain't my boss!" he bellowed, and hit his chest with his fist. "You can't tell me what to do!"

Joey grabbed him by the collar and pushed him outside in front of them. Several of the men followed to watch.

Joey released his hold on Johnny and stood next to his brother-in-law, his arms crossed in front of him.

"Listen, Johnny." Clovis cleared his throat before he went on. "I know you've had some hard times, but I can't have you going around . . ."

Johnny reached behind him, pulled out the .38 revolver he had tucked in his pants, and casually shot them both in the chest.

It was so casual, so easy, the way he did it, the witnesses said later, that they had no idea what he was doing until after it was over.

Two policemen came and escorted Johnny away, just like Aletta had seen in her vision.

★

Aletta finished her story, but before Jerry could say anything, she jumped to her feet and was gone, running as fast as she could out of the clearing. He called to her, but she heard nothing but the voices in her head—her mama's *Come on down to dinner,* Uncle Joey singing, her daddy's laugh. The voices pushed her on. She wanted to outrun them or catch up to them and hold on, she didn't know which. All she knew was that whatever was inside her couldn't be still anymore.

She slogged through the mud at the gate, slipping but still on her feet, still running. She ran like she had when she fled the Rumph kids, faster than she thought was possible.

Jerry ran after her, his sandals flying off his feet after only a few strides. It was a ghostly vision, a dark figure, hair flying wildly behind, followed by a white flowing robe, with the moon adding its own touch of shadow and light to the chase. After crashing into the woods and stumbling over fallen trees and branches, Aletta finally tripped over a tree root and fell gasping to the ground, her hands clutching the earth.

Jerry heard her deep breathing before he could see her lying on the ground in the darkness. He approached her slowly, then bent over her and stroked her hair.

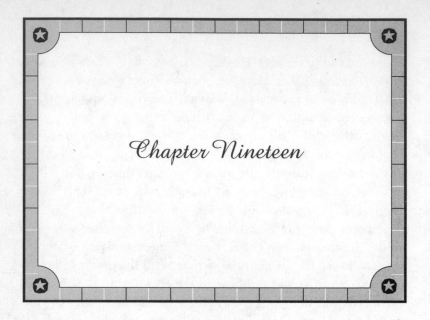

Chapter Nineteen

In Aletta's dream, Isabella walked to each of the women sitting and standing around the room, which was lit by a single candle. They all had dead eyes or wild eyes or eyes closed tightly to the world. She touched them one by one, trying to cut through the fear that hung like smoke in the room. There was a noise and the sound of righteous anger trampling above their heads. Isabella blew out the candle.

Aletta woke up with a start from the dream and lay unmoving for several minutes, unsure if the world around her was real or if she was someone else entirely. Finally, she looked at the clock. It read 8:45. She remembered she'd promised to go to her mother's church this morning for the play. She jumped out of bed, but her legs hurt with every step she took, from running so hard last night. She hobbled to the bathroom, looking at her hands, which were scraped up from falling. *My God*, she thought, *I've lost my mind*.

She hoped Jerry had gotten on a plane to San Francisco already so she wouldn't have to face him, but when she rushed into the kitchen after throwing on some clothes, he stood there wearing a pair of Jimmy's jeans and a white T-shirt, coffee already brewed.

Compared to the ashram outfit, he looked sexy. The thought that she'd had a man spend the night in her house, even if it was on the couch, caused her to pause for a moment. It felt good, like a big step toward freedom from Jimmy, but she felt ashamed too, a product of the nice-girl training she'd gotten from the world her whole life.

"I've gotta go," she said. "I'm sorry. You can't stay here."

His smile faded.

"You look great, by the way," she added quickly.

He padded over to her in his bare feet. "I hope you don't mind I took a shower. I can't tell you how many cow patties I walked through carrying you back to the car. I found these in a laundry basket out in the garage."

She smiled and looked down, embarrassed. "Keep them, and I'm sorry about all that," she said. "I don't know what got into me."

He took her shoulders until she looked up at him. "Don't be sorry. That was one of the bravest things I've ever seen, you telling that story, not to mention how you've lived through it," he said, and kissed her on the mouth. "You're incredible." He led her to the door and gently pushed her outside, handing her the car keys that he pulled from his pocket.

"I'll be gone when you get back," he said, and closed the door.

She walked to the car, then turned around and tapped on the kitchen window with her keys. Jerry looked up from rinsing his coffee cup.

"Thank you," she mouthed.

He put his hands together at his chest, bowed slightly, and smiled.

Her mind was actually calm as she drove to the church, and she felt lighter. Somehow, telling her story had released something from her, something she'd been carrying around a long time. Now she wanted to talk to her mama.

She followed the seven-story-high cross that stood on the

prairie in front of the huge brick building that was the Burning Bush Battle Church, daring sinners to just try to get out of the shadow of the Lord's judgment. The cross could be seen for miles in every direction. Some of the people in town had fought the cross going up because they said it was garish, not to mention rude to people of other faiths.

"What if someone decided to put up a seven-story Star of David?" Janelle McIntosh, the high school English teacher, asked at a town meeting. Her query raised more than one eyebrow in the place, that's for darn sure. Didn't matter though, because the old anti-Christian argument was dusted off and wielded by the church to perfection. Nobody with any power wanted to lose it by being labeled anti-Christian, so the church got its pet project and celebrated a victory for Jesus.

The church parking lot was almost full, so Aletta parked on the street and rushed through the cars and across the blacktop that was so hot it felt soft. Inside the cool, blue-shag-carpeted lobby, she did a double take when she saw the white horse with a gold saddle standing in a corner, but she didn't have time to ask questions.

She opened the big door to the sanctuary and guessed there must be at least five hundred people inside. The sanctuary seemed heavy with a somber air. That and the *shush* of whispering made her slow down a step or two as she searched to find her mother and children. She found them sitting in the center of the middle set of pews and climbed over several people to sit down next to Sissy.

Nadine glared at her. "You missed the opening prayer," she said in more of a hiss than a whisper.

"I'm sorry," Aletta said as she patted each of her children. "I need to talk to you, Mama."

The kids smiled at her with teeth red from Jolly Ranchers. Her mama had been plying them with candy.

"Well, not now," Nadine said.

"But later? It's important." She looked at her mother and felt a little crack in the calloused shell Aletta had formed over her heart.

"Fine, just shush now," Nadine said, then waved at Odiemae Sharp, who was sitting a few pews in front of them.

Aletta took the baby from Sissy and held his warm softness close to her. He snuggled his face into the crook of her neck. The kids were fidgeting already. When the lights went down and the crowd stirred, Reverend Taylor, who looked to have never missed the opportunity to share in God's abundance at the table, walked out on stage wearing a black robe.

"And I heard a great voice out of heaven saying, Behold, the tabernacle of God is with men, and He will dwell with them, and they shall be His people, and God Himself shall be with them and be their God," he bellowed in his most preachery voice. "But the fearful, and unbelieving, and the abominable, and sorcerers, and idolaters, and all liars shall have their part in the lake which burneth with fire and brimstone: which is the second death!"

He pointed to the back of the sanctuary at the end of the center aisle, and everyone turned to see a spotlight illuminate six children dressed in tight red bodysuits. They had red painted faces and horns on their heads. The little devils began to make hissing and screaming sounds, writhing and cackling, loud enough that several babies started to cry. But even as they ran down the aisles toward the stage, Gyp stayed quiet.

Aletta was so surprised at the spectacle she said, "Well, Lord above," out loud.

Several people moved onto the stage in the darkness and stood in three different areas. The six demons ran up the steps and onto the stage, and as they slinked their way to the first group on the right of the stage, a spotlight lit up the scene.

A woman dressed like a prostitute in fishnets, miniskirt, and a feather boa drank out of a martini glass and stumbled around like she'd downed the whole bottle. She gave the glass to a man in a business suit. He pushed it away at first, but then, when she insisted, he took it and drank. Right away, he began to stumble around the stage and hang all over the woman. The little devils ran around and around them until the stage floor opened and out crawled a much larger devil with huge horns, claws, a pointy beard, and a roll around his middle that his tight red bodysuit was ill-equipped to conceal. He stomped over to the prostitute and the man, grabbed them, and pushed them into the hole in the stage, laughing loudly.

Reverend Taylor's voice blared out of nowhere. "Whore-mongers!"

Aletta shifted in her pew and looked at her children, who stared with enormous eyes, especially Randy, who seemed to have stopped in mid-fidget and was riveted to the stage, his mouth wide open. She saw her mother look at her out of the corner of her eye but never turn to meet her gaze straight on.

Next the spotlight lit up a scene of a very pregnant woman in a hospital gown. She lay on a table while a doctor in a white coat stood at the end of the table with some type of machine next to him. He turned it on, and it made a loud roaring sound. He looked to be doing something to the woman with a long hose, but his body blocked Aletta's view. He turned off the machine, then turned around and held up a baby doll inside a large glass jar. Once again the stage opened up and the big devil crawled out of the hole and took the sinners down with him.

"Murderers!" the voice echoed through the huge room.

Now Aletta sat on the edge of the pew. She chewed on one of her fingernails and glanced around to see if anyone else was uncomfortable.

The spotlight swept across the stage and settled on the final scene. A woman and a man sat at a small table. The woman wore a shawl over her head and a long flowing dress. Once again, the man was in a suit and tie. In the middle of the table sat a large crystal ball, which the woman stared into and caressed with her hands.

Aletta breathed in sharply and looked at her mother, but Nadine's eyes were fixed on the stage now.

The woman took the man's hand and looked at his palm. She started gesturing wildly with her arms and cackling loudly. Once again, the little devils circled them until the big devil came out and dragged them down into the hole in the stage. The little devils followed them down, the last one holding the crystal ball over his head before he jumped in.

"Sorcerers!" Reverend Taylor's voice boomed out.

Aletta stood up. "Sissy, Ruby, Randy, get up. We're leaving right now." Shocked out of their trancelike state, the kids stood up behind her. Gyp started whimpering as Aletta roughly stumbled over people on her way to the aisle, her children following along behind.

The entire congregation turned to look at the commotion. Even Reverend Taylor looked out from backstage to see who was causing such a disturbance. They reached the aisle and Aletta practically ran up it to the sanctuary door. Just as she arrived, the door opened and the enormous white horse stood squarely in the doorway, blocking their exit.

A pretty girl about Sissy's age with long blond hair and a white flowing gown sat sidesaddle on top. The horse backed away nervously at the sight of Aletta and her brood charging at him. The girl's face turned scared and ruined the angelic expression her mother had just coached her into.

Aletta took Ruby's shoulder and kept her close with one hand while holding Gyp to her with the other. "Let's go around this way," she said, deciding there was enough room to get around the horse.

Just then, the spotlight caught the horse and the organist hit a chord that vibrated every pew in the house. Gyp had finally had enough and let out a siren blast of a cry. Simultaneously, the stage lit up and Jesus began descending from above, his arms opened wide.

"You're too damn early!" Reverend Taylor whispered without covering his microphone, and laughter scattered through the congregation.

The organist hit another chord as Aletta squeezed past the jittery horse, Gyp bawling in her arms. In spite of the horse's owner pushing on his haunches to get him to go into the sanctuary, the horse backed out of the doorway and knocked Aletta against the wall. Once in the lobby, the huge animal spun around, snorting and flaring his nostrils.

"Help!" the girl screamed, a look of sheer terror on her face.

"Bonnie!" Her mother ran at the frightened animal, which didn't help matters one bit. The horse wheeled around toward the woman, who wore high heels and a bonnet. That scared her out of her bravery and caused her to stumble backwards in a long, slow-motion fight against falling right on her rear. She lost.

Ruby and Randy started laughing so hard that Randy spotted his Sunday pants.

The cowboy who owned the horse kept trying to grab the reins. "Whoa there. Whoa boy," he said.

After making sure Gyp was okay, Aletta looked at Sissy. "Sissy, get her," Aletta whispered, nodding to Ruby. Aletta grabbed Randy's hand and had to drag him out the door while Sissy pulled on Ruby. They escaped into the bright, hot sunshine.

"Thank God!" Aletta cried, and they ran to the car.

"Mama, I can't believe you did that," Sissy said as she sat in the passenger seat trying to quiet Gyp as Aletta sped away.

Aletta threw her hands over her head, releasing the steering wheel for a moment. "I was just tryin' to leave. Who knew there'd be a farm animal the size of a truck blockin' the way?"

Randy laughed. "That lady fell on her butt."

"And that girl looked scared clear out of her wits," Ruby said, laughing with him.

Sissy joined in, and then Aletta.

"Oh, my," Aletta said, as she wiped her eyes from laughing so hard. "Oh, my."

When Aletta pulled into their driveway, the laughter finally died down. "Listen, I don't want y'all to pay attention to that play or anything your grandma Nadine says about the Devil or about anybody bein' sinners, you hear me?"

"That was a psychic lady like you up there, wasn't it Mama?" Randy asked.

She turned the engine off and looked from one of her children to the next as she spoke. "I want y'all to know this right now. I am not a sinner. I'm a child of God and so are you." As she said this, it felt like warm liquid was melting over her heart. "Those people are just scared and mean."

"You think we're gonna get in trouble?" Sissy asked, kissing Gyp on the forehead.

"What for? They had no business having that animal runnin' around indoors with some city girl sittin' on top. It was an accident waitin' to happen," Aletta said.

"It sure was when *we* showed up," Sissy said.

Aletta put her head on the steering wheel, rocking it back and forth. "Oh, my," she said again. "Oh, my."

They found out later that the thirteen-year-old girl on the horse was supposed to represent the church as the virginal bride of Jesus. She was supposed to ride down to the stage where Jesus would lift her off the horse. Then they would take part in a wedding ceremony.

As it turned out, the cowboy finally got the horse calmed down enough to get her off, and her mother shoved her into the sanctuary. She wobbled to the stage on foot, trying her best to look beatific under the circumstances.

At home, Aletta put Gyp down for a nap and went to bed, feeling flat worn out. Her eyes had closed for just a moment when she saw her mother on their front porch at the farm.

★

Nadine went out on the porch when she heard a vehicle coming up the road. She looked relieved as she watched for Clovis's pickup truck. Then she saw Sheriff Calmus's police car. It turned in to the long dirt driveway and pulled up in front of the house.

Aletta walked out onto the porch and joined her.

"Get back inside." Her mama's voice was stern, but it quivered and sounded high and thin. Aletta watched through the screen door as the sheriff walked up the steps with his hat in his hand. He ran his fingers over his crew cut.

"I thought I better come on out here myself, Mrs. Jacobs," he said.

Aletta couldn't really remember much after that. She remembered her mother crumpled on the front porch at the sheriff's feet. She felt the numbness inside that held her for months afterwards as family members from all over came to their home and women cooked more food than the whole county could eat.

Johnny Redding was convicted and sentenced to die in the electric chair, which wouldn't happen for more than two years. It was after everyone left, though, that her mother began to read the Bible and to talk about Satan as if he were standing right in the room with them.

"Listen to this." She called Aletta over to her as she read from her Bible while sitting with the curtains drawn, the darkness curling around her. She was especially fond of Revelations. "And I heard a voice from heaven saying, 'Write this: Blessed are the dead who die in the Lord henceforth." She looked up at Aletta, her eyes ringed with red. "Do you think they're in heaven?"

Aletta held her hands together, her arms twisted around each other. "Yes, Mama." She wanted her mama to stop now, to be her old self and take care of her. She needed to be taken care of. Her daddy and Joey were gone. She didn't understand it, and it hurt inside more than anything, more than the wreck with Johnny, more than on the witness stand.

"But what if Satan was punishing us for our sins? For the demons that have overtaken my sweet little baby?" asked Nadine, her face looking as if whatever was holding it together had loosened somehow and everything had been rearranged slightly differently.

"What demons, Mama?" Aletta ran to her room before she got an answer, frightened to be alone and frightened to be with her mother talking about demons.

The night before they moved to the small house in town, Aletta sat on the floor, rolling her crystal snowball around her with her left hand, then catching it behind her back with her right and rolling it around in front of her again. Her mama was on top of her before she knew what was happening.

"Give me that!" Nadine yelled and grabbed Aletta by the arm, but Aletta held tight to the ball. Nadine finally pried it from her fingers.

"The Devil's toy!" her mama raved. "I should've never let it into this Christian home!"

She ran down the stairs, her hair loose and wild, her feet pounding mean and hard on the wooden steps.

Aletta ran after her.

Nadine flung open the front door and ran down the porch steps and around to the side of the house. As Aletta rounded the corner of the house, she saw her mother at the old well. Nadine held the crystal ball up in a clawlike hand, the moonlight catching it just before she threw it into the open mouth of the well.

Nadine started going to the Sermon on the Mount Baptist Church after they moved to town, and didn't switch to Reverend Taylor's Burning Bush Battle Church until after Aletta and Jimmy were married. Throughout Aletta's teen years, Nadine became less erratic but more rigid. Aletta stopped telling her anything she did with her friends, whether it was a dance, a party, a movie, or trying out for pep club.

"Are you against havin' fun in general, Mama?" Aletta asked her more than once.

She stayed out of the house at Shirl's and Nancy's as much as she could, in part because she couldn't look at her mother without thinking of her daddy and Joey. She would see it in her mama's face sometimes when her gaze met Aletta's, the flicker of a memory. Then a shadow would fall over Nadine's eyes, and Aletta would head for the door.

She didn't have any more night visitors after the sheriff came over that day. She felt like she just pulled shut the window inside her heart that allowed them to come and go. But the images when she touched people got stronger as she got older, and she made certain never to talk to anyone, including herself, about what she would see.

She became very good at pushing them aside like swiping away a fly, and she avoided touching people as much as she could.

★

When she woke up from her nap, Aletta heard music playing and her children's voices singing loudly above it.

Ruby and Randy sang "I Am Woman" with Helen Reddy, taking turns with and then sharing the microphone—Sissy's baton.

"Where's Gyp?" Aletta asked, turning the volume down.

"Mo-ommm!" Randy yelled.

"Right there," Ruby said, pointing to the baby, who lay in his playpen. She grabbed the mike from Randy.

Aletta picked Gyp up. "Did your grandma call?"

Randy spun around on his toes. "Nope."

She was relieved and disappointed at the same time. "Where's Sissy?"

"Mama, can't you see we're in the middle of a show? She's in her room," Ruby said.

"Yeah, with Rusty," Randy said.

Aletta put the baby back down, went to Sissy's room, and opened the door. Rusty was lying on the bed looking at a *Mad* magazine and Sissy was bent over in the closet picking out shoes.

"Gyod, Mama, ever heard of knockin'?" Sissy complained.

"Hi, Mrs. Honor," Rusty said, standing up.

"Hi, Rusty. How's it feel to have a shrine dedicated to you?" asked Aletta. Sissy's room was covered with RC Cola paraphernalia and advertisements. RC pop cans lined the windowsills. Everywhere you looked, you saw the letters RC. She'd even bought a hat made out of RC cans at the state fair.

He smiled and looked around. "It's beautiful, don't you think?"

"Oh, sure. What I don't think's beautiful is a boy in my daughter's bedroom." She paused, then gave Sissy the look, the one without any hint of compromise. "Sissy, no more."

"But they were singin' so loud, we couldn't even . . ." Sissy protested.

"No more, and that's final," Aletta said, and looked at Rusty expectantly, opening the door wider.

"I don't bite," he said playfully as he walked past her.

"Well, I do," she answered.

Chapter Twenty

In spite of the fiasco at the church, Aletta had her best run of business ever that week. Several out-of-towners and travelers stopped in, and the locals seemed to be getting wind of her talent, mainly through the public broadcast system that was Joy's Femme Coiffures.

To Aletta, it didn't seem a coincidence that her life got better after she told Jerry her story. It had been the hardest thing she'd ever done, but she felt different somehow—better. *Maybe I can be happy now,* she thought, but something nagged at her still. She decided not to try to figure it out, though. It was enough for now, and besides, she was too busy. She stayed occupied by telling her customers all about their loves, losses, jobs, homes, children, secrets, and wishes.

Jerry came to say good-bye wearing his robes again, and she gave him a free reading that confirmed what she'd said before. She also added that he and his wife would start some kind of center in Mallin County.

"Mallin?" he asked. "Do you mean Marin?"

"Could be, yes," she said, and he hugged her tight.

Her mother never called, and even though she was still angry as hell about the ambush at the church, the kids needed their stuff back, so Aletta finally had to pick up the phone. She started doodling on the back of a water bill, a nervous habit she had when she was on the phone, as soon as she heard the ringing.

"You can come by later today, but I won't be here. Just get the stuff off the porch," Nadine said coldly.

"I'm sorry about Sunday, Mama, but I don't know what possessed you to think I'd sit through that," Aletta said, mad at herself for apologizing as soon as the words left her lips. She drew a smiley face but gave it wild, spiky hair.

"I thought you might learn somethin', but I shoulda known better. It's outta my hands now," she said.

Aletta's pen stopped. "What's outta your hands?"

Nadine paused for several moments before answering.

"I'll leave the things outside for you."

"Fine," Aletta said and slammed the phone down. She wadded up the bill she'd been drawing on and threw it at the overflowing trash can. Then she realized the bill inside hadn't been paid and picked it up off the ground.

On Saturday, Eugene called to see if he could take her and the kids out for an ice cream cone that afternoon. He stayed at the house into the early evening, and they talked on the porch swing out back for a while. Aletta told him a little bit about what had happened to her in the last weeks, and he just listened. When she told him about the church play, he roared with laughter.

Aletta smiled. "My lands, I almost forgot what it felt like to just visit and not be cookin' or cleanin' or workin' somehow."

Aletta went to sleep that night worrying about the court date she had the following week for the divorce. She was sleeping hard, the kind of sleep that felt like she was on the bottom of a dark, warm lake covered with mud, when Jimmy threw the bedroom door open and stood in the doorway, swaying back and forth.

From the bottom of the lake, she came up for air and gasped loudly, her heart pounding. "My God, Jimmy, you scared me to death!"

"Well, you're killin' me, so I guess we're even," he said.

She got out of bed instinctively, like a trapped animal, not wanting to get stuck in the room with him.

The kids' doors opened one by one. They gathered silently behind their father in the hallway, looking sleepy and afraid.

"You kids go back to bed," Aletta said, her voice filled with sleep and fear. "It'll be all right."

But inside she was scared and wanted them there. They all followed her into the kitchen, and she saw that it was just after two o'clock in the morning. The bars must have closed.

"You're scarin' us all, Jimmy. Please go," she said, crossing her arms tightly in front of her, her blue nightgown too thin for protection.

"Goddammit!" he screamed and banged his open hand on the countertop. "These are my kids. I want to see my kids!"

"Daddy, we'll go with you tomorrow!" Sissy cried.

Ruby twisted her Underdog nightshirt in her hands. "Please don't hurt Mama!"

Randy just cried silent tears.

"*She's* hurtin' *me*! *She's* the one hurtin' *me*!" Jimmy roared.

Aletta flashed on sitting in Johnny Redding's pickup truck and him screaming how Clovis had hurt him so much. She opened the kitchen cabinet behind her and pulled out a huge black cast-iron skillet, the one her mama used to fry chicken for all the farmhands. Aletta held it by the handle in both hands and raised it over her shoulder.

"He was crazy just like you," she said, looking Jimmy right in the eye. "He thought it was my daddy makin' his life bad, but it was his own weakness."

Jimmy laughed a little and waved his hand in front of her face. "What you gonna do with that pan?"

"Daddy, don't," Sissy said.

Aletta could see Johnny's smiling face after the judge threw out the case because of her testimony. "You know what I just realized?" She gripped the handle of the skillet tighter and glared at Jimmy. "I stayed with you to punish myself."

The night was dead outside, and the silence seemed like a threat as they stood there waiting for something bad to happen.

Just then, there was a light knock on the front door. In walked Kathy Kokin wearing the tightest pair of jeans Aletta had ever seen. Her high-heeled cowboy boots made her walk seem more like a strut, and her low-cut ruffled blouse showed off her cleavage. As she approached, smells came with her—a barroom blend of cigarette smoke, booze, and that ever-present perfume she wore.

"Sorry for just bargin' in," she said airily.

Aletta could tell that she and Jimmy had been out together. "You get the hell out of my house! How dare you come over here?!" she yelled, still wielding the skillet.

"Just came to get somethin', then I'll be on my way, Sugar," Kathy said, as casually as if she'd forgotten her purse earlier in the day and had come back to fetch it.

Kathy walked to Jimmy, put her hand around his arm, and whispered in his ear. He grumbled like a sleeping bear, then allowed her to escort him out of the house. She pulled the door closed behind them. Sissy ran over and locked it, even though they all knew it would never stop Jimmy if he wanted in.

Aletta stood there shaking. That Jimmy and Kathy would just walk into her home without hesitation made her feel so violated. It ate her alive that she couldn't protect herself or her children. But one thing started getting real clear. She didn't need Jimmy Honor.

They woke up late the next morning, too late to get to church. Aletta wouldn't have made them go after last night anyway. She herself felt too full of anger and hate to set foot into the house of the Lord.

She had no clue what to tell her children to make them less frightened or affected, so after they ate breakfast, she let them do whatever they wanted. Ruby went out to play ball with the kids on the street behind them, Randy went along because there was nothing on TV except church shows, and Sissy walked to Angie's house.

Aletta changed Gyp, who had blessedly let them sleep in this morning. Just as she put him in his little wind-up swing, she heard cars pulling up outside. She knew they weren't Joy's customers because Joy was closed on Sunday and Monday. She looked out the window and saw several men and women and even some children dressed in their church clothes getting out of cars and trucks carrying picket signs.

A rush of heat started at the top of her head and flowed downward. It felt like her feet melted right into the ground and stuck to it. The signs were about sinning and the devil's work. Charlie Leonard, the director of the church play, carried a sign that summed it all up: SINFUL PSYCHIC SORCERY IS NOT OKAY.

She forced herself from the window to the telephone, where she called Sissy and told her to get Randy and Ruby and take them to Angie's right now. She went out to the garage and threw old toys clear across it on her way to getting the two suitcases she'd taken to North Carolina with her when she was first married. She banged into walls and doorways with them as she charged into her kids' rooms, winding Gyp's swing back up on the way. She threw in clothes with a mother's clarity of what her children would and wouldn't wear even as her mind roared.

Bracing herself, she stalked out to the car in the driveway and loaded the suitcases, careful not to look at the protesters who were now circling in a tight formation in front of her house. She could see out of the corner of her eye that Reverend Taylor had shown up with his pale, sickly-looking wife and was grandly directing the proceedings.

"It's time we shut you down, Mrs. Honor!"

"This is a God-fearin' community, ma'am!"

They yelled at her, but she didn't look up once. Back inside, she picked up Gyp in one arm and his diaper bag in the other. She walked back outside, got in her car, and slammed it into what she thought was reverse, but when she hit the gas, it lurched forward, almost hitting the garage. Hot with humiliation, she ground the gearshift into reverse and sped backwards out of the driveway, causing a few of the parents to pull their children back in righteous indignation.

Aletta drove to Angie's and got her kids loaded up. She headed straight for the highway and Shirl's house in Elk City fifty miles away.

"The Burning Bush folks are tryin' to close down my business. I don't want y'all to have to go through this," she told them as she drove.

From behind her, Aletta heard sniffling, and she glanced over her shoulder to see Ruby holding Gyp tight to her chest. Tears ran out of her big green eyes onto Gyp's soft hair.

"Mama," Sissy said. "It feels like we're cursed."

Aletta thought for a moment about the benefits of running headlong off the highway and into a tree. It might be the best thing for all of them. The thought opened up all the hurt that was hiding under the red-hot anger at herself, her mama, God. When it came through, the hurt just had its own way with her, and she felt like she was cracking open like an egg.

She pulled off the highway onto a dirt road and stopped.

"Mama, where you goin'?" Randy asked.

"I'll be right back." She walked across the dry red dirt and looked out into a field, high with rows of corn. For a moment she could see her father walking the rows, checking the corn, as he used to when she was a child. The vision of her daddy somehow gave her heart permission to go on ahead and split in two, knocking her right to her knees. She hurt so bad she thought there was no way she'd survive it.

But the pain was like a bird that had at last been freed, flying out of its cage in a violent flapping of wings. Right on its heels, right out of the same place inside her heart that the hurt had just flown, came a glorious warmth that filled up her whole body and took her breath away.

She had no idea how long she stayed like that, kneeling in front of the cornfield as if praying to the stalks like gods. Finally, she felt a hand on her bowed head, seeming to anoint her with forgiveness.

"It's all right," she heard a voice say, and she opened her eyes to see a roly-poly making its way up and over and around clumps and clods of red dirt. It was beautiful. She picked up the roly-poly and laughed when it rolled into a perfect ball.

"Isn't it wonderful?" she asked, showing the insect to Sissy, who stood behind her with a hand on her head.

Sissy squatted next to her mother. "You want me to drive?"

They got to Shirl's slowly with Sissy behind the wheel. When they arrived, Shirl welcomed them in as if they'd planned this for months. She took a suitcase from the hatchback. "This is perfect timing, Lettie. The kids are at their grandparents' for a week before they go back to school."

"Thank you, Shirl. I don't know how I'll ever pay you back," Aletta said.

Tom sat in his Barcalounger watching a preseason Dallas Cowboys game with a cooler of Coors within arm's reach, so Shirl hustled the kids out back to admire the new above-ground pool.

"Mama, did you bring our bathin' suits?!" Ruby asked, wiping her nose with the back of her hand, her eyes red and puffy.

" 'Course I did, honey, now go on and play," Aletta said.

As soon as the kids were out of earshot, Shirl asked, "What you gonna do, hon? Maybe you should stay here, and this thing'll blow over." They watched Ruby and Randy take off their shoes and put their toes in the water.

Aletta leaned against the house wearily. "I don't know what I'm gonna do when I get there, but I know I have to go on back." She knew she had to face her life, not run from it or hide from the truth like she'd been doing for so long. She figured she'd rather take a trip to the shores of hell than go home, but right now she didn't have that option.

"I can't believe your mama. I oughta call her myself." Shirl was so mad she could barely hold it in, but she did because she knew it would only make things worse.

Aletta hugged each of her children twice and told them this was just like a vacation and they'd be back home in no time, then she got into the Pig Snout and drove away.

She got home to a deserted Main Street and a quiet house. It seemed like even her friends were keeping their distance. Joy was nowhere to be found, and the lights in her house were off. Aletta felt pretty sure she was avoiding her.

In the bathroom, the pill bottle with the little blue Valiums she'd saved for special occasions was right where she'd hidden it. Every single night lately had been a special occasion, it seemed, and she was very proud of herself that there were still three left. She popped one in her mouth and drank out of her hand from the faucet at the sink, then lit a cigarette and sat on the toilet lid smoking. Within an hour, she went to bed and fell sound asleep, earplugs in and fan blowing.

The dream seemed so real. She stood in the crowd and tried to see what was happening. She couldn't see well enough, so she began pushing her way through. When she saw Isabella, she tried to yell out or run to her, but couldn't move, couldn't speak. Isabella stood with her hands and feet bound to a post that was placed in the middle of a pile of split wood. An old man dressed in black robes came forward, and the people, who looked on with eyes entranced and scared, quieted down. He spoke loudly in a language Aletta didn't understand.

She looked around and saw that the people in the crowd were all carrying signs now, picket signs. When she looked back, the man in the black robes held a torch in his hand. He touched it to the firewood, which went up in a roar of flames. Aletta tried again to scream, but nothing came out. That's when Isabella looked straight at her, as if seeing her for the first time. And as the flames forked up around her face, she calmly smiled, her eyes sparkling with a knowledge that was far beyond the moment of her death.

Aletta woke up but lay in bed for a while, the images of the dream clear in her mind, Isabella's smile touching her heart. As soon as she got out of bed, she looked outside and saw that the protesters were already gathering again. Ten or twelve people, led by the Reverend and Mrs. Taylor, walked in a circle with their signs held high.

THIS IS A CHRISTIAN COMMUNITY
WE DO NOT APPROVE
HONK IF YOU'RE AGAINST WITCHCRAFT

Aletta went to the big stereo cabinet and dug out her Janis Joplin album from the bottom of the stack. She put it on, turned up the volume, and went to the bathroom to get ready. She washed her face and put on makeup, choosing her favorite lipstick, Peaches and Crème.

Aletta belted out the song at the top of her lungs with Janis, and something stirred inside her as she sang, something that felt like courage. She put on her pretty yellow sundress and sandals and turned off the stereo. She walked to the door and took a deep breath before opening it and going outside into the bright sun. People in passing cars slowed to look at the show, but only a few stopped to watch.

Monday morning, people are busy, thank God, Aletta thought.

It hadn't rained in over two months, and the grass under her thin sandals and the trees that lined Main Street seemed brittle and unbending, just like the protesters who stopped and stared. They looked at her as if she'd just strolled in from the Book of Revelations.

She walked straight over to Reverend Taylor, who had sweat beads on his large forehead and upper lip.

"Reverend Taylor," she said, and held out her hand, which he shook confidently. They stared at each other for a moment.

"Mrs. Honor," he said finally, nodding his head gravely, then dropped her hand.

Aletta planted her feet before she began. "I want y'all to know that I didn't mean to upset that horse, but I didn't agree with the message you were sendin' and chose to leave."

"The play is not why we're here," Taylor said.

"Even though that was about the rudest thing I ever saw," said an obese woman holding the hand of a little boy.

Just then, a pickup truck crammed full of teenagers pulled up. At least eight kids sat in the bed and three up front. Aletta recognized a few of the girls as Sissy's friends from school, and the boy who was driving lived one street away. Aletta knew he was a football player and played the drums because Sissy and her girlfriends talked about him all the time. They said he looked like Leif Garrett. The teenagers jumped out of the truck and stood quietly nearby.

"I think that's why you're here. That and my mother," Aletta said, returning her attention to the Reverend.

She looked away again when Joy and Earl pulled into their driveway. Joy's eyes were almost as big as her hair, and Aletta nearly laughed. Joy jumped out of the front seat of their camper truck and marched over. Earl followed a few paces behind.

"We went fishin' at Lake Murray for the weekend, and now what?" Joy asked.

Aletta looked over the group with her hands on her hips. "Burning Bush," she said flatly. "My mama's church."

Joy clapped a hand over her mouth. "Well, if that ain't a cold slap in the face."

"The reason we're here, Mrs. Honor, is *that*," Taylor said, pointing to the sign in her yard. "We are here doing the will of God, because whether you are aware of it or not, you are performing evil works which do not belong in a God-fearing community like the one in which we live. If one sinful business is allowed, it breeds others out of the same devilish cloth."

His parishioners chimed in with "That's right" and "Amen" and "Praise the Lord."

Joy stepped toward him. "This lady here's just tryin' to make a living off her God-given talent, which she has a right to do in this country last time I checked."

Some of the teenagers called out "Amen" and "That's right."

Aletta gave them a half-smile, and Joy winked. Just then, Rusty Conway pulled up with his mother, Betty. Eugene followed closely behind in his Mustang.

Behind them, on the street, Aletta saw Jimmy looking at her as he drove slowly by in a black Trans Am with a huge gold eagle on the hood. Her heart sank.

"Hi, Aletta," Betty Conway said as she walked across the grass eyeing Reverend Taylor. "I've been meanin' to call on you for a long time."

Eugene patted her on the back and Rusty smiled. "Mrs. Honor," he said.

The three of them stood behind Aletta and faced the Burning Bushes.

"I am surprised to see you here, Councilwoman," Taylor said, glaring at Betty.

"Just came to hang out with all you saints and sinners," Betty answered.

Aletta was filled with gratitude. The presence of her friends gave her the strength to gather herself and put Jimmy out of her mind.

"Reverend Taylor," Aletta said. "Do you believe drinking alcohol is a sin?"

He rolled up his shirtsleeves, looking like he was getting ready for a fight. "The Devil's brew, yes we do," he said, and a few of his people clapped.

"What about dancing?" she asked.

"Dancing is one step away from fornication," he bellowed.

The teenagers booed and sneered loudly.

"Well, Ernie's Polka Palace and the Red Dog Saloon have been open for years. I don't see y'all picketing over there," Aletta said, trying to make her voice even louder than his.

"Go home and leave her alone!" one of the teenage boys yelled at them.

Aletta remembered that his name was Jeff.

Taylor glanced at Jeff, then cleared his throat. "Those are not sins of the mind, Mrs. Honor, which brainwash people into serving the Devil," he finally answered.

"Have you ever spoken to one person who has come to Aletta, Reverend?" Joy asked.

"I've heard plenty," he said.

Betty Conway took a step forward. "Then you know she just helps people."

Aletta put a finger in the air. "The reason you're protesting me and not those other places is because you don't like me. I messed up your play, and my mama has convinced you I need a lesson. It's a personal attack."

"This is not personal," he said.

"Oh, yes it is, and that's what I intend to prove in court, and I'll be asking for damages not just from the church but from each of you personally. Hello, Odiemae Sharp," she said.

Odiemae, her mama's best friend, looked down at her feet. Aletta turned to go back in the house, but then turned back around again.

"And one more thing," she called. "Get off my grass!"

Joy, Earl, Rusty, Betty, and Eugene followed her inside.

"Y'all can't look at my house. I've been too busy for house cleanin', " Aletta said.

"Forget about the house. Did you see them?" Joy was peering out the window. "Did you see how they stepped back off the grass? My Lord, you sounded like a lawyer."

"I been talkin' to one way too much lately," she said. She walked back to the open front door. She saw the teenagers still standing around and the protesters marching, this time staying on the sidewalk.

"Jeff!" Aletta called through the screen door. "Y'all come on in!"

He broke out in a wide smile and trotted up the steps, followed by the others.

"Jeff, man, hey, thank y'all for comin', " Rusty said as they crowded into the living room.

"Where were you yesterday? I was tryin' to find you all day," Eugene asked Aletta.

"You were?" she asked, surprised. "I took the kids to Shirl and Tom's."

Betty approached Aletta and spoke softly. "Aletta, can we talk?"

Aletta took Betty back to Sissy's room, knowing it would be the neatest in the house. Betty looked around the room at the RC Cola stuff with a raised eyebrow until a look of understanding took over.

"Is this what I think it is?" she asked.

"Oh, yeah. I told Sissy she ought to have Crush cans too, 'cause that's surely what she has," Aletta said.

"No wonder Rusty's been so full of himself lately," Betty said, sitting down on the bed.

Aletta sat next to her. "He's a good kid."

"He's sure got some crazy ideas about things that Frank's havin' a tough time with. Me too, really."

"Isn't that all teenagers?" Aletta asked.

"I guess so," Betty answered, and then looked at Aletta with an intensity that made Aletta look away. "I'm sorry I didn't call on you after you helped me with my dad. I guess I was pretty embarrassed about the whole thing, but that doesn't mean you don't deserve a thank-you. So thank you."

Aletta started to tell her it was no big thing, but she stopped herself. "You're welcome," she said instead, feeling her face get hot.

"Now I have to say, hon, you've got yourself in a mess with these folks outside. I'm assuming you don't have a business license," Betty said.

Surprise took over Aletta's face. "A business license? Zelma Morgan doesn't need a business license for sewing for people out of her house. Why should I?"

"Because Zelma's an old lady darning kids' socks for a dollar! This is a tiny bit more visible, especially on Main Street."

"But they've left me alone up 'til now."

"They won't with those picketers out front. Reverend Glen Taylor can get what he wants by going that route too. You're operating a business without a license."

"My Lord, that's not what I wanted to hear," Aletta said, and stood up, starting to pace in front of the bed. "I go to court with Jimmy on Thursday, and I'm already scared to death about what this is gonna do to me and my kids."

Betty sighed. "I don't even know if this property is zoned commercial. It might cut off at Joy's place next door."

Aletta caught her image in the mirror on Sissy's dresser. She didn't like how worry looked on her at all. "My Lord, my Lord," she said.

"You do know I'm a member of the City Council, don't you?" Betty asked.

Aletta turned to her. "Of course, I've voted for you two or three times."

"Two times, and thank you. That makes this easier."

"What?"

"Have you ever heard of something called Wal-Mart?" Betty asked.

"No, I don't believe so," Aletta answered.

"You will. It's a gigantic national chain store that's trying to build right here in Okay, off I-40. Me and Jim Greenley have been fighting it because it'll be the end of most of the small businesses. Not psychic readings, though. They don't have that, I don't think," she said with a wry smile. "But I'm losing the battle, and I know it. I can lose it fast or I can make it tough and lose it slow."

"What're you sayin', Betty?" Aletta asked.

Betty stood up and faced Aletta. "I'm sayin' I'm gonna play politics a little and see what I can do about all this. It woulda been hard enough to get this approved even without a mob in your front yard. I've already had a bunch of phone calls complaining."

"You have?" Aletta asked. She looked hurt. "No one's been complainin' to me. 'Til now, a' course."

"I wouldn't worry about it." Betty waved her hand in the air as if she were swatting the complainers aside. "People complain about any change in this town. You shoulda heard the calls I got about the new playground equipment out at Annabelle Park. I got over a dozen complaints about swing sets."

Aletta put her hands on her hips and studied the carpet for a moment. "Well, what should *I* do now while you're playin' politics?"

"You have to be a model citizen for the next few days."

"I don't think I'm the problem here," Aletta said.

Betty sighed in agreement. "Can't you get your mama to call off the dogs for the next few days at least?"

"I'll try," Aletta answered, her stomach knotting up at the thought of it.

"I can't really be seen over here at your place anymore, so I'll have to lay low," Betty said. "And I'm sure I don't have to tell you not to talk to anyone about this."

"Of course not. I've sworn to the Lord above I'll never tell anyone a single thing about what I pick up with my gift, and I'll just use the same rule here," Aletta said, blushing a little. That was the first time she'd ever called her abilities a gift. "Thank you, Betty."

Aletta glanced back into the mirror after Betty left. First she smiled, then she pulled her eyebrows together and looked very worried, then she smiled again. She looked so silly she couldn't help but laugh a little as she walked out of the room.

She went into the kitchen that had been completely cleaned up, along with the living and dining rooms. Earl handed her a cold Coca-Cola that he'd brought over from his house, and patted her gently on the back.

"Thank you all so much," she said, tears forming in her eyes. "I have to make a phone call now. I can't let my kids miss out on seeing how much love there is in this house."

"We ordered a pizza," Rusty said. "Hope you like pepperoni and mushroom."

"I love it. The delivery boy should get a kick out of this one. Are they still out there?" Aletta asked, dialing the avocado-green rotary wall phone.

"Oh, yeah, they're still out there," Joy said from her post at the window.

"Might as well put on some music. Looks like we've got our-selves a party," Aletta said.

"I've got the new Peter Frampton eight-track in my truck," Jeff said. The teenagers all nodded their assent.

"And I've got Elvis in mine," Joy piped in.

"How 'bout John Denver?" Eugene said, finishing off his Coke and keeping his smile hidden from view.

"Come on, Eugene, I thought you were cooler than that," Rusty said. The teenagers acted like they were choking and gagging.

Aletta was laughing as Shirl answered the phone.

"Well, you sound different," Shirl said, surprised. After Aletta filled her in, she said she'd have the kids home by six.

As Aletta hung up the phone, the doorbell rang. Everyone looked at her to see what she would do.

"It's a woman. I don't recognize her as a Burning Bitch . . . I mean Bush," Joy said. The teenagers giggled.

Aletta smoothed her dress, then answered the door.

The woman at the door held herself by the elbows, her lips tight and thin. "Is Tracy Campbell here? She's my girl."

"That name sounds familiar. I'm Aletta Honor, by the way," Aletta said, pushing open the screen door and noticing the crowd of people staring at her from the street. "Would you like to come in?"

"I'll wait for her here, thank you," Mrs. Campbell said.

Aletta found the teenagers huddled in the living room around Tracy as she sat on the couch, bent over, clutching her long brown hair.

"Tracy, your mama's here," Aletta said.

"She doesn't want to go," Rusty replied, looking up from where he knelt on the floor.

"I'm afraid I don't have any say about that."

Behind Aletta, the screen door opened and then slammed shut as Mrs. Campbell stormed into the room.

Tracy looked terrified. "Mom, I . . ." she stammered as her mother grabbed her by the arm and yanked her to her feet.

"Let's go," Mrs. Campbell said. She pulled Tracy out the front door.

Outside, the Burning Bushes cheered for her. Aletta went to the door to watch them leave and heard part of what Reverend Taylor said as they got in their car ". . . rescued from the den of iniquity."

An uneasy quiet settled over the house when she closed the door.

"Rusty, will you give her a call later and see how she's doin'?" Aletta said.

"By God, I was wrong," Joy said. "She was most definitely a burning bitch."

Eugene swung around on the bar stool. "Can't say I disagree."

"And I got the good fortune to have to call another one. Can y'all excuse me?" Aletta asked as she picked up the phone again. The knot in her stomach that greeted her whenever she had to deal with her mama came right up to say hello as the phone rang.

"Hello," Nadine said on the other end of the line.

"Mama, it's Lettie. Now, I don't want you to say anything for just a minute, just listen. I wanted to tell you this that day at church," Aletta said, then took a deep breath before continuing. "We are not to blame for Daddy and Joey's getting killed."

"Aletta, why are you callin' me diggin' up all this old stuff out of the past? I don't want to talk about it."

Aletta twisted the phone cord around her fingers. "But we need to talk about it. It's been keeping us apart for so long . . ."

"I don't think so. I think there's other things that keep us apart," Nadine answered.

"Mama, I can't change who I am. I know you want me to, but I can't," Aletta said, and stomped her foot. "Please ask Reverend Taylor to stop the protesting. I go to court on Thursday with Jimmy . . ."

"What do you mean, you go to court?" Nadine interrupted.

"I've filed for divorce from him," Aletta answered. "I thought I told you."

"No, you did not tell me. Lettie, you've made your bed, now you got to lie in it. There's nothin' I can do anymore. God knows I've tried. I gotta let you go now." There was a click on the line.

"Ugh!" Aletta yelled as she slammed down the phone. She sat there shaking with frustration and hurt for a moment, then she got up and put James Taylor on the stereo. His creamy voice always soothed her nerves.

"Y'all can come back in," she called out, setting the needle onto the vinyl. "Does anyone have a cigarette I can bum? And none a' you kids better say yes."

Chapter Twenty-one

T he way people came and went, it seemed like there'd been a wedding or a funeral in the family. With those protesters out front, it might as well have been a funeral the way it killed her business.

In the middle of it all, Pastor Mueller phoned and told Aletta to read Mark, chapter six, verses one through six, that maybe it would make her feel better to know that even Jesus had suffered indignities in his own hometown.

Gary and Donnie, the policemen, stopped by with their hats in their hands and asked Aletta if she was all right.

"Well, hell no, I'm not all right," she answered, holding open the screen door. "I assume you passed by those folks with the signs?"

Donnie cleared his throat. "Yes, ma'am, we did."

"Well, you can go on out there and break it up any old time. You have my full permission." She waved her hand to show them the way. "I'd even throw in a free psychic reading for each of you just to show my appreciation."

"We can't do that, ma'am. They're not in your yard. They're on the sidewalk, which is public property," Gary said.

Aletta put her hand on her hip. "Then why're you boys here?

If you want a reading, you'll have to pay just like everyone else without a favor to trade."

"Just thought we'd check on you is all," Donnie said.

"Well, I appreciate you boys comin' by. Nice to know y'all are on the job." She gave them a little salute and let the screen door close.

Tom Barber brought the kids home around five.

"Shirl had some things to do, and I needed to get to the city anyway, so she asked me to drop 'em off," he said, setting the suitcases down on the kitchen floor.

"Thanks so much, Tom. It's good to have 'em back, and I'm sure you're not sorry to get rid of 'em," Aletta said, but she was thinking about Shirl. Maybe she didn't want to have anything to do with this mess. Who could blame her? But it hurt anyway.

"Good luck with all this, Lettie," Tom said, then kissed her on the cheek and left.

Aletta could tell Sissy was thrilled and relieved when she saw Rusty and the other teenagers flopped on the couches watching television. Ruby and Randy performed "I Am Woman" for Eugene, Earl, and Joy and got a standing ovation while Aletta rocked Gyp to sleep. Having a house full of people reminded Aletta of when the farmhands would stay at the house when she was little. It felt warm inside her, like family.

That night, after everyone went home, she fed the kids Shake 'n Bake chicken and a can of Chef Boyardee spaghetti, but she couldn't eat a bite herself.

Getting the kids down for bed proved nearly impossible, so it wasn't until around midnight that she remembered Pastor Mueller's phone call. She took the Bible from her bedside table, crawled under the covers and found the verses in Mark, chapter six:

Jesus went away from there and came to his own country; and his disciples followed him. And on the Sabbath he began to teach in the synagogue; and many who heard him were astonished, saying, "Where did this man get all this? What is the wisdom given to him?

What mighty works are wrought by his hands! Is not this the carpen-
ter, the son of Mary and brother of James and Joseph and Judas and
Simon, and are not his sisters here with us?" And they took offense at
him. And Jesus said to them, "A prophet is not without honor, except
in his own country, and among his own kin, and in his own house."
And he could do no mighty work there, except that he laid his hands
upon a few sick people and healed them. And he marveled because of
their unbelief.

The next morning, before her eyes even opened, a prayer was on
Aletta's lips that the Burning Bushes had run out of steam. But by
nine, there they were again. The obese lady and a few of the older
women had even brought chairs and an umbrella and looked like
they were set up to sell lemonade. Aletta called her lawyer for the
third time since yesterday morning.

"They're still here. How bad is this gonna hurt me?" she asked
again.

"It doesn't look good, Aletta. A judge isn't gonna like it one
bit, but it depends on Jimmy. Do you think he'll try for custody?"
Ramey asked.

"God only knows what that man'll try." Her sigh was heavy
with worry. She knew she'd lose every bit of together she'd been
able to muster if her kids were taken away.

A few minutes later, she heard a knock on the door, but when
she looked, no one was there. The knocking got louder, and Aletta
realized it was coming from the back. Betty stood at the back
door, breathing hard and smoothing her hair.

"Well, come in," Aletta said, moving aside.

"Joy let me through into the backyard," she said.

Aletta laughed, surprised. "Did you jump the fence?"

"Good thing I wore pants today, isn't it? I was a tomboy when
I was a little girl, you know. Getting some of my old life back since
you helped me at the party," Betty said, flushed and smiling. "I
even started riding a bike again for the first time in about twenty-
five years."

"That's wonderful. I won't tell you to call next time you want to talk, then," Aletta said. The change in Betty from the party was incredible to her, like there must be two Betty Conways running around town, one mousy and sad, the other smiling and feisty.

"Unfortunately, I didn't bring good news." Betty reached down to touch Gyp in his stroller.

Aletta had taken him on a walk around the house to get him to stop crying. It had worked to soothe him, but made her feel trapped. "What is it?" she asked.

"Nobody will talk to me until they're gone." She pointed toward the front yard. "You've got too much attention on you right now. If they go away, I might be able to do something, but I don't want to pull out my ace until I've got a chance to win."

They talked for a few more minutes, Betty suggesting again that maybe Aletta should move. But inside Aletta's mind, a plan was forming, one that she figured she shouldn't even be thinking about.

Ruby walked in. "Mama, where's my skates?"

Aletta put her hands to her head. "Honey, you can't talk to me right now."

Betty looked worried as she said good-bye and retreated out the back door.

Aletta stood there gazing blankly out the back window, torn about what she should do. In her mind, she called out to Betty to come back, but then decided to hold her tongue. To her amazement, the doorknob turned and Betty stuck her head inside again.

"Did you call me?" she asked.

It took a moment for Aletta to answer. "No, not really. Well, yes, yes. Come in."

Betty stepped back inside, a puzzled look on her face.

"I'm not sure if I should tell you this," Aletta said in a whisper.

"Aletta, I'm one person in the world you can trust. You've got enough on me to get *me* run out of town with you," Betty replied.

Aletta leaned close and whispered, "I promised myself I'd never do this to anyone, but I've also got something on Reverend Taylor."

* * *

Aletta refused to tell Betty what it was she had on Taylor, but that didn't keep them from coming up with a plan, a straightforward and simple one. As Betty was hopping the fence to recruit Joy into it, Aletta heard loud voices out front.

"Mama, it's Silvia," Randy said, running into the kitchen.

Aletta looked out to see Silvia, holding a casserole dish, facing off with the Burning Bushes. Aletta opened the window so she could hear and realized that Silvia was chewing them out in Spanish, her one free hand flitting up and down like a rabid butterfly.

"*Estúpido!*" she yelled and turned to come into the house.

"Well, let her in, let her in," she told Randy, who smiled and ran to the door in his stocking feet, sliding on the parquet floor in the entryway.

The tamales Silvia brought were just in time because Aletta was out of food and had two dollars in her purse. While she and Silvia talked, Aletta watched out the kitchen window. Charlie Leonard, the play director, stood in the street holding a sign out to cars that said: HONK ONCE IF YOU'RE FOR JESUS and then he'd flip it over to read: AND AGAIN IF YOU'RE AGAINST PSYCHICS. Aletta couldn't help but notice he got a lot of one honks, but not that many twos.

Aletta talked with Silvia about the drama outside while keeping watch out the window. It had been about fifteen minutes, and she was just about to pick up the phone when she saw Joy walk out of the salon and glance toward the window. She wore enormous dangling earrings and huge sunglasses with rhinestones along the top of the frame. She carried one of Earl's white handkerchiefs, waving it loosely in her hand as she sashayed, as only she could, across her front yard.

Aletta kissed her hand and put it up to the window.

"What's happening?" Silvia asked, leaning over the sink next to Aletta to look out the window.

"Negotiations," Aletta said, her heart pounding.

Joy approached Reverend Taylor. She stopped several feet from him to draw him away from the group to talk to her.

He hesitated for a moment before walking over to her. They

talked, Joy leaning in close and throwing her head back in laughter twice.

Aletta realized what she was doing—playing the silly woman so she'd seem unthreatening.

Finally, Joy tippy-toed away from him on her red pumps and disappeared inside the salon. Not two minutes later, the phone rang.

"He wouldn't come into your house of sin," Joy said sarcastically, then paused for effect. "But he'll meet you at the church in an hour."

Aletta put her hand to her chest. "What did you tell him?"

"That you were ready to get born again, what do you think? No, I told him it was real important y'all talk alone, that it could bring an end to this whole standoff."

"You should've been an actress, Joy," Aletta said.

"Actress-singer. What d'you think? I coulda been bigger than Judy Garland," she said.

Aletta laughed, surprised that she could. "No doubt about it."

"But then I wouldn't have Early, and I'd be a tormented superstar. Who needs that?"

"Thanks a million, Joy. I hope this isn't affectin' your business too much."

"Are you kiddin'? My stylin' chairs are the hottest tickets in town right now what with all this goin' on. I'm turnin' 'em away. You can still repay me, though."

"How?" Aletta asked cautiously.

"Come on. You can trust ol' Joy. I won't tell a soul. What's the dirt?" she cooed, then called to a customer, "Put that dryer back down, Weezy. You're not done yet."

"I can't, Joy. Anyway, I have an appointment."

"Scaredy-cat," Joy said. "Go get 'em, and call me the second you get back home."

Aletta smiled at the sight of Betty walking out of Femme Coiffures with her straight hair sprayed into a big pouf. Then she started fretting—about Reverend Taylor, but even more than that at this moment, about what to do with her kids. Under the circumstances, she couldn't leave them here with Sissy. She knew the teenagers would be back around eleven, but that didn't make her feel any better.

Silvia tapped Aletta on the shoulder. "Do you have to go somewhere? I can stay with your kids if you would like." Her big brown eyes were kind and welcoming.

To Aletta, it seemed that her own personal angel had alighted right behind her. "What about your baby?" Aletta asked.

Silvia smiled. "My mother keeps him on Tuesdays."

"Oh, that's a new concept," Aletta said, then paused for a moment. "I would be so grateful."

"No problem," Silvia said. She picked up Gyp from his playpen and held him to her.

After giving out a litany of instructions and warnings to her children, Aletta took a five-minute shower, tried on three different outfits, and ran out the door wearing a below-the-knee denim skirt and a red-and-white-checked short-sleeved blouse.

She knew, without a doubt, that this was the quickest she'd gone from preshower to out-the-door since Sissy had been born. She fled like an escaped convict into her car and past the protesters, glancing in her rearview mirror to make sure she didn't see Reverend Taylor or his car. By the time she got to the church, she had sweated through her checks. She found a clean diaper along with some candy wrappers and old homework pages under the passenger seat of the Pig Snout and tried to dry under her arms before going inside. She noticed there were no other cars in the vast parking lot, not even Reverend Taylor's Town Car.

As she walked through the front door of the huge gray brick building, the desire to leave and the air conditioning hit her at the same time. She could hear herself breathe in the quiet of the dark carpeted foyer where just over a week ago she'd been in a tussle with a horse.

She stood there for several minutes just waiting, almost afraid that if she started looking behind the closed doors, those little red devils would be waiting to take her with them into the depths.

"That's ridiculous, Lettie," she whispered to herself. The words seemed to get swallowed by the heavy silence. She peered again down the hallway, and when she looked back, Reverend Taylor stood just a few feet away.

She gasped. "Lord above, you scared me," she said. He scared her bad enough without sneaking up on her.

"Not my intention, I assure you, Mrs. Honor," Taylor said, but the smirk on his face told another story. "Let's speak in here." He opened one of the huge doors to the sanctuary for her. As usual, he wore a tie and smelled like aftershave. His hair was parted and combed neatly to one side of his large head.

"We don't need to talk in there. Don't you have an office in this place?" Aletta asked, glancing in the door.

He touched her arm and looked at her like he knew what was best. "Come along. We're in need of the Lord's presence, don't you think?"

She entered the sanctuary and her stomach turned over. Taylor escorted her, his hand still on her arm, to one of the pews in the center of the room. She couldn't take her eyes off the enormous oil painting of a flaming bush that hung behind the altar, even as she tried to concentrate on the images that were passing through her mind.

"Why don't you sit down?" Taylor said. It was more of a command than a question.

"Did you know I'm able to pick things up from touching?" Aletta asked, glancing at his hand on her arm. "That's how I do what I do."

He chuckled. "Oh," he said, then squeezed her arm slightly before dropping his hand. "Is that how it works?"

"For me it does," Aletta said. "I really think it would be better to talk in your office."

"Unless you have Satan drippin' from your tongue in what you are about to say, I see no reason to go anywhere else."

Aletta felt her resolve wavering and the sweat seeping through her shirt again. Then she realized what he was trying to do. He wanted to intimidate her. "I assure you that nothing will be drippin' from my tongue but the truth, sir, unfortunate as it may be," she said.

"Do you know why we call this a Battle Church, Mrs. Honor?" he asked. "It's because we are battling evil every day. And do you know how many people have come here and found salvation? Can you comprehend how fulfilled your life will be when you release the hand of the Devil and wrap your arms around Jesus?"

Aletta took a step backwards so she wouldn't be standing so close to him. He was a powerful man, and all his confidence made her own a little shaky. "Me and Jesus are just fine," she said. "More than fine. What I'm actually wonderin' about is the state of your soul, Reverend."

He chuckled again and crossed his arms across his large chest. "Oh, you are?"

"As a Christian woman, I find it pretty embarrassing all the way around, I gotta tell you," Aletta said.

"Do you know, Mrs. Honor, who you are talkin' to?" His face reddened and creases lined his forehead. "This entire organization, this building, and all the people who come here are because of me."

"Nevertheless. Never–the–less." Aletta shook her head and dug in her purse for a tissue. "You got a weakness. I know the ladies in the city appreciate it, but I figure your followers might see a problem." She wiped her neck with the tissue and looked him straight in the eye.

"I minister to many people in my congregation, and some of those happen to be women," Taylor said. Now his face was almost crimson.

"I think I'd use another term for it than 'ministering,' myself. Where do you find 'em, anyway? I know you have to go to Oklahoma City. I've heard they hang out downtown mostly, or is it on the south side?"

"I don't know what you're talkin' about," he thundered. "You're the one with the problem here, lady, not me." He turned and stomped back up the aisle toward the door.

Aletta called after him. She had to make him listen. "I know what they look like. I got faces when you were touchin' me just now."

Reverend Taylor stopped but didn't look back at Aletta.

She went on, talking as fast as she could. "I'm sure it can't be too hard to find them. They are in business, after all. I suppose the first place I'd go is to my police friends Gary and Donnie. They were the ones that dropped by my house yesterday. Surely you saw 'em."

"What do you want?" he said so quietly Aletta barely heard him.

"Call off the dogs, Reverend. Get 'em off my property and outta my hair, and do it today." She walked up the aisle past him, but turned back at the sanctuary door and looked at him. "Seems to me the battle you're fightin' is inside your own self."

Walking out of the eerily quiet building, she welcomed the buzz of the world—the birds in the trees making their music and noise, the sounds of cars in the distance. She went over what had happened at least ten times on the drive home and still wasn't sure what he was going to do.

I should've stayed and made him look me in the eye and tell me, she thought, but she'd just wanted out of there.

Out in her front yard, the teenagers and Sissy and Ruby and Randy were yelling back and forth with the Burning Bushes when she drove up.

"Why don't you just mind your own business?"

". . . burning in the fires of hell!"

"Go home!"

"Read the Bible!"

"Hey!" Aletta yelled as she got out of the car. "Let's go inside. Come on."

She herded the kids toward the house.

"We were just tryin' to help, Mama," Sissy said as they walked up the porch steps.

"I know, I know, but that's not the way to do it right now,"

Aletta said. She noticed that Jeff and a few of the others had very red eyes and smelled pretty pungent, but she didn't have the energy to even think about that right now.

Shirl opened the front door just as Aletta turned the doorknob. "I tried to tell 'em," she said.

"What're *you* doin' here?" Aletta asked, surprised and pleased. "I thought you were avoiding this mess."

Shirl pushed open the screen door and hugged Aletta. "Are you kiddin'? I wouldn't miss this for the world. Silvia's changin' Gyp, and Eugene came by. He had to go back to the shop but he wants a call if anything happens."

After they were inside the house, she leaned close to Aletta. "Were you meetin' with the minister?"

Aletta nodded and rolled her eyes.

Aletta called Joy to tell her that it was wait-and-see now.

"What'd he do, steal money from the church?" Joy asked in a whisper. "Oh no, I know, he's a bastard, or—no—a Jew!"

"Joy, you're terrible!" Aletta said.

"Ooh, I got it, this is it, he's cheatin' on that dumpy little wife of his!"

"I'm hangin' up now."

"That's it, isn't it? Who can blame him, really?" Joy said.

Aletta knew Joy enjoyed shocking her.

Aletta hung up, and she and Shirl started dishing tamales onto paper plates. Every few minutes, Aletta looked at the little grandfather clock that sat on the bar under the telephone. She never realized before how loudly it ticked. As they ate, even the kids stayed quiet.

The phone rang, and Aletta jumped.

It was Betty. "I'm over at Joy's. I heard you were back from the church, and I couldn't sit still."

"You called. What happened with the fence jumpin'?" Aletta asked.

"I think I pulled somethin'."

* * *

Two hours later, they still waited. It definitely felt more like a funeral than a wedding now with people standing in corners talking quietly, no music playing, and the kids in the backyard. Aletta finally just pulled the plug on the clock.

"Anybody want a clock?" she asked. As she held the cord in the air, the phone rang.

Sissy answered, then covered the receiver with a hand. "Mama, it's Joy. She says Reverend Taylor just pulled up."

Aletta nearly pulled the clock off the counter, but caught it and put it back, then hurried to look out the window. By this time, Betty had climbed the fence again, not quite so happy about it this time, and had joined the group in Aletta's house. She ducked down behind the bar like a burglar who'd just seen the homeowners drive up.

"Betty, can you call Eugene?" Aletta asked. All she could see was one hand reach up and grab the phone off the wall.

Shirl and the teenagers, who numbered thirteen at this point, rushed the front door to try to hear what was happening.

"Let Shirl listen, y'all, and don't open that door all the way!" Aletta yelled, her nerves causing her voice to sound thin and high.

Aletta watched out the window as Reverend Taylor got out of his car with his arms opened wide and a warm smile on his face.

"What's he sayin', Shirl?" Sissy asked.

"Y'all shush!" Shirl hissed. "He said 'Brothers and sisters,' I heard that much."

Shirl listened hard to his booming voice as Aletta watched him wave his arms toward the house, then raise them dramatically over his head and look skyward.

"He's sayin' that you're saved, Lettie . . . and you took Jesus at the church just now . . . and he witnessed the Light of God come into your body!" Shirl said.

"Oh, my," Betty whispered, still ducking down, but peering up over the counter.

"He did not say that," Aletta said.

"Shhh! He got a personal message from Jesus himself . . .

in that moment that said Mrs. Honor's powers . . . will only be used . . . to serve God . . . from now on in."

"Here he comes! Shitfire, he's comin' this way!" Aletta said, and now it was her turn to duck.

Shirl slammed the door shut and everyone bumped into one another, not knowing what to do with themselves. Reverend Taylor sprang up the porch steps and, without hesitation, pushed the doorbell.

"What should I do?" Aletta asked, squatting next to Betty.

"Go get it, darlin', and act like you just had Jesus himself over for a barbecue for Christ sakes," Betty said.

Shirl shooed everyone away from the door as Aletta composed herself. Finally Aletta opened the door. Her smile was more an exposure of teeth than anything else, giving her a surprised, almost frightened appearance.

"Mrs. Honor! Aletta! Come on out here!" Reverend Taylor boomed at her, his arms outstretched, and for a moment, Aletta thought he was really glad to see her, he was so convincing. Aletta stepped out onto the porch.

He turned to his followers. "Oh, that's just wonderful! She says she was just in prayer after her experience!" Reverend Taylor's voice always seemed to come out in stereo, but then he whispered to Aletta, "Act like you're prayin'."

Aletta put her hands up in front of her and bowed her head dutifully. The Burning Bushes clapped and cheered. Joy had come out to watch, and all the ladies from the salon, in various stages of color and curl, had followed her. They clapped too.

"Praise Jesus!" Reverend Taylor shouted.

"Glory hallelujah!" his congregants shouted back.

"It's a miracle right here in Okay!" the obese lady said, knocking her head on the umbrella as she struggled from her chair.

"That's right. It is! It's a miracle!" Joy called. She grabbed a towel from around the neck of Mabel Sackett, placed it on the grass, and went down on her knees. "I can feel the presence of God here with us right now!"

Reverend Taylor glared at her as members of his church went apoplectic to see another sinner succumb to the power of the Lord. They began falling on their knees too, shouting out prayers and thanksgiving, some of them starting to speak in tongues.

"All right, then," Reverend Taylor said, rushing down the steps. "We better go on and leave Mrs. Honor to her prayers now. I'm sure she's worn out after all the excitement."

Aletta just kept on praying until Joy started blabbing loudly in gibberish as if she too were speaking in tongues. Aletta had to turn her back so she could laugh without being seen.

"She's downright crazy," Shirl said as she stepped out onto the porch, unable to contain herself any longer.

The teenagers came right behind her, and following Rusty's lead, they began raising their arms in the air and shouting. Then, with Joy's encouragement, the salon ladies joined in, capes, curlers, and all.

"Amen!"

"Praise the Lord!"

"Hallelujah!"

The Burning Bushes rushed to the teenagers and to Aletta's children, hugging them and shouting with them. Charlie Leonard ran up the porch steps and pulled Aletta into the yard. She couldn't stop laughing as she got hugged and patted and prayed for.

Eugene pulled up, got out of his truck, and just stood there staring. People came out of businesses up and down the street.

Reverend Taylor was furious as he stood with his hands on his hips, eyes smoldering and jaw set.

"I have to go in now! My baby's inside!" Aletta shouted finally. She looked around and saw Silvia holding Gyp on the porch. Silvia's eyes got big, then she ran back in the front door.

Eugene walked through the melee, took Aletta by the arm, and escorted her into the house.

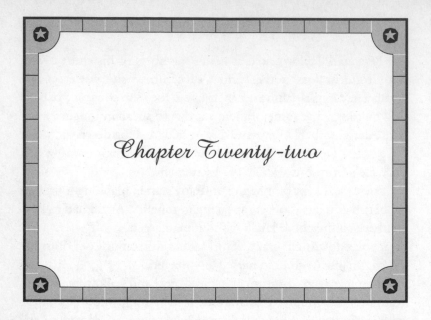

Chapter Twenty-two

"You really are a miracle, you know," Silvia said as Aletta came through the front door.

The tears that came from laughing brought two shades of green back to Aletta's eyes.

The Burning Bushes finally left, and when things calmed down, Aletta looked for Betty to talk to her about the business of the license. She found her in Sissy's bedroom on the pink Princess phone.

Betty motioned Aletta to come in and close the door. "The next vote's Tuesday, and I don't need to tell you that if Jack's gonna get the job, it needs to happen sooner than later while he's still in good with them," she said into the receiver. "Yes, they're gone. Make a few calls. They think she's God's chosen now. . . . All right, yes, fair enough then. By noon, though. We can't wait the whole day."

"What?" Aletta asked when she hung up.

"Somebody we need on our side has a brother-in-law who wants to get the construction contract for the Wal-Mart, so they're anxious as hell to get approval," Betty said. "Sounds like a done deal if there are no protesters as of noon tomorrow. What d'you think? They won't show back up, will they?"

"God only knows," Aletta said, sighing.

"You mean Jesus hasn't told you yet? That's hard to believe," Betty said, smiling.

Outside, at the side of the house, Rusty and Sissy drank warm Coors with Jeff, who had stolen a six-pack from his dad's garage.

A few hours later, Aletta offered everyone who'd helped her a free reading whenever they wanted it. She told the teenagers they had to have written permission from their parents, because she wasn't going to get into the same trouble she had with Rusty and his dad.

"And remember," she said, holding up a finger, "if you fake it, I'll know."

Eugene stayed until after everyone else left.

Aletta saw him to the door. "You know, the best thing about this is all the support I've gotten from everyone," she said. "But the second best thing is it scared Jimmy off for a little while."

"Yep. I almost forgot about him," Eugene said. He leaned over and kissed her on the cheek before he walked out the door.

That night Aletta slept a glorious, dreamless sleep, but when she woke up early in the morning, she got up and looked out the window to make sure there were no protesters. It was just seven o'clock, though, so the only thing outside was Dusty Ray throwing out the *Okay Review* from his bicycle.

An hour later, however, at eight o'clock sharp, the obese woman from Reverend Taylor's congregation stood knocking on the front door.

Aletta opened it reluctantly.

"Hi, hello, I'm Ellen Ann Grimes," the woman said, giggling nervously. "Reverend Taylor said not to bother you for a while 'cause you were probably tired and all, but I thought maybe just one person wouldn't be too terribly much for you to handle."

Aletta couldn't believe it. "Are you asking me for a reading?"

"I'll pay, a' course," Ellen Ann said, digging money out of her purse.

"Come on in," Aletta said, wondering what could possibly happen next.

Randy lay on the living room floor in front of the television eating peanut butter and syrup out of a bowl.

"Go on and play for a while, Randy. I gotta work in here," Aletta said, picking up toys and shoes and things that had somehow gathered since last night.

Randy looked so perplexed when he saw Ellen Ann that Aletta had to laugh.

"What's *she* doin' here?" he asked, getting up on his elbows and knees.

"She wants a reading, honey," Aletta answered.

Randy went to Aletta and pulled her down to him so he could talk in her ear. "But she thinks you're the Devil," he whispered with his hand cupped to his mouth.

"I'll explain later. If I can. Now go play outside with Ruby. It's a nice day."

Aletta turned off the TV, then faced Ellen Ann. "Just yesterday you were out in my front yard callin' me names. I'm not about to start tellin' you the truth if you're gonna get mad at me again. I like you on my good side."

Ellen Ann laughed nervously and put her palms toward Aletta. "Oh no no no, I won't turn on you, Mrs. Honor. To tell you the truth, I wanted to come and see you since you put the sign up, but I was scared."

"So you protested me?"

"Reverend Taylor said you was doin' the Devil's work, but now you're on the side of the Lord. I promise I won't get mad at anything you say," Ellen Ann said, her upper lip getting sweaty.

Aletta finally sat Ellen Ann down on the couch and said her opening prayer. She held Ellen Ann's chubby hands in hers for a moment, then she opened her eyes.

"You live with your mama, don't you?" she asked.

Ellen Ann's eyes flew open. "Yes, I do. Why, how did you . . . ?"

"Your daddy too, but he's much more in the background, isn't he?"

"Yeah," Ellen Ann answered, looking down at her hands in her lap.

"Is there somethin' you want to know specifically?" Aletta asked. She kept picturing Ellen Ann sitting under the umbrella looking like she was queen of the world, lording her moral authority over sinners like herself. Something inside Aletta wanted to tell Ellen Ann the meanest things she could think up, getting her squirming so she could see what it felt like, but over the last few months, she'd actually begun to respect her gift and couldn't abuse it. *A gift from God,* she thought. Besides, underneath all of Ellen Ann's righteous judgment and extra pounds was someone who needed some love and some good news.

"Am I ever gonna lose my weight and meet a man?" Ellen Ann blurted out, like the question had been a creature living in her head looking for a way out.

"All right. Well, you gotta move outta your parents' house first and foremost, if you really want to lose weight or get a man. You've been lazy about it for one thing, sayin' how much you want to lose, but then eatin' like two horses. You can't do that. But a big problem I see is your mama *likes* you fat."

Ellen Ann's eyes got wider, and her moist lip quivered.

"She *gets* somethin' outta you bein' fat," Aletta continued.

Ellen Ann scooted to the edge of the couch and pushed herself up with both hands. She moved her bulk around the room faster than Aletta would have thought possible.

"It keeps me needin' her is why. That's the truth. Oh my Lord in Heaven straight up above, I never told anyone this, but I've thought it. Oh, I've thought it, but then I just can't believe that she'd be so awful." Her Okie drawl got more pronounced the more upset she got. "But she is, she's like that, keepin' my dad under her thumb too, but in a way like you wouldn't know that that's what she's doin' . . ."

"Ellen Ann?" Aletta interrupted. "You don't have to stay there, and you can't blame anybody else for keepin' you fat, 'cause you're doin' it to yourself."

Ellen Ann just stared at her, the sweat running down her temples now. Aletta could tell she was a pretty girl underneath all the flesh, her blue eyes sparkling and her skin creamy and clear. "You've got a job in an office, don't you?" she asked when Ellen Ann still didn't say anything.

"I'm the receptionist at Kerr-McGee out on the highway." Her voice was soothing, smooth, even when she was upset.

"Well, you have a lovely voice," Aletta said. She could tell the girl needed a compliment.

Ellen Ann laughed. "All the men who call ask me if I'm single 'cause they like my voice," she said. "They flirt with me like crazy over the phone, then when they come in and see me, they act like they never heard of me."

"Well, it sounds to me like you have what you need to get your own place." Aletta stood up, took Ellen Ann's hand, and squeezed. "You can do this, you know. I can't tell you what's gonna happen 'cause it's all based on the choices you make. You can have what you want, though, if you do the work."

Just as they finished, the doorbell rang. Aletta's heart did a little skip inside her chest. She had become so accustomed to bad news and bullies, she just assumed the worst. Ellen Ann handed her a five-dollar bill as Aletta opened the door to Charlie Leonard.

"Charlie," Ellen Ann said. "What're you doin' here?"

"Same thing you are, I guess," he answered, and shrugged his shoulders.

By noon, Aletta had seen five Burning Bush Battle Church members, all of whom had participated in one way or another in the protests. She held Gyp on her lap for much of the time as she told them about their lives and problems and desires. She noticed that they had more fear than most people, so after taking a chance with telling Ellen Ann the difficult things, she played it safe with the rest of them.

After Ordell Simmons left, promising to send all of his friends and family over now that Aletta was working for the Lord, Aletta had Ruby go out and throw one of Gyp's baby blankets over the sign. She made grilled cheese sandwiches and Campbell's tomato soup from supplies she assumed had been brought yesterday by her friends, God bless 'em. She was feeding Gyp a bottle when she heard another knock on the door.

"Hello!" Betty called.

"Come on in!" Aletta said, looking at the clock for the first time in hours. Eugene had plugged it back in last night. She was shocked to see it was already one-thirty.

Betty had a worried look on her face.

"Uh-oh, you couldn't get the license," Aletta said, feeling the little creep of defeat making its way into her throat. She held Gyp tighter.

Betty broke into a wide smile and revealed a piece of paper. "And I thought you were supposed to be psychic," she said, waving the paper over her head.

"You got it!? Woohoo!" Aletta jumped up so quickly, Gyp started to cry.

Ruby and Randy came in from the backyard and Sissy hurried in from her room because of all the noise.

"What's goin' on?" she asked.

"Your mom's official, that's what," Aletta answered. "Come here, all of you. Give me a hug."

She gathered her children around her, getting hugs on her legs (Randy), waist (Ruby), shoulders (Sissy), and neck (Gyp). Somehow, Aletta was able to hold the four of them all by herself.

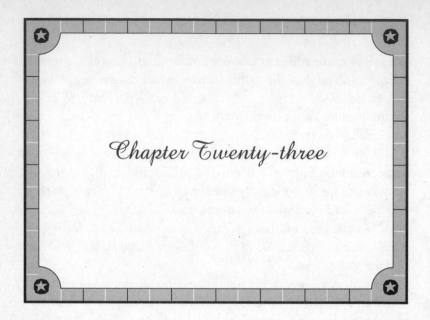

Chapter Twenty-three

At the county courthouse the next day, Doug Ramey approached Jimmy's rumpled, white-haired attorney, Gil Gedds, before the hearing to show him the business license and warn him not to try to go after Aletta as an unfit mother because of her business or he'd call witness after witness who would enlighten the court on Mr. Honor's drunken, abusive, and adulterous behavior.

Joy took off work to accompany Aletta, and they stood outside smoking a cigarette and wishing aloud that Jimmy wouldn't show up, when he did. He pulled into the parking lot in that black Trans Am with the gold eagle splayed all over the hood. He must've traded in the van. Aletta instinctively threw her cigarette down before he could see her smoking, and they ducked back inside until they were called into the courtroom.

They sat in front of the judge, a handsome older man who Aletta thought, by the look in his eyes, might be kind. But when he spoke, he seemed impatient and bitter.

First the judge asked about the four children, emphasizing *four* as if to ask if they had to have so many before blowing their marriage off.

"The children should be with their mother, just as they have been for the last several months while their father has been . . . elsewhere," Ramey said, not wanting to get Jimmy or his lawyer upset.

Gil Gedds stood up and spoke in a monotone, like he'd stayed up too late the previous night and didn't have the energy for any of this. "It's agreed that the children should live with their mother, with visitation rights as follows. . . ."

They worked out the visitation that Ramey had wanted—Jimmy would take the kids every other weekend as long as he didn't drink around them.

What bothered Aletta, in addition to the drinking issue, was that she knew her kids were going to be around Kathy Kokin, and she could barely stand the thought of it.

The judge said it was obvious that whoever got the kids also got the house, so Aletta breathed a sigh of relief at that. Then Ramey asked for a thousand dollars a month, $800 for child support and $200 alimony.

"Judge, my client is willing to pay $400 a month in child support only. With the house, that is more than enough," Gedds drawled.

Aletta almost jumped out of her chair. "That's only twenty-five dollars a week for a whole human being, and there's payments due on the house," she blurted out.

Ramey put his hand on her arm to try to stop her, but she kept going. "How am I supposed to live? God knows I can't afford to hire a sitter. And I have to have a bigger car. I can't even take these kids to the lake on a weekend."

"Mrs. Honor, be still," the judge said gruffly.

Jimmy sat quietly, watching.

Gil Gedds's voice got much livelier now that they were talking money. "Your Honor, the plaintiff has a document which proves that she is running a successful business out of her home on Main Street in Okay, if Mr. Ramey would be so kind as to show it to you."

"All I have here is a business license, your honor," Ramey said holding up the paper. "This is far from proving that Mrs. Honor's business is in any way successful."

Gedds countered. "Excuse me, sir, but it certainly is drawing a crowd from what I can tell when I drive by the location. It seems they're lined up out her door. Or it may be that the people who are visiting are there for a different reason, which the court should know about."

Ramey scooted forward in his chair, his face reddening. "If Mr. Gedds insists on innuendo . . ."

"I have evidence," Gedds interrupted.

Ramey scowled at him and continued, "I will be forced to bring forward evidence concerning Mr. Honor's behavior during the marriage."

"Would you gentlemen like to decide whether you're going to play games or present a case now?" the judge asked condescendingly. "I'm busy."

Gedds answered first. "We rest, Your Honor."

Ramey whispered to Aletta, "If we bring up the adultery, Gedds will bring up the protests. It could go either way, but it's possible the judge has had an affair, and then he'd be sympathetic to that. Or he could be very religious, which wouldn't help you either."

Suddenly Aletta felt exhausted. She didn't want this to get nasty. Surely the judge would be fair. That's all they were asking for was fair. "Just let it go. I can't handle all that right now."

"We rest, Your Honor," Ramey said.

"Is it true you don't even want this divorce, Mr. Honor?" the judge asked.

"Yes, sir," Jimmy said, and cleared his throat. "That's true."

"Given this fact and the fact that Mrs. Honor has a business running in her home where she can care for the children, I rule that Mrs. Honor will receive $400 a month in child support and no alimony," the judge said.

"Imagine that!" Joy blurted out loudly from her seat behind Aletta. "The good old boys win again."

The judge glared at her, then brought his gavel down and left the bench.

Aletta was furious. She couldn't get by on four hundred dollars a month. It wasn't fair. She raced out of the courtroom and into the parking lot, Joy right on her heels. As Aletta passed the black Trans Am, she grabbed the passenger's side rearview mirror and pulled it clean off.

"Oh, girl, now you've done it," Joy said, and took Aletta by the arm and hustled her into her Riviera. She burned rubber on the way out of the parking lot as Aletta blasted out a mouthful of cuss words that would've made an army sergeant proud.

After they got home, they stayed in the car so Aletta could calm down before she went back in to face her children. After just a few minutes, Aletta noticed a black car in her rearview mirror driving slowly up the street behind them.

She slid her butt forward in the seat, ducking down, but she kept an eye on the mirror. "Is that Jimmy?" she asked.

Joy ducked and turned around to look, her pink fingernails on the top of the seat. "Hide that godforsaken mirror," she screeched.

Aletta put the mirror up under her shirt.

"Oh, that's just perfect," Joy said, then looked back at the car. "Shit shit shit, it's him."

They ducked down lower as he passed by, then peered up over the dash to take a look.

"Oh, my God," Aletta whispered, her eyes widening.

"How in the holy hell?" Joy asked.

Aletta took the mirror out from under her shirt. "I must've pulled it off the wrong car."

Joy burst out laughing.

"Nothing mean I do ever turns out right," Aletta said.

"Maybe it belonged to the judge," Joy said. "I bet it did, Lettie. I bet you pulled off that asshole judge's mirror."

Chapter Twenty-four

In between taking care of kids and cooking and cleaning, Aletta gave readings, and in between giving readings, she took care of kids and cooked and cleaned. It seemed she was working all the time, but money was still a constant worry. She did enjoy it when every once in a while someone would show up at her door saying they'd heard about her in Amarillo or Kansas City and had to come by to get a reading on their way somewhere else.

Of the twenty or so teenagers who had been at her house during the protests, only three showed up with parental passes for their free readings. It was crystal clear to Aletta every time she went to the IGA or the bank that there were many people in town who didn't appreciate her business or her, but there were a whole lot who loved her, too. The Burning Bush Battle Church provided many of her customers.

Sissy's attitude, thankfully, had changed toward her mother's vocation. Aletta had become something of a legend among the rebellious teenage population of Okay, so Sissy was one of the most popular girls in school that year. She and Aletta went toe to toe over clothes, partying, staying out too late, and Rusty. As Sissy became more popular, she also became bolder. But she never said a negative word about Aletta's ability or her business, and whenever she was around, which seemed to be less and less all the time, she helped with Ruby and Randy and Gyp while Aletta was with customers.

Every other weekend, the kids would all go with their dad to stay at Kathy Kokin's house, and with the swimming pool and the never-ending supply of junk food, they didn't hate it as much as Aletta would have liked.

One Friday in October, Jimmy called the house. As usual, before he could even finish a sentence, she held the phone out.

"Kids! Sissy, Ruby, Randy, it's your daddy!" She was through with Jimmy Honor and would be thrilled never to have to talk to him again.

Sissy came into the kitchen a few minutes later while Aletta loaded her new dishwasher on wheels. Eugene had found it at a garage sale and fixed it up for her, and it'd been a blessing in her life.

"Daddy can't take us this weekend, Mama. Kathy has the flu or something," Sissy said.

Aletta looked up, instantly angry. "Well, hell's bells, I wish it were that easy for *me* to choose when or if I'm gonna be a parent."

Sissy didn't say anything. She just turned around and walked away.

Aletta felt guilty and knew she'd been bad-mouthing Jimmy and Kathy way too much, but it was like something took her over and she couldn't help herself. It was her guilt that kept her from calling Jimmy and chewing him out. Instead, she called Betty and asked if they could change their plans.

Frank and Betty and Aletta and Eugene had been planning to go to the Strawberry Festival in Ada, but she asked if they could just hang around her house on Saturday and cook out on the grill if it was a nice day.

"Well, Frank'll be tickled pink. There's a football game on," Betty said.

It was a beautiful autumn day that felt the way the color orange would feel if it were a day. Eugene and Frank were inside watching the Sooners beat up on the Texas Longhorns while Aletta and Betty sat out back drinking coffee.

Betty leaned back in her chair and crossed her ankles. "Frank and Rusty got in another big fight yesterday after school. Rusty was playin' his guitar after Frank asked him to mow the lawn," she said. "Rusty said he had another hour before dark to do it and didn't think he had to jump up that second, which I understand, I guess. I don't know. . . ."

"Hmmm," Aletta said. "Does it seem like Frank's bein' too hard on him?"

"He's just worried that Rusty's not gonna amount to anything if he doesn't get serious about school and about life, I guess. You know, Frank's daddy was a no-account bum, so he's real touchy about it."

Ruby ran out in her cowboy boots and chaps, her face flushed and her hair flying out behind her. "There's two men at the door, Mama!"

"Dammit, I forgot to cover the sign," Aletta said to Betty apologetically.

"Let's go run 'em off," Betty teased.

Aletta went to the door and halfheartedly greeted the two young men who stood outside. They both wore jeans and T-shirts and looked a little worn out. One of them held an expensive-looking camera.

"Are you Aletta Honor, the psychic?" the one without the camera asked.

"The one and only," Aletta answered.

"Hi, my name's Brian, and this is Andrew," said the young man with messy brown hair and dark circles under his eyes. "We work for *Life* magazine. We're doing a story on Route 66 and wondered if we could talk to you for a few minutes."

Betty clapped her hands over her mouth, but not for long because she had to use it to yell to Frank. "Honey, *Life* magazine's here to do a story on Aletta!"

Aletta blushed as Frank and Eugene came to the door.

"Well, I'll be damned, Aletta," Frank said, yanking his pants up on his belly.

"Are you gonna let 'em in?" Eugene asked, smoothing his hair.

"Oh, yes, yes, come on in." Aletta opened the door and shook their hands as they entered. "I guess we can go out back if that's all right with you."

Brian asked the crowd that followed them into the yard if they could do the interview alone with Aletta, because they wanted to get a reading. Aletta couldn't tell who was more disappointed at not getting to stay, the kids or the grown-ups.

Brian, his hair falling in his eyes, told her he was the writer and would be doing the interview and getting the reading. Andrew might want to take some pictures later.

"Sounds fine, I guess. What kind of a story is this gonna be?" Aletta asked, surprised at how shy she felt. But after facing down the protesters and standing up in court against Jimmy, she couldn't get too intimidated by much of anything. *What the hell,* she figured. *They're just people.*

Brian pushed his hair aside. "We're doing a road story on traveling Route 66 from coast to coast. It'll cover some of the history of the highway and what's going on with it now. Last night we were hanging out at the Red Dog Saloon just west of here and heard about you from a guy there. You know the place?" he asked.

"You heard about me at the Red Dog?" she asked. Just the name gave her a chill.

"They've got decent pool tables," Andrew said. His skin was smooth, and he seemed so young to Aletta, like a college boy.

"Anyway, this guy said we should stop by here on our way through town, that you were the real deal," Brian said. "So we came to see for ourselves."

"What do we do? You gonna ask me questions?" Aletta asked.

"I think first I'd like the reading, if that's all right with you," Brian said.

"Fine by me, but usually I do them in private for an individual. You know, things can come up . . ."

"Oh, no, Andrew can stay. We're working on the article together, so he needs to know what happens," Brian said.

They sat in the shifting shadow and light under Aletta's big elm tree. It was quiet except for the hush of the leaves as they played keep-away with the breeze. Aletta reached out and took Brian's hands and felt the slight wavy feeling inside.

She closed her eyes, letting the images come forward even as she prayed. She looked pretty in the afternoon sun, and as he looked at her, it was Brian's turn to feel wavy inside.

She opened her eyes, feeling relaxed now and at ease. "Well, thank you, first of all, for the compliment." She smiled at Brian.

Brian looked at her quizzically for a moment, then blushed. "Oh, uh, sure," he said, laughing a little.

Andrew looked at her, then at Brian. "Were you just checking her out? She picked up that you were scoping on her," he said. "I can't believe you."

"I can't help it. She looks good," Brian replied.

"And as a newly divorced lady with four kids, I have to say I don't mind a bit," Aletta said, then closed her eyes and concentrated. "Just something that I'm getting about the two of you. You're really good together. You worked together at another magazine before?"

"Yes, in Ohio, after college. It was for the Ohio Tourist Bureau," Brian said, glancing at Andrew with raised eyebrows.

"One thing is for sure, y'all should stay together, 'cause you're better together than when you're alone. But you've got to listen to each other more. Andrew's not a talker, but he's got good ideas and is a wonderful photographer. And Andrew, Brian may be hotheaded sometimes, but he's a great writer, so it'd be a good idea to just let things go sometimes."

They both just looked at each other and laughed in disbelief.

"This is great," Brian said.

"So professionally, things look real good for you, Brian. Try not to piss off too many editors. Is that who you work for, an editor?" Aletta said.

"That's the boss, yes," Brian said.

"Anyway, you need to play the game and humor them sometimes. You know—pick your battles."

Andrew leaned forward. "Did you hear that, man?"

"I heard it," Brian said.

Aletta continued, closing her eyes again. "But personally, you've got some challenges. You've got a son, did you know that?" She opened her eyes to see his reaction.

His pen fell off his lap onto the ground. "What?" he asked.

"Yeah, and it's not gonna be for a while, but the mother's gonna come after you for some help. Linda? Is it Linda?"

"Lynna? Oh, man, that's not my kid," Brian said.

"Yeah, it is."

Brian pulled his hands from Aletta's and covered his eyes. "Oh, man," he said again.

"You can have a relationship with him. It's not that hard," Aletta said. "But if you don't want to, just know that you'll be forced to one day, at least through money."

"What else?" Brian asked, letting his hands fall to his knees.

Aletta put her hands on his and paused for a moment before continuing. "Well, you're gonna meet someone soon, probably December. You're gonna like her a lot. I even see marriage possibly. Name starts with an M."

"No way," Andrew said.

"Can we return to my career? I like that subject," Brian said.

They talked for another few minutes until Andrew insisted it was his turn, like a kid wanting to ride a pony.

Aletta took his hands and told him about his life in the past and his life to come, including that he'd have three children. She saw that he'd divorce his present wife, but if people were currently happily married, she never told them that information, so she didn't tell Andrew. She told him he'd take some very famous photographs for *Life* and that it was important that he travel overseas to do so.

"Can I come along?" Brian asked.

"Only if you're nice," Andrew answered.

After Andrew's reading, Brian asked Aletta questions like when she first knew she was psychic, what it felt like when she was giving a reading, how the information came through, and all the personal things like what were her kids' names and where did she grow up. Then they asked if they could take her picture out by her sign, so Aletta led them into the house. Betty had been peeking out the window and saw them coming. She ran to the dining room table and sat down, casually swinging her crossed leg.

"Are you finished?" she asked.

"They wanna take my picture," Aletta said.

"Are they gonna take your picture?" Randy yelled as he ran into the room, and that got the whole house interested.

Aletta excused herself and ran to the bathroom to put on lipstick and a little blush. She fluffed her hair up with her hands, then gave up.

All of Aletta's kids, the Conways, Eugene, and now Joy and Earl were outside telling Andrew what they thought would make the best picture when Aletta came out. But Andrew was clear on what he wanted, and he wouldn't let Joy do anything to Aletta's hair no matter how hard she fought. He had Aletta lean against the sign with her house in the background. He said the warm late afternoon light was perfect as he snapped several shots.

"Could you do me a favor and take a picture of all of us?" Aletta asked.

Andrew looked at Brian, who shrugged and nodded. So they lined up, small in front and big in back. Rusty put his arm around Sissy. Eugene tried to step away, but Betty pulled him next to her.

"Now smile," she said.

"The kid's making a face," Andrew said, pointing to Randy. Ruby punched him in the arm, and he straightened up.

"No hitting," Aletta said, holding her smile, and Andrew snapped the picture. It was an image that would sit on Aletta's mantel for many years to come.

Brian pulled Aletta aside before he and Andrew left. "I can't say that I believe you're psychic because the magazine won't print it, but I can say that people in town believe it. Just wanted you to know I think you're amazing. The article won't be out 'til January, but we'll be in touch."

After Aletta herded everyone back inside and Andrew and Brian left, there was another knock on the door. It was Andrew again. He handed Aletta a ten-dollar bill.

"Oh, you don't have to do that," she said.

"You deserve it. You were great," he said, and jogged back out to the truck where Brian was waiting.

That evening, as Betty and Frank and Rusty were about to leave, Aletta pulled Frank aside.

"I'm gonna tell you somethin' about Rusty that you can't tell Betty or him. You have to swear because this is real important."

"I swear. I swear," he said.

As she spoke, Frank looked at her with a look similar to the one he had given her at the Webbers' party when he was cussing her out. After a moment, when he started to understand what she meant, his look changed. Now it seemed he just thought she was crazy. "Are you sure?" he asked.

"As sure as I can be with the abilities that I have," she nodded.

"Well, I'll be damned," he said.

After they left, she walked Eugene out to his Mustang.

"Don't you think it's a strange coincidence that it was some-body out at the Red Dog who told those boys to come see me?" she asked.

"Maybe, or maybe it was somebody who remembered your daddy and was tryin' to help," he said. "Did you ask who it was they'd talked to?"

"I couldn't bring myself to ask. Ain't that funny?" They stopped, and she looked up at him. The evening was just as pretty as the day had been, and she breathed it in. "You're like my daddy in a lot of ways. You're a good-hearted man." She touched his chest with the palm of her hand.

He kissed her then, and as he held her close to him, she just let go, a warm, liquid feeling rising up from her toes. She liked Eugene and trusted him, but she wasn't expecting this feeling from his kiss. She saw him in a whole different way when he pulled away and looked at her before kissing her again.

They kissed for a long time with him leaning on the hood of the car and her leaning on him.

"I should've done that a long time ago," he said when they stopped.

She felt light-headed. "Most definitely."

Drunkenly, she weaved her way back to the house and realized that she hadn't been distracted by the images that came up as they kissed. They had been silent, mute, empty, and she realized she was at a new level of mastery with her gift.

Making out as mastery, she thought, and laughed.

Chapter Twenty-five

Over the next few months, things went pretty smoothly. Jimmy had stopped coming over drunk in the middle of the night, a huge relief, but Aletta knew he was still drinking because she'd get reports from friends and customers about bar fights and drunken scenes. It wasn't the end of his presence in her life, however.

He started dropping by unannounced in the afternoon, usually after work. He would just knock a little as he came in and say, "Anybody home?"

He stood over the open Crock-Pot, spooning into his mouth the chicken and potatoes Aletta had put in for dinner that morning.

"What're you doin' here?" Aletta asked, walking in from laying Gyp down for a nap.

"Came by to see the kids." He replaced the lid on the Crock-Pot and wiped his mouth with the back of his hand.

Aletta looked around, exasperated. This was the third time in two weeks.

"Well, they ain't here, and Gyp's asleep. Jimmy, you're not s'posed to be here. I can't afford to feed me and the kids on the money you're payin'. You eat enough for three people."

He leaned back on the counter and crossed his arms and ankles.

"How you doin', Lettie? I miss you. Ever think about gettin' back together?"

Aletta laughed. "I'm busy." She wished she was big enough to take him by the collar and toss him out on the driveway.

"How 'bout just one kiss for old time's sake?" He smiled.

"The holidays are comin' up soon. I need more money for your children. And the dentist says Sissy needs braces."

He was gone within a minute.

The holiday season proved to be slow for her with everyone so busy shopping, traveling, and having parties. The slower her business, the angrier she got at Jimmy. She worried about money incessantly, but now she didn't share her fears with her kids. During a good week, she was making up to sixty or seventy dollars, but it wasn't nearly enough for the five of them. Finally, just before Thanksgiving, Jimmy came by and gave her a small check in addition to the child support to help her with holiday dinners and gifts.

When their daddy was in the house, Sissy usually left or locked herself in her room, and Randy turned up the TV, but Ruby stayed for every word to make sure she'd be there to protect her mama if her daddy started hitting again.

"This ain't enough to cover the food you eat," Aletta said, looking at the forty-dollar check.

Ruby was scared. She figured that would set him off for sure. She wished her mama would just act grateful, to keep him calm. But he didn't react, just kissed Ruby on the forehead and left.

In mid-December, he quit dropping by completely. The kids went to Kathy's one weekend before Christmas and said she had stayed in bed almost the whole time, and when she did come out, she always had a hat on.

Aletta got through the holiday dinners with the help of Betty and Shirl and their families. But she had almost no money for gifts, so she bought fabric and had Zelma Morgan make them clothes, which they needed badly, for a fraction of the cost of store-bought. She fretted and worried over the clothes, so when all three of her kids were disappointed, it hurt.

Their dad gave them a new Sony color TV, and they were elated. Aletta was so mad, she had the urge to throw it out the window, until she watched her favorite show, *Police Woman,* on it and decided it was nice for the kids.

Eugene took her to a dance at the Polka Palace for New Year's Eve. She hadn't been out socially without her kids since the party where Jimmy picked the fight with Eugene. She allowed herself a few glasses of wine to calm her nerves.

"You sure know how to dance, Eugene!" Aletta exclaimed as he twirled her.

"Bein' single for so long is good for somethin', I guess," he said, smiling and pulling her close.

She felt like she was in high school again, except for one big difference.

"How's business, Aletta?" Iola Little called as she and her husband, Lyle, danced by.

"Little slow what with the holidays," Aletta called back. "Thanks for askin'."

When Eugene went to refill their drinks, she sat in her long velvet skirt watching the couples spinning around. Ray Tettleton looked across the room and saw her.

"Hey," he said before he even reached her, "I just had to tell you thanks for the advice on bringing in Sally as my partner. Business has been great."

She smiled up at him. "I'm so glad to hear that, Ray."

"Wasn't sure if a woman could hack it," he said, and winked. "But she's great."

After he walked away, Aletta thought about the fact that something she had been sure she'd never reveal to anyone just months before was now common knowledge. It was an unfamiliar feeling, being accepted for who she was, but it was a darn good one. Kind of like when she ate Jerry's curry, different than anything she'd tasted before, but sweet and delicious.

At midnight, she and Eugene stood on the dance floor. He spun her around, then dipped her slightly. When they kissed, she lifted one red pump off the floor and allowed her body to melt into his.

In early January, Aletta received an envelope from Andrew that held an 8x10 of the group picture and a 5x7 of her standing next to her sign. There was also a note:

Dear Mrs. Honor,

Here are the photos I promised you. Look for the article in the Jan. 22 issue. By the way, Brian has met a lovely lady named Mary (note the M!) who he's crazy about in spite of himself. We've put in for overseas assignments. There's no word yet, but we haven't been turned down either. Thanks for everything,

Andrew
McMillen

Aletta put the note in her jewelry box for safekeeping and took from her closet a frame that still held an Olan Mills picture of her and Jimmy with their kids when Randy was a baby. She pulled the photo out of the frame and tossed it in the trash. The group photo fit perfectly, but before she put it on the mantel, she retrieved the family portrait and dropped it in the kids' hope chest.

A few days before the *Life* magazine due date, Betty told Aletta she'd talked to Della up at Snyder's Drugstore. Della had promised to call Betty the instant the magazine came into the store, so they could go buy up a bunch of copies. It was 9:15 on the morning of the twenty-second when Della called Betty, and 9:16 when Betty called Aletta. Aletta already had Gyp dressed and ready, so they met at Snyder's at 9:22.

They raced through the old drugstore that was straight out of the fifties, with red leather swiveling stools and a soda fountain, to find Della and the magazines. Betty bought fifteen copies, then almost tore one of them to shreds looking through it to find

Aletta. At first they missed her completely, but Betty finally found the little picture in the center of the eight-page article.

"Well, my Lord, it's tiny, no bigger'n a postage stamp, but you look great. Look, it says 'Psychic Aletta Honor' underneath, see?" she said, holding out the page for Aletta to look at.

"What does the article say?" asked Aletta, shifting Gyp to her other shoulder.

"I'm just gonna read this part next to your picture first, so we can cut to the chase," Betty said. Aletta nodded.

" 'Traveling Route 66 is a journey of American places, but what makes it truly rewarding are the people who make it America. In Tucumcari, New Mexico, we met ninety-three-year-old Navajo Indian Samuel Bearclaw, who has lived in a teepee all his life and remembers hunting on horseback with bow and arrow. He sells his beautiful carved wood figures out of the Tucumcari Five and Dime, which doesn't seem to have changed since it was built in 1889.' " Betty stopped and showed Aletta the picture just above hers of Mr. Bearclaw sitting on the porch of the old Five and Dime holding a wooden bear.

"That's amazing," Aletta said, then Betty kept reading.

" 'We also ran across Aletta Honor in Okay, Oklahoma, . . .' Here it is, here it is," Betty gushed, " '. . . a mother of four who has a homemade sign out in front of her house on Route 66 advertising herself as a psychic. The locals say Ms. Honor has a gift that is as near as they've come to magic, revealing the pasts and futures of total strangers as if they were bedtime stories read from a book.' "

Betty scanned down the page. "Then it goes on about wheat fields and stuff. That's it," she said, and looked up at Aletta, her eyes wide.

Aletta didn't know what to think. It was like Betty was reading about someone else, someone who gets into magazines. That was other people, not her. "They sure did a lot of interviewin' to come up with that," she said finally.

Betty closed the magazine. "That's 'cause they didn't need to say another word. All I know is, you better raise your price, hon."

* * *

Aletta drove home quickly because Gyp needed his diaper changed. As soon as she pulled up, Joy came out of the salon waving the magazine. She met Aletta at the Pig Snout.

"We've got our very own celebrity," Joy sang.

"How'd you get that so quick?" Aletta asked, smiling.

"You may be famous, but I've got connections," Joy said, then hugged Aletta with Gyp in her arms. "Congratulations, honey. I'm so proud of you."

"Thanks, Joy, but I don't think it's that big a deal," Aletta said.

By that afternoon, the line of customers down her porch said it was indeed a big deal. Two of the three Oklahoma City TV stations were at her house by two, and the third one showed up at half past four. Between readings she gave interviews and stood next to her sign and smiled.

"How much do you charge for a psychic consultation, Mrs. Honor?" the first smiling reporter asked her.

"Um, twelve dollars," she said, and then regretted it, thinking she'd just shot herself in the foot. People wouldn't pay that much.

She was wrong. After that first day of doing ten readings, she knew there was no way she'd be able to handle that much every day. By six, she was so exhausted she didn't even care anymore, and her abilities waned badly.

People stood at Aletta's door again by eight the next morning, and because it was freezing outside with a light snowfall, they had to come inside. Shirl showed up from Elk City at nine with an appointment book in hand and a pen behind her ear to "cowgirl" the situation, as she called it. She'd been an executive secretary for eleven years before Tom made enough money in the tire business that she could stay home.

The first thing she did was to go buy a piece of plywood, paint it with the leftover paint Aletta had in the garage, and nail it onto the bottom of the existing sign, covering up the DROP-INS WEL-COME part:

As Seen In LIFE Magazine
By Appointment Only.
Please Call 405-555-2424

"Do you think people will go to all that trouble?" Aletta asked, shivering as she looked at the sign.

"What else do they have to do, Lettie? They can go watch the corn grow or the snow fall with no appointment, or they can come see a world-famous psychic if they make a phone call," Shirl said. "Besides, if you wanna take drop-ins again one day, you can take this part down, but for right now, this is outta control."

Aletta pulled her coat tighter around her neck. "The magazine shows the sign says drop-ins are welcome, so I'll take as many as I can for the next few days."

Just then a white van pulled up across the street. A gaunt, tired-looking man in his thirties got out eyeing the sign and the women. He opened the sliding side door of the van and leaned in. First he pulled out a wheelchair and set it up as the snow fell lightly on him. He leaned into the van again, and when he turned around, he held the emaciated body of a little boy whose arms and legs hung lifeless in the air.

"I better get back inside," Aletta said.

"I'm gonna get to the store. I wanna get back in time to see this one leave," Shirl said, still watching the man.

Aletta sat on the couch with the daddy while the eight-year-old boy slumped in his wheelchair, his head tilted to one side. The man wouldn't give either of their names. He just wanted to know how to make his boy well. Aletta had to tell him that there was nothing he or she could do to heal his son.

The man dropped his head and sighed.

Aletta studied the boy for a moment as she held his bony hand. His thin white skin showed the shadows of blue veins beneath, even in his cheeks. He looked so fragile, but his deep blue eyes shone brightly and he seemed to understand every word.

"Give him some paints and a paintbrush. He can be a good painter, and he'll love it," she said.

"Lady, maybe you haven't noticed. My boy can't use his hands," the father said.

Aletta was silent for a moment, her heart beating a little faster. She didn't want to hurt this man any more than he already had been. Then she had the urge to take the boy's face in her hands. She put her palms on his cheeks and smiled at him. He smiled back at her, his little face turned sideways from the disease in his neck, his dark hair falling into his eyes.

After several moments with her eyes closed, Aletta said, "With his mouth. If you put the brush in his mouth, he'll paint with it."

The father sat dumbstruck for a moment. "Are you serious?" he asked.

"Yes, he is," Aletta said, and kissed the boy on his forehead.

When Aletta came out of the living room, Shirl had set up the answering machine she'd bought at TG&Y. The message she recorded mentioned *Life* magazine twice and said that Ms. Honor's assistant would return the call within twenty-four hours.

"That's what I need, an assistant." Aletta put a hand on her lower back and stretched.

When Sissy came home she begged for the job. She was thrilled to make money and to be so closely associated with her mother's appeal. Shirl and Aletta decided Aletta could handle six appointments a day and have Sundays and Mondays off just like Joy. Sissy would come home after school and return the calls of all the people who'd called that day for an appointment. She'd set appointments for Aletta at nine o'clock, ten, eleven, one, two, and three, and for every appointment she set, she'd get a dollar.

Aletta figured Sissy would blow the money on clothes and jewelry. Instead, she opened a savings account and started putting money away for a car.

Chapter Twenty-six

The phone rang while Aletta was feeding Gyp between appointments. She'd gotten accustomed to letting the answering machine pick up, so she wasn't really paying attention.

"Aletta, this is Odiemae Sharp. I need to speak with you . . ." the machine announced, and Aletta snatched up the phone, holding Gyp in one arm. She had started to dial her mother's phone number twice since the article came out, and now her mother's best friend was calling.

"Odiemae, it's Aletta."

"Aletta, I'm glad you're there. I'm at the hospital with your mama, honey. She's had a bad stroke."

Aletta taped a note up on the door, threw a blanket over the sign, and checked the Crock-Pot to make sure the stew was ready for her kids' dinner. She paced the house until Sissy got home to take care of Gyp. Aletta drove faster than she should have to Deaconess Hospital given that the roads were wet and the temperature was dropping fast.

She entered the building and stopped, instinctively wanting to avoid the smell that she associated with her wreck and Johnny Redding from the first time she ever remembered coming there.

But she made herself think of the births of her four children in this same place and went to the reception desk and found that her mama had been moved to Intensive Care from Emergency. She headed to the elevators, loosening her long coat and scarf in the warmth of the hospital.

She pushed the arrow to go up, and after a few moments, the doors slid open. Inside the elevator, all alone, pale, thin, and almost unrecognizable, stood Kathy Kokin.

She stepped out of the elevator. "Hello, Aletta." Kathy wore a black felt beret pulled down over her ears and spoke in a voice that was as dry as her cracked lips.

Aletta didn't know what to do. By the time she gathered herself, she missed getting in the elevator before the doors closed.

"Kathy, hi," Aletta said too casually, as if they were at the kids' baseball game in the park.

Kathy smiled slightly.

To Aletta, Kathy was suddenly just a person, someone vulnerable and looking for love just like everybody else. A pang of guilt stabbed at her as she watched tears form in Kathy's eyes. She'd seen her in the hospital in her vision. She could've warned her.

"What're you here for?" Kathy asked, blinking back the tears.

"My mama's in Intensive Care. I haven't seen her yet."

"Well, I know you must be anxious to find her," Kathy said, smiling that slight little smile again.

"Yeah," Aletta said. Kathy turned to go, but Aletta stopped her. "What is it, Kathy?"

"Cancer. I'm here for chemotherapy." Kathy held Aletta's gaze as long as she could before turning away.

"I'm sorry," Aletta said quietly.

Kathy just nodded and walked away.

Aletta finally entered her mother's room to find Reverend Taylor and Odiemae Sharp sitting next to Nadine, tubes up her nose and in her arm.

"I'm so glad y'all are here with her," Aletta said, and hugged them both, the events of the summer meaningless under the circumstances. "How is she?" She strained to keep from crying.

"Not that good," Reverend Taylor answered. "She was out for a little while."

"What d'you mean 'out'?"

"Her heart stopped, honey. They had to revive her," Odiemae said. "She hasn't woke up yet from the coma, but they're hopeful she's gonna pull through."

"Can I be alone with her for a minute?" Aletta asked.

After they left, Aletta sat down next to her mother and for the first time in her life thought she looked frail. Her permed gray hair was separated on the sides where she'd been lying on it, revealing her pink scalp. Her eyelids were closed tight over deep sockets, and her mouth was thin and pale.

"Oh, Mama," Aletta said leaning close enough to smell her mama's familiar scent. She almost felt like a little girl again.

She stayed with Nadine for several hours. Many of her mama's friends from the church came in to pray and sit. Reverend Taylor and Odiemae sat vigil with Aletta until suppertime. After they left, the room was so quiet, all Aletta could hear was her mother's shallow breathing. The white blanket on her bony chest rose and fell, rose and fell. Aletta touched her face and smoothed the thin, silky, gray curls back off her forehead.

"I wish I could change everything for you, Mama," she said, and took her mother's hand. The tears that finally came were old, the tears a little girl had wanted to cry a long time ago.

She went home when visiting hours were over and told her children about their grandmother and about Kathy.

"Gosh, does Daddy know?" Sissy asked about Kathy.

"I'm sure he does," Aletta said.

Sissy tried to call Jimmy, but he wasn't at Kathy's house. Aletta felt pretty sure he'd bail out quickly in a situation like this and assumed he was out drinking somewhere, but she didn't say anything.

The next morning Aletta woke up at five-thirty and couldn't go back to sleep, so she got up and baked chocolate chip cookies to take to her mama. She let the kids lick the bowl and mixer before sending them off to school, then dropped Gyp off with Silvia on her way to the hospital.

Walking in with the *Life* magazine and a foil-wrapped plate of cookies, she told herself to remember her mama was in a coma. But when she entered the room, her mama had her eyes open and lay propped up a little.

A nurse was tucking the covers around her.

"Mama!" Aletta said.

"Hello, Lettie," Nadine said hoarsely. "What the hell happened to me?"

Aletta was surprised and, if truth be told, happy to hear her mother cuss.

"Well, I guess you had a stroke and your heart stopped for a minute. It was a clot in your blood is what they said." Aletta glanced at the nurse.

"I already told her, but she didn't believe me," the nurse said, smiling.

"I'm so glad you're awake, Mama. How d'you feel?" Aletta asked as the nurse excused herself.

"Not so good." She didn't look so good either. She was pale and looked frightened.

With her mother awake now, Aletta wasn't so sure how to act around her. It was easier when she was unconscious. Aletta tried to remind herself how she felt yesterday and gently put her hand on her mama's.

"You must be real scared, Mama."

"I've always been so healthy," Nadine said.

"I know, and you will be again."

"The doctor says I'm still not outta the woods."

"You're strong as a horse. You'll pull through just fine."

"If I was you I wouldn't talk about horses after that scene at the church," Nadine said, and laughed a little.

Aletta could see her mama now, coming out from behind the bitter old woman she'd become, and it made her heart hurt with the missing of her all these years she'd been gone.

Aletta chuckled. "I expect you're right."

"What's it gonna be like, Lettie?" Nadine looked at her. She seemed so small.

"What, Mama?"

"When I die."

Aletta took her mother's hand in both of hers. "Well, I'm sure it's beautiful. . . . I know you believe in heaven."

"Yeah, I *believe*, but *you* know for *sure*," Nadine said, not shifting her gaze from her daughter.

Aletta paused for a long time before answering. "What do you mean?"

"Well, I saw you in that magazine and on the TV."

"And?"

"And, it sounds like you know about things," Nadine said.

Aletta laughed bitterly and looked out the window. "You had to get that from a magazine?" she asked.

"No, I remember when you was a girl. I know you can see the other side," she said.

Aletta kept looking out the window to help her hold back the tears.

"Can you see your daddy and Joey?" Nadine insisted.

Aletta looked at her mama and a tear escaped down her cheek. "Daddy's been tryin' to talk to me." She remembered at the party when she had helped Betty contact her father. He'd said there was someone who wanted to speak to her. She knew it was her daddy. He'd been there by the fire with Jerry and at the cornfield on the way to Shirl's, too.

Nadine let out a short laugh, and tears came to her eyes. "Well, what's he sayin'?"

"He wants us to love each other, Mama. That's what I think he wants the most."

Aletta leaned over and held her mama and they cried together, and the tears were pure somehow, coming from a place untouched by judgment or shame.

"Oh, my," Nadine said after a few minutes, "tenderness always undoes me. We're just a coupla blubberin' gals, ain't we?"

Aletta nodded as Odiemae Sharp walked into the room. "Oh, I'm sorry. I'll come back later," she said when she saw them.

"No, no, it's okay, Odiemae. Come on in here," Nadine said, wiping away her tears with a tissue.

"You sure?" she asked.

"Come on in, Odiemae. She's doin' a lot better." Aletta blew her nose. "Odiemae's the one that called the ambulance for you, Mama."

"That figures. We'll prob'ly end up croakin' on the same day," Nadine said.

"I hope not, the way things are goin'," Odiemae teased, and Aletta laughed.

"See what I have to live with?" Nadine joked back.

This was a side of her mother Aletta had never seen, and she realized she really didn't know her at all.

Odiemae stayed for an hour, but Aletta stayed until lunchtime. Nadine kept falling asleep, but when she was awake, they talked about the *Life* magazine article. Nadine showed Aletta her very own copy of the magazine and told her she'd seen her on two different TV stations. When she had to leave, Aletta put six cookies on a plate for her mother and took the rest for her kids.

She woke Nadine up to say good-bye. "Mama, I have to go, but I'll be back later, okay?"

Aletta wasn't sure whether she had heard her or not until she got to the door.

"Lettie," Nadine called, her voice small and weak.

Aletta turned around. "Yeah, Mama?"

"It wasn't your fault," her mother said, her wispy silver hair forming a halo on the pillow, her smoky blue eyes looking straight into her daughter.

Aletta stood there for a moment just holding her mother's

gaze. Something inside her, something hard and calloused that had grown over her heart to protect her from the pain of her mother's unforgiveness, just melted away from her and turned back into its original form, a daughter's love for her mama. "Thank you," was all she could say, but the words came straight from her heart.

Aletta walked past rooms with people lying in bed, sick and suffering, as she headed toward the elevator. She noticed an old man in one of them leaning toward the ground from his bed, trying to find something. She walked past, then turned around and went into the room.

"Can I help you find somethin'?" she asked.

He looked up at her, age spots dotting his face and balding head. "Dropped my darn remote control," he said, his voice clearer than his rheumy eyes. "Nurse takes forever to come, and my legs aren't workin' that well."

"Easy enough." She looked under the bed, found the remote, and handed it to him.

"Thank you," he said, looking up at her. "You remind me of my daughter. She's pretty like you."

Aletta smiled radiantly. "Would you like some cookies?" she asked, and held out the foil-covered plate.

His eyes lit up. "Homemade?"

She nodded. "Chocolate chip, made this morning."

"Honey, you just made my week," he said.

That afternoon after school, Aletta was getting the kids ready to go visit their grandmother when the phone rang. Sissy picked it up and gave it to her mother.

"Hello," Aletta said.

"Mrs. Honor, this is Dr. Sweetney from Deaconess Hospital. Your mother's had another stroke. She's still alive, but you should get here as soon as possible."

Aletta left the kids with Sissy. Driving to the hospital, she had the strangest experience. At one point, it felt as if she were watching herself drive from just overhead. She had a sense that everything was just fine, and there was nothing to worry about. When she got to the hospital and turned off the engine, she had no idea how she'd gotten there.

She found several of her new Burning Bush friends in the waiting room outside Intensive Care. Odiemae hugged her tight.

Dr. Sweetney came out when he learned she was there. He looked younger than Aletta expected him to, with dark hair and dark hazel eyes behind glasses.

"Your mother's had another stroke," he said quietly. "We were hoping to let her get stronger and recover from her first stroke before going in, but we had to do an emergency bypass. She's very weak and unstable."

"What are her chances?" she asked.

"Honestly, not very good. I know this is hard, but we need to know from you if we should try to resuscitate if she goes into arrest again." He took off his glasses and began cleaning them with a tissue he fished from his pocket, but he never took his eyes off Aletta.

She could tell this was difficult for him. After they discussed it at length, she told him to let her mother go if her heart stopped. Aletta knew Nadine would want that, to go with dignity.

"Thank you, Doctor," she said, and laid her hand on his arm. "We appreciate everything you're doing."

Inside the room, Aletta thought her unconscious mother looked like something out of a science fiction movie with all the equipment hooked up to her, and she wished she could take her home. Instead, she sat down and took her mother's hand again. This time, she didn't cry. She didn't need to.

"I'm just gonna stay here with you, Mama," she said.

Once again Aletta had the sense of peace she'd had in the car. For the first time she could ever remember, she didn't need anything from her mama. She had no idea how long she sat there before she knew her mother was gone. Dr. Sweetney and the nurses confirmed this with their machines, but Aletta already knew. She laid her head on her mother's chest and held her in her arms.

Before she left the hospital, Aletta went to the old man's room.

He took one look at her and turned off the TV. "Did you lose somebody?" he asked.

She nodded. "My mama."

He put a hand over his heart. "She was blessed to have you as a daughter."

"You think so?" she asked.

"I know so," he said.

As she entered the elevator, Aletta took a deep breath. She had an overwhelming desire to be with her children.

The funeral services took place at the Burning Bush Battle Church on the following Saturday. Aletta chose not to speak, but asked Rusty to sing.

"What about 'Stairway to Heaven'? That'd be perfect," he said.

Aletta shook her head. " 'Blue Eyes Crying in the Rain' was her favorite song, Rusty." So he agreed.

The moment he touched his fingers to his guitar and brought forth the first few notes of the song, Aletta was transported back to the farmhouse on a spring evening, listening to Joey.

In the twilight glow I see you
Blue eyes crying in the rain
When we kissed good-bye and parted
I knew we'd never meet again
Love is like a dying ember
And only memories remain
And through the ages I'll remember
Blue eyes crying in the rain
Some day when we meet up yonder
We'll stroll hand in hand again

In a life that knows no parting
Blue eyes crying in the rain

Rusty's voice was so sweet and clear, there wasn't a dry eye in the church when he finished. At the end of the service, Aletta stood up.

"We're gonna have a big reception at my house, so y'all please come and help celebrate my mama's life," she said.

It was remarkably sunny and warm for February, and Aletta opened the front and back doors of her house. There had been at least a hundred people at the funeral, but it seemed like the entire town showed up for the reception party.

Everyone brought a casserole or dish of some sort. People who were just driving by came in to see what was happening. Aletta went to each of her friends—Joy, Shirl, Betty, Silvia—and thanked them for all they'd done for her.

Aletta was sitting at the dining room table talking to Eugene when the phone rang.

"Aletta, it's Jimmy."

Instinctively she held the phone out to yell at the kids to pick it up, but then she put it back to her ear. "Hello, Jimmy," she said.

"I called to give my condolences about your mama," he said. "I know y'all had a tough time, but I'm sure it was hard on you, losing her."

"Thank you. I appreciate that," she replied, and realized the hate she normally felt for him was either on a break or was gone for good, she wasn't sure which. "How's Kathy? Y'all still together?"

"Yes, we are. It's tough, but she's braver'n I could ever be," he said.

"You tell her I send a prayer for her healin'," she said.

Jimmy paused for a moment before answering. "I'll do that, Aletta. That'll mean a lot to her. Means a lot to me, too."

A little while later, Odiemae Sharp pulled Aletta aside.

"I've been wantin' to tell you this, Aletta, but everything's been so crazy. Just before your mama had that second stroke, I was there with her. She said somethin' I didn't understand but I thought you might. She said, 'I wisht I wouldn't have thrown away her gypsy ball.' That is what she said exactly. Does that make any sense to you at all?"

Aletta hugged Odiemae for a long time before she was able to speak. "It makes perfect sense."

Aletta hugged Betty and Rusty before they left.

"You did such a great job," she said to Rusty.

He beamed. "People seemed to really like it."

"Everyone's been tellin' him how good he did," Betty said.

Aletta just looked at Frank, who smiled proudly. The Conways had been a happier family since Aletta had told Frank his son was going to be a country superstar with his name on the Okay water tower and a street named after him, the street the huge Wal-Mart sat on.

On the twenty-first of March, the first day of spring, Aletta loaded the kids into her pastel pink '57 Chevy. She'd been making more money than she ever thought possible for an uneducated country girl, and the first thing she'd done was buy back her Chevy from the man who'd bought it from the car lot.

She drove to Eugene's and honked. He came out wearing a swim mask and snorkel, and she laughed.

"This is crazy, isn't it?" Aletta said as she turned onto the country road.

"Sure, but that's what makes you so much fun," he answered.

They turned onto the road Johnny Redding had missed when he picked Aletta up long ago. She held her breath as they pulled up to the big old farmhouse. It seemed like her mama and daddy and Uncle Joey could walk out onto the porch and greet them. She used to avoid this place, not wanting to remember because it hurt too much, but now it made Aletta smile to think of them. The people who lived there now had kept the place up good, and it looked almost the same as when Aletta was a child. They had agreed to her plan and were getting free readings in return.

Ruby and Randy jumped out as soon as the car stopped, and

ran to check out the small mobile crane that sat next to the boarded-up well. Aletta watched her kids run around the land she used to when she was a child, and she laughed with delight.

Eugene got out of the car and walked over to his friend Mitch, a beefy guy with a land grading business. He leaned against the well and shook Eugene's hand.

"Are we really fishin' for a crystal ball, or were you pullin' my leg?" Mitch asked.

Eugene smiled. "I know it sounds a little off the wall, but she wants to try," he said, glancing at Aletta, who was stroking the bark of the old oak tree. "Thanks again for doing this. It means a lot to her."

Mitch shrugged. "No problem, but didn't you say it was dropped more'n twenty years ago? It'll be a miracle if we find it."

"That's true, but you don't know Aletta," Eugene said. "We'll get started in just a minute, all right?"

He walked over to the huge tree and joined Aletta. "Is this bringin' back some memories?"

"Oh, my Lord, so many," she said. "That dead crow dropped right here in front of Johnny and my daddy." She pointed to a spot on the ground where tree roots gnarled the surface.

"How's it feel to remember?" he asked, and put his hand in turn on the trunk of the tree, feeling its surface.

She looked at him, thinking and feeling for just a moment. "You know, it's fine. I know they're all together now, and they're right here with me too," she said, and put her hand on her heart.

He took her in his arms, and they stood under the tree, holding each other.

Aletta now realized she could make it just fine on her own, without a man, but it sure felt good to be held.

"You know," he said finally, his tone serious, "I need to confess somethin'."

She stepped back and looked up at him curiously. "What's that?"

"Remember when the Chevy used to break down all the time, so you'd have to bring it to me and leave it?"

" 'Course I remember," she said.

His face reddened. "Well, I . . . I did things to it on purpose, so I could see you more often."

She looked straight ahead, gazing at Ruby and Randy chasing each other around the well. Finally he reached out and touched her shoulder, a worried look on his face.

She glanced down at his hand, then looked up at him and smiled playfully. "Darlin', I knew that a long time ago."

About the Author

★

DAYNA DUNBAR is a native of Oklahoma and
currently lives in Los Angeles, where she is also
a screenwriter. This is her first novel.